THE HOLLOW MIDDLE

By

John Popielaski

THE HOLLOW MIDDLE

By

John Popielaski

Published by Unsolicited Press

www.unsolicitedpress.com

Printed in the United States of America.

ISBN: 978-1-947021-40-2

Grateful acknowledgment is made to the following for permission to reprint copyrighted material:

American Journal of Botany: An excerpt from "Community Development Following Gamma Radiation at a Pine-Oak Forest, BNL," by Richard Stalter and Dwight Kincaid. 2009.

Bob Swerer Productions: An excerpt from *Alone in the Wilderness.*

Counterpoint, LLC / Soft Skull Press: An excerpt from "The Country of Marriage," by Wendell Berry. Copyright © 1971, 1972, 1973 by Wendell Berry.

The Cut: An excerpt from "How Much Can You Really Change After You Turn Thirty?" by Melissa Dahl. Originally published on www.nymag.com on November 24, 2014.

The Guardian: An excerpt from "Artist Nails His Scrotum to the Ground in Red Square," by Shaun Walker. Originally published November 11, 2013. Courtesy of Guardian News & Media Ltd.

Houghton Mifflin Harcourt Publishing Company: Definitions from WEBSTER'S NEW WORLD COLLEGE DICTIONARY, 4/E. Copyright © 2013 by Houghton Mifflin Publishing Company. All rights reserved.

Reyes, Philip: An excerpt from *Faith, Hope, and Love… With Autism,* "This is the story…," by Philip Reyes. Originally appeared on January 24, 2015 at faithhopeloveautism.blogspot.com.

Scientific American: An excerpt from "Eye Contact Triggers Threat Response in Autistic Children," by Sarah Graham. Originally appeared in the March 7, 2005 edition.

Sinclair, Jim: An excerpt from "Don't Mourn for Us," by Jim Sinclair. First appeared in *Our Voice*, Volume 1, Number 3, 1993.

For the inhabitants of all the hollow middles. And I thank the following for all they have done, intentionally and otherwise: the forebears and the blood relations, Susan, Lupe, Tito, Jude, Dapper Dan, Ping, Jim-Bob, Secret-Agent Man, Pittsburgh, Summer, and, as always, Henry Taylor.

Contents

THE
HOLLOW MIDDLE

Chapter One

Nothing is remarkable about the lightening hour and the mild fairgrounds air, and nothing is remarkable about the peeps and ribbits in the meadow where the birders, loyal to migration schedules, stalk when there is light to glimpse a little rarity, and nothing is remarkable about the yonder man, bespectacled, whose respiration is the stuff of late-stage hibernation.

His name is Albert Lesiak. He walked four miles from a bar across the bridge, reclined against this log, and aimed his double stare in the direction of the Connecticut River for a time before he jackknifed into Lethe. This sort of thing occurred more frequently when he was young. He'd wake beside the ocean, under snow, in cornfields, cars, chairs he failed to keep from yielding to the tipping point, on roadsides, rooftops, automatically sprinklered lawns, in houses that turned out to not have been his own. Because he never suffered an arrest or damage he deemed irreversible, because he never died, he started to believe that he was under the protection of a figure out there somewhere. Then he started wondering why his protector didn't do a little more for him, like make him more appealing to the ladies, for example, or instill in him sincere ambition, or allow him to detach from his material concerns, perhaps recalibrate his mind and soul to be at home inside the bony frame of an ascetic.

The Albert Lesiak you see before you is the product of a compromise. Since penury did not agree with him beyond the age of twenty-eight, since money for the sake of money got him thinking of the odds against a camel passing through a needle's eye, and since he found a woman he could live with, he acknowledged tacitly he would release whatever force had helped him thus far from having to be bothered any further with the enterprise of shepherding this sot, this social drinker (terms which Albert planted at the two poles he envisioned as the bookends of his being) toward greatness, which he thought, with modest application, he could reach in due time on his own. The adventure might be sweeter for the solitude.

In the meantime, he required occupation so that he would not appear to be the outcast that he knew himself to be. To *seem* an outcast would not do. Without a certain revolutionary goal in mind, he reasoned that, whatever imprint he would make upon the world, he'd have to bide inside a system meant to stifle.

He discovered that a buttoned shirt, a patterned tie, a pair of khakis, and a sense of humor offer camouflage for disaffection. People who keep steady hours don't attract too much suspicion. And, if one takes on a job that wields no power over anyone of consequence, that person has few limitations placed on how long he may fly beneath the radar. So, when Albert's mother-in-law once asked him what inspired him to become an English teacher at a Catholic school, he rubbed his stubbled chin and ruminated for a moment over a cheesecake crumb that wedged itself between two molars.

"I don't know," he said. "I like to read. You never really know what happens to a person when he reads."

Such comments indicate that biding sometimes wears on Albert. Sometimes he believes he is afflicted with a sort of Stockholm syndrome, a phrase he looked up in a dictionary once. The certainty of definition gave him leave to think about what goes on psychologically to let the hostage feel such tenderness extending toward the captor. Even after sixteen years as a teacher, Albert is not quite certain who his captors are. Some days it seems his students, who themselves are hapless and controlled but wield the well-concealed malevolence of children, hold him hostage. Other days he is certain the administrators, who are calculating in a pleasant way but are also serfs to mortgages and dream-like visions of retirement, erase in geological time his individuality, his essence. And then some days, when he's clear that he is free to go at any time, he's certain he is both the hostage and the captor. Typically, the sun does not shine on those days.

Sometimes he believes that cognitively he is dissonant and asks himself how can a person not be thus afflicted when, on the one hand, his spirit flutters when he reads about Thoreau's refusal to remit his taxes due to an objection of the moral basis of a war with

Mexico, and, on the other, he who is aflutter takes no action to determine what is to be done with what's deducted from his modest pay biweekly.

No dissonance or syndrome adequately explains the current vegetal repose that Albert's in. The summer solstice is eleven days away—so the debauchery that led to this condition may have simply been intuitive, a reenactment of a pagan rite that helped the ancients to make seasonal peace with the unknowable. It's not unusual for Albert to invoke the Norse, despite his Slavic bloodline, as he stumbles headlong toward oblivion during what he likes to think of as the festival of light. School is out—so this could be his way of saying he has put away the person he has had to be in favor of the person he believes he is. All manner of existences whose beings are, in essence, latencies have shown themselves since May—so Albert's self-indulgence may just be his way of joining them. The difference, though, is that where turtles, toads, chipmunks, black bears, daffodils, and so on seek the water and the light and the reproductive rendezvouses to keep the species going, Albert seems a miser, barren, fallow, insular, inward as if sitting on a treasure that he will not share because he fears it will not be enough or may produce some complications.

He is not a sire. Such a bender therefore warps no kid. For many years Albert feared paternity, imagining how much it would extract in money and emotion to conceive and bear and house and feed and clothe and educate and upkeep and amuse a child until at least the age of eighteen. Because he'd long grown distant from the wish and the imperative to add another offshoot to his family tree and keep his blood and last name extant into perpetuity and because he'd long lost the character plasticity he thought was necessary to relate to children properly, he rarely dwelled on what he might be missing and was disinclined to think of this omission as unnatural or as something that would mark him as disloyal to his species. If he does not regard genetic sacrifice as noble, he at least considers it unselfish, a partial abnegation of the ego, a small gift to a world that did not bear a billion living humans all at once until the early 19th century. Although he is still capable of love, he rationalizes that withholding progeny is his way of acting locally and thinking globally, his renunciation of his claim on everything his branching lineage would inevitably have consumed, disposed of, soiled, subjugated, lorded over, and exhausted.

Such withholding and such renunciation went from theoretical to, if the bond of marriage was to hold till death and infidelity was held at bay, irrevocable when Albert's wife received word that, even with the reproductive advances and the three attempts to reverse what nature had said no to, she would not be a mother. Mary Lesiak tried hard to get her husband to consider adoption as a worldly good that rectified in part the terrible injustice of a child drifting parentless toward adolescence and adulthood. But Albert was adamant in his belief that blood should raise blood because who knew what happened when you tinkered with the natural order. There was, of course, the fear that the adopted offspring might seek answers to the ontological questions that adoptive parents do not have the wherewithal to stem. There was, of course, the question of how many hoops prospective parents had to jump through and the question of how much would be required from their bank account before they would be granted the enormous and ennobling burden of caring for someone else's already dramatic life. So Albert considered his potential for paternity as something of a phantom limb, an appendage that he thought about involuntarily from time to time with sadness and nostalgia, knowing that a part of the original was lost, but also with a weird relief in his belief that such an integral component of the corpus was removed from him without his consultation and through no fault of his own, and that the otherworldly agent he had formerly relieved of any obligation sort of owed him one for that.

***

A foot shod in a hiking boot applies a modicum of rousing pressure to a lower limb. These are times that Albert dreads. Called back to consciousness before the carbon dioxide in his blood could dissipate sufficiently and leave him with at least the hope of mental clarity at some point in the day, having to recall his carriage of the night before and gauge just how regrettable it should be viewed as in light of the social compact, failing to recall much of anything at all, and clutching his pressurized head as though it were a hand grenade endangering the family men in his platoon, he looks at the offending boot.

"Are those new Keen Durands?" asks Albert.

"Relatively new."

"These are Keen Durands," says Albert, lifting up his left foot. "Got them for my birthday not two weeks ago."

"Are you all right?" asks the Samaritan.

"Depends on what your standards are. I'm probably affected still by the intoxicants."

"Do you need help?"

"No. But thank you."

"You're sure?"

"My computational facility is less than facile, I admit. But based on past experience, and I'm aware there are no guarantees, I'm confident that this will pass." Albert shields his eyes and looks up at the man from whose neck dangle quality binoculars. "Do you know who you look like from this angle? John Updike." Albert clears his throat.

Narrow, bird-like, smirking slightly as if used to privilege, Updike's face looks down at Albert. "How old are you?" asks Updike.

"Do you have the time?"

"It's a little after six."

"I'm forty-four. I feel like groaning." Albert takes his glasses off and sets them on his lap. He puts his hands together at the palm edge, covering his face from chin to forehead. He drags his hands down and allows his index fingers to dig out the gunk that has accumulated in the inner corners of his eyes, and then he runs his middle fingers horizontally across his eyebrows, using ring and middle fingers as massage tools on his temples. "I suppose I should arise and rejoin the race." He rests his hands flat on the ground and pushes to improve his sitting posture. "I may need more time."

Updike looks through his binoculars at the island in the river, and he asks, "Are you a father?" The question's intimacy is mitigated by the island-looking.

"I have not been blessed," says Albert. He puts his glasses back on and adjusts them. He looks likewise at the island. "I take it you're a Pater Noster?"

"Catholic?" Updike asks, panning his binoculars deliberately until he's looking up the river.

"Strict Lapsarian."

"It is a blessing," he says, lowering the binoculars and holding them with both hands at the level of his chin. "I have three girls and a boy."

"It seems the pity tide has shifted. Now I pity you."

Updike smiles and brings his binoculars back up to his eyes. He scans the east bank of the river.

"You're a birder, too, I'm guessing, in addition to the fatherhood," says Albert.

"Do you pity me for that, too?" asks Updike, panning slowly to the right.

"I get the birding. I can tell a catbird from a titmouse. Who's not fond of bird life? I have feeders at my house." Albert takes deep breaths as if he really needs the oxygen. "Looking out for any species in particular?"

"I am looking," says Updike in the calm and steady tone of someone who narrates for a nature documentary or for the portion of a golfing tournament that takes place on the putting green, "for the common teal. The cattle egret, if I'm lucky."

"I keep meaning to get better at identification," Albert muses. "Birds, trees. I think that part of our experience is rapidly diminishing."

"No sudden movements," Updike whispers as he crouches, training his binoculars on the meadow. "There's a pair of sandhill cranes at ten o'clock. This is unbelievable. I heard that one was spotted down in Stonington, but this is unbelievable."

"Are they endangered?"

"Not officially, but with the rate of habitat destruction I don't see how they won't make the list before long."

Before deciding he's reclined enough and should assume the stance that served our ancient forebears in the grasslands, Albert cleans his spectacles, reorients himself, and follows the trajectory of Updike's quality binoculars. Albert has long admired creatures who've been muscled out of places they had come to know so intimately that leaving must have been the sort of ache it's better not to have a language for, and so he feels what someone lost inside himself must feel when he's positioned just so to experience the uplift of the morning light, which doesn't quite illuminate the spectral pair of sandhill cranes—two birds that should not be here but, since *should not*, fit inside the solitude so perfectly they must have known what they were doing when they bypassed all the places somehow marked as spoken for.

Away from the river, past the blind of beige reeds, meadow yields to marshland, and the cranes, assured by Updike's practiced stillness and his distance, flap their silent wings at one another, lift as if for takeoff, then splash down in shallow water, bowing to each other as if meeting for the first time. They leap and leap and leap and circle one another in a dance expressing such kinetic joy that Albert is ashamed of his inertia, his aloneness, his awareness that he has no sense of what it's like to feel their kind of liberation, to just up and let the body go so wholly into motion, tethered all the while to a companion and to ritual. He knows their lives stretch back to their beginnings, and he knows his own is lost and broke its link to kinship and tradition long ago.

"You know," Updike whispers, his binoculars still trained, his lips near motionless, "the sandhill crane has one of the longest fossil histories of any bird. Goes back at least two-million years. Some ornithologists say five. These are basically the same birds that did the same dance back then. How's that for continuity?"

Albert watches as the cranes continue, disappearing finally behind the reeds that ring the far side of the marsh.

"What are they doing now?" Albert whispers.

"They could be tending to a nest," says Updike, still looking through his binoculars but dispensing with the whisper. "Could be foraging. Could be resting up before they fly out to Nebraska. Hard to say unless you go back there and have a look. But I try to tread as lightly as I can. Leave no trace and all that."

"Why don't you have a camera? How do you prove what you've seen without a camera?"

"I know I've seen what's on my life list. Cameras seem to violate the spirit of the thing." Updike lowers his binoculars, lets them dangle from his neck, and says, "I've bothered them enough for one day, I suppose. Good luck to you. I hope you find your way."

Updike takes the rutted trail upriver past the lateral river marker, footstep after fading footstep validating Doppler via Albert's one good ear, and disappears into the owl-guarded cedar woods, in search of something else to go completely still for and observe as if in observation something in him is replenished or restored and then, in opposition to his culture's tendency to stake a claim, just lets the witnessed go, not interested in the capture even of an image to peruse and ponder over in his den, his shoeless feet at ease upon an ottoman, the spirits in his snifter swirling counterclockwise now and then beneath his nose.

I hope you find your way, thinks Albert. *What the hell is that supposed to mean?*

Albert, though the beneficiary of a liberal education, harbors reservations when it comes to his ability to decode a person's tone, especially the tone of someone he suspects is his superior in some way. Nuance, he believes, although he sometimes argues otherwise, is just another form of obfuscation, one more scale the shifty lay upon the open eye, another ball of cotton the deceptive stuff inside the cupped ear.

Was he sarcastic? Did he mean, like, existentially, I'm lost? My soul is doomed? He doesn't even know me, and he spends his Saturday mornings chasing birds that aren't even there most of the time. Although he didn't seem like the sarcastic type. He did wake me up. That showed some concern. He seemed like a good guy. Maybe . . . maybe he thought I stumbled here last night, not knowing where I was, and meant I'm going to have to fight a little through the fog to find my bearings and get home. That's probably what he meant. That's a fair enough assessment. Okay.

Rising after such nights is an undertaking. There is no telling how the head is going to react to a sudden change in altitude, no telling if the stomach will rebel and rumble suddenly, the body bent hard at the waist, the hands on knees for structural support as the digestive system's normal course is violently reversed, no telling if the corpus has absorbed the blows of inconsiderate abuse and will resume its functioning as usual. There's little doubt that history repeats itself. The trick is in predicting what exactly will recur and when.

Albert thus assumes the six successive postures depicted on the evolutionary scale, although he feels no sense of triumph on ascending to the sixth. A slight stoop in his shoulders, his tendency to slouch, hints at his potential to regress, but presently there is no question where to place him on the scale. Even with the slouch, he's over six feet tall. He looks out at the river, and he waits a while for the compass needle in his brain to flutter less. His eyes are blue and bloodshot, and they water with the breeze. He turns and scans the marshland once more for the cranes. He envies their easy disappearance, their acceptance into landscape. It occurs to him that the pride he takes in biceps whose circumference is a couple inches greater than the average, the pride in bulk and bulge, runs counter to his admiration of the cranes whose strength and grace and vanishing are effortless, in tune, and are in no need of a mirror or an inner voice to confirm that they exist.

So what's the point? he wonders. *Mass and acquisition. See and be seen. Why can't it be that easy to retire or to fly away?* The alcohol must run its course.

Albert stares out at the reeds leaning marshward in the breeze.

His mouth goes briny, and his stomach swells. He spits the frothy spittle of the dehydration sufferer and takes deep breaths. It's all about imagining a balance and believing it's achievable before the body is quite ready. Mind over matter.

The swell subsides. The beads of sweat that bubbled from his forehead start to dry.

Okay. Okay. It's time to go. No big deal. A few miles to go.

Albert walks along the trail that parallels the bending river south, and he negotiates the deep ruts that the bored kids and the rough adults in lift-kit trucks gouged out for jollies. Frogs take refuge in the murky water as he nears. He passes casing after casing left behind by litterbugs who shot at deer or clay pigeons or Busch cans or a tree whose trunk got in the way. He passes a pile of asphalt shingles left by someone who believed his freedom would have been infringed if he had paid the small fee for disposal at the dump. To Albert these are but the recent signs of man's dominion—inconsiderate, unthinking, counter to the ethos of the commons. When he sees such signs, he can't help thinking, more or less, of what Chief Seattle is reputed to have said:

"Every part of this country is sacred to my people. Every hillside, every valley, every plain and grove has been hallowed by some fond memory or some sad experience of my tribe. Even the rocks, which seem to lie dumb as they swelter in the sun along the silent shore in solemn grandeur, thrill with memories of past events connected with the fate of my people, the very dust under your feet responds more lovingly to our footsteps than to yours, because it is the ashes of our ancestors, and our bare feet are conscious of the sympathetic touch, for the soil is rich with the life of our kindred.

"And when the last Red Man shall have perished, and his *memory* among white men shall have become a *myth*, these shores will swarm with the invisible dead of my tribe, and when your children's children shall think themselves alone in the field, the store, the shop, upon highway, or in the silence of the woods, they will not be alone. In all the earth there is no place dedicated to solitude.

"At night when the streets of your cities and villages be silent and you think them deserted, they will throng with the returning hosts that once filled and still love this Beautiful land.

"The White Man will never be alone. Let him be just and deal kindly with my people, for the dead are not powerless."

Sadness floods through Albert when he thinks how little is held sacred, how little is perceived as lost. Try telling someone with a flat-screen television and a mortgage and a riding mower and a laptop and a dream of college-educated progeny that, if he wants a fuller, more authentic life, he should be mindful of the solemn grandeur and the cherished, long-term memories of rocks; that, if he wants the dust to be more loving and responsive to his footsteps, he should lose the shoes and socks more often; that, if he has an inner life and sense of history, he should feel haunted by the native dead, the souls of those the white men so efficiently dispossessed.

If you're like Albert, you don't say a word (unless you've had a few) because you know the sacred and the secular are mismatched rams, the former waiting for the final head-butt to relieve it of the stress of balancing on the precipice so long. You yourself, although you're always open to the possibility and really want it to be true, can't always wrap your brain around the sentience of a rock, and, despite your excellent grades in two college courses on Buddhist thought, your fluency eludes you when you try to posit how it might be possible. You yourself were raised believing in the need for arch support. You are a tenderfoot and thus don't like to contemplate too much the always rising mountain of discarded shoes you've added to for many years. You argue with yourself that you were not there at the dispossession, that your forebears took a later boat, that you have little reason to feel haunted by the spiritus mundi that you are not unwilling to acknowledge probably exists. You'd rather whistle past the graveyard. You do not say a word, but, if you're like Albert, you are bothered, gnawed at by a sense that you are not at peace—with your surroundings, with yourself. This feeling doesn't follow you with the insistence of a Fury, but you sometimes wonder if it's always there and you have simply missed the subtlety, the understated, native way that Chief Seattle's prophecy about invisible returning hosts who will not leave the latest iteration of the settlers alone has maybe come to pass. If you're like Albert.

Ask ten people what the word *Connecticut* means, and it's unlikely even one replies, "*Beside the long tidal river,* of course. From the Algonquian, *Quinnehtqut.*" Ask ten people in Albert's town who inhabited the place before them, and a few might mention the Gildersleeves, the Goodriches, and the Hamiltons—the families who said there should be boundaries and unearthed the stones to build the walls, who cleared the forests for tobacco fields, who quarried brownstone, horse after horse, block after block, and shipped it down the river to the cities. Their names are on the wooden plaques that hang beside the original front doors (or the convincing replicas) of the historical houses, stops on the Old Homes Day tour the town conducts each spring. Ask a random person why the Wangunk Meadows Albert walks through are called the Wangunk Meadows, and, if you have stumbled on a person who has lived around here long enough to have a deep opinion about the nature and rate of change, he might say the name has something to do with the Indians that used to live around here. Unless he is the sort of person who uneasily occupies this time and space, he does not mention that the records show the Wangunks sold a hundred-fifty square miles on both sides of the river to the whites for thirty coats in 1662. He does not wonder if the whites used magic or persuasion or religion or threat of musket ball to seal the deal or if its terms were mutually understood or if the winter of 1661 had been so brutal as to make the deal appealing to the Wangunks on a strictly wanting-to-survive-another-winter basis. He does not try to sink his supply-side mind into what the whittled homeland might have meant to people whose physical and spiritual existence hinged on access to the animals and the fish, the river and the woods. He does not try to see through Wangunk eyes the little reservations they were left with (250 acres for the one, 30 for the other), does not try imagining how tightly squeezed their bodies and their spirits had to feel in order for the last few Wangunks to decide in 1765 that it was time to finally leave and disappear.

So Albert walks through here thinking about how way leads on to way, how one night he is passed out on the fringes of a meadow steeped in darkness and in the morning he is lit again and making incremental progress toward a road he knows leads home, how one day a pair of sandhill cranes are somewhere Albert only thinks of as point A and another day they are engaged in something more transcendent than kabuki in a marshland it is obvious they love and where there is no question they belong, how century after century this meadow was essential to a people who were mindful not to leave a nasty trace, and now it is as if their culture is a freak thing from a myth from which we pilfer names (Connecticut, Shenipsit, Wangunk, Mattabassett, Meshomasic, Pecausett, etc.) so it seems as though we give a shit about maintaining a connection to a time, a mindset, and a way of life we couldn't wait to leave behind. If Albert believes his presence here is an offense to the invisible hosts, the Wangunk dead, he doesn't feel unduly haunted or as if he's acting in the spirit of a conqueror by being here. In fact, he wishes there was some revealed procedure he could follow, some symbolic ritual he might perform, some rite to reconcile what cannot be altered to what has been changed for so long that there seems no use in trying to articulate an individual apology to the deceased whose wrongs have lingered generation after generation unredressed.

Why wake the sleeping dog? Why beat the dead horse? Why not let the dead bury the dead? Albert couldn't say exactly except that, as a person raised sporadic Catholic, he's a sins-of-the-father sort of guy and believes in the restorative nature of contrition, of confession as an act that has the strength to lift the burdens of the past from the shoulders of the present. The problem is that his reconciliation toolkit is not equipped to fix what Albert would like to fix. The Church is not inclined to give advice on how a person might attract an audience of the Native dead, and, even if there is a handbook or divining rod, the doctrine is inherently stingy when it comes to interfaith apology. Involuntarily, Albert thinks about the three wise men and what they symbolized about the known world at the time. So Albert dispenses with the letter of the law, and he imagines that he understands enough about its spirit to attempt what modest reconciliations lie within his purview. He attempts to keep his unilluminated mind aware of any mundane opportunity through which he might with little action effect some small-scale good that someone watching from a slightly different plane might see as evidence that Albert is guided by a heart resigned to keeping what exists within its narrow sphere from getting any worse, from getting cracked or trampled on or elbowed out or excavated or undervalued in the context of the modern world's economy. When such trying fails, which he has learned it probably must, he understands it's proper to at least express to the worsened his sorrow, which is not Seattle-quality sorrow or Wangunk-quality sorrow, but it emanates from a place that Albert's certain hasn't changed since it was first inhabited who knows how many moons ago.

If Albert believes his presence here is an offense to the invisible hosts, the Wangunk dead, he somehow still feels loved. He isn't sure by what, but for the moment he is unconcerned and does not feel a pressing need to get an English name attached to something he suspects attachment will diminish and confine.

He leaves the last of the marginal woods and sees the fairgrounds filled with light, the sort of light that he imagines must have been envisioned by the Yahweh writer as he worked on page one. Albert squints. He passes by the long, rectangular enclosure, post-and-rail fenced on three sides, where the truck-pulls take place three or four times annually. Albert went once out of civic duty, and he tried to get excited by the brawn of those machines, but he was most impressed with what appeared to be an organized suspension of society's truncation standards as to shorts. He suspects that such suspensions have to do with a nostalgia for the sort of liberty that Catherine Bach embodied in the role of Daisy Duke from 1979 to 1985, and he will not heap derision or scorn on someone who is not ideal for trying to recapture that. Beyond the truck-pull area, he passes the long, rectangular pavilion under which the livestock are exhibited for one week each October at the harvest fair, which Albert attends because it helps to entertain the thin illusion that his produce doesn't mostly come from far away.

Albert looks for Updike's car, but there is no one here. He must have walked, and this impresses Albert since so few these days walk substantial distances away from their insulated homes and enter woods or meadow with no other purpose than to see what it is like to spend a fraction of this fleeting life on foot. He's not expecting anyone these days to be like Stephen Talkhouse, the legendary—but at one time very real—Montaukett who existed in the 1800s, who routinely walked twenty, thirty, even fifty miles in a day because he never felt above his natural means of locomotion and declined to delegate his walking to a horse.

Albert stops and tries remembering who said that walking is an act of humility. It was probably Wendell Berry. Or Gary Snyder. Albert leans toward Gary Snyder and resolves to work on memory improvement. For now, as he resumes the walk, he sees the wisdom in the sentiment but wonders how humility is expressed by simply doing this. He reaches the swinging gate and turns left onto the paved road. He walks perhaps a hundred feet and stops to see if there is any sign of life inside a crushed shell of a painted turtle spring and reproductive pressure and tradition tempted into hazarding a trip across the asphalt. Albert feels depressed relief when he discovers there is none because he wonders what he could have done if he'd seen movement or the glimmer of existence in the eyes. This, according to the myth, is not supposed to be the way the turtle got its crooked shell.

Albert continues east and, in the distance, sees another shell, but this one seems intact and making progress toward the center of the road. He hears the whoosh of a vehicle approaching from behind him, and he runs, although he knows there is no way he will be fast enough. A pickup passes him. The turtle's head goes in. The turtle disappears beneath the truck that does not slow or swerve, and Albert's sure the shell has given way to tires once again, although it does not register that he hasn't heard the crunch. He gives the truck the finger as he runs but feels the deepest of the gloom or rage or disappointment lift as he picks the shell up, turns it this way and that as he inspects for cracks, and sees that it is still in one piece, that the turtle is a turtle still.

Albert hates to put it down in the direction it was headed because he knows it will at some point head back and attempt the crossing once again. Why can't biology respond more quickly to the perils humans mine the way with? Why can't the turtle bend a little and be less beholden to the inborn route? He lays the turtle on the grass and waits as its appendages emerge and it resumes its ancient pace away from the indifferent road.

"What the fuck's your problem?"

The power of the upraised middle finger is a curious thing. In this case, Albert's moved the driver of the pickup to pull over, get out, and approach him at a brisk pace and with the sort of involuntary inflation that accompanies aggression in a rooster. Albert saw the glow of brake lights, saw the guy's approach in his peripheral vision, but he took a first-thing's-first perspective and ignored him while the turtle found its bearings.

There is, of course, a necessarily unreflective aspect to aggression, so, when someone puts an index finger up and says with just that finger *Please wait a moment, bald aggression, while I tend to something more essential,* aggression does not know exactly what to do because it cannot simply stand still reconsidering its recent path in life without experiencing the early stages of the diminution of its adjunct rage, which, in these types of situations, often has the lifespan of a mayfly. The aggressor steps a little closer, close enough that Albert feels the puffs of breath percussing on his nape when the aggressor, as if doubting whether Albert heard his inquiry the first time, repeats, "What the fuck's your problem?"

Albert supposes that expressing what the problem is and asking the aggressor to be mindful of the posted speed limit and the likelihood of turtles crossing here this time of year would not resolve this confrontation to either's satisfaction. Albert therefore takes his glasses off, wheels around, and squarely head-butts the aggressor's nose—a strategy retained from youth, a muscle memory recalled—and the aggressor falls and introduces into Albert's day a stressor hitherto not evident.

Albert's unfamiliar with the woods on this side of the road because it's private land, but he does not have far to go to reach the next essential road. There are no houses, no nosy windows. No fear of bumping up against the residential and veering off to circumvent the civil eye. No fear of getting lost.

He jogs in until he hears the fugitive cover whisper it is now advisable to slow his noisy pace and to consider how not to make the big mistake. How deer can live their whole lives this way Albert does not have the time to think completely through, but he is conscious that for now they share a similar condition and it wouldn't be ridiculous to try a little deer-think and rely on natural cover and the ginger step to get him undetected to the tree farm where he can adopt the unsuspicious, civilized, and thoughtful stroll. He must admit that fleeing is invigorating, that he does feel quite alive, but what is wrong with how he lives his life that this is what it takes to conjure up vitality? Is this mid-life? Is this the crisis? If so, this can't be solved by purchasing a muscle car. Would he mind so much if someone quiet in a tree were looking at him through the crosshairs of a sight and pulled the trigger, ending things in pure defiance of monotony, releasing him to see what else is out there? And then he comes to the conclusion that deer-think probably does not entail rhetorical questions and the inner monologue to this degree.

Albert reaches the edge of the woods and takes a knee, squinting as he tries to gauge the risk of this exposure. It is possible that the aggressor has recovered consciousness and is so embarrassed by his inability to follow through on his aggression that he has no interest in broadcasting his defeat or seeking Albert for a rematch and simply drove away, but it is also possible that the aggressor's brain is swelling, pressing perilously against his skull, and that a passerby has called an ambulance and the police are making inquiries and Updike, having seen the birds he hoped to see today, has made his way back to the fairgrounds' entrance and reported his encounter with Albert, who, in this scenario, would be immediately promoted to a person of interest. Albert reasons that this second situation is unlikely so far because he hasn't heard a siren yet. Nonetheless, this is one of those rare occasions when Albert wishes he had yielded to conventional wisdom and agreed to buy a cell phone. Then he could have called his wife and asked her to do a little research and conduct a short reconnaissance mission, reporting back to him via cell phone before he made the big decision to emerge completely from the woods. He remembers reading somewhere or seeing something on Discovery or PBS about how the Neanderthals may ultimately have been done in as a species because their larynx limited their vocal range and left them with a language that could not express the range of thought that characterized the Homo sapiens who then went on to rule the world.

But always, it seems, there is the other hand. Albert does not want to be a ruler, and he wishes that he didn't have to be a part of what's become of Homo sapiens. He pities the Neanderthals, imagines what the world would look like if their rivals hadn't had the insurmountable advantage of a more accommodating voice box. Progress can't go on forever. Someone or some force of nature will at some point put a foot down, and Albert's confident that when the time comes, if he's still around, he will be ready. No, he does not want a cell phone. He is glad he's not connected. He'll negotiate what lies ahead alone.

He stands erect, looks right and left, and enters Millane's tree farm, walking down a broad lane flanked by maple trees ten or twelve feet high. He wonders where these trees will go, what new development they'll help seem more organic, more in tune with the ideal. What pesticides are used here? What time of year are they applied? He's grateful anyway that the tree farm occupies the last part of the flood plain and the town will not permit construction here. But those pesticides go somewhere, and that somewhere must be sick of them by now. Albert makes a mental note. It's quiet. Birdsong. No human or machine. He's confident that no one who might travel on the road that's to his left a couple hundred yards could see him through the trees. His shoulders relax. He reasons that, when he emerges, in the interest of projecting nonchalance, he'll cross Route 17, turn left, and stop into the Citgo station for a coffee and the paper and a pleasant word with the attendant, who will therefore not suspect a thing.

Albert checks his backside pocket to assure himself that he is in possession of his wallet still. He rarely carries cash these days, a practice he's aware the banks have engineered, and he's been meaning to incinerate his debit card and figure out a safer, less shadowy place to keep his currency than in the local branch of an enormous bank. In a credit union. Underneath a paving stone. Divestiture, a total break, if he is serious. He makes a mental note.

He strides across the two-lane road as if he's proud to be bipedal, but his head swims when his stubbled chin is held this high. He feels how red his eyes are, fears a little for his soul.

Just moderate, he thinks. *Just keep it together a while longer. There's a bed at the end of the tunnel. You have no obligations on your time today. Nowhere that you need to be.*

This business of being beholden to the hour and the minute jacks him sometimes, makes him feel he has enlisted himself into an army whose commanding officers will not articulate a mission or a cause. He'd be content with five divisions: morning, forenoon, afternoon, evening (gloaming when he feels poetic), and night. With earlobe and elbow room. With broad ways to negotiate. He'd be content to scrub the temporal divisions altogether, tickled and at home if time were Henry's stream, which he could enter and emerge from at his leisure—trunks or no trunks, one toe or the whole shebang.

"Will that be all today?" the man from Bangladesh behind the counter asks.

"Yep," says Albert, "just the coffee and the paper. Busy here this morning?"

"No, not yet. All is quiet."

Albert swipes his debit card. "All right, have a good one."

"Please give your wife my hi."

Chapter Two

There is nothing like the balm of coming home.

Albert looks around at what's returned, at all this is the season for.

Despite the evidence in favor of resilience, Albert sees it all as tenuous and fragile, balancing on a wire above a canyon, someone in a suit and tie at either end engaged in cell-phone conversation, waiting for the word to come down from the lawyers so that they can finally tuck their phones back in their pockets, stretch their stiff extremities, and crack their alabaster knuckles prior to beginning the at first unnoticeable vibration that will in waves be magnified and cause it all to flail and spaz, to lose its breath before it all concedes there is no longer any point or purpose in resisting what the shamans saw in visions and predicted years ago.

I'm so hungover.

Albert trudges up his gravel drive, whose inclination causes him to lean uphill a little and accentuates his stoop. He lays his coffee cup in the recycling bin beside the woodshed. He closes the lid and pukes in one convulsion.

Breathe, just breathe, he tells himself. *Mind over matter.*

He hopes that this expulsion has rebalanced things inside him and set his melancholy humor straight, and he imagines how his strength and clarity will flow back once he's able to lie down a while. He climbs the seven crooked concrete steps that lead up to the patio at the back of the house and notices his wife, whose back is turned.

An herbicide container dangles from her left hand, and a spray nozzle extends exterminator-style from her right. Albert watches as she sidesteps, moves from weed to weed, and douses each green sprig in milky jizz that stains the paving stones and leaves a lot of poorly drawn chalk outlines to remember all the mute decedents by. Each application Albert feels as her endorsement of the hard-to-wrap-the-brain-around, industrial, systemic, corporate scale of death that has become too easy to pretend does not exist because it has become so difficult to seriously believe a grassroots movement could exert the sort of budging force required to dissuade the massive entities involved from marching onward, flanked by their platoons of lobbyists and lawyers, with their EPA- and FDA-approved campaign of national toxicity. So Albert feels a different kind of rage, a different sort of sadness than he felt when, homeward-bound, he saw the turtle struck defenseless. He possesses no authority over that indifferent road, and, despite his intermittent vigilance and his occasional successes, he is not its caretaker, is not charged with shepherding the turtles past the hazards to their breeding grounds so that their ancient form of life might soldier on.

But here, within the four pins that delineate his acre, Albert is responsible for caring what goes down, for caring that what lives here is respected, is not doused or elbowed out or stepped on or run over or subjected to the backhoe or, in broad, romantic terms, unloved, and that has meant he does not fertilize the grass, he does not dig haphazardly, he does not mow at normal speed, he does not let his dog lord his domestic status over those who are still wild, he does not walk without awareness of his footfalls, he does not poison wasps or bees, he does not poison weeds, and he does not believe the promises of companies like Monsanto. Though his dreams of emulating Jains are not sustainable or realistic, he at least can keep in mind the spirit of those words Seattle may have said in 1854:

"The white man must treat the beasts of this land as his brothers. I am a savage and do not understand any other way. I have seen thousands of rotting buffaloes on the prairie left by the white man who shot them from a passing train. I am a savage and do not understand how the smoking iron horse can be more important than the buffalo that we only kill to stay alive. What is man without the beasts? If all the beasts were gone, men would die from great loneliness of spirit, for whatever happens to the beast also happens to the man."

"Would it kill you to kneel down and pick a weed?" asks Albert. "It's a little early for an application."

His wife keeps spraying and does not turn around.

"You know what that's been linked to. And that doesn't bother you? This really doesn't bother you?"

She says nothing.

"You're pissed because I wandered last night."

Mary is intimately aware of her husband's position re Monsanto, re Dow, re Bayer, re Trans Canada, re Chevron, re BP, re Exxon, re the frackers, re the mountaintop removers, re the EPA, re Congress, re existence in a world that she agrees is as industrial as it has ever been, that she agrees is mercilessly run by slaughterers, by spewers, by despoilers, by contemporary Molochs who will not be satisfied until there's no more money to be won. But, unlike Albert, she is not above admitting that a poison, on occasion, has its uses, that, in this case, she is willing to accept the possibility a little poison labeled detrimental to aquatic life may wind its way down to the watershed in order that her problematic back is spared the added strain of bending for the stretch she would require to manually say hell no to the continued propagation of these unsightly weeds.

Such sightliness and seemliness are virtues in the suburbs, and she's not above admitting that she likes her yard and house to look a certain way, that is, in keeping with the tidy ethos of the neighborhood. Unfortunately, her husband does not share this ethos, which he has made clear he views as superficial, all show, no substance, *Edward Scissorhands* absurdity. Hence the weeds, hence the snapped tree that's been hanging by the shed since the ice storm last November, hence the unpruned shrubs, hence the unraked leaves, hence the mess, hence the stuck garage door and what is left unfixed, hence everything. So, yes, if she is limited by a bulging disc and opts to spray a little *Roundup* on the patio in the interest of basic seasonal beautification, to do what Albert, as the man, should weeks ago have done, she will not hang her head and be included on his list of the environmentally indifferent. She holds him culpable for putting her in this position to begin with.

She sidesteps, sprays, sidesteps, sprays, tracing a clockwise arc until she faces Albert. Her cheeks are chubby, ruddy with the slight exertion, and the bags beneath her eyes convey exhaustion with this way of life, with Albert's inconsideration, with his absence and return, with just the two of them, no mediating force to buffer what they say, no layer of illusion to rely on for civility. They are the product of a blind date and the grim determination to transform what evidence they saw of their compatibility (their love of Scrabble, hiking, and tippling, for example) into something lasting. They lived together elsewhere, in Albert's small house by the lake, for two years before they bought this one, and he proposed not long thereafter, saying, "I think we should get married," because premarital cohabitation could potentially have posed a problem for him at his school if rumors started circulating after both their names were published in the Real Estate Transactions section of the Sunday paper, and a parent or an administrator who was old-school doctrinaire began suggesting that a teacher living in a state of sin was not a proper model for, indeed performed a dangerous disservice to, the taught and was, according to the letter of the law, a candidate for termination as set forth in an appendix of the contract, which, in legalese, said do not scandalize the school and do not truckle like a libertine to turpitude. And so their marriage, predicated largely on a practical defense against opprobrium and unemployment, lacks the romance, lacks the mystery and chemistry that lubricate the seized relationship and ease it past the countless frictions that consign so many to the junkyard of divorce, which, in the Church's eyes, is absolutely turpitudinous.

"You had your chance to weed your way," she says. "Still drunk?"

"The weeds don't magically disappear, you know. They still need to be picked postmortem."

"That'll give you something to do once you recover." She looks toward the driveway. "Where's your truck?"

"I'm not picking poisoned weeds. You started it. You finish it."

"You had that much to drink? Nice job."

"It's an affliction," Albert says, heading toward the sliding door that leads into the kitchen.

"Everything with you is an affliction. The end of school. Easter. Christmas Eve. Thanksgiving. Your birthday. Friday. You're not doing this the whole summer."

"I need a nap. Please keep the volume down."

"Don't ask me where the Advil is, and you can find someone else to take you to wherever it is you left your truck last night," she says.

"That's sweet," says Albert over his shoulder. "I'm almost emotionally overwhelmed."

"Emotionally," she scoffs. "You're not capable—"

Albert slides the door shut. Her voice is muffled by the double pane. He only has the one good ear, but he is certain she is saying that whatever region of his brain had jurisdiction over his emotions was severely damaged long ago.

He knows how slender is the line between the sound mind and the skewed. It scares the ego out of him when he's inclined to feel reflective. His grandmother, after all, had become so disconcerted and confused, her memory so fragmented toward the end, the pieces of the once remembered so minute and scattered so far by the psychic winds, that Albert had to redefine what he had theretofore believed about the nature of the personality. His mother has shown signs. He sometimes feels his own capacity for recollection slipping, but he tends to write off slippage to the alcohol or to the natural, mild retardation of a person's recollection powers at a certain age, a fact of life that isn't necessarily a portent of the mirror-shattering disease.

But what his wife refers to is an incident that happened over twenty years ago on a Saturday in June of 1987, an incident she wasn't there for and was not aware had even taken place until she heard about it from her husband.

That day Albert was a young man, drunk, and standing upright in the bed of Bob Orr's F-150 when Bob Orr disregarded what he knew about inertia and, given the green light by a prefrontal cortex that was not yet fully developed and was therefore not prepared just yet to adequately render an assessment of the risk on the horizon, made a hard right onto Hallock at a speed that to this day is in dispute. The angulating turn continued Albert on the trajectory that they (Bob Orr, F-150, Keith Donovan, Pat Joyce, and Albert) had all been on a fraction of a second prior to the unforeseen ejection and sent Albert sailing headfirst onto asphalt, skidding to a stop upon his grated back and shred posterior, presumed dead by his companion knuckleheads. This incident was not the first time Albert went off, involuntarily or otherwise, in one direction while his friends, whom he considered on occasion unadventurous or, when he was riled, cowardly, stayed put and safe. He did not die that Saturday, of course. His friends were genuinely relieved that he revived there on the road and spirited him to the emergency room, where the attending doctor, smelling Albert fumy from afar and tiring of trying to decipher bits of English through his slur, dismissed his poor condition as the mere product of immoderation, nothing that a good night's sleep, ibuprofen, hydration, and a life-evaluating hangover in the morning wouldn't cure, and sent him home. Skull-fractured, brain-contused, Albert was assisted home and guided to his front door. He retired to his bed where he slept the sleep of the almost dead, and, in the morning, vomited with terror in the toilet. Albert's mother was no stranger to her son's occasional matutinal catharsis, but that Sunday what she heard unsettled her because, despite her efforts, she could not recall the goddess of the morning asking so much of her son before. "This isn't a regular hangover," he admitted, and she drove him to the hospital in Stony Brook, where he began his convalescence and redemption. It turned out to really just be Albert's one-year break from alcohol, a record that still stands.

His mother maintains that Albert's personality had somehow crossed the Rubicon and changed in some way she could not quite put her finger on when he returned in May of 1987 from his freshman year at Geneseo.

There was the one night early on, when Albert turned left on leaving someone's festive house instead of taking what a clearer mind would have discerned to be the right that led back to the dorm. He was untethered for a while—wandering in darkness and emerging after he could not determine how much real time in a cornfield he was frightened had a consciousness intent on misdirecting him because it did not want to let him go. And so he ran until he met a wire fence that flipped him over into someone's yard in which the largest satellite dish he'd ever seen was basking like a stoner in the starlight, into someone's yard from which a black dog rose and chased him, flipping over, back in. And there was total darkness once again, and afterward, despite the marshaling of all his mental powers, Albert had no power to remember whether he kept running once the territorial ambitions of the dog were slaked or how he came out to a road where he found a small apartment building standing behind a row of sky-high junipers. He only knew that this was not the place he had been trying to return to, that a lot depended on his sense of which direction spoke to him, which one was chanting "Home." Like a heliotrope or moth, without the plotting logic of a language, Albert had the inkling that, when all else fails and you've been turned so thoroughly around you're aching for a lodestar, it is always best, if it's an option, to direct yourself toward light. So he determined which horizon was the lighter, which was likeliest to cast behind him all this darkness, and he leaned and fluttered and reeled in that direction. In one of those occurrences that could be read in any number of quotidian ways, Albert saw himself assuming the proportions of a problematic hero coming back from the unknown with only a divine's dead reckoning to guide him when he looked up from his feet and saw a sign that said the road that he was on was called AURORA WAY—a sign that he believed communicated to him personally as clear as day that he was heading in the right direction, toward the morning light, and that he would not have to face another tribulation on his way to what he saw more clearly now than ever was his temporary home. And thus he was directed safely, proving to him he was under the protection of a loving God. Perhaps, when Albert made it home that May and brought that sense of temporary with him and that sense of mystical, his mother sensed the mindset of the refugee in him and understood that he preferred to be unsituated, wayward, seeking, drawn to darkness he could feel adventurous and mystical and unseen in and then emerge from when the existential funk he found himself immersed in passed. But all of that had nothing to do with Albert's entry into higher education, and it wasn't fair of his protective mother to assign the blame to Geneseo for this disturbing wrinkle in her first child's personality, which she'd been sure for eighteen years she really knew. But before he left for college, before he sent the applications in or even read through one brochure, her son was on the lookout for what he could not help feeling he had lost, and he is on the lookout still.

But Albert's wife, unlike his mother, does not blame an innocent state school for her husband's inability or his unwillingness to come down from the crow's nest like a normal person and connect with her emotionally, to be compassionate, to empathize, to touch, to wear the wedding ring, to be affectionate about the eyes and by such simple signs of human tenderness and kindness show that he is capable of love. When she looks out the kitchen window and observes him putting cracked corn out for deer or taking care to search for toads before he lets a foot fall on the grass or sitting with a cardinal stunned by its encounter with a windowpane until it has the wherewithal to shake it off and fly away, she wishes that it felt as natural for her husband to extend himself to her and put himself in her place as he so naturally extends himself to them and puts himself in theirs.

But wishing has a way of turning into disenchantment when it goes on long enough, and the prospect of attaining the wished seems a hopeless, cruel illusion. Then a person must take steps to shore up self-respect, or else a cornerstone of personality will go to pieces and the edifice will groan and list. Although Mary did not abandon hope completely and, in that regard, did not just let her cold fish of a husband off the hook, she did at least assign a cause to her illusion; and, in that assignment, she was freed to let the blame and burden weigh on Albert's shoulders or inertia's or biology's or Bob Orr's but not on hers.

It took a few years before she recognized the mean streak in him was a mean streak and not simply the occasional sarcastic lob she took at first as humor. When, while they were having dinner on their first date, she brought up the topic of the relative ages of companions past and said to him, "I was just thinking, you're the youngest person I have ever dated," and Albert said, "That's funny. I was just thinking you're the oldest person I have ever dated," she was caught off guard and stung a little but could not help laughing at his timing. But timing, she discovered years later in the kitchen, isn't everything and can't replace commiseration or concern or the expression of a thought left unattended by a punchline, unaccompanied by irony, that wiseass. Timing can't replace an open heart, and so the humor in what Albert said appeared to her diminished once she understood that he was using it to ward off something she had grown exhausted trying to discern. She couldn't understand the origins of Albert's meanness and was curious about the wilderness from which it may have come. She pieced together what she could.

Mary had found it strange and somewhat saddening when she and Albert started dating and she'd hold a sprig of mint or lilac just beneath his nose to see if his olfactory arousal mirrored hers, and all she could elicit from him was "Hmm. Smells good."

When they went hiking in the woods above the Salmon River and she paused on the trail, struck by something unseen, unheard, untasted, something that could not be touched, and said, "I love that smell," and Albert said, "What smell?" and she said, breathing deeply, "Cedar. Don't you love that smell?" and he said in his flat tone, "It does smell good," she started to suspect that he did not partake in one-fifth of the world that she experienced, that he was shut off from the joy she took in taking in the scent of something, understanding it, communing with it in a way that otherwise would not be possible. She pitied him for what he might be missing as she would, without volition, pity someone who was blind or deaf.

Now and then she tested him, attempting with an unobtrusive question to discover if he had detected the pervasive smell of heating oil after cleaning the furnace, the eggy smell of propane when the pilot light went out, the cozy smell of woodsmoke in the air the first time that fall, the sulfurous smell of roughly forty-thousand gallons of untreated sewage discharged due to human error into the Connecticut River early one July, and so on. Each time, nothing.

And so she finally asked him, "Do you have a sense of smell?"

"Not really," Albert said. "Not since June of '87 that I know of." He related to her for the first time the circumstances of his launch and his reentry and his landing on his skull, which must have reconfigured, he supposed, the delicate circuitry so that his nose was not as useful as it used to be. "It isn't something that I miss," he said, but she was not convinced. And she was right.

He would have liked to close his eyes and swirl his shapely beer glass counterclockwise just beneath his nose, discerning malt notes, picking up the citrus emanations, recognizing that the profile he inhaled and registered meant Galaxy instead of Citra hops. He would have liked, midsummer nights, to sit out on the patio and from the breeze receive the essence of the weeping-cherry blossoms wafted from the front yard and be lifted by the sense that he achieved a kind of temporary oneness with a live thing in the world. He would have liked to lounge and to divine without articulation what he'd have for dinner. He would have liked to render an informed opinion on the stickiness or dankness or whatever weed-related noun was in when Jim, his friend from childhood, came up for a visit, grinned, and opened up a plastic baggie as if offering the opportunity to step on through the looking glass, inquiring as he flexed his eyebrows, "What do you think of *that*?" He would even have liked to be the harbinger of malodorous approaches if only to show proof that he was in the same expressive community as everybody else.

So she was right, and she pitied him for knowing she was right. But Albert's one of those benighted souls who thinks that everything, especially the bad things, has a purpose and was orchestrated from on high, and, further, he is one of those who takes great solace in the relative disasters others suffer and, by such comparisons, regards his own disasters and regrets as manageable and prime contributors to what he likes to think of as the evolution of his character.

And that is why, from time to time, Albert likes to think of Phineas Gage, whose damaged skull went on display at Harvard Medical School's Warren Anatomical Museum in 1866.

Thus thinking one night by the fire, after his relaxed consumption of a certain barrel-aged barley wine and in the middle of his coming to an understanding with a certain barrel-aged Scotch ale, which, combined, accounted for his openness and his effusion, Albert told his wife the story of the foreman Phineas, who oversaw a crew whose job was to remove the geological obstacles that still lay in the way of Progress and replace them with the railroad tracks that would assume their little role in the enormous enterprise of making quaint the notion of an endless and terrestrial frontier. The way, of course, to wave goodbye to such obstructions back then was to bore a hole in said obstruction, add explosives, fuse, and sand, then tamp until compaction necessary for an obstacle-obliterating charge was, in the foreman's narrow-eyed experience, achieved. On a Wednesday outside Cavendish, Vermont, the leaves preparing their autumnal flare, the foreman Phineas tamped and, somehow, just this once, he was responsible for the production of a spark that set the charge that launched the slender tamping iron through his left cheek, behind his left eye, through his left frontal lobe, and out the top of his skull, through which, according to the doctor who attended to him thirty minutes later, the pulsations of his brain were clearly visible, which circumstance, combined with the continued consciousness and outright equanimity of Phineas, made the accounts of how the accident transpired virtually impossible for a respectable physician such as Dr. Williams to believe. Albert told her that, despite some setbacks in his convalescence, Phineas recovered, more or less, and lived for twelve more years. This part always heartens Albert since it shows that one can take a serious blow and reel a bit and shrug it off and make one's peace with circumstance, surviving what the books agree should not have been survivable. Providing far more uplift than a thing with feathers, Phineas is Albert's hope. If Phineas could forge a life for twelve more years with one eye and a healed-up hole from cheek to skull, then Albert's long-term prospects should be solid, nothing to debate or doubt or worry over. And this part always heartens him because, when the comparisons are drawn, his near-death experience, even if in the accounting we include the life-long (heretofore) olfactory impairment, was a head bump, on the order of a splinter or a hangnail or a thing of no account and which a man would simply fold into his life and then forget—no wringing of the hands, no *Woe is me*, no looking backwards impotently at what was done.

Albert's wife, however, seized on something altogether different, did not see the theme as the resilience of the human form and did not read the story of the former foreman Phineas Gage in a comparative light, a light that shed its minimizing grace upon the glorified bump that Albert's head had once sustained. Instead, his wife discerned the meaning of the story in that "more or less," which Albert explained to her a little based on what he could remember reading from the doctor who took over Phineas's case, one Dr. Harlow, whose report regarding the behavioral effects of having had a tamping iron suddenly propelled through cheek and brain and skull was written up as follows:

"The equilibrium or balance, so to speak, between his intellectual faculties and animal propensities, seems to have been destroyed. He is fitful, irreverent, indulging at times in the grossest profanity (which was not previously his custom), manifesting but little deference for his fellows, impatient of restraint or advice when it conflicts with his desires, at times pertinaciously obstinate, yet capricious and vacillating, devising many plans of future operations, which are no sooner arranged than they are abandoned in turn for others appearing more feasible. A child in his intellectual capacity and manifestations, he has the animal passions of a strong man. Previous to his injury, although untrained in the schools, he possessed a well-balanced mind, and was looked upon by those who knew him as shrewd, a smart businessman, very energetic and persistent in executing all his plans of operation. In this regard his mind was radically changed, so decidedly that his friends and acquaintances said he was 'no longer Gage.'"

Although, to Mary's knowledge, no one (except Albert's mother, who placed the blame for his alleged transformation elsewhere) who knew Albert prior to the accident lamented that the Albert they knew post-accident was intellectually or psychologically or behaviorally or otherwise rejiggered or diminished (not including the olfactory impairment), that he was, for lack of qualifiers more precise, "no longer Albert." But she had heard stories of him making breakfast for his friends the morning after a debauch and had heard stories featuring Albert the Generous, Albert the Loyal, Albert the Loving, Albert the Easygoing, Albert the Social, Albert the Forgiving, Albert the Fun, Albert the Human—Alberts she at best had seen but fleeting glimpses of, and, after hearing of the temperamental changes Phineas underwent post-tamping iron, she convinced herself the accident and not acculturation or the physical and philosophical impossibility of stepping in the same river twice had remade Albert into Albert the Fitful, Albert the Irreverent, Albert the Indifferent, Albert the Impatient, Albert the Capricious, Albert the Vacillating, Albert the Distant, Albert the Ghost of Alberts Past.

A simple look at the chronology she worked from indicates the error of her diagnosis. Although there was compelling anecdotal evidence of pleasant Albert pre-accident, she disregarded or selectively forgot the other anecdotal evidence she'd heard that pointed pretty unequivocally to a dangerously unstable Albert before his head bounced off the pavement: his decision to bed down adjacent to a homeless man named Adam on a sidewalk in Manhattan; his projectile vomiting upon his friend's fiancée as he celebrated the arrival of the winter solstice; his liberation of a poached lobster off his friend Ed's boat because he had been reading recently about Guevara y Bolivar and at that moment saw himself (envisioned, really) poised nobly at the vanguard of a lobster liberation movement, which, later, David Foster Wallace would give voice to in his essay "Consider the Lobster"; his involuntary soiling of himself one evening and his subsequent removal of his underwear with scissors and his subsequent insertion of the underwear inside a can of Chef Boyardee he had recently decanted and his subsequent windup and throwing of the stuffed can over his drug-dealing neighbor's house and into his drug-dealing neighbor's yard to right a wrong his drug-dealing neighbor had committed against him in the past; his tendency to go hermetic during intervals that neither he nor those around him could predict; and his perspiratory outbursts when a social situation pressed upon him and he felt he had no way of getting out, no exit to return him to himself. And although there was compelling anecdotal and eyewitness evidence of misanthropic Albert post-accident, she disregarded or selectively forgot the other anecdotal evidence she'd heard and all the eyewitness evidence she'd seen that pointed pretty unequivocally to empathetic, altruistic Albert: his refusal to avert his gaze from the impoverished on an urban street and his involuntary lack of condescension or patrician pity when he handed over money his companions argued would be used for alcohol or drugs; his minor ministrations (getting mail, delivering food, listening) to their neighbor Dorothy whose cancer was intent on shutting down her lungs; his natural inclination to look after elderly neighbors and shovel out their driveways before his own or clear out what a storm blew down before they shuffled out and harmed themselves; his easy way of making friends and knowing people up and down their street whom she had never met; and the unarticulated love he showed to and the tears he shed for her own father, skin and bones beneath a blanket on a deathbed.

It didn't matter to her that events and times did not cohere. She didn't really hear when Albert had mentioned that the latest evidence suggested Phineas Gage's behavioral decline moderated later in his life, suggesting that social recovery, the imposition of some structure on a wrecked mind, may significantly reduce the long-term damage done to brains that suffered injuries like Phineas's and Albert's. It didn't matter because Mary was never really comparing the pre-accident Albert, whom she had never met or known firsthand, to the post. All along, consciously or not, she was comparing the post-accident Albert to her non-accident father and her non-accident grandfather. The more she saw of Albert and the more she learned about his personality, the more she learned about his worldview and his ethos, which were not the ones that she was taught by her parents and her grandparents, who were not inclined to criticism and who did not harshly judge, who played musical instruments with unencumbered joy and sailed and did artistic things with wood like fashion walking sticks and wooden ducks and cared about how maple syrup was produced and, if they had a dark side, they did not let it cast a gloom upon their optimistic dispositions, did not let it burden those who did not have to bear it.

Albert knew that he could not compete with that, and he did not intend to try. So when his wife complains or makes a snide remark about his meanness or remoteness and attributes it to damage in whatever region in his brain has jurisdiction over his capacity for intimacy, emotional availability, and happiness, the kind that finds expression in a song, a sail, a carved duck, or an interest in the tree-to-table journey maple syrup makes, he takes a breath and tells himself she does not know a thing about neurology and takes another breath and tells himself whatever damage his brief arc and cranial collision with the road inflicted on his brain was in the interest of a grander plan and for a purpose he is in the process of trying to discern. He knows for sure that something of the plan and purpose was communicated to him, something was revealed, conventionally, politely, in a letter from the hospital that hadn't seen fit to admit him and perform a CT scan the night before his mother drove him frantically to Stony Brook. The settlement seemed like a sign, and when he thought about what he could do with fifteen-thousand dollars of the hospital's money and, without consulting a financial planner or a person in possession of an elder's cautionary wisdom, suddenly decided he would buy a piece of land in Maine, which he had never been to, *that* seemed like a sign. With the help of someone sweet-toned at directory assistance, Albert got the numbers of some realtors in the 207 area code, and he made inquiries, receiving in the mail days later cheap brochures that featured, in his price range, cabin after cabin in the woods, where he imagined that the world he knew would not be too much with him. Sight unseen, except for the accompanying photographs below the brief description in the listing, Albert picked out one camp, rustic, twenty feet by twenty-four, that sat on eighteen wooded acres and had shadowed views of a secluded stream that seemed as though it might be therapeutic and a natural way to help him iron out the cognitive kinks he intermittently experienced while convalescing in the first few months. Because the possibility of seizures was statistically still high despite his dutiful ingestion of his daily doses of Dilantin, Albert was not allowed to drive up to the closing and appealed to his reluctant brother, who agreed to drive him but, because he harbored brotherly resentment against Albert for profiting from what he could not help regarding as his older brother's alcoholic tendencies and his associated idiocy and, most of all, his dumb luck, his ability, when all was said and done, to be indemnified, protected from himself—because he did not have, like Albert, an apparent guardian angel to confer such windfalls on him, Albert's brother charged a hundred dollars for his services and said that Albert would have to be responsible for all expenses there and back. Albert agreed and, for the first time in a while, felt at ease because he sensed that he was buying something that would always be there for him to retreat to, bodily or in his mind, whenever he grew tense about the possibility he'd someday have that seizure or grew weary of the burdens of an occupation and the steadfast habits the respectably employed are generally expected to adopt or grew reclusive, restive when he argued with his wife.

***

Hungover and exhausted, he recalls his cabin and his land as he discovers on a corner of the kitchen table yet another foster-parent pamphlet asking him, addressing him directly, "Can you help these children find a home?" and then becoming unabashedly imperative, commanding Albert, "Be a part of someone else's childhood memories."

Chapter Three

Albert shuts the bedroom door and pulls down the shades. He lies down on the bed and stares at the ceiling, does a quick review of his behavior in the past twelve hours or so and does not fare too well in the accounting. This will pass. It has to, or the living with himself will start to seem like a landfill of discarded, twist-tied moments he can never feel completely rid of or distinct from because he knows that in his lifetime they would always be in some stage of decay, and he would be to blame for their continuing emissions.

What makes things worse is that he knows he should be happy and his inner being should be in a state of heliocentric ecstasy and solar union as the summer solstice nears. He hears the birdsong out there and is honestly ashamed, upbraided, but the chemical reaction that he started last night has to run its course, which, from experience, he estimates will take the day. The best that he can do is to consider it cathartic, jettisoning something heavy he could not have carried much longer anyway and getting acclimated to the lighter weight, suspecting, hoping, despite his history, that there would be illumination or emotional growth of some sort or at least relief at his journey's end; but he would rather hang his body in the closet for a while and inhabit just the half-ounce that a goldfinch occupies and have his winter-dulled exterior burnished naturally, his yellow brightened sans volition for the spring and summer and express himself without his usual repertoire of reservations interfering with his inborn song, which in his half-ounce form would simply come to him and out of him as something free of mediation that he does not have to think about. But, because he can't escape himself and always gets lost in a bamboo forest when he tries to follow the confusing map that is supposed to lead him down the Noble Eightfold Path, he's left to contemplate what he and all his molecules are doing in the here and now or what they could be doing in the over there a bit and then.

Like a robin or a goose that lifts its resident body into the accepting sky and flies, depending on the season, north or south to find its needle's worth of refuge in a haystack of a place awaiting occupation once again, to find reunion with a landscape it remembers in its fragile bones more fondly for the absence and to be assured of wholeness by reunion, Albert, lying down, looks forward to his leaving here, which will become the left behind, the deprivations and the trials and the climate he can tell have oriented his internal compass north, northeast. Unlike the migratory goose, however, Albert's movement will not be cooperative nor an example of transcendence via group dynamics, will not coalesce into an aerial V that lifts the spirits of the groundlings; and, unlike the migratory robin, Albert's aim will not be reproductive, will not culminate in his protection of a speckled, light-blue egg in which the basic hedge against mortality resides. His movement must be solitary. In a sense, his aim is not to be.

In the twelve months after Albert became the outright owner of a piece of land he'd only met the one time, prior to the closing, when he with his brother weaved through eighteen acres of enclosing hemlock, pine, and cedar, following the orange tape that someone had tied at intervals to branch tips so that what were really four imaginary lines became an almost tactile boundary inside which Albert would be the human consciousness, the one who made decisions on just what would stay the same and what would change here—in those twelve months during which he convalesced without a drink and grew accustomed to the mental clarity of someone who perceived himself as saved, he did not visit his dominion once as it contracted in the winter months and thawed come spring, releasing turtles, tree frogs, black bears, all practitioners of dormancy and hibernation back into the world that was, to in-absentia Albert, diminished while without them. In those twelve months, while he was living in his old room in his parents' house, dependent on his mother for his transportation to and from the classes he now took at Stony Brook because it made sense in the context of his convalescence to accept his limitations temporarily and transfer, Albert's property, instead of being categorized in Albert's files as something solely geographical and corporal, something on an average bearing of N 84° W 1,018 feet, more or less, to an iron pin; thence on an average bearing of N 8° E 803 feet, more or less, to an iron pin; thence S 82° E 996 feet, more or less, to an iron pin on the westerly line of the Morton Road; thence southerly by the westerly line of said road 766.5 feet, more or less, to the point of beginning—in those twelve months, Albert's land existed to him more as something hypothetical, more as something that a healing mind was free in idle or in anxious moments to inhabit disembodied and romanticize and dream on. In those twelve months, Albert's dreams and visions and romantic notions took on something like the substance of reality, a sort of parallel reality in which he, the very soul whose name was writ bold on the deed of record, did not figure largely, if at all.

That first June after Albert's convalescence he stood in his room and tapped the barely used eraser of a pencil on his upper lip and tried to estimate the prescience of his checklist, tried to judge if it accounted for the less inevitable contingencies, the ones a Champlain-caliber quartermaster would foresee and with his pencil obviate, including certain afterthoughts and just-in-cases on the checklist to allay the mind and reassure it of the long and glorious history of reasoned readiness. The time had come to leave this life and live another, motherless one for the next four weeks.

But first he closed his eyes and tried to picture how, when he'd awake up there alone come sunrise, need would lead to need and want would lead to want, he being insufficient to make do with what was there already, not possessed of porcupine or ermine or coyote birthright knowledge or the wherewithal to take the treading-lightly, living-off-the-land approach of every other being who inhabited his eighteen acres or passed through them as if boundaries were offenses to the shared predicament of being, before division into kingdom, phylum, class, order, family, genus, species, earthlings, definitely earthlings first, and thus ignored the boundaries as a ghost would not be troubled by a door, would not acknowledge it as hindrance to admission but as the creation of a willful sort who had been taught through generations that the secret to a happy life was to believe that such defenses and delineations had the power of a talisman to keep the mounting evidence of his brief tenure out.

So Albert envisioned morning light through cobwebbed

window and his body rising from the plywood bed and figured that the beneficiary of a good night's sleep required a substantial pillow, sleeping bag, and foam mat. Check. He saw himself, his bare feet on the floor, in embryonic contemplation of the enterprise of simply rising, and he further saw himself, a figure in the process of renewing consciousness and putting on identity's accouterments, remembering the violated tree's imperative to cover up what nakedness his briefs did not address, withdrawing from his duffel bag one of many pairs of clean socks (check), one of many t-shirts (check), and one of two pairs of jeans (check) that he put on without condemning the ancestral spirit of inquisitiveness and the disturbing, soul-befuddling can of worms it opened for the rest of us. Before he saw himself go out the door to urinate in any of the many areas he designated for that purpose in the woods, he saw himself slip boots on. Check. Outside he saw himself beholden to no pressing material need, no want, except that maybe prior to the sun's ascent the morning's chilliness says sweatshirt. Check. He pictured leisurely returning up the steps, across the deck, the stream rush like the voice of some intelligence requiring translation just beyond. If the weather that he pictured held (if not, then rain gear—check), he saw himself stay on the deck and pick up one of several water jugs (check), tilt a little of its contents in the coffee pot (check), sprinkle in a bracing dose of Morning Blend (check), and place the pot on one burner of the two-burner propane stove (check) he lights with either matches advertised as waterproof (check) or one of several lighters (check). Albert saw himself reclining in an Adirondack chair (check), his head's slow swivel left to right inviting him to estimate the per-square-acre density of his respiring woods and guess at the extent of the roots undergirding what would starve and topple left untethered, to observe from point of mostly stillness the sprung stream and imagine what it must be like to be a brook-trout fingerling submerged and buffeted without a guardian in what, from point of mostly stillness, seems to be unmerciful froth, to gaze upon the bluish, breeze-swayed flame as though it were Frank Mesmer conjured, comeback, snapping out of it when his attention fixes on the pot top percolating and he pours the coffee steaming into his ceramic cup (check) and opens up the Coleman (check) to get the cream (check) he pours conservatively in before he teaspoons (check) two heaps of sugar (check) and stirs, as always, clockwise. He saw himself, caffeinated, cracking three eggs (check) in quick succession on the sloped side of the iron skillet (check) that first he lubricated liberally with butter (check), scrambling delicately with spatula (check), and serving on a plate (check), the rye bread (check) that lies thereon just barely buttered with it did not matter which of several knives (check). He saw himself, among a woodland full of crumb and morsel seekers, as a Burgermeister Meisterburger, as a first-world emblem of the too-replete, and saw himself repairing to the privy, to the privacy of door- and latch-outfitted outhouse where he keeps his toilet paper (check) protected from the mice to whom a certain point upon the evolutionary line has not arrived and who are therefore stymied by the mystery of his cylindrical tin (check). Albert saw himself pump twice the sanitizer (check) and cup his culture's oozed defense against bacteria and microbes in his palm and rub his hands together like a large raccoon beside a stream or like a human in a boardroom contemplating the material potential of his greed. He saw himself meander like a monastery person past the punk wood, past the moss and fungus to the rushing stream in which he holds his five-gallon bucket (check) submerged as if he's trying casually to drown a witch and saw himself direct his lop side back past healthy poplar, hemlock, pine, returning up the steps and setting down the bucket on the deck. He saw himself determine that he did not accidentally entrap a fingerling and add a cap of bleach (check) to the water, saw himself dunk in the breakfast instruments (including fork—check) successively and scrub each lightly with a sponge (check) containing dish soap (check), arranging them inverted on a table for the air dry.

Albert's reckoning and his envisioned elsewhere were, like all imperfect meditations, interrupted by a figure from the clung world, by his redhead of a mother who inquired from the kitchen in a neutral voice about the last of his provisions (check). O, encroachment. O, maternal trepidation. O, umbilical cord, you phantom limb. O, apron strings. "I'll be right down," he said like someone woken from the otherworldly rhythm of a dream, trying quickly to extinguish the distraction and pursue by steady respiratory means the fled spell. Albert breathed.

He closed his eyes again, breathed in, breathed out, and saw himself in his woods, returning from an evening constitutional, his arms extended to approximate the balancing device a tightrope walker might employ in his attempt to get from point A to point B without descending like a rag doll to the canyon floor or to the avenue from which the city folk look up and marvel at his willingness to venture netless into the unknown. Albert saw himself returning to the dimming light across a stream-spanned cedar, little more than quite a log now, bridging bank to bank as if the windfall had accorded with the woods' projected sense that it would be nice to have a crossing here for when the water swells and skunk or porcupine or ermine has a pressing interest in a shortcut to the other side. Albert saw himself evaluating risk, the odds that he might slip and fall and puncture or impale his greenhorn flesh or torque a ligament or bone beyond what its Creator reckoned a late-model, largely sedentary Homo would in general have necessity to flex, the odds that he might crack his recently rehabilitated head on any basically immovable stream-bed rock and drown in two or three feet of compelling water, drawing the alive for miles around to make a beeline for the bridge feast. Unprotected ultimately, Albert took what measures he could take: pain reliever (check), first-aid kit with red cross (check), a copy of *How to Stay Alive in the Woods: A Complete Guide to Food, Shelter, and Self-Preservation*, bookmark set securely in the start of "Part Four: Safety," featuring chapters on "Keeping Out of Trouble," "Getting Out of Trouble," "Emergency Aid," "Backwoods Medicine," "Survival Kit," and "Being Ready" (check). Albert saw himself simultaneously accepting the unavoidable cliché that nothing lasts forever and his competence to indefinitely stall the Reaper's summons, saw his boots shuffling his stranger-in-a-strange-land corpus to the point of no return, his being a kinetic vessel, touching down intact, in one piece, campside, walking up the steps, across the deck, and sitting in the Adirondack chair to let kinesis be, to look back at the woods where he had been, to see how close was darkness on his heels, to see he did not fear. Albert saw himself become a deeper shade, a form becoming featureless, like something changed by time-lapse into nothing, an ocular *non grata* in the moonless woods until he rotates a depressed knob clockwise and a deep, percussive hiss hits his tympana as propane floods a tempered-glass enclosure and the quick, fricative rasp of match or flint strike poofs illumination from a lantern (check) he hangs up on a blacksmithed hook as though conducting a 19th-century locomotive onward to a brighter future, shedding light to undermine the modest, backwards night and prove that darkness long ago lost the power to subdue. Albert saw himself immediately believing that the impotence-of-darkness proposition is demonstrably untrue and saw himself considering the long, illustrious history of *vanitas*, the peacock feathers we have fanned, the silverback gorilla chests we've drummed from one felled forest to the next, the expectation we are owed—entitled to—at least our roughly eighty allotted years and anything short of the actuarial average is a crime, a gyp, the sort of hoodwink that the Dutchmen sold the Wappinger Confederacy on. Albert saw himself tilt back his head and wonder like an amateur astronomer or wordless stoner at his little lantern-centered solar system, at the particle mosquitoes and the particle moths who in their buzz and flutter, in their bloodlust and their lightlust make him nod *aha* at the systemic levitation of it all and at the existential counterpoint that has to be the fall, the corporal shrivel, the collapse, and the dispersal outward once again and at the simple, simple truth that he is but the particle Albert—a buzzer and a flutterer and a temporary luster and, like all things great and small, a perfect candidate for, if looked at in the right light and with the proper spirit, the epiphany of free-fall and the grand reunion that is always looming anyway. Insect repellant fortified with Deet (uncheck). Albert saw himself come down to earth and give in to the right brain's hankering for one night's worth of Western literature (check). He saw himself remove the lantern from the hook and hold it out before him in the manner of the hooded figure he spent hours of his youth examining inside the foldout album cover of *Led Zeppelin IV*, which was not formally titled and which featured four mysterious symbols that, despite his microscopic efforts, he was never able to definitively decode and so was never sure that one was linked to Jimmy Page and one to Robert Plant and one to John Paul Jones and one to John Bonham, who at thirty-two gave up the ghost September 25th, 1980, after drinking heavily and choking on his vomit in a guest room at Jimmy's Old Mill House in Clewer. Albert saw himself proceed inside and shut the door to keep out the particles not conducive to the ripple-less condition he prefers to keep this pond of his reflection in. He saw himself hang up the lantern and lie down upon the plywood bed, a book held up before his eyes as though the answers were encrypted letter after letter, sentence after sentence, page after page in there, awaiting someone calm to sneak in and decipher them. Albert saw himself absorbing, practicing the intellectual osmosis of the college boy who thinks he's more substantial than a college boy, who thinks he's plumbing depths a college boy does not possess the respiratory know-how or the mental fortitude to plumb, who thinks that when he surfaces he won't be even slightly sickened as he decompresses in a room that's growing dim, the condensation on the lantern's propane canister descending drip by drip like paratroopers to the floor, becoming one with it until evaporation works its magic and the process of becoming otherwise goes on. Albert saw himself close up the book and do the conscious in-and-out thing with his breath and saw himself with heavy lids outlast the propane light. He saw himself get up and wiggle on his sandals (check) and saw himself encircle with a pointless tenderness the band around his skull and click the button on the headlamp (check) whose beam he follows to the table on which rests his almost indestructible Tupperware rinse cup (check) in which his toothbrush (check) and toothpaste (check) lean like embodiments of the suburban bored whom someone with a four-wheel-drive has dragged out to experience the character-building deprivations of the woods. Albert saw himself, a beam disciple, following the light out to the deck on which the water jug remains at his disposal, saw himself fill up his rinse cup and walk down the steps and to a point that is sufficiently camp-removed and in the woods a little deeper where the leaf and needle litter offer some encouraging semblance of filtration and the comfortable illusion that the daily human effluent can be broken down completely and not leach into the sphere that so depends on some politeness. He saw himself, a beam of light, disturbing the nocturnal, fearing that, if he should turn a certain way, he'd see a pair of reddish eyes approaching to inform him that his light-head is a rudeness. He saw himself, a beam of light, just brushing, rinsing, pouring what remains inside his rinse cup on the fluoridated foam so that no trace of whiteness would be evident tomorrow. He saw himself, a beam of light, concluding his existence on this day by humbly urinating on the fluoridated foam to further its dispersal and remembering something brave that Wendell Berry once wrote down: "I come to you / lost, wholly trusting, as a man who goes / into the forest unarmed." Albert saw himself considering that and feeling at peace without the canister of bear spray (uncheck) he had purchased when, because he was so far from here and did not have the proper visualization tools, it made more sense to demonize and fear. He saw himself, no beam of light, walk toward the camp and up the steps and to the plywood bed in darkness.

Albert's mother called to him again about the last of his provisions. Albert looked out his bedroom window at his Blazer, which was fairly packed. Despite what he would leave behind, he felt bogged down, a college boy defined by baggage, tied by form and content and tradition to the motherland no matter how far ultimately he got from that indelible home, another fraudulent adventurer alighting in a foreign place that he will try to rearrange to make it seem more like the old place he could not abide while he was there in body. Albert made a mental note to not be bound to rearrangement, and he tied a tight imaginary string around his favorite finger to remind him to accept on its subsistence terms this place that he was going to for just the second time.

So that first June after Albert's convalescence, spirits buoyed by the lack of seizure even after his prescription for Dilantin was with guarded optimism not renewed, he carried down his duffel bag and told his mother in the kitchen that he thought he'd checked off everything that he would need and would make do without whatever he forgot. She held out the provisions checklist and reviewed what items she had placed inside the cooler and what items, such as bread and cereal and mustard that was not yet opened, she had placed in paper bags with paper plates and such because, while perishable, such foodstuffs did not need proximity to block-ice in order to maintain their edibility.

"Although," she said, "the mustard will once opened."

"I know, ma, I'm not retarded," Albert said when he meant to thank her, not just for the mustard tip but for her managing to spot him through the modern post-knock reclamation process, which involved a lot of driving and a lot of waiting while there was no getting younger and a lot of redirecting weeping energy toward avenues conducive to the positive vibrations generally prescribed for long recoveries, to spot him unconditionally, to spot without resentment, when she might have wanted to assert that the parental obligation, even in America, expires once the child turns eighteen, forgets where he has come from, and begins to make a big production when he judges that the parents' love infringes like a Stamp Act on his sense of independence.

"No one said you were retarded," she replied. "The doctor says you're fine."

"What's that supposed to mean?"

"It means nothing. It means you're fine."

Albert was not encouraged by her declaration. People who are fine don't need to hear assertions of their fineness, which condition is the given and, as such, remains unspoken until it is unsettled and adulterated and the path back to that coveted default setting people think of fineness as turns out to not be lined with primrose and necessitates the therapeutic hand of language to assist the wobbled and the loop-thrown back—in mind first, and, in fact, in body, second.

However, Albert had been feeling he was past that, thought he was already back; but now, because a well-intentioned declaration jogged his memory, he was not sure and wondered what would happen if, while he was soaking in the peace of eighteen acres, he was taken out of nowhere by that seizure whose unlisted odds his realist neurologist had assured him in their final interview were diminished since, without Dilantin even, he had still not had a seizure, though he'd cautioned that the odds would never be so long as they would like.

"It could be today," the doc had said. "Or sixty years from now. Or never. It's impossible to say."

The latitude of long-range forecasting let him keep the options open. Anything can happen. Albert wondered if the crows would come first, cawing as he twitched or played the pine cone in the still life, debating beakwise whether they were bound by scavenger morality and their intelligence to wait until coyotes got to him and there was no uncertainty that he was carrion or whether they'd be doing humankind a favor, holding up their symbiotic end, in hastening the *bon voyage*, the *it's been real* of this defective member, culling from the herd this Albert-shaped imperfection, leaving behind no secrets in the bones, revealing the inherent foppery of clothes.

"You know your father wishes he could go," said Albert's mother as she wedged a bag of his provisions in the backseat of his Blazer. "He was telling me this morning how he's looking forward to accruing more vacation time and going up there with you sometime. Help out with repairs and whatnot. You know how he is with repair."

"I know. He told me. I was there."

"That's right. That's right. I've been so busy."

"It's better this way. We could use some time alone." He paused. "You know what I mean."

"No drinking," she said. She wasn't quite beseeching.

"Ma, I haven't had a drink since last June. It's been a year. The doctor said it's no big deal if I have one or two."

"I don't care what he said. He doesn't know you. No drinking. What does moderation lead to?" She paused. "Promise me. No drinking."

"I'll be fine," said Albert. "No drinking, Ma."

He pecked her on the left cheek and did nothing with his backhand when he noticed that a little of this morning's application of the moisturizing wrinkle-staller Oil of Olay was transferred to his lips, which he preferred, according to his narrow reading of what constituted masculinity, to keep un-glistened. He started up his Blazer, whose ignition lent a seismic note to his departure and whose muffler perforations likely violated New York's 1988 emissions standards. He reversed his inconsiderate conveyance down the short drive onto Norwood. Waving to his mother as he tried to prove to her through gradual acceleration that, outside the convalescent bubble, he would not revert to last June's maniac, he wondered how long character improvements in a troublemaker's profile had to undergo the head-to-toe inspections before the people modified the Volksgeist, bent a little, and agreed that there was precedent for long-term transformation and agreed that the duration of improvements seemed indicative of a substantial shift inside their Otis Campbell, who for years had made them feel more upright, stable, capable of pity.

Albert waved, and he supposed that coming back would be more difficult this time, although he could not put his finger on exactly why. But if, as he believed, it was as Heraclitus argued and you can't step in the same river twice, what difference did it make *when* you did the stepping? What difference did it make when Albert came back? Why should changes he'd encounter on his next return be more a tribulation than the ones he met with on his last? Be careful where you step is all the returnee can do. And so he waved a while after he no longer saw her because he knew she was still out there, hand still raised, adjusting to the little preview of mortality that flickers every time we say goodbye to someone whom we love.

Albert passed Mullany's house and Shepherd's, Doty's, Butler's, Hull's—all structures whose interiors he intimately summoned to his mind without intending to, the way you summon places childhood concentrically unveiled to you and ingrained with arboreal patience in your heartwood, places set on hedged- or fenced-in little lots that in his mind did not exist in isolation but were intricately linked and as entwined as any ecosystem that a lower-order native as a matter of survival and exuberance learns in secret to negotiate. Albert passed what he still thought of as the field that Mr. Thomas owned and never saw a need to post with prohibitions warning off the children such expanses draw. All houses now. All territory claimed. He felt foolish, letdown suddenly in the heart to have believed once that the field would always be the field. Foolish not to have considered, even as a child, that his own house and Mullany's, Shepherd's, Doty's, Butler's, Hull's—the whole neighborhood—had in their turns usurped their own space in a field, which had been forest, which, if you go back a little way, a certain people whose affiliation Albert did not know the name for then had thought would be forest more or less eternally. He drove and wondered if the river, having been stepped into for the trillionth time, came back around and let the steppers enter the river as it used to be. No mercury. No dams. No tires. Nothing slick on top. No lead. No fishhooks.

What's the point of wondering that? That river is downriver. Always was from where I stand, and always will be. Still.

Long Island Sound is not a river, and he did not consider stepping in as he strolled from slip to slip and paused at certain pilings to consider from a new perspective the allure of harbor water and the hold it takes of someone peering at it from the creaking dock as he kills time until the ferry comes and carries him sixteen miles farther north, where Bridgeport has no power to arrest him with nostalgia and does nothing for him but provide a highway, which a person of a certain turn of mind might liken to a river if the median and shoulders didn't seem so stranded and so hostile to the life he thinks of in his river dreams as relatively unified and riverine. Albert did not think of stepping in Long Island Sound. He did, however, look with interest to his left, beyond Lord Jim and all the moored boats that had spent the winter shrink-wrapped in a boatyard, and he saw the Lilco smokestacks looming red and white like massive barber poles, and he remembered where the secret breach was in the fence, the one they had to walk a ways through woods to get to, the one that said to him and Long Dong, "Psst. This way, boys. Ignore the signs," the one they folded back and crouched through with their Ugly Stiks and Penn reels in the winter when the water out there had grown inhospitable and striped bass gathered at the hot spring where the power plant expelled its heated water through a pipe, creating for the stripers a Caribbean anomaly, a winter home away from home, a temperate zone. Each visit was an exercise in catch and release, a reeling toward them from the wilderness the possibility that they could live this way, outdoors, by wits, and kill when necessary as they would have in the old days but were free of any obligation to produce their proof of that today and were at liberty to simply voice their admiration for the captured piscine beauties, to be steady with the barb removal and give back the lips in good condition, and to lay with cradling hands the stripers in the water where they always floated for a moment as if faced with a decision, always chose at last to fishtail suddenly and swim back to the warm place they were hooked from. Albert wondered if they ever did communicate to others in their school what they had learned of the unknown.

When the ferry docked and Albert embarked, he climbed the metal stairs that echoed every footfall, and he walked across the top deck to the starboard aft-rail corner where he stood for several minutes, motionless, like something Henry Moore had sculpted, staring downward at the passengers and vehicles still boarding, thinking of how constant movement constituted such a national distraction. Then he moved a little, being human, and he panned his gaze from left to right to take in the familiar from on high: Danford's, The Steamroom, JK's, Billy's, The Village Way, The Schooner, Port Wind—establishments he'd been denied admittance to (depending on how seriously the bouncer took his job), establishments he'd reveled in and sometimes left with dignity and of his own accord and sometimes been thrown out of, establishments he had some nights reposed behind and seen through different eyes at first light.

His clear and current eyes looked past the merchant nature of the village center, up the wealthy hill, and settled on the landscape's highest point on which a widespread building made of glass and bricks held up a silver cross like an antenna situated in the hope of crystalline reception, held the cross as close, in purely physical terms, to God as those who followed in the loving footsteps and the founding spirit of the four French Sisters of the Order of the Daughters of Wisdom had been able to afford.

Unlike the newborns taken early or diminished prematurely, Albert had been born on schedule, of sound mind and durable body, in a mostly sterile operating room in Saint Charles Hospital twenty May thirtieths ago without the undue drama that he starred in in his later years, long after he'd attained the age of reason. The only complication on that maiden birthday was the webbing that connected little piggies two and three on both feet, a deformity his mother's obstetrician said was easily correctable with her permission. Ever since that sunny afternoon when Albert was five or six years old and sitting barefoot on his front stoop doing nothing when Manny, who lived four doors down at 214, pedaled by and stopped in to be sociable and looked down at the ground at nothing in particular the way kids who straddle bicycles will do and noticed something not quite right with Albert's podiatric picture and, without intending to embarrass him or be malicious, asked about those Siamese toes before he took a sneaker and a sock off to reveal to Albert five articulated toes, no webbing, which made sense to Albert as he studied them and realized that all along he'd been outside the norm—since then, he'd been of two minds on the subject of his mother's calling of the audible that said there was no need to differentiate and left her first-born's toes, as she explained to him as Manny rode away, as God had made them.

On the one hand, when Albert, reclined unburdened on a flame-retardant couch or cradled by a hammock lightly swung, gazed painterly upon his fused toes and he wiggled them as if to make them say hello and all is well, he ranked his mother up there with the four French Sisters who, on February 7th, 1907, did not turn their backs on or avert their eyes from but threw wide their arms to welcome those initial twenty-seven children, homeless and disabled and relinquished, sent by train to those angelic Sisters who in allegories would be Love; he ranked his mother up there with the great defenders of the leprous and the hare-lipped and the lazy-eyed, with all the saints (canonized and otherwise) for whom the sheen of flesh and vanity and the opinion of the shallow world meant nothing, held no warped allure, and so he spent a good proportion of his free time seeking gratitude's wellspring, hoping to return to her with even just a few cupped drops for starters.

But, on the other hand, he had to make his web-toed way alone through Babylon, where augmentation, reconstruction, realignment, lifting, tucking, and all manner of undoing the aesthetically displeasing work that God or Time had done was pretty much becoming (or already had become) a way of life.

Albert still looked at the silver cross and thought about the

Yellowstone eruption or the reconfigured plague or the astronomer-evading, damn-we-did-not-see-it-coming asteroid that would lay low the current rulers of the earth and wondered what their curious successors centuries, millennia removed would make of all the silicone and plastic mingled with the bones and hardy whatnot they'd discover in the graves. How easy would it be for them to comprehend how vital attractiveness was back then? How difficult for them to make the pieces of the puzzle fit together and to figure out what possible roles the fake tit and the plastic face had played in that mysterious and long ago and almost lost society? Would these discoveries become their Bog Men? Their Stonehenge? Albert had no idea. He liked to entertain the larger questions on occasion, ones for which he knew there were no answers. For now he wanted to remain a little closer to the knowable and the pedestrian, and he was certain that, unless his corpse had been interred in permafrost or in a peat bog, no one in the future with an interest in forensic archaeology would poke his head up like a meerkat from the grave in which the once-Albert had completely yielded to the not-Albert—no one would call over to a colleague elsewhere at the dig and say, "The second and third phalanges of this one's feet appear to have been webbed at birth. Perhaps his parents had been cousins. (Laughter) Nothing plastic in here, though." *No,* thought Albert, *there would be no way for anyone to know.* The webbing would have long since decomposed. He wouldn't even rate an interesting footnote in that future's scientific literature.

But in the complex, subtle, highly critical, and eminently chancy rituals involved in the attraction of a mate, such curiosities were duly noted. Albert chose to limit his exposure and did not wear sandals publicly.

He looked still at the silver cross, then lower, wondering which window looked into the room in which his mother, beat from labor, had recovered, and he wondered why she hadn't simply told her obstetrician, "What the heck. He's getting circumcised anyway. Let's do the toes as well." Why spare his toes the one pain and allow his penis to experience the other? Why keep God's work original in one case and remake it in the other? *Who knows,* thought Albert, who smiled and imagined someone dressed in white emerging from the alley next to Billy's and holding him at scalpel-point, demanding that he make the split decision: "Your penis or your toes." *Toes*, he thought. *No doubt. Please, spare the penis. Part the toes.*

Like pilot fish that shadowed the indifferent shark, two jet skis flitted in the ferry's radiating wake, past Lilco's smokestacks and the channel-marking buoys and the scrub beach and the dunes that rose in the direction of the pinkish mansion in which Foghat had reputedly resided once, and then the jet skis separated from the P.T. Barnum when the inlet widened into open water, wrecked without remorse the picturesque arrangement, jettisoned the harbor's calm as liberated brats will do. The silver cross grew thin, then graduated to a glint. Port Jefferson became a picture postcard and, receding knot by knot and swell by swell, became a variable impression in the distance and in Albert's mind, and so he said goodbye by turning from the haze.

He scanned the coastline to the west and tried to find the indentation of Setauket Harbor, where he knew Ed Mendel's little pirate boat was moored, unless its captain had gone easy on the coke last night and risen early and got heroes from the deli and a case or two and stroked the rowboat to the mooring with a friend or two who had no work lined up that day or no employment aspirations for the summer. How pleasant it would be, Albert thought, and how relieving to kick back on the right side of the Evinrude, his starboard arm all leisurely upon the gunwale, Ed obeying the harbor's posted speed limit and its admonition to produce NO WAKES, the saline breeze invigorating to the nostrils, the beer ice cold and plentiful and canned, the nowhere-in-the-world-to-be feeling, the option to go fishing or to waterski or to just bob out there and think about the depth and listen to the Dead and talk about the quality of cheeba currently in circulation and be certain something monumental would transpire that night because the rumor was that Bighead managed to obtain a quantity of mushrooms from mysterious quarters. Fucking Bighead.

For a while Albert leaned back against the rail and kept on looking west and tried to put in words exactly what he hoped to find in Maine that he could not find here and what he hoped to be up there that he could not be here. What was he, after all, without community, sans context? No one, really. Anyone. Why leave the people whom he intimately knew, the people by whom he was intimately known? They knew too much, he guessed. But so what? It stood to reason that, if Heraclitus's river was a different one each time the foot stepped in, the foot, in fairness, should be mutable as well and seen, by virtue of accrued experience, as different from the foot that stepped before. Except it rarely seemed to work that way.

Here he was, a year removed from his collision with the pavement, a year removed from alcohol and rash decisions and urea-saturated pants and rude awakenings and public shame, a year into his long-term plan to really model gratitude, a year into a poetry apprenticeship that made him almost thank the fracture for directing him that way. But everyone who knew him knew his history and waited for it to repeat itself, saw Albert's feet still planted in the same position they'd been in before they flew out of the bed of Bob Orr's F-150. As if the impact had not shattered him and the ensuing year had not put back together a distinct Albert. As if his feet would always lead him back to feel nostalgia by the riverside. As if he could not walk away from what he was once in that river. Maybe they were not far from the truth, and it was best to simply have his feet convey him to a river where his intimates and he had never been, had never dipped a toe in. Still. If there was anything the head smack taught him, it was how like butterfly wings memories can be and how it helps to smell the milkweed.

The ferry sailed on.

Albert smiled and remembered being out with Ed around the Middle Ground last June about a week or so before his fracture. They had passed the Stratford Shoal Light, heading east as Ed stood tall in tinted specs, his bleach-blond mullet trailing in the breeze. The cooler was already half-filled with the lobsters Ed had poached since they had left Setauket Harbor, and the longer Albert sat by them attempting to determine if he really could intuit suffering emanating from those eyes the harder it became for him to argue that, in human terms, it made no sense to empathize. Before they got as far as Shoreham, Ed throttled back and looked around to verify no witnesses on the horizon, and he gaffed the buoy line that he began to haul in hand over hand. Albert put down his sixth or seventh beer and chose a lobster from the cooler, holding its face close to his, adjusting to account for claw range.

"Ed," said Albert, "I believe this lobster wants its freedom, man."

Ed looked over his left shoulder to where Albert sat beside the Evinrude and paused the haul. "Don't you throw that fucking lobster off this boat."

"It's a liberation matter, Ed. Look into the eyes. Oppression's writ there, Ed."

"Then go join Greenpeace. Don't throw that fucking lobster off this boat. I swear to God."

"Lobster," asked Albert face to face, "were you born free?" He nodded the lobster, faced it toward Ed, and nodded it again. "Ed. Born free. Born *free*, Ed." He held the lobster at arm's length over the gunwale, outside the boat.

"I'm telling you. Do not—"

"Fly. Be free," said Albert as he released his grip. The lobster free-fell momentarily and plunked like a flat stone in the water.

Ed let go the trap-line, whose immediate uncoiling was a lesson in what happens when a mortal does not guard his precious time more carefully, and took two giant steps for steaming mankind toward the stern where smirking Albert rose and backed a little, tensing to absorb the blow that he was certain would land shortly on his port-side since he knew that Ed was born a righty and in no mood to be feigning with his left. But when it came to punches, Albert's face was fairly practiced in absorption, and he took in good fun and in stride the one that Ed threw, nothing much, a knuckle-sandwich landing sloppily on his cheekbone, sending Albert into a spastic sort of scuba-diver backflip a foot or two to the starboard of the Evinrude's propeller. Albert surfaced and he backstroked for a while, soaking in the high sun, feeling the exposed joy that a manatee must feel before a speed-obsessed Floridian goes medieval on its belly. Of course there had to be infringement on the peace. He heard and felt the rumble of the Evinrude's ignition, and he saw what had been mellow water roil underneath the engine and the oily cloud of its exhaust as Ed leaned forward on the throttle and began to pull away. Suspended like a child between the wanting to believe that what he hoped would happen would and the desire to get on with it and see the world for what it was, Albert watched as Ed and the Garcia steadily diminished as they headed west, until that speck that he had faith was still Ed and the Garcia disappeared around a point he couldn't judge how many miles distant. This was problematic. If a Seal Team Six member surfaced at that moment with a Sig Sauer P226 and pointed it at Albert's head and promised to dispatch him, making him a mere statistic, just another in the country's rapidly elongating line of victims of a violence that's so easy with a gun, unless Albert could, without a moment's hesitation, answer accurately the Seal Team Six member's inquiry about how far it was to Long Island's shore, he'd pause, say um, and close his eyes while guessing ten-point-five miles because he knew the Sound was twenty-one miles at its widest point, which more or less was the vicinity he thought he floated in at present, and because Long Island seemed as distant from him as Connecticut and because, when all else failed, he figured that he might as well split the difference. But he might as well be shot by Mr. Seal Team Six as try to swim ten miles, or even five. Of the top ten non-disease-related ways he did not want to die, drowning tied with choking on a Fireball at number six. So Albert floated on his back and looked up at the clear sky, picturing his body as a piece of driftwood going slowly, slowly with the flow.

He closed his eyes. He still made the subtle flipping motions with his hands and feet, but he relaxed. He thought Dead Sea. Thought buoyancy. Thought buoyancy and dozed, the water's rhythm lulling him and maybe, too, the alcohol was humming him a pleasant, poison lullaby. This went on and this went on, and then, inside the small absurdist theater in his head, he heard offstage the sound of something distant flapping, possibly a flannel sheet or possibly a flag or possibly a heron or a cormorant preparing for a solo liftoff or attempting to attract the reproductive interest of a female via wingspan emphasis. The sound grew louder, and his driftwood body swelled a little with the water. Also offstage, someone yelled as if through cupped hands, "Hey, man, you all right?" and Albert looked up at the blue sky and reduced the autopilot flipping motions he'd been making with his hands and feet and felt his feet sink as he went more vertical and saw two guys upon the canvas stretched across the two hulls of a catamaran, which vessel struck him suddenly as the epitome of grace.

"Are you all right? What are you doing this far out?" They seemed relieved that they were not addressing the anticipated corpse.

"I'm fine," said Albert. "Just floating. I was made to walk the plank."

The two men looked around. One said, "What plank?"

Albert said, "My friend and I did not see eye to eye on a bioethics issue. He'll be back."

"Well, in the meantime, do you want to come aboard and have a beer?"

"I do," said Albert, who then swam to them and grabbed the hand one of them extended.

"How long have you been in there?"

"Half hour. Hour. Hard to say. I might have dozed off for a while."

They drank their Buds and talked about the weather and when bluefish schools would boil through and how a friend could leave a friend without a life vest in the middle of the Sound.

Albert explained, "He likes cocaine. We drink a lot. It gets tempestuous, but he'll be back."

"You could have died, man. We barely even saw you."

"True. God bless the manatee. But thank you for the rescue. Thank you for the beer. Beautiful vessel. Beautiful beer."

Midway through the second beer, Albert saw a boat come round the point around which Ed and the Garcia had disappeared before. "I think that's him," said Albert, and the three of them sat lined up on the canvas, seagull style, facing west and watching as the speck cast off its speckness. "Yep, that's him." They watched as Ed pulled up and idled maybe twenty feet away.

Ed shook his head and smiled. "Get in, asshole."

"Aye, aye," said Albert. "Thank you, guys. I mean it. Thank you." And he did a leaning jackknife off that Jacqueline Onassis of a cat and swam in six or seven strokes to the Garcia, climbed the ladder he unfolded and reclaimed his cushioned spot beside the Evinrude. Ed passed the peace pipe, and the ripple in their little sea was smoothed out with a smoke.

Now that, thought Albert standing on the top deck of the P.T. Barnum, heading steadily toward Connecticut, *was living.* And he wondered if his coming life would ever yield that sort of *oomph* again, that sort of psychic oneness with the world that opened up when he was willing to kick back and say, without saying, "Come what may." This second trip up to his eighteen acres, Albert's ownership of which, he always told himself, his fractured skull made possible, might, he hoped, provide him with the yea or nay he needed to move on.

The long drive up put much behind him: Port Jefferson, Norwood, family, friendship, place-sense, what he knew, how he was known. Listening to the gospel of the internal-combustion engine testifying over Eisenhower's Interstate for mile after asphalt mile, Albert, when not distracted by the radio, was slapped by how incongruous the journey was, how patently unnatural to maintain a speed of seventy for almost seven hours in order to traverse four-hundred miles for the purpose of briefly seceding from society, retiring for four weeks into woods that weren't all that different from the woods (in Connecticut, in Massachusetts, in Vermont) that grew much closer to his home, that weren't all that different (except that his were not the old growth) from the woods the whites had felled since 1492 with the persistence of a cancer. Hard, then, not to think that he was just a sort of cell dispatched by something vastly biological to venture to a distant part of what had been a healthy and holistic body and begin the decimating occupation of that tiny, eighteen-acre region hitherto so very much unlike the kingdom of the laid low and the overbuilt. *Hard,* he thought, *but not impossible. Think pine. Think hemlock.* About twenty miles after exiting the Interstate, Albert drove slowly into Garland, passing by the green and gold sign that reminded passersby of its establishment in 1818, by cornfield after cornfield, by the town hall and the historical-society building, turning left where 94 abruptly ended at the tee where sat the Garland Store and Post Office. He passed the fairgrounds and another cornfield, turning right on Center Road, hemmed in on either side by woods, and drove until he reached the cornfield on the left that was the landmark he and his brother had bypassed last time when they missed the unpruned entrance to the discontinued Morton Road, down which his camp sat four-tenths of a mile on the right. Discontinuance or not, to call the Morton Road a road was to disseminate a false impression, to play loose with language, to express a sense of humor, maybe, where the joke was that you're free to call a thing whatever you would like, but simply calling something something doesn't necessarily make it so.

As Albert pulled in the Morton Road, he tried to fathom how deep were the inland-sea-sized puddles he was inching toward and felt the tires slide a little with the mud as they sank in and sloshed. The puddles thinned and disappeared, replaced by a persistent trickle as the road descended, steepening, and Albert bucked from side to side not quite in concert with the creaking Blazer as it crawled upon and over rocks it could not go around because the narrow way, constricted left and right by poplar, pine, some hardwood, brooked no deviation. For a moment, he imagined someone in another vehicle approaching from below, and Albert wished he knew the custom in such situations, who possessed the right of way and who would have to throw his tranny in reverse, returning to his point of origin by side and rear views, because there was no sliver of a shoulder to repair to with a wave to let a traveler in opposition pass. Because imagination can trade places rather quickly with reality, he worried that in backing up he might go off the relatively solid roadbed into tree and mire and entanglement and thus become the anti-hero of a story that would no doubt be disseminated by the person he imagined was approaching from below as soon as he could make it to the Garland Store, where Albert would thenceforth be ashamed to show his face because what sort of man can't back his own truck up a hill. The wave of worry made him press down on the brakes and stop to reassess if he possessed within himself the right stuff to effect a backward egress. He closed his eyes and visualized reversing flawlessly and put his mind at ease, and then he realized with open eyes, remembered from the only other time that he was here, that down below, beyond his property, the progress of the Morton Road was interrupted by a stream strewn here and there with boulders, and, although it might be technically passable by someone who could not care less about the undercarriage of his vehicle, the odds that someone would approach from that direction, he assured himself, were slim.

Anxiety subdued, he rolled his window down and looked around. He felt a little first-world silly having stressed out in the presence of so many trees, so many vertical, outspreading lives exuding oxygen and calm.

Breathe in, breathe out. Something, nothing. Is, was. Repeat.

Albert raked his version of a Zen garden for a while and discerned the rock wall standing still among the trees and undergrowth that slowly claimed it for their own, took back in due time what a farmer had unearthed and stacked to form a certain line between his field or pasture and the three-rod Morton Road, which at the height of its utility had measured forty-nine-point-five-feet wide. Albert looked at all the thin trees vying with the scattered ancient ones and wondered what had happened to the old economy that made the land beyond the wall unviable to farm, that made the man who once had visions of a life here throw up his calloused hands and sell the land for little, thinking elsewhere must be better. How long ago was that? Twenty years? Fifty? He considered what it must have been like to have lived and worked here in the thirties, and he wished that he possessed the wisdom to observe a forest and determine just by noticing a few particulars about the trees how long ago the forest floor was but the sun-drenched realm of seedlings. And he wondered what the plans were of whomever owned those woods beyond the rock wall now. He doubted there could ever be tract housing here or strip malls in his lifetime, and what reason, he conjectured, would there ever be to level woodland for the sake of leveling? He felt this place was safe from depredation for a while. Here he saw the not Long Island. He saw little evidence of a transformative economy. He saw abandoned farmland yielding meekly to the woods. He saw cheap land that no one seemed to want unless what one was looking for primarily was to be left alone, to be enfolded like a wild thing inside the woods.

Yes, he thought, *this is the ticket. This is where I want to be,* and he continued inching down the maybe half-rod Morton Road again and closed his window so the overhanging branches on the driver's side could not get in.

Without the dangling strip of orange tape the realtor last year had knotted to the cable stretched across the entrance, Albert, his eyes so used to looking for suburban landmarks like a boner of a mailbox or a trimness symptomatic of the ailment that is curb appeal, would have continued slowly past the twig-colored cable, would have missed the untrod, unwhacked byway to the unfamiliar kingdom that did not exactly whip the cornets out to welcome him with a majestic flourish. He got out, unheralded, and he unhitched the cable from the lower portion of the tree whose upper portion had gone punky and had given way since he had last been here. Albert waded through the knee-high grass and brushed his right foot back and forth to warn what toads or mice or sexton beetles might be here that something indiscriminate and burdensome was coming, and a frog of some sort sprang once to the woods. More power was exhibited in mercy, he agreed, than in severity.

He entered in his mental ledger one good deed.

He drove through cautiously, looking left and right for any signs of fleeing life. Detecting none, he inched the Blazer on, flattening the boggy grass with parallel tracks, and came out to the dirt and gravel clearing where he parked. Oppressed, he walked toward the clearing's edge, where cedar, pine, and hemlock seedlings vied with one another, rising brightly toward the light, and he unzipped and pissed beside the little trees and felt that owning woods was worth it just for this. No neighbors, no police, no penis being cited for indecency when nature called. No one asking him to be beholden. No one asking him if he required help.

The camp sat in a depression shielded from the clearing by a line of pine and hemlock. Sided with vertical pine strips with the bark still attached, the camp appeared at first to be a dense stand until you caught a sliver of the stovepipe's silver and discerned the dirty window and became aware the stand was like a palisade that ended where the grayish fascia board and needled asphalt roof began. Albert bounced on down the duff path bordered by two lines of cedar six-by-sixes to the rough-hewn cedar decking, slick in spots with moss and fungal slime, that ran along the right side of the camp for twenty-four feet, turned left, and stood a moment on the front deck, troubled by the possibilities the open door portended to a mind accustomed to the sanctity of locks and even latches.

Albert remembered what the realtor had said: "A lock will only keep the honest people out." The tradition, too, the realtor suggested, was to leave the doors of hunting camps unlocked so that, if someone hunting in the area got hurt or started going hypothermal, he would have a place to turn to. "But it's entirely up to you." Since Albert had assumed that there would be no reason anyone would want to enter here except in an emergency and that, if someone did decide to yield to rural curiosity and have a look around, he'd have the decency to honor Albert's trust and latch the door on leaving, Albert, as far as he remembered, had experienced no reservations when he left last year with just the latch he had secured to guard an acquisition, a possession, he now realized he'd left defenseless.

He stood to the left side of the door and pushed it all the way open. Peeking in, he banged his left hand on the outer wall a few times and expected to observe the sudden movement of an animal whose rabidity would laser in on him, and suddenly he wished his hand could drop down Eastwood-style to a sidearm that would render the uncertainty less taxing. When he heard no scurrying and wasn't charged, he ventured in and peered beneath the plywood bed and peered beneath the lower bunk and peered behind the woodstove and peered behind the hardwood piled in the corner and uncocked real slow-like the internal hammer whose concussion he had been expecting to absorb.

The only threats he saw did not exhibit threatening behaviors (raising hackles, baring fangs, bluff charging, and the like)—behaviors that inspire men to action (picking up a blunt-force-trauma sort of object, talking softly to convey a sense that we are all in this together, climbing up a climbable tree, or just plain fleeing like a lion-shadowed antelope, anything except inviting contemplation in and waiting with your legs crossed in a lawn chair while a list of options is compiled and considered, waiting with your fingers, fingertips to fingertips, before your pursed lips, conveying to the cocked aggressor you are not sure what to do). The only threats he saw were biological and widespread, sprinkled everywhere as if the mice had feared they would get lost in here and needed to deposit landmark after fecal landmark to allow them to retrace the hound-befuddling trail they blazed through Albert's dream of solitude. But he was not above cohabiting with field or deer mice. He believed he understood their plight and did not *want* to be an instrument of their extermination, their expulsion.

Albert knew that it was in his nature to humanize, but he also knew it wasn't necessary to confer human qualities on these trailblazing mice in order to acknowledge that they held the prior claim, that this was their home, their land, more than his, no matter what the papers said. He knew he did not have to think of them as thinking as he did in order to extend compassion to them. He had only to acknowledge they could suffer as legitimately as he could. Who didn't suffer? Words were not required. Neither was a human brain. So, what to do about the problem here presented?

Albert walked out to the lawn chair on the deck, where he imagined he breathed in an atmosphere whose lower concentration of infectious particles was probably more conducive to arriving at a more humane decision than he could arrive at on the inside, where the line that history had drawn between humanity and mice seemed starker, seemed to call for traps or poison. Albert sat and tried to picture what the scope of suffering would be like in the aftermath of a deliberate poisoning campaign. Fievel after Fievel growing dizzier and dizzier behind the walls and dying there unloved or staggering outside in the hope of a revival in the light and hemorrhaging internally as a fox or hawk or owl hears the rustling, snatches up the easy meal, and sickens likewise, Albert's landscape ultimately littered like a creepy wasteland just because he couldn't deal more sturdily with his, his kind's, inherent kernel of repugnance and conditioned gravitation to the quick fix. No, that outcome would not do. He wished the world community would one day coalesce and grow vociferous in condemnation of the evil that conceived of hemorrhagic means of pest control.

A cabin mined with snap traps would sound positively medieval in the middle of the night. The peanut-butter dollops calling out to whiskered noses, promising to cure the huddled of their hunger, seemed but sweet perversions of the post-fall human mind, devising always tortuous snares and sly enticements to achieve a little broken neck here, a trapped leg there that the defenseless mouse would have no choice except to gnaw and leave behind as though the fourth leg were the burden. Albert's admiration for the little fuckers grew, and in his burgeoning appreciation of the mouse's concentrated brand of toughness and tenacity he found the story he had heard of the New Hampshire man who had been cutting trees down on his woodlot, probably imagining his place in this life was secure, and whom the universe had picked to somehow fall face-up and have a leg be shattered and immobilized beneath a fallen tree, whose many years of patient standing there had fused in it a stoicism that contributed a heavy psychic element, a messing-with-the-frantic-human's-psyche sort of stillness to its weight. A sense of certainty came over Albert as he considered how, if he were likewise pinned, he would assume his story had been written, wind down, breathe less, let go—the coyotes and the ravens and the burying beetles coming in the end to pick apart the person who he sometimes felt was masquerading as this character named Albert and was lucky to have lasted in the troubled role this long. But this New Hampshire man was certainly not Albert. He used his shirt to tie a tourniquet around his upper thigh and used his Buck knife to begin the severance. He passed out, woke up, went back to cutting. Passed out, woke up, went back to cutting. Finally, he dragged himself away, his leg detached like a prosthetic he decided did not fit correctly anymore. Two miles' worth of dragging, and he made it to the road where he was rescued by a passerby and driven to a hospital. Albert tried to picture no one passing by, no merciful extension, the New Hampshire man just dragging what was left of him inside the darkness of a cabin wall to die a death that seemed to render all that effort, all that life force, pointless. *No*, thought Albert, *I would not wish that suffering on a man. I would not wish it on a mouse.* And so.

Albert went inside and used the yellow broom to sweep the droppings into piles that he then collected in the dustpan and deposited outside. He opened all the windows, swept the beds and wiped some dampened paper towels over counter, over cabinets, over tabletops and breathed as though his cilia were insufficient to prevent the airborne particles from entering his lungs. When he was done, he took a seat upon the deck again and breathed more deeply, wondering how much he couldn't see. What lurked in them there woods? What microscopic creatures whirled like dervishes about his head? What lived inside the cabin's ceiling and its walls? What entered him with every breath? He had reason to believe himself his own worst enemy, the entity to really fear, and he'd achieved a fragile peace thus far with that marauder. *I have been protected. I will be protected.* He believed.

Albert tilted back his rehabilitated head and looked up at the limited sky the trees permitted any groundling thus positioned to contemplatively eye, and for a moment he believed he would experience a bout of vertigo or tunnel vision, which assailed him mostly as he slouched toward class and which he always feared as dark-hearted harbingers of the seizure that had not yet come, and, when the rush of dizziness or narrowness did not materialize, he felt more fortified than he remembered ever feeling in his natural habitat, the suburbs, which a part of him regarded as an unforgiving wall against which he'd been banging his not quite conditioned head since middle school, at least, while those who loved him and who did not see a wall looked on and wondered what was going on inside.

His head still tilted back, his eyes still looking past the treetops to the circumscribed sky, he let what he was hanging onto float away (he knew that it would float back down and land on him at some point like a gondola, but for the moment the motif was buoyancy) and thought about the serious risks and troubles people more adventurous and logical than him accepted as a part of moving boldly through this life and leaving self-absorption to the sad sacks of this mind-blowing situation we have here. Albert knew that he was not, genetically or temperamentally, among those sorts who sought to be, who let themselves for the advancement of the commons be propelled by rockets into orbit, circling the motherland it seemed to him offensive and ungrateful that they'd want to ever leave. *That's ultimately the purpose*, Albert assumed. *To leave.* But where would he be, where would any of us be, if someone blessed with fortitude wasn't always standing at the forefront with an outstretched index finger pointing onward to a place or to a way of life that wasn't known? *Perhaps*, he thought, *in Eden still, the water pure, the conscience clear. Perhaps wiped out in Ethiopia not too far from the get-go because the wish to stay put turned out not to be adaptive.* Albert may not be the one to lead, he may not like whom he has followed, but he followed. *So*, he thought, *I'll let a little sorrow in and mourn again the simple failure of an O ring, mourn the Challenger's explosion seventy-three seconds into a similar sky, lament what vaporized, what drifted down through catastrophic sky, through water, landing softly on the ocean floor three years ago.*

The interlude concluded. Nature called.

He walked around the angled deck and wound his way upon forgiving pine duff to the outhouse, which was four by four and light blue. The last time he was here, accompanied by his brother on the day he signed the papers, was the first time he had used an outhouse, such a liberating structure being outlawed on Long Island. He recalled the light metallic clink of latch on catch, the hula dance of breeze through treetops, and the peering down into the hole that did not seem at all as pestilential as he'd feared. He had sat down, felt on some frontier he could not put his finger on, and wondered how long it would be before the hole was filled to its capacity and how exactly someone went about a proper outhouse decommissioning. What he was sure that he did not recall, however, was that ragged hole in the plywood's bottom, where the sheathing almost touched the ground. *No big deal*, he thought. *That's easy to repair.*

He pulled open the door, the spring creaked, and he saw no spot upon the square floor that wasn't inch deep in the droppings of an animal he could not at that time identify. He did know that they were not left there by a mouse, a moose, a deer, a bear, a fox, or a coyote—beyond that, he could not be sure. So. To the woods. A little deeper into the woods to do his business as a truer primitivist, a person who was so far gone that he might have some difficulty coming back.

When he returned he figured that the dust inside the camp had settled so that he would not on his reentry introduce too many plaguy particles into his lungs, and he could start unloading his supplies from the Blazer. Shouldering a duffel bag toward the camp, he noticed how the camp's rear left, where it was propped up by successive cinder blocks, sagged more prominently than he remembered, and he got the sinking feeling that the simple infrastructure here, his interloping presence here was under an impersonal attack. *Be rational,* he thought. *Be rational.* He raked the Zen garden that he kept on standby in his mind. *There's no attack, you freak. Just maintenance. Just basic maintenance.* That, however, was unsettling enough because of his incompetence, his lack of practical experience, the absence of a wall jack, the feeling that the whole thing would at some point have to come down, and he'd have to somehow start anew.

***

Well, thinks Albert, hungover, wanting to reclaim the clear mind and return to Maine as he has done each summer since that first extended stay, *I guess there was no point in worrying about anew.* Nothing much has changed there. Albert's eighteen acres on the Morton Road are not much different than they were twenty-four years ago. He is an apostle of inertia. The trees grow. The camp still sags. The roof leaks. Long ago, he ceded the interior to the mice. He sleeps inside a tent when he goes up there now. He does his business in the woods. He longs to go because he does not want to be that guy who wakes beside the river and considers dry pants an accomplishment. He does not want to raise the lamentation for the past that earnestness cannot retrieve. He does not want to butt heads with his fellow man because of differing interpretations of the rights of turtles. But he has to. The shoulder voice is clear that it's a must. It's easier, when he can feel he's tilting at a dangerous degree, to leave. So when his head clears, he will leave and be the person he believes he is alone, when no one who opposes his ideals will be around to challenge him to stand his ground.

Chapter Four

In 1947, in the heady years that followed Victory, on five-thousand acres in the geographical center of Long Island, long after every native was exterminated or resigned to reservation life or city life or town life or another mode of settling things, and not too long before the residential post-war creep extended like a skin condition this far east, the U.S. Army base known as Camp Upton formally ceased to be and became the Atomic-Energy-Commission-administered (and then the Department-of-Energy-administered) facility known as Brookhaven National Laboratory. Surrounded by oak and pine forest, the Lab was naturally fortified from the enemies then eyeing the Nation, but, because a Nation cannot leave security entirely to geographic advantage in an age when threats may come from above, there were, nearby, surrounding the Lab like a palisade, more Nike missiles in position than the Lab would ever need. In keeping with the age-old notion that there is safety in numbers, more weapons were the only things that put the collective mind at ease. This ease was mere illusion. On some level (psychological, spiritual, schoolyard), a Nation that recently vaporized so many innocent people with two unprecedented Bombs expects that karma or the all-seeing eye atop the pyramid on the backside of the dollar or whomever oversees the basic and generally accepted what-goes-around-comes-around ethos cannot permit such violations of compassion to soften into history without direct address, and so such a Nation sleeps with one eye open. In the meantime, Science is the sage that promises to answer all.

Many educated, intelligent, science-loving people whose roots were not far removed from European soil flocked to the Lab with dreams of service to the shining city on the hill but also to the arduous and cumulative and often morally gray endeavor of human knowledge or betterment or, God forbid, enlightenment. If you accept that these were not bad people, not minions devil-sent to carry out a diabolical, insidious project to remind the world that it requires absolute evil to define absolute good, do you simply write them off as well-intentioned nerds whose thick and black-rimmed spectacles were fitted with the wrong prescription from the outset, rendering them incapable of seeing how their ant-like contributions would in time destroy some unsuspecting future members of the Colony?

It takes a certain sort of person to appreciate a hermit thrush and its unintentional ability to lift a human's spirit with its singing, a certain sort of person to look upward with humility at the reticulating branches of an oak that's been around so long it must in some sense pity humans their inherent brevity, to marvel at its water-uptake genius and its respiration, its sequestering of CO2 without reminding anyone that such a service should be recompensed. It takes a certain sort of person to accept that certain places on the earth have long been spoken for and are not meant for a clear-cut or a cul-de-sac or mineral extraction or an interstate or any of the multitudinous mutilations profit says it is okay and perfectly natural, nay, inevitable to perpetrate.

Back in 1960, it took a certain sort of person to reflect, on entering the forest that belonged now to the Lab, that nature was created to be put at man's disposal. It took a certain sort of person to walk in with nothing, no ancestral sense of kinship with the woods, no sorrow in the lonely knowledge that the road toward Progress had to be unmerciful, with nothing but the satisfaction that he found the raw material for an experiment that other cytologists and ecologists (and maybe even physicists) would wish they'd had the kindled wisdom to conduct.

So the eminent cytologist Arnold Hicks Sparrow had the Lab's maintenance crew fence off 123 acres of the pine-oak forest that had grown according to natural laws for generation after generation, and, on November 21st, 1961, Dr. Sparrow led the team that bombarded the center of those woods with cesium-137 gamma radiation for up to twenty hours each day over the ensuing seventeen years, ending quietly sometime in 1978. The genesis of the experiment was the understandable fear that the USSR could at any moment bomb New York or Washington or someplace nondescript that no one in the Pentagon would expect; the genesis was the *que sera* reaction that we might as well determine what the fallout would destroy botanically and cellularly so that our brightest minds could get a handle on the finer points of Armageddon ahead of time. As early as 1962, the biologist/ecologist George M. Woodwell noted without apparent irony or angst that "cesium-137 gamma radiation altered the normally stable pattern of ecosystem behavior." The Drs. Sparrow and Woodwell detailed, with the sort of creepiness that only a tone of clinical detachment can convey, the effects of anywhere from two to several thousand roentgens on trees, plants, aphids, ants, and deer mice, which for some reason they did not refer to as deer mice but as *Peromyscus*. Five concentric circles ringing their respective zones extended out from the center, the region of the most intense irradiation, which the scientists referred to as "the dead zone, the zone of total kill." In the study's conclusion, Dr. Sparrow wrote, again without apparent irony or angst: "The dead oaks and pine in Figure 1 are mute evidence of the lethality of gamma radiation." No one mentioned that the half-life of cesium-137 is 30.17 years. No one mentioned whose unfortunate role it was to finally remove the irradiated soil and where that unwanted soil went. No one mentioned if the soil, so unwanted, was removed at all. And, certainly, no one mentioned anything about apologizing to that mute, abused, and unloved patch of earth the Lab refers to unofficially as the Gamma Forest.

Because of the Lab's stated commitment to exploring peaceful uses of nuclear radiation, because the seven Nobel Prizes awarded to twelve of its scientists since 1958 are a testament to the Lab's humanity and its pioneering spirit, there is no need for apology. On occasion, the Lab may reluctantly acknowledge that the blazing of the sort of scientific trails we are discussing here may sometimes call for some remediation to clean up the necessary messiness of genius, but the Lab is clear apology has no place in an institution whose existence is dependent on the will to not be bound to anything as unenlightened as the troubles of the past.

So the Lab celebrated in 1947 the commissioning of its Graphite Research Reactor. So it puffed its chest out just a little bit more in 1958 when it turned on its High Flux Beam Reactor. So it ran its white fingers through its oiled hair in 1959 on opening its Medical Research Reactor. So its thumbs strained its suspenders when in 2010 its Relativistic Heavy Ion Collider promised to unlock the secrets of the stubborn universe. But, of course, the Lab was well aware that, when you play with fire long enough, you can expect a burn or two. You can't help that. It is the nature of the beast. You can, however, keep the injuries from your neighbors for a while—until the neighbors get to wondering about the smoke that seems increasingly to waft from your serene direction.

After decades of denying it had anything to do with the mounting anecdotal evidence of rare tissue cancers in children who lived around the Lab's perimeter, of breast cancer in women whose faucets poured water drawn from the aquifer beneath the Lab, of brain, lung, testicular, esophageal, and other cancers among the Lab's employees, after decades of intensive, focused obfuscation, the Lab admitted in 1997 that its spent-fuel pool at its High Flux Beam Reactor had been leaking six to nine gallons of tritium-contaminated water per day for a period of twelve to twenty years into the aquifer that provides water for over a million of its neighbors. The EPA assured the people that the leakage posed no threat to public health.

Whether the Lab enjoyed this moment of unburdening and found it so cathartic that it wanted to share more, or a higher power than the DOE demanded it go public with its findings, isn't absolutely clear. What is clear, though, is that the Lab admitted that its Linac Isotope Producer was a likely source contributing to the three tritium plumes that emanated from the Lab. It admitted the existence and pinpointed the location of the Graphite Research Reactor spill site. It admitted to a Building 830 pipe leak that emitted cobalt-60, hydrogen-3, cesium-137, plutonium-239, and americium-241. It admitted to radiologically contaminating soil at the Particle Beam Dump and the Alternating Gradient Synchrotron Experimental Area. It admitted to a Bubble Chamber spill area. The Bubble Chamber was "used for the storage of drum- and liquid-filled scintillation counters. Scintillation oil is mainly composed of mineral oil and trimethylbenzene." It admitted to a trichloroethylene spill area. It admitted that for three years in the Meadow Marsh, adjacent to the Gamma Forest, it discharged raw sewage containing aluminum, cadmium, copper, iron, lead, silver, zinc, and other inorganic compounds to examine the effects of such discharges on natural systems. It admitted to contamination at Building 702, which contained a graphite pile, biological shield, control rods, and other equipment. One concern here was contamination via the "experimental holes." According to the Lab's "Graphite Pile Removed, Area of Concern 9, Final Closeout Report," "One of these, known as the animal tunnel, was employed to irradiate animals." It admitted to PCB soil contamination at Building 96. It admitted to mercury soil contamination at Building 464. It admitted to fifty-five biological, chemical, and radiological waste pits containing arsenic, barium, beryllium, the hepatitis virus, et cetera. It admitted to Area of Concern after Area of Concern.

It admitted no malfeasance, and it issued no apology.

As far as Albert knew, when his father started working at the Lab in 1984, there was nothing to apologize for. The recession of the 1970s and early 1980s hit the Lesiaks hard. Albert learned about privation somewhat, but this knowledge came in little lessons he took little solace in at the time.

For example, when he made his peace with the reality that he would never own a Members Only jacket in that brief historical window when, among the children of his middle school, such a ridiculous possession was considered cool, he knew how shallow such desire made him seem. He'd seen the images of the distended bellies and the fly-bespeckled foreheads of the children starved in Ethiopia, and he knew that he was blessed. What bothered him was that he did not feel content with that degree of blessedness and that he knew such ingratitude was like a slap across the chiseled faces of those children who were too infirm to raise their hands in self-defense, too weak to shoo a fly. So when his father got that job and Albert began receiving an allowance and began to spend a little of it on a six-pack now and then and grew a little maudlin one night as he pondered what he knew of the inequity of life as late-night television glowed ghostly in his face, he sponsored a child in Ethiopia based on one of those commercials in which someone who exuded empathy said, "You could save a child's life for less than fifty cents a day."

His father's good fortune, therefore, did not go unshared. And life went on at Albert's house without excessive worry. Though he knew that something vaguely nuclear went on at the Lab and though his father sometimes told the family over dinner he had been inside the HFB reactor in the morning to perform routine maintenance and joked that afterward his skin glowed green and all day he felt stronger than he ever had before, Albert was intimately acquainted with his father's sense of gallows humor and never seriously considered that in 1984 the government would put civilian life in harm's way. Besides, as a member of the Plant Engineering Division's Heavy Equipment Mechanic Operators, his father mostly worked outdoors, in the sunshine, the fresh air, and sometimes the woods, outside of the reactors that were built to keep the radiation in. In one of the December editions of the *Brookhaven Bulletin*, for example, which his father brought home every Friday, there's a photograph of Albert's father operating a backhoe, digging a hole at the corner of Princeton Avenue and Upton Road, where his HEMO colleague Howard Bell later used a forklift to carefully lower a fifteen-year-old Moerheim blue spruce they planted in honor of the Christmas season. That was the sort of thing Albert figured his father mostly did.

It wasn't until the 1990s, after Albert had left home and moved to Washington, DC, and Virginia and Mississippi and Queens and finally Connecticut, that the *Bulletin* occasionally published, in addition to the week's cafeteria menu, the results from the softball and bowling leagues, the classifieds, and so on, articles about the General Accounting Office's investigation of the DOE's responsibility regarding the tritium leaks, about the water pumped out of the High Flux Beam Reactor's spent-fuel pool, about the Lab's switch to thermoluminescent dosimeters, which were touted as state-of-the-art in gauging a worker's radiation dose, from the film badges that had been worn before by workers such as Albert's father.

It wasn't until the January 18, 2002 edition of the *Bulletin* that the "In Memoriam" section on page three mentioned that "Albert Lesiak, who died on February 26, 2001, at the age of 61, had joined the Plant Engineering Division on August 6, 1984, as a heavy equipment mechanic operator. He had left the Lab on December 4, 2000."

The *Bulletin* never mentioned that Albert's father had left the

Lab on December 4, 2000, because cancer had been brutally efficient in destroying his esophagus and was almost finished with the rest of him.

Chapter Five

Albert's wife, assured that he by now would be in dreamland, flips her sandals off and walks back into the house. She takes the foster-parent pamphlet from the corner of the kitchen table, relieved he hadn't flicked it to the floor, sits down on the sofa in the living room, and dreams of parenting. Their Chihuahua-slash-Italian greyhound Charlie Watts hops up with her and stares with bulbous eyes and shakes as if in need of an embrace. Albert's told her to be happy with the dog's love. It will never yield to brattiness or to rebellion or to the need to see the world. It will never ask for money as a proof. It will not stab you in the back or in the heart or in any other body part that you hold dear. She puts her arm around Charlie Watts and pulls him close to her. She wishes loving Charlie Watts could be enough.

Mary acknowledges the fear of being stranded on the tide-assaulted island that is old age, drenched and dried out, drenched and dried out, no one from the dwindled ranks of the beloved to step forth, pledging solemnly to moderate the rate of her erosion. She has played the game of who will be the first to pass, and she suspects for several reasons that it will be Albert. Then what? No life insurance. No offspring. Their circle of friends barely an arc. By then she will not even have the love of Charlie Watts. Things will dim. The din will muffle. Organs she relied on for so long will ease her into the idea that she will be let down. Morbid, maybe, to consider shutdown at the tender age of forty-four, but she would like assurances that someone bound to her by love will be there to extend to her a hand that she can hold as a reminder of the stake she still has in the world that she will soon be letting go. And even if she is the first to go, she isn't certain Albert would be liberal with the hand.

The trick is to appeal to that part of Albert that can't bear to know there is a light bulb shining in an empty room, to know that, as the meter wheel revolves, he's paying an enormous entity to burn a little more for nothing. Even if it's only pennies, it's the principle.

When he considers the waif's abandonment and says he's sorry but he likes his privacy and quietude too much and says, aside from privacy and quietude considerations, blood should raise blood anyway (there's trouble enough in that), the trick is to explain to him that for their sacrifice, which should be purely borne in the conviction that it helps to fit a misplaced being more securely in the world, the state will pay them $746 per month for a child between the ages of zero and five, $756 per month for a child between the ages of six and eleven, and $819 per month for a child twelve and over, far more than they would need to raise the child properly. She can see him calculating the expenses in his head, and she can see him brighten when he figures he can profit from a kindness, maybe use the surplus to begin improvements on the camp he has been talking about for years and show the boy (it probably will have to be a boy) the property that will one day be his. That sort of continuity will probably appeal to Albert. *Yes,* thinks Mary, *that's how I'll approach this.* She now regrets having sprayed the poison on the patio and fears that Albert, when he wakes, will still regard her as an antagonist.

She lies down on the couch with Charlie Watts beside her and holds her cell phone up before her face as though the screen contains a major secret she would like to know about her future. She uses both her thumbs to click the keys and watches as the homepage of the Connecticut Department of Children and Families appears. At the top left corner of the page, she clicks Adoption/Foster Care, which takes her to the Heart Gallery where she has been many times before and where the photographs and stories of Children Available for Adoption in Connecticut are exhibited according to no particular organizing principle. She scrolls down and sees that eleven-year-old Anthony, who loves math and wants to be an engineer and looks together in the photograph, is twelve now, and she wonders if the DCF, to give the kid a fighting chance, should leave out references to trauma and behavioral anomalies. She knows, of course, that such omissions would be unfair to everyone involved, but she remembers back about six months ago when she emailed Anthony's photograph and story to Albert, who wrote back, "What kind of trauma are we talking about? Was he molested? Was he dropped on his head? Did he witness a murder? DCF should really clarify what trauma means. And I don't like that bit about 'challenging behaviors.' Red flag there. Sounds like a euphemism for a deviance that would likely get us sued somewhere down the road. Next." She wonders how much money it would take for Albert to agree to take in Anthony, and Mary doubts, if she is being realistic, that $819 a month will be enough. *The camp,* she thinks again. *Just emphasize the extra money will be used to redo or, think big, rebuild the camp.*

She scrolls back up and lingers on the photograph of Jake and Ryan, whom she has not seen before. They are ten-year-old autistic twins who seem, posed together in a park-like setting, neither happy nor unhappy. They neither smile nor frown. They emanate a flatness, sort of similar to Albert. Ryan isn't verbal, but he can communicate through a device known as a Dynavox. Jake can basically read and speak in sentences, though he isn't ready to relinquish flashcards. Mary saddens when she thinks of him progressing, of him becoming ever distant language-wise from Ryan. She doesn't quite know whom to feel more sorry for—for Ryan who might wonder why he was not blessed with the ability to send his words into the air or for Jake who might feel guilty that, by comparison, he was. How cruel debility is. How relative and scattershot. *What the hell did these kids do to deserve this? Or what did their parents do? Where are they?* She switches screens and Googles *autism.* As she figured, she finds nothing definitive about a cause: "Autism is a brain disorder . . . The degree to which genetic factors play a role is not yet clear . . . Prenatal issues may substantially increase the risk of autism . . . Studies indicate environmental factors may exacerbate genetic predisposition to autism." In other words, who knows.

She switches back to the Heart Gallery and looks at Jake and Ryan again. *Albert never smiles in photographs either,* she thinks. *He comes from a long line of silent people, and he doesn't like to speak unless he has to or unless he's had a few. They have some sort of neurological issue. He has some sort of neurological issue. It says here they like to camp. Albert likes to camp. He likes the silence of the woods.* She guesses that, if she suggested they communicate by flashcards, he'd be willing. *This might work,* she thinks. She allows herself to dream, but still she thinks it would be better to begin the conversation by reminding Albert of the financial benefits. $756 times two. $1,512 per month. Once she establishes that fact, she can appeal to Albert's virtue and his sympathy for underdogs and his sense of there-but-for-the-grace-of-God-go-I.

Mary Googles *autism flashcards* in the meantime. Most of them are colorful and divided into squares in which a common, necessary object for which the autistic child cannot find the right word is depicted: a plate of food, a glass of water, shoes, shirt, television, toothbrush, dog, the usual. Some of the flashcards are designed for certain settings. One for school features twenty squares with pictures of a pencil, backpack, lunchbox, bus, the usual. Some are seasonal, for Christmas (stocking, candy cane) or summer (beach ball, popsicle). She scrolls down and sees that many of the flashcards feature pictures of children's faces in a range of attitudes to help facilitate emotional expression: happy, sad, angry, upset, surprised, frightened, bored, tired, calm. She likes how there is no room on the card for ambiguity, how something as abstract as an emotion is conveyed with just a picture, a boy smiling or a girl with something like a Zen peace on her face. How nice it would be if in the evening when she's sitting on the couch and Albert is sitting in his chair and not a word has passed between them for an hour or two and there is no emotion but a surface interest in the news or *Jeopardy!*—how nice if she could simply pick up the emotions flashcard, wave it slightly to attract his focus, place her finger on each successive square until she touches the one that best expresses what he feels just then, and have him do the same with the emotions flashcard lying on the table next to him so that they know where each one stands without the language thicket sprouting up between them to obscure what is essential.

Mary figures that to adequately communicate with Albert without a word she'd only need two flashcards: one for the necessities and things he always loses (things he always asks for or desires or pretends to be incapable of getting for himself), and another for emotions. She gets a piece of paper and sketches out a large box, which she divides into twenty smaller boxes. At the top of the page, she writes Things Albert Needs/Wants/Asks For

Regularly. She tries to boil Albert down to the basics.

In the first square of the first row, she draws a picture of a mug and underneath writes COFFEE. Above the mug and to the right, she draws a tilted carton and in little, legible letters in the middle of the carton spells out CREAM. Above the mug and to the left, she draws a tilted packet with the bottom right corner torn off and a few granules starting their descent and in smaller, no less legible letters in the middle of the packet spells out SUGAR. *That,* she thinks, *should cover the first hour or two of Albert's day, his slurping time.* In the second square, she changes her perspective, goes for the aerial instead of the side view, and draws a plate on which she centers a sandwich fringed with lettuce. On the right side of the plate, she draws a pile of potato chips, and on the left she sketches a pickle spear. Beneath the plate, she spells out LUNCH, a crunching time. She wonders what it must be like to be a man and wife who sit across the kitchen table from each other, passing cream or salt or half a muffin and conversing as if they believe not solitude but interaction is their natural state. How personally and mutually fulfilling that must be.

She stares at Albert's empty chair and pictures him poking his plate with his index finger to pick up the last crumbs and hears him grunting as he stands and walks his plate into the kitchen where he leaves it on the counter, and she pictures him looking around a while, shuffling papers, opening drawers, before retreating to his room, the door to which he softly shuts as though the life she leads outside it is unbearably tumultuous.

In the first square of the second row, she draws a pair of boxer shorts, although some time ago there was the gradual transition back to briefs, and underneath them spells out UNDERWEAR. She draws and spells out, draws and spells out: SOCKS, PANTS, SHIRTS, NOSE-HAIR SCISSORS, DOG LEASH, GLASSES, WALLET, KEYS, REMOTE CONTROL. She looks over the images, the words, and sees there is no tumult. Just monotony. The same scenarios each day, each week. The same words uttered like an incantation that's so sly the chanters do not realize the spell they're under has been cast by them, or, if they sense a hex-ness in the words, they let that slippery realization slide because it's easier to think that when they find their keys or nose-hair clippers or whatever and engage them in their narrow functions some small gap or void in their existence has been filled and they, unless they tend already toward the Gnostic, have little reason to start contemplating life as something not so narrowly materialist, so practically defined.

Mary hears Albert snoring in the bedroom. He is so predictable. In several hours he'll awake and thus commence the sighing time, the period of why, the period of sorry, of dependence, of belief in turning over the new leaf, of sweetness. He will be a ceiling starer and a tosser and a turner, unsettled and inert, in search of little rescues.

In the first square of the last row she draws a pill bottle on which she spells out ADVIL, and in the second square she draws a glass with a slightly rippled liquid line below the rim and draws three squares in suspension and spells out ICE WATER underneath the glass. In several hours, with or without the flashcard, she will extend to him two orange pills and a refreshing-looking glass, and he will be abashed and she will take that as a sign of truce, of gratitude. She'll leave without a word and close the bedroom door. When she returns within the hour, she'll see that he is less morose and less puffed about the eyes and wants some sign that he will be admitted back into the circle that the other humans orbit in. This means physical contact. In the third square of the last row, she draws a feminine head, with flowing hair and full lips, in close proximity to a penis, and beneath them spells out HUMMER/SEX. Albert will say, "Can I get a hummer?" She will show a countenance of resistance and then remove the covers and his briefs and start a kind of nodding genuflection. He will rise eventually and fuck her from behind, and some implicit tenet of domestic life will thereby be restored. After separate visits to the bathroom, they will talk a little guardedly about his night. When she has heard enough she'll say, "I'm making chicken burgers. Can you eat one or two?" In the fourth square, she draws a plate on which she centers what appears to be a chicken breast she flanks with small potatoes and a salad. She writes DINNER. Albert will shower, and the night before will be a figment. In the fifth square of the last row, she draws a can on which she spells out BEER. Albert will open up his little fridge and spend a moment in deliberation. She will mention Jake and Ryan shortly after, stressing how important it would be for everyone involved to experience normalcy.

By six o'clock Albert has showered and is sitting in his chair, his stockinged feet up on his ottoman, his left hand curled possessively around a Duvel glass from which he sips an excellent American interpretation of a hefeweizen at responsible intervals. His right hand clutches the remote control, and, as soon as one newscast goes to a commercial, Albert clicks over to another one and then returns to the original channel as if on cue, as if he has internalized to the second the duration of commercial breaks. So far he's seen nothing as to whether anyone had been driving past the Portland fairgrounds early in the morning and had pulled over to confront an unknown middle-finger-wielding man who wheeled around without a word as civil prelude and administered a head-butt that concussed the aforementioned driver, sending him in serious condition to the hospital where he is still recovering tonight. By 6:15 and the beginning of the weather, Albert feels as if he were a fugitive from justice who just learned the search for him had been called off and he could go back to whatever life he finds it in his heart to live. He stares a while at the tile on the wall and at the bird made out of smaller, green and blue tiles above the woodstove, and his confidence in freedom renewal wavers somewhat when he entertains the possibility that the head-butt story wasn't big enough to make the news or that it made the five-o'clock edition but not the six and that the search is very much in progress, news or not. *No*, he thinks, *it's big enough. It's got everything the six-o'clock news becomes erect for.* The fear of an assailant on the loose and possibly a danger to the citizenry, who would not be aware of this potential danger had it not been for the news team's tireless devotion to delivering its audience the news they really need. The opportunity to nudge the audience toward civic duty and exhort the heretofore reluctant witnesses to call the police department's Tips Hotline if they have any information regarding this disturbing case. The promise that the case continues and that the news at six will bring you all the breaking details in the case as soon as they become available. *No,* thinks Albert, *it is big enough. I'm in the clear. He must have simply gotten up and driven off. He may be looking for me, but he didn't report me. And for that I drink to him.*

Albert sips his hefe and directs his realigned attention to the television, steadily increasing the volume so that he can hear the sports report above the high-pitched clatter of the dinner knives and forks and pots and dishes Mary scrapes and rinses before depositing them like car-wash quarters in the dishwasher. Many of their battles are waged this way, no words, just sounds that they diminish or increase in more or less proportion to the fluctuating level of annoyance each feels for the other. An adjustment here, an adjustment there. It is a favored method of engagement since the battles typically are brief and any martial implications of a short-lived din can easily be written off as misinterpretation or the day's steam or inattention, so the battles rarely blossom into wars.

Mary is still drying off her hands when she walks into the living room and to the Hitchcock coffee table that parallels the couch. She sits down and takes the foster-parent pamphlet from one of the two drawers, placing it on the tabletop.

"I know you probably saw this this morning," she says.

"The foster thing again? We've been over this."

"Before you say no, just hear me out."

She opens the laptop on the Hitchcock, goes to the DCF's Heart Gallery page, and scrolls down to the photograph of Jake and Ryan.

"Is this about the kid with the unspecified anger issues? I told you—"

"No," she says. "They're twins."

"Twins."

"Ten years old. Autistic. Jake and Ryan. Jake can communicate in full sentences, but more often he uses flashcards."

"Flashcards."

"Ryan isn't verbal, but he can communicate using a Dynavox."

"A Dynavox. Am I dreaming this, or are you just fucking with me because I didn't come home last night? I already told you driving wasn't an option. Which reminds me—"

She holds the laptop so that Albert can see the photograph of the boys.

"They seem a little flat."

"Like you," she says. "I think you'll like these kids."

"No."

"Before you say no, I want to do a little experiment. I made two flashcards out of cardboard. Hang on."

Mary goes into the kitchen and takes the flashcards from the vacuum closet. She holds one up and says, "This one is for, as the title says, things you need, want, or ask for regularly. So, for example, if you're having trouble finding your glasses, you just point here, without saying anything, which shouldn't be a problem for you, and I'll help you find your glasses."

Albert seems interested.

Mary holds up the second card and says, "This one is to help you express yourself emotionally. I basically just copied this one from an autism website, but I added LOVED, INTERESTED, BUZZED, CONTEMPLATIVE, HUNGOVER, and TRAPPED to make it an even fifteen. We can add more later if we need to. So, again, if you're feeling upset, for example, you just point here, without saying anything. I'm not sure what we do, though, once the feeling is expressed and how I figure out what's upsetting you. We may need more flashcards."

Albert gets up and points to INTERESTED.

"In the flashcard idea," he says. "Not so much in the autistic-twin adoption. We only have about eight-thousand in the checking account as is, and now you want to raise two kids?"

"The state will give us $1,512 per month, tax free, to foster them. The state will also cover all their medical expenses."

"Yeah," says Albert, "and what happens when it comes time to adopt them?"

"The state assistance stops, but we can foster them indefinitely. It's only eight years until they're eighteen."

"And then what?"

"Think about the meantime. It won't cost close to 1,512 a month to care for them. Think about what we can do with the extra—for us and for them. You can finally fix up the camp or build a new one if you want and take the boys up there in the summer. Think about what you'd be giving them. The woods. The peace and quiet. Explain to them the differences between a Douglas fir and a spruce. Think what you could teach them."

She sees Albert grow contemplative and feels that he is softening, searching for a reasonable objection to this new appeal to his humanity. He gets up, and she hears him move a couple cans and bottles back and forth until he finds what he is looking for and shuts the beer-fridge door. He pads his socked feet toward the beer-glass cabinet, surveys briefly the transparent sacristy he likes to think he keeps in his unholy-seeming house because it is the dust-verboten repository of the vessels of the ritual that Albert believes is ministration to his spirit, which the glassware, stemmed and shapely, help to escort forth or summon home with gravitas and dignity and style that mere indulgence and remorse have never overshadowed. Albert opens the paned-glass cabinet door and cradles with his ring and middle fingers a tulip glass he places on the cluttered counter. He fills the glass halfway with a barley wine he's aged since last year, and he watches as the carbonation rises two fingers and then settles. He puts his nose into the glass and sniffs once. Nothing. He takes his nose out, swirls the glass, inserts his nose and sniffs once more for nothing before he fills the tulip to the rim and sips. While he is thus engaged in this communion, Mary double-checks some figures she had earlier written on the pamphlet's backside.

Albert returns to his chair and says, "We just don't have the room. We have 1,174 square feet of living space. Divide that by four, and we are cramped. As it is, it's hard enough to get away from one another." He pauses. "You know what I mean."

"I know," she says, "but we also have an acre. And we can finish the basement. Add a big bedroom or two smaller ones."

"So build a camp and do the basement," he says with a magical wave of his hand.

"It's doable," she says. "Each year we'd be getting $18,144 from the state. Over eight years that amounts to $145,152. We make more than 110 a year. We'd have enough."

"145,152."

"145,152."

Albert shakes his head. "I can't start parenting at forty-four. I'm not fit." He raises his glass.

"We'd be better parents than the parents they have right now. Come on. It'd be good karma."

"Since you're such a fan of karma, tell me what these poor bastards did to deserve their parentless, autistic, Dynavox, flashcard fate."

"That's one way of looking at it, I suppose. The other way is to believe we can make things better for them, draw them out, provide for them. I'd rather see it that way."

"Today I woke up by the river and head-butted someone I don't know because he almost ran a turtle over. Would you want me for a father?"

"I would if I were them," she says.

Which means, he knows, not really. After all, Albert doesn't sail a Sunfish to Point Judith as her father used to sail, and Albert doesn't concentrate his presence in a wood-shop as her father used to concentrate his presence, and Albert has little sense of family history to pass down to a young'un as her father used to pass their family's history down to her, and Albert is not the last one standing at a party, the responsible and sober one who tours the quieted house, collecting cans and bottles and locking doors and shutting lights and making sure there are no fires as her father used to stand and tour and collect and lock and shut and make sure, and Albert doesn't offer or extend himself with ease for friendship's or for duty's sake as Mary's father used to offer and extend himself without a second thought when someone needed him to sacrifice his talent and his time, and Albert doesn't smoke a pipe as Mary's father used to smoke a pipe and in the process model reassurance and paternity.

But Albert will have to do.

"I would if I were them," she says again.

Albert sips his beer and thinks of Updike from this morning, Updike who felt sorry for him as if childlessness were a pathology like cancer or the clap. It then occurs to Albert that the birder's pity maybe wasn't caused by Albert's lack of progeny, per se, but by the shut-in Updike recognized the inner Albert as, a person doomed to stare at his four personal walls and all his mirrors and perhaps to push aside a curtain and peek outside a window on occasion, someone who, because he doesn't know or has forgotten how to let another person in, will not himself go out to ask of the begotten and begetting world about the beauty and the substance and the mystery of invitation and exchange.

"I need to take a leak," he says, and, when he stands, he notices the barley wine has buzzed him, rather pleasantly so, which recognition makes him wonder why such pleasantry can't always be enough, why he so often takes the reckless turn and dances in the woods with all the others who believe they follow in the spirit of the liberal Dionysus. Albert's father wasn't like that, wasn't one to weave and stagger, wasn't one to cry out to the sky, "God damn, I bear a burden," and, believing that he knew how he could make his lot more lightsome, slurred and stumbled onward toward more alcohol. So why is Albert? Why did the apple fall so far from this particular upright tree?

Albert urinates and pictures how his father used to sit upon the cushioned kitchen stool, his torso leaning toward the jetty of a counter, legs crossed, left on right, his form, already uniformed in labor blue, illuminated barely by the stovetop light at five a.m. His left hand held the coffee mug, his right the cherry Middleton, the most delicious, in his estimation, of the thin cigars. In one sense, he was statuesque, possessed the grace and dignity that fortitude exudes. He seemed at first a figuration that was not inclined to elsewhere, but you knew, by lineament or intuition, that his inclination and his stillness were a smokescreen, just the way he marshaled strength, and that he'd move by six and go to work and do as he was told to do because his four kids and his wife were not the burden and because he wanted those four kids to be as little bowed and slouched about the head and shoulders from what the world would claim was their allotment of the world's weight—by his labor, by his hands, he wanted them to be as little bowed and slouched as possible, to shrug off what the world would try to load on them and to believe that by his hands and by his labor they would one day have the means to choose the path they skipped down, to become, like him, laborious if they so chose or learned or artistic or adventurous or leisurely or any of the adjectives that he, when young, assumed would not apply to him because it seemed foregone that he was meant to operate and to repair the earth-removal machinery with his stoic brothers for the father's always coughing excavation business, which died slowly of unspoken causes sometime during the recession of the seventies.

Albert drips and zips and feels so much the squanderer, the ingrate. When his father lay, a stickish figure on his deathbed downstairs, he rose up perhaps a centimeter to reciprocate his son's embrace, his teacher-son who had with sorrow to return to his existence in Connecticut because it was the last day of his February break, and whispered above the wrecked esophagus, "You were everything I ever wanted in a son," and Albert cried and his father rasped, "Don't cry," and Albert choked out, "I love you," and his father rasped, "I love you. Don't cry," and Albert went in the half-bathroom where he cried and could not gain composure, could not manly up about the eyes, and finally drove away and took the ferry north, and on the next day took it south again because that morning, while he stood before a freshman English class, his father finally died.

It took a while for Albert to recognize what his father, suffering his own travails as he moved closer to the valley of the shadow yet still thinking of the troubles of his son, had given him: a sort of absolution for his years of idiocy and ego, basically a free pass to get on with life and not dwell overmuch on how he could have acted oftener in the interest of the family honor in the past, or could at least have thought a moment longer on how the carousal and abandonment of sense that he had scheduled for a certain night would be the spring of such distress for those who shared his name or blood.

It's over now. It's done. You are forgiven. Live. I love you.

For a while Albert believed his father's final words to him were really just a well-intentioned lie, the sort of thing one told a child who was not attractive or athletic or intelligent or popular because one understood the long-term implications and importance of developing a child's self-esteem, especially when the unforgiving world was poised to chip at it and contradict it.

But Albert was not a child when his father died. He stood there, thirty-two, and listened to his father's final words to him and cried as if what he had learned in catechism had no power in this case to palliate or to redeem. One might think that nature in its let's-get-on-with-living wisdom would have had some practical provision kick in shortly after Albert lay his flower on the casket, leaving it with all his grief, which is unseemly for a man to cling to like a blankey fringed with satin as he wanders toward the yet to be determined joys and tribulations of his life. But Albert went home and thought about his father's final words to him and wished there were some flagellation protocol by which he could just whip the woe right out of him. He thought about those words when he was crystalline and sober, and he thought about those words when he was circular and stewed. He thought about those words when he walked steadily through the woods with Charlie Watts, and he recited them in lieu of prayer while he was sinking like a lobster trap into the deep. He knew that he would push that boulder up the mountain once he saw it sitting at the bottom, and he knew that he would be bowled over time and time again because his strength was limited and he was always in the way, but he was baffled as to why he couldn't, on occasion, step aside and walk around the resting boulder or step aside and let the boulder hurtle on while he ascended and took in the view or yodeled or considered where to post a cautionary sign.

Things began to change one morning when, while opening his mailbox, Albert discovered on the ground beside the post a plastic tip to one of those thin cigars his father used to smoke. It was the color of a hardcore smoker's teeth, the tinge of yellow he remembered, but he couldn't tell for sure if it was from a cherry Middleton or not as there was nothing on the tip to indicate the manufacturer, and there was no tobacco remnant in the tip that

Albert could put up to his imperceptive nose and sniff a few times on the chance he might detect a note of that aroma that his memory had recorded in the old days when his nostrils flared and he possessed the right connections to distinguish scent from scent—a note of that aroma that his memory had recorded as synonymous with his father, as inseparable from his identity as was his sunken chest, his crooked nose, his blue eyes, or his voice that said such things as "Spiders are our friends." Albert was not averse to reading more into coincidence than realism would allow, but even he, despite his wanting to believe that tip was a deliberate sign his father left to say hello, did not believe the tip was more than a temptation tossed out of a passing window by another American litterbug. But two days later, Albert was yawning on his patio and, as he came out of his stretch, he saw a plastic tip beside the silver can he used for woodstove ash. He briefly did suppose that it was possible the pilot of an open-cockpit plane had flown above the house the night before as he or she concluded his or her enjoyment of a thin cigar, removed the remnant flecks of that enjoyable tobacco to be stowed away for future pleasure, and then jettisoned the empty tip which plummeted and bounced a few times on the patio before achieving equilibrium beside the silver can by which the mundane Albert would discover it come morning. *No,* thought Albert on second thought. *Who's abdicating his fidelity to realism now? Something is afoot.* And for the next two days, on and off, he dwelled primarily on that.

Dwelling basically involved Albert staring with his actual eyes at one corporeal object or another without the object's essence or its full dimension registering in Albert's brain, and it involved him straining his transparent or his inner or his mind's eye to discern just what the afterlife was up to, what it was about, and how much interaction with this side Albert was on was generally allowed. Was it a good sign or a bad sign that two tips had materialized before him in two places there was little doubt he would eventually be? Was it a sign for help, his father crying, "Pray for me"? Was it more like a pleasant note, a postcard sent from someplace where the climate and the realized spirit perfectly align, the message short, expressing the sender's sole regret: "Miss you. Wish you were here." That sort of thing. Albert thought that way for a couple of days and did not experience an epiphany and did not come to a settlement or conclusion, though he did recall, the few days after his father had died, at odd times, entering a room where he could have some privacy and sitting on his old bed or the toilet or his father's toolbox or his father's ottoman and praying, hands clasped, eyes closed, "God, if it is possible, please send a sign that's not too cryptic telling me my father is all right. And Dad, if you can hear me, send me a sign to let me know, wherever you are, you're all right. Amen." Albert was on the lookout for about a month following his father's death, and like the person who adopts a poker posture over the stonework of the wishing well or like the person who walks into the empty church and toward the altar and ignites a candle as if the ignition and the flickering light would show the lost soul home or change the course of a disease, Albert looked and looked and wanted to believe but, absent the observable development, he never felt more rooted in the world. In one sense, Albert was done with signs because he knew that, even if he got one, it was up for multiple interpretations anyway, an ink blot that your mindset or your heart turned into something relevant to you; besides, it had been about a month since his father had died, so the immediate grief-assuaging element of a sign had been substantially diminished anyway. So, although he hadn't sworn off signs entirely, he had gone back to relegating them to the periphery, the outer reaches of his life. Of course, the first and second thin-cigar tips swung the pendulum the other way and knocked all thoughts of relegation out the window, and, although he didn't understand the temporal complexities of sign delivery or why there had to be such lag time, he was, as far as his attunement to the otherworldly signals was concerned, considerably revived.

Thus, Albert was on the lookout for the third one, which he found one bird chirp of a morning at the end of April, two days after he had found the second one and nearly two months after his father's merciful death. It was beside the mailbox post, where he had found the first one, and he picked it up and carried it with the mail back up the gravel drive. He didn't try this time to translate what it meant because he guessed by this time that such signs should not be subject to reduction, weren't meant to be interpreted as "Hello, my son, I love you" or "Goodbye. It's been nice knowing you" or "Take care of your mother to make up for all the disappointments," weren't meant to be like Chinese characters that any Anglo could remove the Eastern mystery from by running his know-it-all finger down the right page of a Chinese-English dictionary. Albert sat down on a patio chair and looked toward the silver ashcan just in case. He lay the mail upon the table, and his fingers moved the tip around so he could study it from every angle and in several shades of morning light as if it were an arrowhead he'd found in Wangunk Meadows.

Albert was fine not knowing who had left it there, and he was fine not knowing why the object was revealed to him because, as he revolved it, he discovered that such objects were but signposts to the past and took the finder out of himself and let him hover in that privileged zone, the one we have no name for. He could suddenly see his father floating on an inner tube in their aboveground pool, his infant sister's fragile head cradled egg-wise in their father's sunken chest, which Albert could hear his father telling her was Albert's bird's nest once. And Albert could see himself at thirteen years old accompanying his father on his second job, which was to clean the bank adjacent to the Triple Crown at night. Their presence there was practically conspiratorial, a secret that they rarely shared, Albert emptying the paper-laden garbage cans, his father vacuuming the crew-cut of a carpet or polishing counterclockwise the resistance of the safe, the two of them the only people in that somehow ghostly place. And Albert could see his father sitting next to him when they were older, two versions of the same man on the stoop, his father reaching over to accept a sip of Albert's Watney's and declaring to his curious son, "Tastes raunchy," as he gave it back and raised his Schmidt's and smiled with his new teeth, saying, "This now. This is beer."

Albert put the tip up to his lips, inhaled, exhaled, and he realized he'd had the wrong perspective all along. True, he'd been a troubled son. He'd crashed two cars. He'd wet the bed. He'd cracked his precious head. He'd leaned back too far in too many chairs. He'd woken with the two black eyes that Christmas. For the first time, though, Albert regarded such behaviors as equivalent to the cyclical disasters nature rolls out every year—tornados, hurricanes, lightning strikes, wildfires, blizzards, floods—the ones that everybody talks about years later because they were such exclamations to the cadence of their lives and overshadowed the predominating periods of placidity and wholeness Albert now reckoned he'd been negligent in giving the memory airtime they were due. The lingering suspicion that his father's final words to him had been a well-intentioned lie now lifted like a fog that had obscured the view from Albert's dearest bridge, the one that spans the river whose apparently eternal flow is really a sublime reminder of the constancy of alteration.

***

Albert emerges from the bathroom and considers fatherhood anew, what it confers, what it exacts, what it is bound to leave behind. Perhaps, he thinks, at forty-four, it's time to stop considering himself as just a son—to share, to branch out, to don the mantle of the patriarch, to gather round him fostered progeny who nod when he pronounces. *Maybe*, he allows. However. But. He wonders who will stand by him when he is prone and fading, who will bow and mourn and be so tearfully reluctant to depart. Who will return when he is gone and sob and pray when no one's watching and absorb the tears with some material and cast their bloodshot eyes about for some communication, a believable sign as an assurance that, despite the sorrow and the gaping absence, Albert is whole and very much all right? He warms to the idea of being flanked, when he is on his back and on the verge of levitation, by an older version of the twin autistic boys he tried his best to shepherd through the yammering and cliquey world. He wonders if they'd hold up flashcards picturing two teary faces to express that the inevitability of his departure makes them sad or if they would, by then, have outgrown flashcards and be able to articulate their feelings and their thoughts without assistance but, as overcome with filial emotion as Albert had been, say nothing but "I love you" and then cry and wait for him to tell them they were everything he ever wanted in his sons. He wonders what it would be like to just let go, assured that he'd passed on what valuables he could pass on, had shared his favorite books, had shown them where the river was and who its natives were and hunched with them beside it as they sought the sandhill cranes, had shown them snakes and toads and turtles and all manner of the practically defenseless and exhibited the quality of mercy, had sat down with them in silent observation of the mayflies, had explained to them the three tips he had found and who his father was, had left to them his little camp and his unharvested eighteen acres. He wonders whether, if they start to doubt if he had meant it when he said that they were everything he ever wanted in his sons, they'd both go on the lookout for potential signs and find three DirtWolf bottle caps in places where they often stand or see a man who looks like him, same hair, same shirt, same posture, walking with a butterfly net or fly rod by the river and be baffled by the symbolism for a while, alternately assured and unconvinced, until they realize that they themselves are really what he left for them to stumble onto on an ordinary day and plumb and be at peace with.

Maybe, he allows. However. But.

They are not blood, and aren't all the inextricable bonds, the deepest loves, the truest obligations traced back to the blood? Mother, father, sister, brother, daughter, son—all points connected, sans volition, on the bloodline. Sure, there's continuity in blood, the past communing tributarily with the future. There's security and comfort and the cookout ease of the familiar in the physical resemblances that generation after generation reappear, recur. There's the existential question answered, the assurance that, in death, you still have iterations in the world, your representatives who do not have to say with words, "I have his eyes, his nose, his webbed toes, his propensity to tipple and atone."

But this would not be that. This would be him plucking from the oceangoing river two defenseless boys who did not ask to be released, did not indite their shaky signatures on a contractual line before a neutral notary and formally absolve the points along their bloodline of the bond, the love, the obligation to dive in the river and forsake their own lives even if they cannot save the boys, even if it's just to prove they could not have lived without the boys. Albert tells himself he's not cut out for such a rescue operation, not equipped for voluntary blood-unrelated acts of sacrifice or valor. He's only out there in a kayak, drifting down the selfsame river himself with just a lightweight paddle that allows him, in his solitary estimation, only slightly more directional control than those two floating kids, chucked in who knows how far upriver, counting on their pruny hands and feet to keep their faces high enough for oxygen—only slightly more directional control than those two floating kids possess.

Albert resumes his usual position on his chair and sips his warming barley wine. He looks at Mary, who is looking at the laptop.

"I don't know," he says. "They're not blood. Mary, there are always complications, anecdotally and in the literature, when blood's not raised by blood."

"That's stupid," she says without looking up. "What literature?" A pause. "What do these two care about blood?"

"I don't know," he says. "Who knows?" He sips. "Can that be answered by a flashcard?"

"Just try the flashcards first."

"I need to get my truck tonight," he says as though the urgency of this concern, which has lain dormant all day, suddenly resurfaced.

"I'll take you," Mary says. "Just try the flashcards first."

"I will," he says. "But it may have to be when I get back from Maine. I was thinking of leaving tomorrow. Or maybe Monday. I'm really not prepared. Maybe some flashcards tomorrow."

"Fine," she says, closing the laptop. "Did I tell you that your mother called?"

"When?"

"When you were out."

"What did she say?"

"Not much."

"What did she want?"

"She didn't say. Let's go get your truck."

They walk out, and it is daylight still. They will return before the darkness and settle like two turkeys in the tree of their routine.

Chapter Six

Albert wakes this morning in his bed. Queen sized. Clean sheets. No river flowing by reminding him he lacks direction. No one walking by, inquiring about his health and wondering what happened in his life that led him to his occupation of this place. On paper this is his dominion, and he feels benevolent about his rule. His brain and bowels feel at ease, no percolation, in a state that's not at odds with daily regulations. He remembers that, like him, his pickup's in its usual place, secure, unlocked. His wife is up already, practicing the quiet motion, delicately matutinal, that says to him it's pointless to attempt to pinpoint where. Charlie Watts lies sprawled beside him, a watchdog whimpering and twitching on occasion, temporarily off the clock. The sun illuminates the room. Birds of every inspirational denomination sing. Normality seems musical and sociable today and calls him sleepyhead and tells him, "Rise and shine. It is a beautiful day to be alive." Albert does not disagree. He does not add a qualifier or consider a condition. Certainly he understands the purgative worth of wrath, the refuge to be found in sullenness, but he does not feel drawn by their appeals today. Whatever flecks of wrath he sported yesterday, whatever cells of sullenness he hosted then have been transmuted by some alchemy into pure contentment, that estate in which the organs sit right and the little place you occupy within the world feels as organic and pollution-free as an Inupiat's before the Contact.

Albert thinks about what he will do today, the preparations to be made if he's to head to camp. And when he thinks about the bother, he resolves, *There is tomorrow, and tomorrow there will be tomorrow.* No, he will not practice the philosophy of rush today. He strokes the length of Charlie Watts, looks at the subtle tree sway out the window, and is grateful to the chlorophyll for greenery. What else? He has to call his mother back and hear the homeland news and reaffirm his loyalties. He mentally pencils in a second cup of coffee and a phone call. Then he rises.

Albert notices two flashcards lying on the nightstand, and he wonders what it must be like to rise each morning unassisted by a language, the diversity surrounding you still untagged in this day and age, undifferentiated by the words we all agree will stand for certain things and streamline our communications. We organize, deceive, uplift, demean, inspire, puzzle, sadden, ostracize, include, convert, disrupt, calm down, et cetera with words. To wake each day and be outside of that agreement and that streamline seems monastic almost, but the vow of silence isn't voluntary and the cloistering is not within a monasterial community with the intent of being separated insofar as possible from the profanations of the world. The vow has come down from on high. The cloister is a single body that must mingle with the wordy others who were blessed with free range, who were granted knowledge of the secret handshake, who were given the invisible key that liberates some of the internal mystery and lets the store of endless words out to go up against the others, to engage in discourse and in intercourse, and to accomplish what they can in terms of sensibility.

He looks at Charlie Watts whose tail flogs Mary's pillow.

"How do *you* do it?" Albert asks. "You seem pretty happy being wordless."

Charlie Watts goes belly up and seems as joyful as a dolphin. Albert does a quick scratch on Watts's chest and watches as the angled leg goes charging in the air. There's something to be said for wordlessness, expression that does not get lost in the translation into words. He supposes you cannot reduce the world to words any more than you, depending on your comfort zone or motive, can reduce the world to money or to facts or to the sense that there is something out there you'd do well to pay due homage to while you are of sound mind and body. He picks up Charlie Watts because the dog's knees aren't what they used to be and softly sets him on the floor. He picks the flashcards up and walks without a word toward the bedroom door he quietly opens as if his commitment to the silent treatment has begun. It does not, on this happy morning, enter Albert's mental field of vision that, in Mary's estimation, he has been a student of such treatment, an astute practitioner, a master even, for as long as she has known him; and, on this day of clarity, it does not creep into his consciousness that she, aside from her desire to become a mother to the motherless, would like an unadulterated, honest, and unmoody word with him, the kind that you can point to on a flashcard and remove, like that, the vehicle of ambiguity that can upset the apple cart that is a marriage's dynamic.

He makes his usual stops. Bathroom. Kitchen. Chair and ottoman. He sets his coffee on the little table that abuts the right side of his chair, sits down, and puts his feet up. In an instant, it occurs to him that out in public such a posture can imply an air of attitudinal entitlement, a relaxation that goes counter to the ethos and suggests you feel yourself above the generally accepted seating doctrine. Such instants signal the beginning of vacation, the removal of his work-shoed self from the employment ranks and the insertion of his barefoot doppelganger into the expansive field of summer, which could not care less about achievement or an ironed shirt or leadership. In such instants he can glance back at the academic year's annoyances and small oppressions, knowing they will fade in no time, growing dim as he gets used to the idea of evening light a-lingering. He smiles when he thinks about the elevation of his feet upon his cluttered desk when he was in the empty classroom weeks ago, no students scheduled for him to instruct that period, no member of the administration on his calendar to meet politely with, to nod to, to address as Mr. Last Name in the presence of the students. He smiles when he thinks about his feet thus propped and some administrator, Mr. Morehead, jiggling the universal key in Albert's doorknob as he did some weeks ago, politely entering, asking, "Got a minute?", waiting for the English teacher to uncross his legs and put his feet back like a good subordinate upon the nine-by-nine asbestos tiles so that Albert did not appear, by virtue of his mellow pose, his hands behind his head and all, to be receiving Morehead's visit with a posture someone passing by might read as unprofessional or disrespectful, a mockery of hierarchy. Albert didn't plan to be a dick. Had Morehead, waving his hand at Albert's raised shoes, asked him, "What's the meaning of this?" Albert would have told him that he was pretty sure his penchant for propped feet went back to a poor-production-quality filmstrip that he saw in third or fourth grade. In it two black-and-white, 1950s-looking men were in an office setting. One was standing, jokingly accusing his reclined colleague of malingering. Improbably, a doctor then walked in and began to talk about the circulatory system and how raising one's feet above the level of the heart improves the blood flow.

"That's why, when someone's dizzy or in certain kinds of distress, we elevate that person's feet above the level of the heart," the doctor said.

"Huh," the seated man said. "And all this time I thought I was goofing off."

Albert smiles. He wonders how much he's forgotten since he saw that filmstrip, why that simple scene sticks with him and affects the way he sometimes lives his life.

"What are you smiling at?" Mary asks, looking up from her phone.

Albert picks up a flashcard, points to HAPPY, points to CALM.

The phone rings.

Neither moves because their screening process since they discontinued caller ID dictates that they freeze until the answering machine clicks on and they determine by the tinny, disembodied voice the call's priority. The message-less hang-ups vex them, and on such occasions they indulge the silence for a moment, wonder who it could have been. A telemarketer? A friend inviting Albert to join him for a new beer? A sibling hoping to retard the subtle degradation of the sibling bond? Vexation hits him hardest since he doesn't have a cell phone and is thus dependent on the landline if he wishes voice-to-voice communication, which he sometimes does when he is home alone between the hours of three and roughly five, when Mary's still at work and he anticipates garrulity upwelling in him as he starts to sip the day's first beer, the one that puts the world aright and fortifies his circulation so that, briefly, for a microcosmic Golden Age, he's unassailable.

"Hi, it's only me," his mother's voice says from the answering machine. "Okay, I guess you're out. I'll . . ."

"Ma," says Albert when he picks up the phone. "What's going on?"

"Oh, not much. Is everything all right?"

"What do you mean?"

"Nothing. Do you have a cold or something?"

"No."

"No, it just sounded like you might have had a cold or something. How's Mary?"

"She's all right."

"Is she home?"

"She's right here. Do you want to talk to her?"

"No. Listen," Albert's mother says, "the reason I'm calling is I got a letter from the Department of Energy the other day."

"For what?"

"They oversee the Lab. They want me to sign something releasing them from liability."

"For what?"

"Daddy's death. It seems that they're admitting they may have caused his cancer."

"Well," says Albert, "they're a little late."

"The letter says that, if I sign, they'll send me a check within a week for $250,000."

"250,000?"

"Yes. What do you think I should do? I'm asking all of you."

"You're not even suing them and they're offering 250,000? Why now? What are they hiding? They know something we don't if they're offering that much out of the blue without being sued."

"It's not just us. They're making offers to anyone, or to the families of anyone, who worked at the Lab, it says here, for more than 250 days from 1947 to 1993. If they got cancer, they got an offer. There's a list of cancers."

"Is anybody suing instead of signing?"

"I don't know."

"I'd call a lawyer."

"I did."

"And?"

"We'd have a good case, but it could be in court for ten years."

"I guess I'd take the money. Even if it is blood money."

"If he had just died," she says, "I think I'd sue and see what happens. But it's been eleven years. I don't know. Your brother thinks I should sue."

"And then their lawyers would say that Daddy smoked for forty-some-odd years and got cancer that way. How would we prove he got his cancer from the Lab?"

"I don't know."

"What do Kathy and Krissy say?"

"Kathy says just take the money. Krissy's not sure."

"How much would a lawyer cost?"

"I don't know."

"I guess I'd take the money," Albert says.

"You think so?"

"It's up to you, ma."

"You don't think it's wrong?" she asks.

"It's all wrong. But he's dead. What else is there to do? We're not cut out for long-term litigation."

"No," she says, "we're not."

"At least you'll be a quarter million richer. You could move out of Krissy's if you want."

"We're splitting it five ways," she says. "Each of you kids will get fifty, and I'll get fifty."

"Keep it," Albert says. "It's yours."

"It's all of ours," she says. "Don't be ridiculous."

The conferral of a handsome sum of money on a person whose self-image's foundation largely rests on his belief that he's immune to the transformative effects, the character alterations that in subtle and in wide-eyed ways accompany a windfall can induce in such a person, in whom the impression of asceticism as an ideal abides, a fretting over whether such material improvement will embolden him to say "So what?" when it appears he may the whole time have been harboring inside his flannelled self the hypocrite he scoffed and threw tomatoes at when he was in the audience that scoffed and threw when yet another troubling example of hypocrisy was brought to light. The fretting can take many forms. In Albert's case, he puts the phone down, turns the water on, and washes, in the manner of an un-harassed raccoon, his hands. He looks out the window as the birds take turns at being peckish on the feeder roosts and feels the fretting calmed by the prevailing sense of avian cooperation, all the feathery examples of civility that seem to reign in times of plenitude. There are, he thinks, these moments when you have the power to become what you have long professed, to prove to doubters your avowed convictions have not been a pose. There are, he also thinks, these moments when you have the option to just cave and, by your caving, say that principles are fluid and adaptability, historically, has been a huge advantage and the world will soon forget your moral failings if you overshadow them with something big like Christopher Columbus's revealing to Queen Isabella an enormous chunk of the unknown or like a record of donations and an easy smile that disarms the people who might otherwise be prone to question you and your morality if you exuded gloom.

"What was that about?" asks Mary

"The Department of Energy," says Albert, "which apparently oversees Brookhaven National Laboratory, where my father used to work, will give my mother 250 grand if she releases them from liability for my father's death. It looks like we'll get fifty thousand out of that."

"Wow. That came out of nowhere."

"It's not a life-changing sum."

"No. But still."

Albert spends the next few hours on the laptop, learning what is public knowledge now about the Lab. He reads about the incidences of a rare soft-tissue cancer in children who live around the Lab's perimeter, about the tritium plumes that flow in three directions from the Lab, about the residential breast-cancer clusters that defy the averages, about the Gamma Forest and "the dead zone, the zone of total kill," about the leaks that emanated from the sealed reactors, about the Particle Beam Dump and the Alternating Gradient Synchrotron Experimental Areas, about the "experimental holes" and animal irradiation, about assurances and pat denials issued by respectable officials, about the onward march of science and the Nobel Prizes, about the Lab's commitment to humanity and to the dogged exploration of the peaceful uses of nuclear radiation. Albert tries to hear the conversations that accompanied the cost-benefit analysis whose figures clearly showed it was acceptable to leave a trail of *x* bodies over *y* years, necessary, even, to produce them as collateral damage, cellular sacrifices to the grander cause as long as they achieved the endgame Albert, armed only with an English degree, cannot conceive of and cannot imagine ever justifying such a corporal toll.

"I don't think I can take the money," he tells his wife. "The government is basically admitting that they killed my father and a quarter million is the number they assume will be enough to calm whatever moral reservations we might still have with their sentencing the poor guy to a slow, corrosive death and with their waiting eleven years to basically say they saw it all coming, this should cover it."

"Maybe she should sue."

"That's not the point. They let him die because they knew there was a number they could cover that would let them off the hook. It doesn't matter what the number is. It's just the way the system works. And what does it say about me if I'm there with my hand out at the end of the complicity line? It says that I forgive them, which I don't, and that I sold my father out."

"What's the alternative? It's been eleven years. What's done is done. Move on."

"There is no statute of limitations on dispensability," he says. "And what's the alternative? The alternative is to bow out, to sever all ties, to not participate. Complete withdrawal. Opt out. Thoreau it. No more government, no more Citibank, no more Bank of America, no more TIAA-CREF, no more AT&T, no more Comcast, no more Monsanto." He pauses. "The alternative is to live off the grid. Go solo. Like we talked about a hundred times."

"Off the grid," she says with skeptical amusement. "You say that every summer, and every fall you say it isn't practical."

"It's different this time," he insists. "My father was immensely practical and died at sixty-one—before he even drew Social Security. I'm tired of the bullshit. Aren't you? I'm tired of feeling that the whole façade is going to collapse for real and that we're going to be directly underneath it when it does." He pauses. "We can live off the grid. We have the land already."

"Well," she says, "why don't you at least take the money before you unplug? The Department of Energy doesn't need it. It would be their contribution to your little revolution."

"I don't know," he says. "It's something to consider, I guess, as a means to an end." Albert paces, rubs his chin hair as he contemplates. "Maybe." He pauses, rubs his chin as prelude to a pair of minor declarations. "I'm not going to Maine today. I have to think on this."

"Okay, you go think."

"I'm serious."

"Okay."

"I'm serious. We're forty-four, and what are we? Taxed to no end. Bound to Citibank. Bound to Bank of America. Bound to TIAA-CREF. Bound to AT&T. Bound to Comcast. Who knows what the fuck we are to Monsanto. We exist to make our contributions to their fortunes. We're complicit. We'll retire, if we're lucky, suffer medical catastrophes, fight bitterly with the insurance company we gave who knows how much to, and we'll die. At home and tubeless, if we're lucky."

"What happened to happy and calm?" she asks, pointing to the flashcard.

"I'm taking Watts for a walk," he says. "I can't think in terms of flashcards now. Watts! Let's go."

***

Albert drives about a half mile down the road and turns right, drives slowly past the cranberry bog where he released a palm-sized snapping turtle last May, and wonders if the turtle lives there still or tried to make the perilous return trip to the fairgrounds in front of which he'd found it lying upside down in the eastbound lane, miraculously unscathed. He turns left on Cox Road, past Kelsey's Pond, and comes to the beginning of the dirt road that leads in to the state forest.

A mile in, he makes a U-turn, pulls into his usual spot beside the road, releases Charlie Watts, whose life seems suddenly widened by the smells of the woods. They walk not quite a half mile down the road in the direction they had come, and Watts, a guided missile, turns left where the trail starts and climbs the rutted hill that ATVs and rain take turns eroding. The trail turns rocky, ledgy, notwithstanding the occasional stretch of mud. The glacial boulders here and there remind Albert just how briefly we've been resident. A little higher and the rockface rises to the canopy, the ledges overhang, and Albert can't help imagining the natives up there practicing the art of patient observation. Time and time and time. The trail's ascent is gradual, but Albert's lungs pump harder and his breathing speeds up for the first mile and then levels after that, a period of acclimation that amuses him when he compares this hill, the Fire Tower Hill, whose elevation is 916 feet, to higher mountains he has been on. Elevation, though, is immaterial. His hiking here is not about attaining to a view or planting his imaginary flag and looking up when he has gone back down a hero to the lowlands, bolstered by the sense that he has somehow conquered that height and can therefore go about his lowlands life with greater confidence and clarity, a big man. Albert comes here to commune, to blend in, to obscure himself among so many trees and practice breathing. It is rare he sees a person walking back here, and he knows there is a bear around here somewhere, which awareness lets him feel a few leagues deeper in the woods than he would map-wise seem. He kids himself that he would like to be that bear, an unwashed, primal, and uncultivated being who emerges from the forest when the spirit moves it to investigate the scents and share in the abounding seeds that hang around for songbirds, outwardly unbothered by its kind's diminished numbers, lumbering, lumbering, returning to these nine-thousand acres when the sheltered people get too curious or frazzled or defensive, taking with it unobtrusive ursine goals: perpetuation of its bearness via cub production, storage of sufficient fat for winter, procurement of a cozy hole far off the beaten trail, no redolence of man, no evidence of bushwhack. Bear indivisible.

Watts pauses at a trail fork. Sometimes, when the day is open and the mind's unburdened and an hour more or less is of no consequence, they bear right, take the long way. Most times they bear left, as they do now, and hike up to the ridge where four concrete footings and the rusting steel that formed the anchorage show where the fire tower stood.

As they bear left, Albert looks up toward the ridge and sees what he believes at first he does not really see. About a hundred feet above them, fluffed up, stockstill, ears pricked for reception, eyes subjecting them to canine inquisition, a coyote stands, betraying no fear, no aggression. Albert stops and leashes Watts, whose eyesight isn't what it used to be, who seems to wonder why this sudden outburst of restraint at this point in the woods. For maybe thirty seconds, Albert and the coyote make their mutual appraisals. Then, just briefly, the coyote sways from side to side, turns right, presents its bushy tail, and trots away. Albert waits a few minutes to allow for distance. Feeling privileged for the glimpse, admitted to a world that's miserly about admission, he continues up the ridge with Watts still leashed. Up there, there is more light. He sits down on a mossy footing, fiddles for a second with a rusty bolt, and looks around. Watts sniffs. How easily and silently some forms of life can disappear. How easily and silently some forms of life can make the elsewhere here. No hands to wring. No baggage. Absolutely clear on the essentials.

Albert sits there for a while, easy, silent. He unleashes Watts and watches as his aging dog retraces with his nose where the coyote was. Albert looks at all the trees, imagines wildfire, wonders where the fugitive coyote would retreat to then. It's one thing to evade an interloper and his dog, another to outrun a fire and remain unsinged. Either way, he guesses, it's about retreat, about the flight from or surrender to the well-positioned and relentless forces that your instinct or experience informs you that, no matter how fierce you believe your heart to be, how just you judge your cause to be, you cannot beat.

Albert tallies what exactly he would be retreating from: a government whose General Accounting Office auditors attached a value of a quarter-million dollars to his father's radiation-shortened life; a mortgage which, when Albert's in the mood to mortify the flesh and stares at the afflicting figures on the amortization schedule, renders Shylock's sin so quaint that Albert has to wonder when the Christian world rejiggered its traditional interpretation of the immorality of interest, shrugged as if to say to Jesus, "What else can we do?", and said okay to usury; a five-year truck note on which he has four years left, a note whose final payment will feel like a lullaby whose sweet refrain is "Free and clear" but whose deceptive subtext will subliminally usher in the notion of inevitable decline and a mechanic's intervention and the line between fair-market price and highway robbery; a debit card and credit card whose engineered convenience makes him feel like a de-facto advocate of a society, a new-world order in which coins and paper money go the way of wampum; a 403B account that in his lifetime will not yield what everyone asserts he'll need to keep pace with inflation and maintain his accustomed living standard in the dream state of retirement and wage release.

That is the dream, Albert thinks, fiddling with the rusty bolt again. To be released. To be what in a perfect world you would already be. A conservator of lions or a landscape painter or a circle maker or among the foremost experts in the art of sunrise observation or a scrimshaw dealer who appreciates the special sorrow of the walrus and the whale or a restorer of the world's discarded brooms. So why not? Why not, when there is potential dissonance or confrontation in the middle distance, squarely gaze on it for thirty seconds, sway from side to side, turn right, present the pure indifference of your backside, and, untethered, trot away?

Well, for one, he thinks, *I like my ranch house, which I sided, which I roofed, which I'm attached to. I like its modesty and how it sits upon the grassy hill and is obscured a little from the street view by the maple and the weeping cherry tree and grants me keyhole insight into kingship. Surrender and there's that.* The pleasant garden and the pleasant patio a-flower, the pleasant shed beside which cracked corn draws the deer, an acre, a shy acre on which woodchucks, rabbits, squirrels, chipmunks, field mice, moles, garter snakes, American toads, the usual, are not pushed out, a place that will in fact be his in fourteen years. *Fourteen years*, he thinks. They'll fly by like the last fourteen, and then what? When he looks back on those fourteen years of mortgage payments, automatic bank deposits, home improvements, cashless purchases, biweekly contributions to his laggardly retirement account, refueling, refueling, refueling, hangovers, blowjobs, reruns, phone calls, Google searches, central air, oil heat, and so on, will he be just another unknown citizen, a good guy, steady, who does not complain in any significant way and, in his practical obedience, does his small part for the exclusive enterprise that is his country and is easily forgotten when he peters out and dies? An easy guy to eulogize and file? Will he be just another in an aging nation of recliners, watching *Alone in the Wilderness* on PBS again and listening to the narrator say, "Thousands have had such dreams, but Dick Proenneke lived them," wishing he'd been born with Dick's resolve and moved his whole life into the Alaskan bush, as Dick did in 1967, and lived there as a fully realized throwback, having no internal reservations that he should be living some other way or somewhere else, for over thirty years?

Albert fiddles with the rusty bolt. He likes it here. He thinks of the coyote. Wild. Of the timber rattlesnake he almost stepped on last week as he walked the ridge with Watts. Wild. Of the anecdotal black bear out here somewhere. Wild. Maybe that's as wild as it ought to be for someone whose formation took place on a fenced lot on Long Island, which was wild once but had the wilderness bred out so long ago it's hard to see the wilderness or even just the period before the power lines as other than a myth, a shared delusion founded on supposedly a speck of truth, a state the books say once existed but that doesn't feel true, has the aura of the alien, because if you believe it absolutely, that the time you long for wasn't all that long ago, is barely out of reach in geological terms, then you must countenance that sinking feeling that suggests the road ahead, no different from the road behind, is just a moneymaker for the well-positioned and the forward-thinking, just a way to make believe the present is in need of serious improvements, which are ever and anon on that horizon, that imaginary line beyond which nothing like a netless ocean or an uncut continental forest free of market pressures ever lies. A needle drops unbidden on a vinyl record spinning on the Pioneer in Albert's brain, and "Stairway" plays.

My spirit is crying for leaving, Albert thinks. *I've stood looking. I would like to hear the forest echo with laughter. Not developer or lumberjack laughter but the sort of laughter Robert Plant was thinking of, dryad laughter, the forgotten elemental lilt, the laughter of the sentient being picked up by the human ear again.*

But that is hard to square with the statistics. In the past ten years, he has read, the earth has lost an average of six-thousand acres of forestland, along with all its stunned inhabitants, per day. Per day. Four acres of woods are lost per minute. At that rate Albert's eighteen acres wouldn't last five minutes. He looks down at the trees and tries to estimate 210 feet by 210 feet and tries to picture four such swaths no longer there, replaced by cattle or a Taco Bell or a secluded house in which a spider would be hard-pressed to find refuge and a lawn that's fertilized and watered as if it is central to a village's subsistence. Still, there's hope. Take this place, for example. In 1903 these woods found a stout defender when the State of Connecticut bought seventy acres for $105 and protected them from the prevailing ethos via legislation, designating them the country's second State Forest, which, since then, has grown to these nine-thousand acres, practically nothing in the context of six-thousand acres lost per day, but something inspirational regardless, like bagpipe music playing as the thinned ranks that still stand against the onslaught and rapacity of an indignant Empire disregard what the enormous toll suggests about the likelihood of their success and soldier with the breathing music on.

"I think Dick Proenneke is my piper," says Albert, who puts his hands on his knees. He rises from the fire-tower footing, checks himself for ticks, and looks around to locate Watts. "This way, Watts. Watch out for the coyote." They walk along the ridge a little ways, turn left, and head downhill. Watts slaloms ahead. "Dick Proenneke is my piper," he concludes. "He has to be."

Chapter Seven

Albert possesses, as do many people who have hit their heads on asphalt roads or sampled angel dust by accident or lost the steady rhythm and the compass of the old religion, a conviction, an unshakable belief that random happenings or stray thoughts featuring a pleasing seam of relevance or memories long dormant suddenly remembered at a time that seems too opportune to be dismissed are signs to be interpreted, pieces of the existential puzzle that must be at first encountered out of context, looked at downside up and upside down and sideways, and inserted in the right position if the larger picture is to clarify. And when he judges that the signs are dutifully and accurately interpreted, the pieces situated so the fragment sharpens, coalesces, and the vision that had previously been only hinted at is billboard-sized and unified, the execution is what's left, transferring the exuberance and buoyancy of the dream, of the epiphany, into the workaday and tempered world, the one in which it often makes more sense to live vicariously through someone who has done what will remain a restless hypothetical for many in his fan club.

"Do you remember Dick Proenneke?" Albert asks Mary as he freshens Watts's water bowl when he gets home.

Mary has the scrunched look of the stumped decipherer. "Is this another one of your Pat McGroyne jokes? Because I don't get it."

"No," says Albert. "Dick Proenneke. The guy who retired, built his cabin in Alaska with hand tools, lived there by himself until he was like eighty? On PBS?"

"Yeah, yeah, I remember. What about him?"

"I want to do what he did. A variation on what he did. He was fifty or so when he started. So I've got six years on him."

"You're going by yourself?"

"No. A variation on what he did. You're in on this."

"I'm not living in that camp. It's disgusting."

"New camp. New outhouse."

"So you'll take the fifty thousand?"

"If my mother signs, I'll take it."

"Then what?"

"Phase one. Lay the groundwork."

She shakes her head and sits down on the couch.

"Listen. I go to Maine tomorrow or the next day and begin the demolition. Tear down the cabin. Tear down the outhouse. Clear things out and take a fresh look. Do a little feng-shui evaluation," Albert says as he slowly moves his hands karate-wise before him. "Maybe take a couple trees down if I have to. Do a little site work. You come up one weekend, come up for a week, whatever, and we figure the dimensions, figure where the new camp goes. Once that's settled, I can figure out materials and whatnot so we're set to build next June."

"O-kay," she says.

"Okay," says Albert. "Good enough. This next part might sound somewhat radical at first."

Mary rubs her eyebrows with her thumb and middle finger, starting from the middle of the brow and rubbing out.

"I mean, if we go off the grid, it is, compared to how we're used to living, pretty radical. This next component, though, is less unusual than it used to be before the housing crash." He pauses as if to allow a period of inquiry. "It makes sense for us, I think, if we're committed to withdrawal, to strategically default."

"Meaning what?"

"Meaning we stop paying our mortgage. We're not too far from being underwater anyway, and it'll be nine months before the bank begins foreclosure proceedings. So we can live here for a year, and in the meantime we save over twenty-thousand dollars."

"Foreclosure."

"*Strategic* foreclosure. Look it up. It doesn't have the stigma that it used to have. It's relatively common now. It's practically the little guy's sole defense against the depredations of the banks."

"And what about our credit?"

"It'll take a hit. But who cares? We won't need it in the woods."

"No," she says, shaking her head, "that's crazy."

"What's crazier? Paying, month after month, year after year, a huge bank all that interest on a property that isn't worth what we bought it for, or moving on and getting clear of that enormous debt and living on our own?"

"What about the money we've put into this place?"

"It's gone," he says. "Unless we wait until the housing market bounces all the way back and try to sell the place then. We could be dead by then."

"And what do we do when the bank comes after us?"

"We have a non-recourse loan. They can only take the house, which we concede. We're basically free and clear if we default."

"And what if we decide, say, two years in that living off the grid is not for us?"

"That would be a problem. But it *is* for us. You know it is. We're forty-four, we—"

"No Jake and Ryan then."

Albert knows that he can never be Dick Proenneke and can never blaze the same trail, even if the underbrush and overstory have restaked their claims and make it seem as though no human heretofore has had the nerve to come this way. Once blazed, always blazed, regardless of the obscurations. He knows he cannot be original by following, cannot attain authenticity by using someone else's map or playing hopscotch with the footprints of a bona fide adventurer. It isn't 1967. Albert knows he won't be a lone man in the wilderness of recently annexed Alaska. Albert knows that he does not possess Dick Proenneke's manual intelligence, his natural feel for the autonomous constructional arts, and won't be using handmade tools and won't be chopping down his own spruce or devising some means to retrieve them from the distance, won't be peeling off the bark himself or planing with no hurry the unevenness from the logs or notching joints with masterly precision so that one log practically becomes engrafted to the next until the walls are raised or fashioning a fireplace and chimney out of stones he witched out of the landscape with his own hands and bore home. Albert knows he won't be radiating Dick Proenneke's cheerful, camera-ready patience, which makes living in the backwoods by oneself look easy and organic, as if anyone of basic sensibility and physical endowment and a mind not thrown by lonesomeness can do the same. Albert also knows that he possesses something that the record shows Dick Proenneke never had: a sudden inclination to extract from State care two autistic boys whom he envisions would do better in unregulated woods, no specialists, no whoop-de-doo, just four souls variously deficient, differently damaged, repairing as a unit into the unknown. Not Dick Proenneke territory certainly, but close enough.

"Talk to the foster people," Albert says. "Explain to them our situation. See what they have to say."

"Our situation? Our situation is about to be a train wreck."

"Don't be so dramatic. We have a year to work this out. If it's not for them, it's not for them." Albert looks in the refrigerator. "Anyway. Phase one. Strategic default puts over twenty thousand in our pockets. Next, we stop contributing to our retirement accounts and cash them out next May. That'll be another sixty, maybe seventy. With the Department of Energy's fifty and what's in our checking, we'll be well over a hundred. And if we become foster parents this year, we get what?"

"756 per child per month. 1,512 for both of them," she says.

"That's right, that's right. Another eighteen thousand, give or take. A new camp won't cost more than ten. And then we're independent."

"What happens when the money runs out?"

"You'll be surprised how long it lasts when we get rid of our expenses. No power bill, no phone bill, no—"

"I'm not getting rid of my cell phone," Mary interjects.

"No cable bill. No credit cards. Maybe one for an emergency. No insurance on the house. No—"

"No health insurance."

Albert pauses. Intellectually, he knows the modern health-insurance system, in which people pay a certain monetary sum as an anxiety-soothing hedge against the probability of future illness, has been extant for about a century, with origins in the still imperial England of Lloyd George, and knows that being uninsured does not necessarily mean one's organs, sensing economic vulnerability, would fail any sooner than the organs of the comfortably insured and does not necessarily mean a nasty bacillus would have a preference for an orifice of the uninsured and bypass all the open mouths and nostrils of the people who had seen their primary-care physicians for the proper prophylaxis. But, viscerally, he's forced to entertain some major reservations now about intentionally removing the insuring hands that have been cupped beneath him since the day that he was born.

She's right. A person who is forty-four should be more circumspect and should be able to depend more confidently on his supposedly developed frontal cortex to assess severity of risk and to advise, "If I were you, I wouldn't," and should step away with care from the crevasse that tempts him with its passable appearance, solid-seeming and serene, instead of stepping gingerly ahead, applying gradually increasing pressure on the one foot, then the next, and, by repeating suchlike cautionary footwork on the first leg of the journey, gradually arrive at the emboldening conclusion that the risk is overblown and that the well-intentioned frontal cortex shouldn't be so motherly and stifling when a person is still relatively young and has the fortune to retain a spirit of adventure, which is tempered now, the forty-four-year-old crevasse adventurer assures himself, with life experiences a well-developed frontal cortex would have told him not to have, and he got through those harrowings just fine.

Besides, Dick Proenneke did it. He went without insuring his endangered health for over thirty years. Unless Dick had set aside a certain sum to cover his insurance premiums and flew his bush plane into Anchorage or Fairbanks once a year to get his annual physical. That doesn't seem like Dick. And, anyway, Dick crashed that plane, escaped with minor injuries, and gave up personal aviation altogether, which renunciation would have made the annual physical more burdensome. Perhaps Albert doesn't know Dick.

How does someone who does not avail himself of checkups and preventative care and recommended pharmaceuticals make it all the way to eighty? That's just Western Medicine talking. Be on guard when Western Medicine starts talking. Watch your wallet. Watch for side effects.

What Albert cannot lay upon the Western medical tradition, though, is family history, his future writ, potentially, in the language of genetics and inherited catastrophe—his father's esophageal-cancer death, his maternal grandmother's slow-motion Alzheimer's death, his mother's pattern of dissimulation in the disconcerting face of her own worsening forgetfulness. His father's death is not so much the overarching existential threat, is not so much the fate he thinks is likeliest and therefore does not fear the most. His father smoked religiously, which Albert does not. His father worked among the half-lives of cesium, tritium, and other brands of radiation, worked among the dumps of benzene, mercury, and other sorts of terminal chemicals, which Albert, as far as he can see, though sight is not reliable here, does not. And so he hopes that, if disease can be primarily environmental, he is in the right environment to not develop that one.

Still, genetics.

So he worries sometimes when he vomits or has heartburn, worries that he's thinned the lining of his delicate esophagus a little more, inviting cancer cells to congregate and bloom and make him hack and cause his stomach to be surgically raised and cause him to be further ruined by the radiologists and chemotherapy technicians and reduce his rich voice to amphibious dimensions, all croaks and hisses, waiting, always waiting for the turmoil to be over.

That is not so much the overarching existential threat. At least his father, physically debilitated and exhausted by the cells' sick mind games, was identifiably his father even at the end and recognized him as his son and had, at least, the sense his story, even when he died, would not be over all the way. He somewhat saw his future, even if his present was a mortal drag. Such is the continuation promised by one's offspring, the relieving transfer of mortality's baton.

But Albert's grandmother, though a mother and a grandmother and beyond, with actual blood relations in this world, did not, in her mind, take the next step on the human timeline, say her present-world farewells, secure in the successional belief that those she left behind would follow her in due time. In a sense, she made the journey in reverse, returning to her young adulthood, to her youth, to her not yet departed parents, who were vibrant, her not yet departed brother, who was vibrant, and regarded everyone, related to her or unlinked, at first, politely but as people who were see-through, nothing to her, which is why she spoke to everyone so often of the dead, who were to her just elsewhere in the world, and then developed such a deep dread of and banshee-like resistance to the present, wailing when her daughter tried to help with her incontinence, flailing in the night when she awoke and saw the strange man, who explained again with a heroic patience, "I'm your husband, Ann," lying in such scandalous proximity to her, evading sometimes somehow the security measures that her husband in his heavy-lidded desperation put in place, and looking, always looking, for the people dear to her who were no more, reminding everyone who saw or heard her of the death knell that is always poised to rock our inner ears.

That is the overarching existential threat, that Albert is on his unwilled way toward becoming his succeeding generation's version of the hollowed-out, untethered, short-term-middle-term-and-pretty-much-all-utile-terms-of-memory-deprived but otherwise relatively healthy specter doomed to stare and wander in this unfamiliar world, expecting always to encounter the desired and familiar other in which he is young and all his dreams cohere and where he lives has not been fractured and where the people he is certain he still lives among have not been scattered to the winds. *That* is the fate he dreads the most because it strikes him as the likeliest, the one genetics and environment have quietly conspired in, the one that will, by slight degrees, just now and then at first, misplace the keys to his identity, his selfhood, his location in the mind, the one that will reprogram over time his inner GPS, which scans the world's coordinates and then reports to him without a question, "You are here." He knows there's nothing he can do about genetics. Someone rolled those dice before his time. What troubles him is that he has not done his long-term prospects any favors, that his formerly fractured skull, his past and present drinking, and his general negativity and gloominess have probably enhanced what factors lurk in the environment and pull a certain person with the requisite predisposition to the side and start their tinkering with what originally was quite a steel trap of a memory. What kind of old age will it be if he is wandering from tree to tree on his eighteen acres looking for his formative house on Norwood Avenue, the friends he shared the halcyon experience of unencumbered childhood with, the siblings he could not imagine distant, the parents yet unravaged, all powerful, all knowing? Poor Mary looking out the cabin door, her mind imagining the worst, her lips muttering as if a muttered wish might alter her reality for once and suddenly produce her shadow of a husband from the shadows of the woods, "Not again."

Albert looks at Mary, who's still waiting for an answer to the implied question of health-insurance coverage. *Why am I so yellow?* wonders Albert. *Why am I, at forty-four, hoping,* hoping *to go out the way Dick Proenneke did—a conscious concession to the toll of age, a dignified retreat from his beloved wilderness, a stroke indoors in California as if something in his hardy constitution said, "We're rupturing this vessel for your own good. No droopy lip. No burdensome paralysis. Dick Proenneke, this is it"? I'll cross that bridge,* thinks Albert, *when it requires crossing. Dick Proenneke went into the woods, with insurance or without, when he was fifty. I am forty-four.*

Albert says to Mary, "Did Lewis and Clark have health insurance? Did Ernest Shackleton? Does Eustace Conway? I don't know."

"Who's Eustace Conway?"

"The actuarial tables will tell you we've got time before we need the serious medical attention. Decades probably. Statistically. Policy-wise, it doesn't matter. It's out of our hands. The health-insurance question has been settled by Obamacare. Be insured or pay a fine."

"That's true."

"And I was thinking of trying my hand at writing some commercial stuff for extra money."

Silence.

"And if you talk to the foster people while I'm up there, tell them I'm at a writer's residency in Vermont or someplace for a month or so. That sounds impressive. Tell them I'm an English teacher. Beloved, really. Tell them I'm a poet." He pauses, fishing. "Tell them I'm a landowner." He nods. "I don't look too bad on paper."

"Who's Eustace Conway?"

"Another guy who does what needs doing. He takes care of business."

"What is that supposed to mean?"

"*The Last American Man*? Elizabeth Gilbert pre-*Eat, Pray, Love*? It's around here somewhere. I have to pack."

Although she sees some serious logistical flaws in certain outlined features of his plan and more or less expects him to consider it by summer's end as just another windmill, Mary can't help feeling in possession of what she is pretty sure is conjugal joy because her husband spoke to her today in an inclusive, you-and-me-united kind of way for longer than he'd spoken to her in the eight years they've been married or, for that matter, in the fourteen since they met; and, plan or no plan, maybe they have turned a conversational corner, which she's long regarded as the first negotiation on the road to marital fulfillment, to collaborative union, and, perhaps, to equitable orgasm distribution whereby "First come, first served" is no longer the abiding *modus operandi*. Anyway, she feels alternatives to discontentment.

Chapter Eight

Albert turns the stubby key—and nothing. He removes it, blows on it, and tries again. The inner locking mechanism clicks, is sprung, and he unhooks the padlock's horseshoe portion from the eyelet bolt screwed halfway through the treated post. He stretches out the cable so it roughly parallels the entranceway and lays it on the ground so that it doesn't interfere with all the seedling hemlock, fir, pine, and spruce and doesn't weigh them down as they try hard to grow out of the shadow of established trees and tippy-toe it toward the sunlight. Albert notices two furrows in the earth and smiles on the inside at the industry of mole or shrew.

He drives his pickup in about ten or fifteen feet and shuts it off this time instead of leaving it to idle.

"Let's go, Watts."

The entranceway is densely flanked by trees that have grown up and out and deeply evergreen, and the grass and weeds are mid-shin high. Albert waves his right foot back and forth as though it were a dull scythe, warning frogs and toads who might be hiding that a heavy being has arrived. He steps and waves his way into the little clearing, looks around, and everything is as it was, as he remembers. Watts is systematic in his vacuum-like investigation of the place's scents. Albert walks back up the driveway, moving twigs and branches, gently tossing slugs aside to moisture elsewhere. He drives slowly in and does a five-point turn and situates his truck so that it's pointing roadward and allows him room behind to pitch his tent. He walks into the woods and, in an act that he considers one small indication of this place's liberating atmosphere, he urinates without concern for neighborly intrusion or the health of peonies. He zips his shorts and surveys, and he wishes that the course of forest management since Contact could have gone a different way, could have been less focused on commodity. But this, these eighteen acres, Albert considers his protectorate, except he doesn't feel at all imperious or lordy. "Okay," he says. "Unpack. Make camp. Relax."

He flaps the tarp and spreads it like a tablecloth upon the open ground, avoiding little cedars on the fringes, little firs, encapsulations of a shade of green that is a life assertion as inarguable as any airtight axiom. He squares the two-man tent, which realistically provides accommodations for the average breadth and culled necessities of one man, tugs and smooths the corners like a hovering mother who's concerned about appearances and what the world thinks. He puts the graphite poles together, slides them through the guideline sleeves, and bends them into arcs as he inserts them in the grommets, staking the ephemeral shelter to the packed earth as if it might blow away despite the windbreaks on all sides and tautening the purple rainfly just in case. He slides an office-cooler jug of water closer to the open tailgate, which he climbs so he can also slide the cooler with provisions to the more convenient access point. He jumps down. Tests the knees. He sets the silver-legged, black bubble of a Weber grill on the ground at a remove he judges sparks would be unlikely to singe the rainfly from.

He wipes his hands, unfolds a camp chair, sits, and faces the direction of the old camp, which is thirty feet or so beyond a pine stand, set in a depression with a stream view, listing like a wooden houseboat to the port side, chances for recovery appearing dim. Albert thinks about destruction, the intention to undo, and whom he'll have to kick out if he means to settle here. He leans his head back as if getting a professional shampoo and listens to the hermit-thrush cascade, the flute tunes floating down from hidden elevations in the canopy like spray shot through with sunlight, hanging rainbow after rainbow as reminders of the spectrum. He can't tell if one is singing to itself in vernal joy or if it pours itself into a courtship song to which the courted trills her airy variation or if the dryadic music is ecstatic, beaks-held-high, parental confirmation that, in this predacious world, the eggs are nesting peacefully. Whatever Albert's grooving to, the solstice is approaching, the solstice is approaching. A barley stalk of light brushes Albert's upturned face. He wishes it would linger, wishes it could hold that angle for the night, rendering unnecessary the encirclement of the elastic strap around his poorly oriented head, unnecessary the illumination of the headlamp, unnecessary the becoming what sticks out as really not nocturnal in the dark. Dick Proenneke must have known the idyll of the long day. But he must have known the flipside, too, the long night.

***

Things dim. Albert crawls behind a beam of light, unzips his tent, and enters, tailed by Watts, when it appears that all the birds have finished singing for the night.

Albert lies, hands on chest, and stares up in the country darkness like a man before the casket lid is lifted for the wake, a man whose eyelids the mortician had not in his pursed-lip judgment seen the need to glue shut. Albert's never heard well, having most days just the one good ear to work with, but he sees the wisdom, the potential for expansion in depriving oneself of a prime sense on occasion to convey to a deficient one it's not forgotten even if it's failed him often. Optic deprivation is at work here. Simply being outdoors, in the dark, and grounded is contributing to the development of a dimension he has not experienced in full or apprehended since—he judges he's in no position to submit a ballpark estimation even. His least reliable ear, because it finds this modest elevation or the current barometric pressure or the rural quietude agreeable, has popped, and Albert hears in stereo with what he thinks must be approaching owl-like acuity.

He can't sleep now. His ears are wide-eyed.

Rustle, twig snap, flutter, pitter patter, squeak, shriek, sniff, a gathering in the yond of hitherward coyote yips. Watts growls from time to time, then puts his head back down to signify he overstated the severity of the alarm. Watts knows the language. A variant, at least. And Albert, supine, immobile, clothed, and covered up, no operable sense of smell, is but a misfit here, a wayward form, an inhalation/exhalation from afar, who hears the language of the woods tonight but has no tolerant interpreter, no independent means, not even Watts, to translate into rudimentary communiques what's being said, what's going on outside the thin synthetic material on which his rough, omnivorous, unminty breath is, particle by particle, producing condensation as if, by immersion and by willingness to learn, he has been elevated to the status of a dew maker. Eventually his eyelids yield to traveling exhaustion, and he snores as if announcing to the nightlife he's arrived.

***

Before the sunlight filters through the eastern trees and through the rainfly and the tent and through the phosphene screens of Albert's inner eyelids, a persistent beep arises in the dream world and demands to be acknowledged in the material one.

"What the fuck?" asks Albert, his growly elongation of the first and third syllables conveying to curled Watts a depth of irritation lack of elongation doesn't have the time to properly convey.

Watts, who sometimes runs purely on voice recognition, weakly wags his tail against the tent wall. Swish. Swish.

About a mile distant, up the hill and down the Center Road on which Albert had driven yesterday, is Thomas Dairy Farm, whose daily rituals begin around the time the cocks should be saluting skyward with their beaks and doodling the day's first crows; except, there are no cocks, just farm machines proceeding often in reverse.

Albert sheds his sleeping bag and tent. He slides the two-burner stove to the tailgate's edge and threads its hose's fitting to the propane tank. He rummages like a conscientious, declawed bear through a dry-goods bag and finds the coffee and the pot. He tilts a water jug at no great angle over the tailgate's edge and fills the silver coffee pot with water, halfway fills the percolation carriage with the coffee. He opens up the propane valve, turns the knob for burner one, which hisses like a tire leak, clicks the lighter, and sets the pot upon the flame, that sign of human dominance, that sign of what would humans do without it. He walks a sanitary distance into the woods and urinates on leaves and needles, making spur adjustments to avoid the ants and spiders who did not anticipate precipitation, looking this way, looking that, for something primal or majestic staring back, but there is only Charlie Watts conducting the eternal olfactory reconnaissance of canines everywhere.

Albert pours his coffee, lightens it, sweetens it, and stands some minutes with his arm crooked, sipping to reduce the heat and volume, listening to the faint lows of the milk cows, lows arriving through the trees like water barely lapping at a lake shore. He looks into his coffee, and he thinks about the cream, where it was squeezed from, how it became, how it got cartonized, what splashes each day over decades probably have done to arteries that once knew no constriction.

He sits down in his camp chair and has no idea how long a milk cow lasts. Five years? Twenty? And what happens at the end? A quick death—stroke or heart attack? Or is there lingering requiring a bullet to the brain? A sledge? A throat slit? Does someone sympathetic from the rendering plant arrive and put in motion some professional procedure whereby everyone involved is fairly certain that they did right by that faithful cow? Or is the spent cow tractor-dragged or bulldozed, stiff-legged, to a distant corner of a field and left for the coyotes and the ravens and the sexton beetles and the men who like to shoot the coyotes and the ravens once the milk-cow carcass is sufficiently diminished and the scavengers seem troublesome and pesty, enemies to the livelihood, again? Albert wonders if, ten-thousand years ago, the cattle could have somehow risen up against domestication, or if an eastern mystic far beyond his time could have emerged and cogently prefigured to an open-minded population how the negative vibes of bovine subjugation would forever ripple outward, we might have the tranquil bovine look in *our* eyes, we might be a species of the meek and the content, our jaws moving casually sideways as we chew and take a natural joy in periodic relocations in this pastoral life we share with others, free of pettiness and grandiosity. He wonders if the dairy farmers over yonder ever think this way, and he concludes that such considerations probably disqualify him from participating realistically in farm life.

There comes a point, he guesses, when survival or efficiency or simple maintenance of manliness determines that you cannot care about the end-of-life realities of milk cows, about the cramped conditions milk cows spend their lives in and the basic absence of mobility, about the possible cruelties milk cows suffer at the hands of someone for whom dairy life is not the culmination of a childhood occupational dream, about the bullet holes or poisoned meat in dead coyotes, dead ravens, dead lions in the dust of Kenya, dead vultures in Zimbabwe dust, Namibia dust, about the severed hands of mountain gorillas shot and hacked by Congolese poachers for export to the Asian markets. There comes a point, he guesses, when the quality of mercy is so strained that it becomes, at best, the quality of indifference, the quality of gaze aversion. For a moment, Albert hears in his head the dour David Gilmour singing "On the Turning Away." The milk cows low still in the distance. Albert cannot figure out how not to turn away from them, how not to think about himself as milk cow lowing from the confines of a stall so that a person sitting at his ease and sipping coffee near the solstice cannot say he didn't know.

Like many people who have no experience negotiating non-cash economies, Albert wonders how a person like himself, descended from a college course on the Romantics, would be able, should he really move his life up here full time, to make ends meet when the impressive acorn pile he amassed, his cash reserve, his value and utility in the wasteland of the cash economy, runs out. If somehow he was blessed with the possession of a cow, what then? Where keep it? How provide for it? How care? How coax the milk? How store it? How move the cow when sickness or a worse fate fells it? How make it through the winter when the currency is gone?

Albert gets a second cup of coffee, sits back down, and puts his free hand for assurances on Watts's head. Beyond the stream, hidden in the deeper woods, a deer snorts. A denizen. A native. A practitioner of pure subsistence. What, in theory, Albert wants to be. Not hunted, though. Not hunted. If inside him is the hunter that the distant forebears used to be and he is able to perch motionless for hours in a tree until a deer appears and doesn't fear what might come from above, and he is able to become an instrument of death and do the disemboweling and the skinning and the carving and, again, the storing, what becomes of that Albert who, though not officially, was in his fiber a devoted follower, a philosophical disciple, of Saint Francis, of the Jains, embodiments of harmlessness? Becoming, finally, after all the false starts, all the Lents, a steady and invested vegetarian might be the way to go. A conscience cleaner. He sips his coffee, pets Watts. But even then a lot of trees will have to make way for a garden and the necessary sunlight, and what lives in them and on them will be chainsaw struck by massive rearrangement to accommodate a good intention, a decision to pursue what may or may not be the lesser of the evils. Albert sighs because of life.

He gets pressed by more immediate concerns and finds himself rewishing that the porcupines, against whom he bears no vendetta for exhibiting fidelity to their rodential nature, hadn't gnawed a secondary entrance through his outhouse wall, already rickety, and let go with a carpet bomber's flair for coverage on the plywood floor. He finishes his coffee, and he wishes thus because the current primitivist bathroom situation unsettles what he takes for granted should be the reflective interlude, the natural rhythm of matutinal evacuation, which is nigh. When Albert first came here and discovered the incursion, he decided, once he poked his head inside the door, against remediation since he didn't know what happens on a microscopic level when those fecal pellets break down, what potential killer might go airborne, what footnote in the literature he might become if he scooped up and swept and sat down and each morning breathed his Oms in that confined space, trusting that his pulmonary fortitude or his cilia would be enough to carry him through each morning's movement past the specter of infection.

He remembers reading of the Australian hiker on the Appalachian Trail who was relieved to have arrived after so many footsteps at a shelter for the night and swept in preparation for his short stay, performed the usual housekeeping hikers typically perform before they settle in. The Aussie didn't know that, as he stirred the unseen world and as the dust rose, he inhaled the hantavirus, courtesy of deer mice, and would soon be laid quite low. He didn't die. He made a full recovery. *But,* Albert thinks, *why take the chance? Why clean? Let sleeping microbes lie.* He takes his toilet paper roll and garden shovel, and he bushwhacks what he senses is at least two-hundred feet into the woods. As he does not assume the posture of The Thinker, he determines that the first thing he will build here next year is an outhouse and resolves that it will be impregnable and sterile. O, the bodily necessities, the unavoidable appointments.

Albert comes back from the woods. He sticks his garden shovel like a dagger in the dirt and stows his toilet paper in a Ziploc bag. He sanitizes his adventurous hands and stands like someone on the verge of heading west who suddenly has doubts about Manifest Destiny and isn't certain, after all the preparation, that he wants to move and thereby make himself a rugged individual, a capital A American who is on board the prairie schooner drawn by the doctrine, other claims be damned. They say it is no tragedy when someone who has lived a long time dies, and that may be. And Albert goes back and forth on whether sentience can be reasonably attributed in this hemisphere to a cabin that has stood here for so long the paperwork is not clear on the year of its construction, only indicating it was built in 1900, plus or minus. A monument's a monument, and, consciousness or not, it's been imbued. Albert hates to undo handiwork. He's loath to pull the plug. A usurpation of the natural course is really not for him. But why let the poor camp sag? Why let water seek its lowest point inside of it? He wonders if it suffers. He searches for a reason for kinesis, wants a thing he learned to underpin his action. Every act of creation is first an act, declared Picasso, of destruction. Could be empty art talk.

Albert tries to conjure up exceptions to the dictum. He is stumped when he considers the example of an oak tree. Does a seedling start out as an act of destruction? You could say the acorn dies or loses, anyway, its acorn-ness. You could say the open space is lost, has given way to shadow and to majesty. *Okay. Let's go with Pablo. Let's head west. Let's do this.*

Albert levels his ladder on the leafy, duffy ground and leans it at an angle he deems safe against the center of the cedar fascia board that runs the rear length of the camp. A reputed fact he picked up somewhere comes to him, reminds him of the shifty line between the here and the hereafter: half of all falls from elevations three times the faller's height result in death. Albert takes a step back, looks up, adopts the posture of assessment, and estimates the height of this side of the roof to be no more than ten feet, which will put his head at no higher than sixteen feet when he is standing on the roof. Two feet to spare. The roof, though, pitches upward toward the front, increasing from what Albert guesses is a three pitch to a six, statistically increasing his awareness of mortality. *Slow and steady wins the race,* he thinks. *Tread lightly.*

He walks back to his truck and puts his tool belt on. He slides the hammer handle through the silver ring, secures the diagonal-cutting pliers in the leather pocket, picks up the pry bar, picks up the shingle remover, and returns a-jangling to the ladder. There is domination in ascension, domination in deciding you were granted the authority, the justification to undo. Albert climbs and steps upon the roof and surveys, but more meekly than Balboa on the mountain overlooking the Pacific and without the fibrillating dream of riches and indigenous upheaval. He looks down and sees Watts beside the ladder, looking up.

"Go lie down, Watts. I'll be up here for a while."

Albert makes a mental note to locate Watts before he throws any material from the roof. He wonders, if he falls, if Watts could make like Lassie and communicate to someone his degree of desperation and his canine inability to rescue Albert himself. Albert looks over the edge and pictures himself an angled figure on the ground. *No sense looking over edges now,* he thinks.

He decides upon a shingle seam and pushes the remover like a broom. He lifts the shingle, watches as the asphalt granules tumble, bends with the remover, slides the shingle to the side, continues. As he finds his demolition rhythm, he would like to sing a work song to declare his solidarity of purpose, but it's just him and there's nothing in his culture that he knows of sung specifically for this. He measures progress by the shingle pile he's amassing near the ladder top. Up and sidestep to the left, up and sidestep to the left, monotonous, he moves. The sounds he makes, frictional, clanging, respiratory, are conventional asunder sounds, but they do not drown out or otherwise discourage birdsong that seems bursting with the ecstasy of reproduction and the solstice coming. Albert plods on. *Destruction first,* he tells himself, *and then creation.*

Pablo never stipulated that destruction must be wholesale, though. So Albert feels no compulsion to become another merciless quadrantal juggernaut, erasing life as he proceeds. He pauses to allow the frantic carpenter ants evacuation and adjustment time, but pausing probably is not sufficient for atonement or for straightening out the karmic kinks that radiate from forced dispersal. Albert waits while the earwigs and the pill bugs and the spiders and the beetles and the caterpillars and the insects that are practically translucences—the whole retiring, fine-until-Albert-came, roof-based ecosystem—seek another seam, another home, away from this methodical marauder. Towering, Albert stands motionless and figures this is history writ small: the sad migration from the loved savannah, the spirit-crushing final look and leaving generations of ancestral dead and geographical intimacies behind because the jungle's being logged or drilled, the exodus from somewhere birth-dear where the old reliable soil doesn't give up what it used to, where the water merely trickles or no longer flows, where structures rise, where boundaries harden, where possession has become the true religion, where the human voice has come to bellow to the voiceless, "You must go." Albert watches the diaspora, consoles himself by reasoning that one day he will be again by far outnumbered by the quiet dwellers of the new roof, which resettlement will be, he reasons, a creation aspect of the teardown presently underway.

As he continues with the racket of removal and identifies himself with the despair of forced migration, the idea occurs to him—not like a light bulb switched on but like a soft glow from the east—that, when he wears a collared shirt and patterned tie and stands before his slumped students like a stubbly sage of questionable authority and warns them, as if it could paralyze or kill them, of the literary danger of indulging sentiment, he's still a faithful Eliotic soldier after all these years and needs to find his nerve and champion articulately for once the worth and substance of the sentimental when it's earned and needs to come up with a lesson, an entire unit even, to make clear, to crystallize just what he means about emotional expression being earned, about expressing feeling unapologetically, with authenticity, with disregard for the bloodless pose, with no care for the elevation of detachment as the true perspective. What's the point of being a recruiter, though, without some sort of follow through, some action or some program with a circulatory system that transforms the intellectual or the emotional or the ethereal expression into something real? He can't keep pointing to the textbook excerpts, hoping that some students will just magically absorb Thoreau, who speaks in riddles to the cell-phone generation and inspires in the screen-devout the condemnation of indifference. A pond of lily pads and blank stares.

Albert fishes. Edward Abbey maybe. Show them how the feeling, the disgust, the outrage, the gut reaction, which an oilman or an executive or Eliot might greet with condescension and dismiss as sentiment, becomes removed from the abstract, becomes the call to action for the characters, becomes the call to action for the more devoted readers, becomes earned. The feeling, the idea, becoming something to contend with, something actually dangerous in the world.

Albert pauses. He will have to go back to Aristotle. Or to Plato. He confuses them with regularity. The older he becomes, the more he must reread. Art imitating life. Life imitating art. So many fine, imaginary lines and shades of meaning and causation chains. Pedagogically, it doesn't matter in the long run. Albert will depart Connecticut a year from now, or two, and live here off the grid with Mary and perhaps two kids and be, at last, the change he wants to see in the world, praise Gandhi.

When all the shingles and the tarpaper are detached and piled neatly near the ladder top and Albert has walked the roof as though he were afflicted with the crippling shyness and the downward gaze, collecting all the roofing nails that have in the destructive scrum come free, he climbs down the ladder, conscious of the OSHA voice that cautions him against the false step, walks around the area on which he plans to rain down the debris, and sweeps his right foot lightly along the needles and the leaves in search of the covered toad, the covered newt, the covered snake that has no notion of the grand piano that's about to fall upon its hiding place. But all seems clear. He climbs back up, picks up a sheaf of shingles, six or seven thick, and heaves it over the roof's edge. The sound of landing rises to him like the sorrow of a child being bottom-flogged by father with a leather strop, once, but once with the conviction of the patriarch. Albert looks over the edge and sees no sign of life. He sees Watts by the tent. It's critical to be deliberate. Albert lifts another shingle sheaf and heaves it. When the pile that was on the roof is now the pile on the ground, he climbs down, walks around it, and inspects. He picks up scattered nails and puts them in his pockets. All seems clear.

Albert climbs back up the ladder, and he pauses near the top. He looks behind him half-expecting to see someone who is not Watts looking up at him, perhaps in silent inquiry regarding the commotion. Albert thinks about his senses, wonders if the five are all he has. It seems a slim tool kit sometimes, insufficient for the odd jobs. He concludes that speculation this high on a ladder violates the stricture that that voice is always issuing, the voice that's always saying some version of *Don't fall.* So he ascends, as far as it is possible, without reflecting on the extrasensory and its potential to reorient his cocked head of a life.

Albert picks up the pry bar, and he heads up-pitch. Working from the outside of the roof in, he kneels and sets the pry-bar claw against the seam and hammers the back until the claw is wedged. He pushes down on the pry bar, applying even, gradual pressure so there is no sudden giving and no sudden tumbling over. The nails shriek, the plywood lifts, and he continues down the eight-foot seam. He works his way around until three sides of the plywood are unfastened, and he pulls up on the plywood, using the remaining fastened side as fulcrum. Albert looks in, baffled by the excremental dunes that porcupines have left behind.

He drags the unhinged plywood toward the ladder, lays it so that the uprooted nails face downward, and returns to face what he's uncovered. Two unknowns confront him. One is whether down below and cornered, waiting to let go the fury being cornered says must be let go, a porcupine is bristling like a reed patch in a breeze. And one is whether down below and dormant, waiting to let go the particles disturbance says must be let go, a respiratory illness is awaiting inhalation to continue the involuntary cycle of the dust-bound. Albert kneels, takes a deep breath, holds it, and lies prostrate on the roof, his head and shoulders dipping in the opening. His eyes adjust. He looks around, sees nothing but more excremental dunes. He crosses off the one unknown and comes back up for air.

Before he stands the whole way, he can tell his head has lightened. He is dizzy. Basic certitude is put on hold. He waits with hands on asphalt-speckled knees and wonders what the wobbly head will do. The one spell lasted three days. Albert almost saw the doctor then, but most spells pass like cumulus clouds that briefly block the sunlight and allow anticipation for its glorious return to build. While Albert waits for the passage, there is no escaping the idea that it's a reap-sow sort of thing, his brain reminding him of all the trauma and the trouble that he put it through. So while he waits, he understands that, if this is the seizure, stroke, or aneurysm that will do him in, it's no one's doing but his own, and he is fairly grateful that he made it this far. No blaming the protective spirit for abandonment. No bargaining for an extension.

Dostoyevsky suffered seizures and reported feeling an acute awareness, a euphoria, a flash of ecstasy before the spastic onset. Albert supposes that the mystic prelude must have made the seizure something to look forward to, a sudden punctuation to the insight mortals aren't meant to linger too long in the presence of. But Albert, who has tripped before, does not suspect some Huxley-type door is opening for him to take a scales-have-fallen-from-his-eyes look through and has no sense that a curtain has been pulled back to allow him one quick peek to blow his mind before he's sent back to his body. He just feels, as things spin, that his chickens have come home to roost and that the mystery is in his history of always coming back to equilibrium and steadiness and ordinary clarity instead of shutting out the light.

Albert breathes. The spell goes slowly by. He straightens. Except for what is green appearing more intensely green and what is blue appearing more pervasively blue, the world has not changed. He looks around. It's vivid all right, but vividness could just be relative, his eyes recalibrating after the confusion. He looks a while at the closest white pine's intricate needlework and at its layered bark. Solid. Real. He tests his steadiness by looking quickly up, which sometimes throws him for another loop and sends his hands back to his knees. But he goes treetop. He goes sky. No sway. No vertigo. His head stays tilted back, but Albert's eyes pan down—treetop, short branches, longer branches, porcupine. Porcupine.

The porcupine is first a shadow, or a rather unusual bole, upon a white-pine branch that's maybe fifteen feet away from Albert and maybe six feet higher than the elevation that his head now occupies, and then the eyes announce themselves, the outline of the mouth, the softness-seeming that goes counter to the first thing people think of when they think of porcupine, the quill defense. This porcupine does not appear defensive. Part koala, part beaver, part the peace of Buddha, it just clings and bares its buck teeth a bit because they can't be cooped up too long, and stares back. If there is fear, it doesn't show. If there is sadness or a sense that things around here are about to go quite differently, it doesn't show. If there is friendliness or grudging tolerance or a this-land-is-your-land-this-land-is-my-land mutual-possession sort of attitude, it doesn't show.

But, even when it comes to humans, Albert's not a great interpreter of body language. He can read the basics: the condescension in the lip of a superior; the shrug that lifts the student's shoulders just enough to get the point across that knowing isn't everything. But fluency, that force that puts one at his ease in a country that is not his own, eludes him. And so he stares, awaiting some spontaneous translation to enlighten him, to bridge the gap. But Albert cannot read the language of the porcupine.

"What's up, buddy?" Albert asks. No reply. He makes the clicking, tsking sounds he makes when he desires to convey to chipmunks who seem skittish that he means no harm. The porcupine is stoic.

"I didn't know you used this place," says Albert, motioning to the four-by-eight opening where the sheet of plywood used to be, where what had been a refuge is exposed. He stares up at the porcupine. "Help me out here, Saint Francis." No reply.

With the conscience of an interloper, with deliberation, with not wanting to disturb his clung observer, Albert goes back to prying. He kneels down, works the claw in to the next seam without a hammer, pries a little, and looks up to see if prying has affected the perspective of the porcupine. It hasn't. So he pries and looks, pries and peers, and motionless remains the porcupine until Albert lifts the second sheet of plywood, sidesteps toward the ladder, laying quietly the second sheet upon the first. When he looks up, the sight of movement startles Albert until it hits him that the porcupine is in the middle of an unenthusiastic scratch, which soon subsides and gives way to the hind leg finding purchase on the stout limb once again. You do not often hear of human admiration alighting like a monarch's scepter on the porcupine, but Albert's admiration alights on this one as his motion is again arrested and he looks now, like a subject, up. The balanced fact impresses him, the perfect fit, the stoic sizing up, the taking what will be in stride, without suburban passion, with no recognition of imaginary lines, with certain solace there will always be the trees. What would happen to the porcupine without the trees? Albert fails to picture what a clear-cut here would look like. He looks around. Impossible. The trees on Albert's eighteen acres aren't going anywhere if he has any say in their existence, which he does because his name was properly recorded in the registry of deeds and this is still America, whatever that means. Nothing to the nationless. He knows that. Nothing to the porcupine, a creature of the pure allegiance, inextricably a local. He knows that, too.

He tries to visualize the porcupine's inception, the gestation period, the spring birth, he would guess. He tries to visualize the porcupine's miniature emergence one day, hairless, quill-less, he supposes, somewhere in these woods. He tries to visualize the gauntlet that it waddled through, the predators that it evaded, the little-room-for-error learning curve, its teachers. He considers how much might have been self-taught. Why does it not seem to fear him? Maybe he should throw some bent nails with no great velocity at it to teach it that it should. He wishes that he had the working knowledge to distinguish gender, age, to know how long the porcupine has lived and has to live so he can temper expectations of attachment, or indulge them, and decide on name or no name. Besides the outhouse plywood, what does it prefer to eat? What time of night does it prefer to stroll? Near structures or in deeper woods? How close might Watts get and not cross the line beyond which is the zone of self-defense? What happens when it dies? Does it drift off toward a secret graveyard like an elephant who knows the natural end is nigh, or is it simply stricken and laid low, its eyes the first to go, then tenderness by tenderness to bone? Albert makes a mental note to get to know his neighbor, to sink in a camp chair and enjoy a beer tonight while he consults his *Reader's Digest North American Wildlife, An Illustrated Guide to 2,000 Plants and Animals*, which his wife discovered years ago in excellent condition while she rummaged through the FREE shed at the dump.

Albert removes the last sheet of plywood from the upper, steeper-pitched part of the roof and lays it gently on the others near the ladder. He scratches his head where it was fractured and wonders why the builder didn't go with a conventional roof—a regular ridge beam and at least a seven pitch on either side of it to work with gravity and shed the water more efficiently. It makes no sense to have the steep part of the roof slope down and join the shallow, where the water has the opportunity to pool and, with the patience water's sometimes known for, wait for even just a pin prick of an opening to whisper, "Water, this way." Too much faith in flashing.

Albert looks inside the space he has uncovered, looks appraisingly at what the porcupine had going on in there, imagines how dense the darkness must have been, and cannot figure how the porcupine got in. Where is the hole? He looks back up at the pine limb, at the portly-seeming porcupine still clinging there, observant, non-judgmental.

"I'm sorry, buddy," Albert says, feeling like a wrecking ball, a bulldozer, anything whose reason for existing in the world is to undo.

The cabin he is standing on seems suddenly a sunken ship, a manufactured thing abandoned to the elements, permitting claimant after claimant to come in and sniff around and live a little while in a place that mostly had abandoned the disturbance of the built world and allowed some quiet lives to benefit a while from the industry of human hands. He thinks of how a reef can blossom from wreckage, how a refuge can emerge from ruin.

He resolves that he will be as mild as he can as he continues to demolish. He will not use the sledge to bring the walls down. He will not set fire to the floor. The natural lumber (the pine-board siding with the bark still attached, the cedar beam, the hemlock deck) he'll lay back in the woods. He'll leave a sheet or two of plywood leaning on the woodshed for the porcupine to gnaw and scratch. The rest he'll haul with glass and shingles to the dump. He'll make his humanist apologies along the way and ask Saint Francis for assistance with forgiveness.

"I'm sorry, buddy," Albert says to the porcupine still clinging to the limb. "But I will leave the trees. I won't cut down the trees."

Albert climbs down the ladder and walks over to the pickup. He pets Watts, drinks some water. He gets a box of heavy-duty plastic garbage bags, a surgical-looking respirator mask, and a shovel. He climbs back up the ladder, puts the mask on, and steps in the opening where the porcupine once lived. He opens a bag and shovels in a load of dusty fecal pellets. He thinks of Cotton Mather's *Wonders of the Invisible World* and how the wonders can be anything, the devil in a dust mote, the divine inside a porcupine.

By six o'clock, he's borne six bags of dusty feces down the ladder and lined them up like Easter-Island moai on the deck's edge, where they stare with no expression toward the stream. By six o'clock, there is no plywood on the roof to walk on, just the center beam and ceiling joists on which Albert does not walk as though he were a Mohawk on Manhattan girders. By six o'clock, he has one foot on one joist and another foot on a joist that's sixteen inches distant, balancing, and looks up at the steady porcupine that has observed his humanly ups and downs all day.

"All right. I'm heading down. Goodnight." No shifting. No reply. "All right. I'm heading down. Goodnight."

Albert walks his stiffening limbs toward the pickup, where he finds the Ziploc bag that keeps the toilet paper. He blows his nose, examines the black-snot patterns, wonders if the mask did anything except to temporarily allay the respiratory fears. He blows until the snot is clear, breathes deeply, has no reason to believe his lungs are self-correcting and a match for fecal dust, but he believes it anyway. He can't say why, but he feels alive.

He picks up Charlie Watts with one hand, pets him roughly with the other, and looks him in the face. "What's up, you little dirtbag? I don't want you fucking with that porcupine, Watts. Good boy," says Albert, as though Watts has put his porcupine concerns at ease, and places Watts back on the ground.

Albert situates the grill a common-sense distance from the

truck and sets the camp chair next to it. He takes a newspaper from beneath the passenger seat and loosely crumples pages he arranges in the bottom of the grill and shakes the tilted charcoal bag until the belly of the grill is full.

In solitude, with no electric buzz, no screen aglow, the consolation of a fire is a deep one, a connection that says Godspeed and permits all forms of human misfits to go forth, to fan out and take residence in wasteland and in wilderness, beneath the urban bridge, beside the rail-yard, in the yet unpeopled woods whose worth has not yet risen to the point at which the slickers representing market forces say they must be felled. There is, in the ignition, a release, an inarticulate communication with the cubicle your soul's become, and if your world is ordered by linguistic sequence and by meaningless, anti-depressant-caliber routine, you simply stare into the fire and feel there's something ancient and essential and more lasting than your national boundaries going on in there; but you, who still hold on to early lessons focusing on citizenship, can't quite get past the wanting it, the inarticulate, the ancient, to be just a hair less mystical, a hair less nimble as it dances and entrances like a shroomy Deadhead outside the confining jurisdiction of the languages you know. So Albert stares, his right hand touching Watts, who also stares, two figures soothed and stumped, smoked out, squinting as the paper-fueled fire dies down, casting sparks that float and fade to black, and slowly the briquettes begin to glow.

Albert hangs the grill lid half on, half off, letting in the oxygen, letting the concentrating fire breathe. He leaves the fire for a moment, feels around inside the cooler, and retrieves a can of Gandhi-bot. He stares a moment at the label art, and, even though he's seen the picture many times, he smiles at the odd depiction of the robotic Mahatma. He pours the Gandhi in a slightly tilted tulip glass and puts his nose close to the poured beer, the rising head, picking up, he thinks, the prickle of the hop bite. He takes a slow sip, picks up bitterness, which gives way to citrus notes, to malt notes, to alcohol, the brewer's balancing act.

"My goodness," Albert says to Watts, whose tail wags, "that's what I'm talking about." He brings his glass and his *Reader's Digest*

North American Wildlife hardcover to the camp chair, and he situates himself a temperate distance from the grill. He locates *Porcupine* in the index, flips to page 44, and reads about the average length of head and body (18-23 in.), about the average length of tail (6-11 in.), about the long, stiff quills, which, "contrary to popular belief, the Porcupine does not shoot. When threatened by the weasel-like Fisher or some other predator, it turns its back to the enemy, raises its approximately 30,000 quills, and strikes out with its tail." He reads about the slow-moving gait, admires any creature whose default pace is ungainly amble. He checks the coals and takes a sip.

He reads, "The Porcupine is a large nocturnal rodent. If seen during the day, it appears as a round, dark shape high in a tree. At night it clambers from tree to tree, often causing serious damage by feeding on buds, twigs, and bark."

Albert sips. He walks back over to the camp and climbs the ladder, looking at the limb to which the porcupine had clung. He looks from limb to limb, sees nothing, climbs down, and returns to tulip glass and camp chair. He sits and sips and tilts his head back. He estimates two hours left of daylight. Albert welcomes in the evening buzz and wonders what it must be like to live up there, without the baggage, naturally arboreal.

Chapter Nine

Mary hasn't heard from Albert in almost three weeks. In her marital experience, such vernal separations are the norm. He heads north come mid-June, as reliable as any other migratory species drawn away by the return of life to someplace less hospitable in other seasons. She is used to that, and she looks forward, in a way, to life without him and his yellow-toothed mouth to feed, his clothes to wash, his "What was that?" rejoinders to her enunciations, his loud digestion, his inaction, his silent reading. In his absence, she relaxes and has people over and does not tread lightly and is not compelled to answer for a dead toad in the driveway or a barley wine gone missing from his beer fridge or for water run too long or for excessive toilet paper in the bowl or for a light left on, illuminating an empty room till morning, or for simply standing in a place that Albert would like to be. Sometimes, when she's sewing in the silent kitchen or she's on the sofa sketching out her vision for the vegetable plantation, Divorce comes waltzing in her otherwise contented mind like someone caped and dreamy saying in a devilish tone, "You know you want it," and, before she has the time to entertain the possibilities and repercussions, waltzes out and leaves her wondering why Albert has no desire to communicate.

Is it too much to ask for him to have a cell phone for emergencies? Is it too much to ask for him to periodically confirm that he's okay and still alive and wondering in his loneliness if she's okay and still alive? What is a marriage otherwise? It weighs on Mary that her husband doesn't suffer loneliness like she does sometimes, weighs on her that he feels no compulsion to reach out to her, to use the payphone at the Garland Store to call her and console himself for three minutes with his wife's voice, weighs on her that she apparently occupies so little space in Albert's mental and emotional landscape that he feels no pull to write her a letter, which she knows would pose no hardship for him to mail when he goes to the Store, which is also the Post Office, for necessities like ice and beer and the paper. What is wrong with Albert, what is wrong with her, that he feels no desire to communicate or correspond—even if it's just for show, to put her mind at ease?

In summers past, although she had her doubts about his fortitude and wherewithal, it wouldn't have surprised her if her husband, answering internal unrest, left her for the woods, said nothing to prepare her, sent no word, and never came back. A dick move, certainly. In retrospect, unlikely—but within the realm of possibility. This year, almost three weeks into Albert's annual silence, Mary isn't wondering if he'll return and how she'd cover the expenses by herself. This year Albert left with a plan, which he, all husbandly, shared freely with his wife: the demolition of the old camp, his share of the DOE settlement, their strategic mortgage default, their modest savings, the cashed-out retirement accounts, the possibility of foster-parent money. The plan will probably fall through, she guesses when she's pressed by realism. But for now it is a plan, as promising as any. She intends to do her part.

Mary enters Sweet Harmony. She glances at her phone and sees that she's a little early.

She looks up at the menu board behind the scone-filled glass counter, orders a hazelnut coffee (soy milk, no sugar), and takes a look around the place. The tables are arranged in no presentational order, but she sees an official-looking woman with an open laptop and a projector that she's aiming at a blank wall. The woman shims one leg of the projector and seems satisfied the blue projection on the wall is leveled and centered. The woman looks up and smiles when she notices that Mary is observing her.

"Are you with DCF?" Mary asks.

"I am."

"Am I the first one here?"

The woman looks around at patrons scattered here and there and says, "I think so, but I'm expecting a few more people."

Mary nods. She finds it somewhat odd that the Connecticut Department of Children and Families chose a coffee shop in Middletown as the venue for its Foster-Parent Open House, but she says nothing. Mary works as an office manager for United Cerebral Palsy-Hartford, which administers group homes in the region, and she often deals with state agencies, including DCF. She guesses DCF chose Sweet Harmony because it's free to talk to people here. She would prefer a little privacy, some pretense of discretion, but she supposes there is nothing here to hide, and she's aware what's first to go when state agencies are told to scrimp. She gets her coffee, and she takes a seat three tables from the laptop and projector. Eventually, another woman in her forties and a couple quietly arrive, make modest purchases, and sit in similar proximity to the laptop, the projector, and the welcoming, official-looking lady, who, once her audience is situated, checks her watch and stands up.

"My name is Lisa Ward," she says, "and I'm a social worker with the Connecticut Department of Children and Families. I'm here to give you an overview of our agency's mission and philosophy. I'm also here to explain to you the licensing process and requirements, and, if you choose to pursue becoming foster or adoptive parents, what you can expect in terms of the assessment and home study. Most importantly, I'm here to answer any questions you may have, so please feel free to ask a question at any point during the presentation. First, though, I'd like to hand out this informational and FAQ sheet, which you probably already received when you first contacted our office."

She moves among the three tables, handing out the pamphlets with a smile, and then walks over to the blank wall and dims the light in that part of the establishment. She taps on her computer, and some bullet points appear upon the wall.

"I'd like to dispel a few misconceptions," she says, straying a step or two from the laptop. "There is no upper-age requirement to foster or adopt a child. If you are twenty-one years of age or older, you are eligible. There is no income requirement to foster or adopt a child. We only ask that you have sufficient means to provide for the child's care independent of the subsidies. That's just a safeguard. You will not be asked to provide care independent of the subsidies. There is no home-ownership requirement. Some people are under the impression that renting will disqualify them from fostering or adopting. That is not true. There is no marriage requirement to foster or adopt a child. Some people are under the impression that single people are disqualified. That is not true. The same goes for

LGBTQ+ singles or couples. You do not need to be heterosexual to foster or adopt. Another misconception is that the foster or adoptive parent is responsible for the health-care costs of the child. There are some exceptions regarding certain adoption situations, but generally that is not true. The child is covered by the State of Connecticut. Another misconception that often scares people away from fostering or adopting is that the foster or adoptive parents will be saddled with the costs of the child's college education. Again, there are some exceptions regarding certain adoption situations, but generally that is not entirely true. The State of Connecticut will subsidize the equivalent of tuition, room, and board at Central Connecticut State University. So, if your child were to attend a school that costs, say, fifty-thousand dollars, you would have to pay the difference. So there is legitimate cause to be frightened in that case."

The audience of four politely chuckles.

"The other items on this list we can address as we move along. But, before we move on, are there any questions?"

She waits a moment and then changes the Power-Point slide to one headed MISSION AND PHILOSOPHY.

"Okay. I'd like to briefly talk about DCF's mission and philosophy regarding foster care and adoption. First and foremost, our mission is to protect children. Some people are under the impression that children in foster care or up for adoption are somehow delinquents. Children enter foster care or adoption through no fault of their own. They are abused, neglected, and/or abandoned. They need to be protected. Ultimately, in terms of foster care, our mission is to support and preserve families. That means reuniting children with their biological parents whenever possible. That's the goal of foster care.

"In terms of philosophy, we do believe that, whenever possible, it's best to place a child in a home where the parent or parents are of the same cultural and language background. This does not mean you cannot foster, say, a Latino child if you're white. It just means that we try to take those differences into account in the placement process."

She pauses and looks from table to table, the computer glow

illuminating her face from below. "I know this is a lot to take in. Can I answer any questions?"

Polite, negational head shakes from the caffeinated, pursed-lipped four-person audience.

"Okay. Good. Let's continue." She changes the Power-Point slide to one headed FOSTER CARE AND ADOPTION.

"I'd like to discuss some important differences between foster care and adoption and what those differences mean in terms of expectations. As I mentioned at the end of the mission part of the presentation, the primary goal of foster care is reunification. That is *not* the case with adoption.

"When DCF deems it necessary to remove a child from the biological parent—it is often a single parent—we give that parent a list of things that must be done in order to regain custody. Your goal as a foster parent, and it's a selfless one, is to provide that child with a safe and stable home while the biological parent does what has to be done and satisfies the court. For many people, foster care is difficult—gut-wrenching, really—because it is, ideally, temporary, and that child whom you cared for and, in many cases, came to love has to leave you. For many people, that departure is emotionally devastating.

"The situation is often considerably complicated, emotionally speaking, when the foster child is an infant. While it's true that 50% of foster children are over eight years old and 30% are over twelve, it's also true that the department has a shortage of foster parents who are willing to take babies. Obviously, the majority of people who are interested in adoption would like to adopt a baby. However, there are not a lot of people who are willing to care for and love a baby who, if all goes well, they'll have to give back to the biological parents. It takes a certain kind of person to do that.

"Now, if you're considering becoming a foster parent with the expectation of adopting the child you foster, I want to caution you. Although foster care *may* lead to adoption, I wouldn't count on it. If you go into foster care with the expectation of adoption, the odds are you're going to get your heart broken. That's why DCF will not license a home for both foster care and adoption.

"If you have your heart set on adoption, I'd suggest you not consider foster care. As I mentioned before, foster care is not for everyone. It's often extremely difficult to let go. Unlike with foster care, the goal of adoption is to permanently place the child in a loving home. Remember, a child who is in adoption is there because parental rights were terminated, either voluntarily or because the court said so. If you adopt a child, that child is yours and isn't going anywhere. And that's not for everyone either," she says, her lips coming together, forming a straight line, neither frown nor smile. "So, before you sign anything, you have to decide what's right for you.

"Before you decide what's for you, I'd like to talk about some numbers to help you make an informed decision. I know you're here because you want to make a difference in a child's life, but, having fostered and adopted two children myself, I also know that welcoming a child into your home entails a pretty significant financial commitment. There are several ways that DCF helps to make that commitment less burdensome.

"Now, if you're considering fostering a child, you should know that DCF's financial assistance in that case is fairly straightforward. First of all, all medical expenses relating to the care of the child are completely covered. Second, most other expenses pertaining to the child are covered by the monthly stipend."

A chart detailing the various stipends appears on the wall.

"As you can see, the stipends vary slightly depending on whether there are twenty-eight, twenty-nine, thirty, or thirty-one days in a month. The reason for that is that we base the overall monthly stipend on the daily per diems that you see here. So, if you foster a child between the ages of zero and five, you receive a monthly stipend in the range of $746.17 to $797.63. Between the ages of six and eleven, 755.87 to 806.93. If you foster a child who is twelve or older, the range, as you can see, is 818.96 to 875.44. Now, we also have cases that we refer to as Medically Complex. If you foster a child whose situation is deemed Medically Complex, the monthly stipend ranges from 1,352.27 to 1,445.53. These children may have relatively mild medical conditions such as asthma, but they may also have, say, severe cerebral palsy and require a lot of care. Parents who foster such children must attend the Medically Complex Certification Course to become certified. As you can see here, some children require Therapeutic Foster Care, which applies to various serious situations, cerebral palsy often being one of them. As you can see, the monthly stipend for Therapeutic Foster Care is significantly higher, ranging from 2,641.03 to 3,056.91. In such cases, the foster parent also needs to be certified. Generally, unless the prospective parent has prior experience, a very strong desire to foster such children, and/or the necessary free time to provide such care, we do not recommend that first-time foster parents take on Therapeutic Foster Care or serious Medically Complex situations."

Lisa Ward takes a deep breath and, with the exhalation, says, "So. Hopefully the compensation picture regarding foster care is pretty clear. Any questions? Anyone need another coffee?" She smiles and looks from table to table.

"Okay. The compensation picture regarding adoption is a bit more complicated. Now, if you're considering adoption and the child you adopt has absolutely no issues and is perfectly adjusted, you are unlikely to receive a subsidy from DCF. Unfortunately, the sad reality is that very few children up for adoption have absolutely no issues and are perfectly adjusted. Very few."

The Power-Point projection switches to a slide headed SUBSIDIZED ADOPTION PROGRAM.

"In recognition of that sad reality, we have what's called the Subsidized Adoption Program, which we created to help special-needs children in DCF care to get adopted. The idea is that, if we assist adoptive parents financially, we'd have more success in placing children in permanent homes as opposed to leaving them in foster care until they age out." She pauses. "I've never cared for that phrase 'age out.' It sounds so . . . I don't know. But that's what happens. They age out of foster care, and then they're on their own or, if they have serious medical issues, they remain in State care. That's why adoption is so important."

Mary believes her.

"As I mentioned before, very few children do *not* qualify as special needs. For that reason, if you decide to adopt, the child will most likely receive some sort of subsidy benefit. Now, what qualifies a child as special needs? Basically, we regard a child as special needs if, because of one or more of the following conditions, we are having a hard time placing him or her with an adoptive family. As you can see here, an obvious obstacle to adoption is a child's physical or mental disability. Another obvious obstacle, and a fairly common one, is the child's difficulty in adjusting emotionally—to foster care, to school, to people. Waiting to be adopted, year after year, can really mess a child up emotionally. A less obvious issue is the *likelihood* that a child will develop a physical, mental, or emotional disability. This could be because of a fetal issue that has not yet manifested, or this could be because of trauma in the child's past. In any of those cases, we regard the child as special needs.

"A child will also be considered special needs if he or she is over the age of eight. Most people simply want to adopt a younger child, and being over eight years old really diminishes a child's chances of being adopted. Another issue is that, if a child is over the age of two, certain racial or ethnic factors are likely to hinder that child's adoption. I know I said earlier that DCF strongly prefers to place children in families of similar cultural and language backgrounds, but often that is not possible. So, for example, if we have a three-year-old African-American boy up for adoption but no prospective African-American adoptive parents, we would much prefer that that child be adopted by a qualified, loving white family rather than remain for who knows how long in foster care. But the racial issue can be an obstacle, which is why we consider such a child to be special needs.

"Another, distinct obstacle is when we have siblings up for adoption. DCF strongly prefers to keep siblings together. Under the best of circumstances, adopting a child can be quite an adjustment. For many prospective parents, having to adopt two or more children is a deal breaker. So, even without the other obstacles I've mentioned, siblings up for adoption are considered special needs."

Mary thinks of Jake and Ryan. Ten years old. Autistic. Twins. Stuck, according to what Lisa Ward just said, in pre-adoption Purgatory. Cursed with special needs. Mary wishes she could somehow tell them help might be on the way. She wishes she could somehow tell her husband that there *is* financial assistance for adoption, that they wouldn't have to foster those two boys indefinitely, that they would not just be a shadow of a family. She wishes Albert would join the human race and get a fucking cell phone and be open to communication with his wife like any other normal husband.

Lisa Ward taps on her computer, and the projection on the wall now reads WHAT DETERMINES AMOUNT, TYPE, AND LENGTH OF SUBSIDY.

"Okay. As opposed to foster care, the economic variables related to subsidized adoption are more numerous, but they're not too complicated. Most importantly, the subsidy is determined solely on the basis of the child's special needs. That means that, if you are considering adopting a child, there is no parental income requirement to determine if your child is eligible for subsidy payments or other adoption assistance because the *only* determining factor is the child's special needs. Also, if you adopt a special-needs child, DCF will reimburse you up to $750 to cover the expenses related to the adoption.

"In terms of subsidy amounts, you can see here that they are pretty similar to the foster-care amounts we saw earlier. So a special-needs child between the ages of zero and five would receive a monthly adoption subsidy in the range of 701.51 to 749.89. Between the ages of six and eleven, the range is 724.13 to 774.07. If the child is twelve or older, the range is 798.95 to 854.05. For Medically Complex adoptees, the range is 1,352.27 to 1,445.53. So, the adoption subsidy is slightly lower than for foster care, but it's comparable.

"In terms of subsidy length, although there is the occasional exception, the special-needs child will receive the monthly subsidy up to his or her eighteenth birthday. However, generally the child will continue to receive the medical subsidy until the age of twenty-one.

"For the most part, the subsidy terms will be determined and clearly stipulated before the adoption becomes legal. For example, a child's eligibility for the 100% Medical Expense Subsidy is determined during the adoption process. So there are no surprises. If the child does not qualify for that subsidy prior to adoption, which is unusual, there are situations where the child can qualify for it after adoption if, for example, the child has a condition that existed prior to adoption but was somehow missed and now requires treatment. This is somewhat unusual, but there are cases in which adoptive parents notice something, after the adoption has been finalized, and ask DCF for a subsidy to address that situation because it would have been granted pre-adoption had DCF been aware of the condition. In that case, you'd file what's called an Application for an Adoption Subsidy After Finalization. The only time that subsidy would not be granted is if it is determined that the condition definitely developed after the adoption. When in doubt, though, DCF will err on the side of subsidy.

"Now, other subsidies. As with children in foster care, children who are adopted from foster care are eligible to apply for the college tuition/post-secondary education reimbursement program. As I mentioned earlier, that would cover the annual equivalent of tuition, room, and board at Central Connecticut State University, which I think is currently at about $25,000."

Lisa Ward pauses and looks down at the notepad next to her computer. As if speaking to herself, she says, "Mission. Philosophy. Differences between foster care and adoption. Subsidies." She looks up, smiles, and says, "We're almost done."

A picture of a sinuous, black-topped road appears on the screen. The heading reads THE ROAD TO FOSTER CARE AND ADOPTION. The road, a simple, single lane, runs from the bottom left of the screen to the top right, where the road disappears, presumably continuing to some unseen region tinged with happiness. Mary tries to imagine herself and Albert on some portion of the road that isn't there. She pictures the road continuing north-northeast, through Connecticut, Massachusetts, briefly through New Hampshire, through Maine to the unpaved, discontinued Morton Road down which her husband drove, as far as she knows, three weeks ago. She pictures herself and Albert and Jake and Ryan finally stepping off the road and onto eighteen acres and, that easily, existing theretofore as a happily adjusted forest-dwelling nuclear family free of certain pressures and demands inherent in existing as consumers in mainstream American society. She wonders if that's the right stop. For the boys. For her and Albert. She would like to raise her hand and ask Lisa Ward's opinion, but that portion of the road is imaginary, suggestive of the promise of long-term relationship development, and can wend so many ways. For all she knows, the road ends at the ranch house where she's lived alone these past three weeks, the ranch house that, when she and Albert and Jake and Ryan live there together, will be so full of love the windows will illuminate. Why ask Lisa Ward about a hypothetical situation, an imaginary road?

Along the wayside of the screen road, circled numbers indicate the stops a person traveling the foster-care/adoption road must make. Stop one is Attend Open House.

With her pen, Lisa Ward points to stop one, looks out at her four-person audience, and says, "You are here." She points to stop two and says, "The next step is to schedule the home visit, which is basically just a personal interview. Prior to the social worker arriving for the home visit, we will have done a background check of all members of the household. During the home visit, your social worker will do a preliminary assessment of the home environment. A more thorough assessment will be conducted in the later home visits," she says, pointing to stop four. "As far as the interview, we're mainly trying to get a sense of you, your personality, your motivation for becoming licensed. That sort of thing. The interview also allows you to ask your social worker any questions and get a better sense of the road ahead.

"Now, the next step is a bit more involved." She points to stop three. "The pre-license training involves attending classes over a ten-week period. The purpose of the classes is to help you understand where children who are in foster care or up for adoption are coming from, what they've been through, and the psychic and emotional tolls those experiences can take. So we'll discuss, for example, the impact of abuse and neglect on these children. We'll discuss the trauma of separation and loss. Those issues are crucial because they often delay the normal stages of childhood development, so we'll talk about what those normal stages are and what delayed development may result in. Oftentimes, no surprise, the results are behavioral. So we'll discuss how to cope with certain behaviors, especially focusing on the critical difference between parental discipline and punishment.

"Whether you're seeking licensure as a foster or adoptive parent, we'll discuss what we call permanency planning. In terms of foster care, this involves such issues as birth-parent visitation and, as mentioned earlier, the ultimate goal of reunification. I know it's difficult as a foster parent, but we have to discuss why the birth family is so important and how you can help to maintain that connection until reunification. We'll also talk about and prepare you for what happens if reunification doesn't work. In terms of adoption, the permanency-planning discussion mostly has to do with certain pre-conditions for certain adoptions. This could involve a stipulation that says, for example, the birth grandparents have some visitation rights. Again, we'll discuss the importance of the birth family and how, by helping your child have a better sense of it, you can help your child's emotional health.

"Even if, in the case of adoptive parents, there is no ongoing contact with the birth family, we will discuss, as we do with foster parents, the importance of life books in helping the child to understand his or her family history and to understand that those memories of the birth family are not in conflict with the child's love for and life with the adoptive or foster family.

"Those memories and that family history are extremely important to the child's sense of self. The life books are especially important when there are issues of diversity involved. We will help you discuss with your child the concept of difference and what it means in our society. It can be confusing for a Latino child, for example, or an African-American child to be adopted by a white family and to live in a white neighborhood and go to a mostly white school. We can help you help that child work through the confusion. The life books can be effective in helping such children have a better sense of their personal narratives, their history.

"At the end of the ten weeks, we will provide you with a wealth of resource information that covers everything from how to say goodbye to your foster child to the adoption healing support group to tax information to how to avoid lead poisoning. You will have a lot of help along the way.

"Now, once the pre-license training is complete, your social worker will conduct a home study, which will consist of two to four visits. As with the initial home visit, you will have the opportunity to ask your social worker any questions you may have. However, whereas the initial home visit is primarily a personal interview, the focus of the home study is on assessing the conditions in and around your home and whether they are suitable child-wise. If things look good early on, you can probably expect two visits. If there are some issues that need to be addressed, you can expect three or four.

"Your social worker will assess your home on the basis of a number of criteria. We will provide you with a detailed checklist toward the end of the pre-license training classes. But, to give you an idea, the cleanliness of your home is an important consideration. We check for safety issues such as childproof window locks, tamper-proof electrical outlets, smoke and carbon-monoxide detectors, properly installed railings along stairways, things that are probably already in place. We check to make sure that any cleaning chemicals, alcohol, and guns that you may keep in the house or garage are properly stored and not accessible to children. If you have not had much experience with children before, that's okay. Your social worker will help you to childproof your home.

"We also assess the bedroom situation in terms of adequate space for the child, age-appropriate furniture, fire exits, et cetera. If you have pets in your home, we will assess their demeanor and whether we consider them to be compatible with children. If you have a yard, we will assess it with an eye toward the safety of the child. For example, if you have a pool, is it adequately fenced? If you have a swing set or other playground apparatus, is it up to code?

"Some people initially feel defensive about the home study. Please remember that the basis for the home study is not aesthetics but safety. So, if we ask you to address a particular issue, it is not a criticism but an anticipation of a safety concern that could arise if a child were to live in the home.

"Aside from the home assessment, you will, during one of the home visits, have a TB test and undergo first-aid and CPR training. After the home study, you will be licensed to foster or adopt. For foster parents, the time between starting the licensing process and actually taking a child into your home will be about four months. For adoptive parents, because of the attendant legal issues that need to be taken care of, it typically takes between six months and a year."

Between six months and a year. Mary wonders if her husband will be able to sustain for that long the noncommittal, low-intensity, financially conditional parental interest he evinced before he left for Maine three weeks ago. Sitting in Sweet Harmony, with her cell phone but alone, she wonders if, up there, alone with Charlie Watts, Albert even thinks of those two boys or if he just saw dollar signs when he was buzzed on beer or light and said she should look into foster care—said it because it didn't really matter to him one way or the other, said it the way he says her hair or nails look good. She tries to imagine Albert in pressed pants and a button-down shirt, welcoming their social worker into their home for the first visit, the personal interview. She tries to imagine what might barrel from his mouth (or what might saunter) when the social worker asks him what his motivation is for wanting to adopt. Will he explain to her that he and Mary got the conversation going on the basis of the subsidy? Or will he be more positively lucid, explaining how they always wanted children but had not been physically blessed and now want more than anything to share their lives with those two vulnerable boys?

Never mind that now. Mary tries to imagine what Albert will say when she informs him she would rather they adopt, not foster, those two boys, what he will say when she informs him about the home visit, the ten-week course, the home study, the six months to a year. Past experience is no predictor. Depends how many beers he's had or wants to have. Depends what book he's reading. In the present, absent even rudimentary communication, for the purposes of Mary's speculation, Albert does not exist—except as what he was three weeks ago. There is no telling.

"Questions?"

Mary raises her hand.

"Yes?"

"My husband and I are considering adoption. He's a teacher. And a writer. Sometimes he'll get a writer's residency, and he'll be gone for a few weeks or a month working on some writing project in Vermont or wherever. Would that kind of absence hurt our chances to adopt or?"

Lisa Ward says, "No. Absolutely not. As long as we're sure that the child will continue to be cared for in your husband's absence, it presents no problem. Single parents are allowed to adopt, so you'd just be a single parent for a few weeks or a month."

Mary raises her hand again.

"I have another question. My husband's at a residency right now. That's why he's not here. My other question is, if he's away at a residency during some part of the adoption process—like if he's not there for the first home visit and the personal interview—would that present a problem?"

"It would. If two parents are applying for licensure, DCF requires that they both be present during all parts of the process beginning with the home visit. Everyone needs to be on the same page. If your husband has advance notice of when he wouldn't be available, we would take that into account and could work around it. It would delay that adoption process a bit. But, yes, he has to be there."

"Okay. Thank you."

Another person's hand goes up.

"I don't anticipate this happening," the woman says, "but, hypothetically, what happens if my job moves out of state and we have to relocate? Would the subsidy continue?"

"It would. As long as you notify DCF sixty days in advance, you'd see no interruption in the subsidy."

"Thank you."

Lisa Ward takes other questions. She reviews the application procedures, hands out a checklist that bullet-points her talk tonight, provides her contact information, and says, "I hope you all will decide to foster or adopt. I know from personal experience that the process can be daunting, but I also know from personal experience how rewarding it is to take a child who has been through so much into your home and to love him or her as your own. It really does make a difference in the world. Thank you for coming tonight."

Everyone smiles. The four-person audience rises.

Mary disposes of her cup and leaves Sweet Harmony believing Lisa Ward, believing in the transformational capacity of selflessness.

It is slightly after seven on a Thursday at the end of June in Middletown on Main Street. Sunlight still. Mary pauses for a moment by a parking meter on the sidewalk and is certain, subsidy or not, they will adopt those boys. She's certain all those ways that hitherto had seemed directionless, misguided, leading to the sterile calmness of an existential cul-de-sac, actually led to this. To acclimate herself to the idea of motherhood, she'd like a little alcohol.

She walks to the corner of Washington and Main and teeters on the sidewalk's lip and waits for WALK. She crosses Washington and walks past Luce's, Mike's Barbershop, the firehouse, Whole Foods, the Buttonwood Tree, where Albert read his poetry once, Saint Vincent de Paul, where someone who reminds her of Grady from *Sanford and Son* asks her for a cigarette. She tells him that she's sorry but she doesn't smoke, and he replies, "I see how it is." She has never wondered such a thing before, but now she wonders if that man had ever been in foster care when he was young, if he had once hoped to be adopted, if the man's belief in how the world works could have been transformed by even temporary parental tenderness. She crosses Grand Street against the light and turns left into Eli's, which is not as crowded as it typically would be at this hour on a Thursday since the Wesleyan kids have scattered for the summer.

Although she likes the place, she doesn't enter it, as Albert invariably does, with the peculiar pilgrim's ardor, carrying within the article of faith that beer is transcendental, spiritual, a godly nectar, an epiphanic liquid, its incarnations extending back seven-thousand years, past Buddha, past Jesus, maybe past Ra, the curious elixir able to effect in the believer the beautiful sigh that is the intimation of apotheosis, the quick-flick mayfly assurance that it's possible one day, after circling gamely in the light, to be at peace, unbound. And she is not inclined to sacrifice the liver and the brain and the fragile capillaries in the nose as evidence of her fidelity to an unorganized religion in which the body counts as such a burden. But she enters, not without a flickering of joy, and passes the enthusiasts, clean-shaven, hirsute, wiry, portly, slovenly, tidy, clear-eyed, bleary-eyed, mostly male, mostly smiling, all aglow. She passes on her left the bicycle suspended from the ceiling upside down, the phone booth now defunct. She passes on her right two cushioned armchairs situated at a distance that is, in the bar din, conversational, passes two barber's chairs flush against the wall and campy. She consults the blackboard beer list hanging on the wall across from the bar and feels intrusive, like an interloper, because two hipsters flank the menu and her consultation requires that she stare between them without appearing to be nosy, but they do not mind her and she wonders if their lack of interest has to do with her declining powers of physical attraction as she inches deeper into her forties. It would be polite to glance at her at least, but then she hears them talking passionately about the relative merits of Chaucer versus Shakespeare, and, in terms of self-esteem, she's slightly boosted once she classifies these two who didn't have the common decency to glance at her as nerds.

Mary's beer-selection process is purely nominal. She does not possess Albert's esoteric knowledge regarding styles, ABVs, IBUs, hop varietals, malt bills, astringency, and so forth, so, if she finds the beer's name to be ticklesome, she chooses it and does not dwell on what she didn't choose as Albert's wont to dwell. She leans her breasts in toward the bar and orders a Captain's Daughter from the skinny, neck- and forearm-tatted man who threw her husband out eight years ago. At least he and Albert harbor no hard feelings. Albert and his trail of reconciliations. "Thank you," she says. She sips the rim pour down to carrying level and repairs to one of the cushioned armchairs, where she sips again and is intensely pleased with and feels oddly proprietary about her selection. She hopes that Albert hasn't tried this beer, that she is its discoverer, because she'd like to find it in a beer store and bequeath a four-pack or a six-pack to his beer fridge to express her pleasure at his unannounced return, whenever that may be.

She takes her cell phone from her purse and wishes she could text or call him to discuss what she discovered at Sweet Harmony tonight, to make him believe her the way she believes Lisa Ward. She wonders if he was as much a solitary creature prior to his fracturing his skull, if he could share then, say "I love you" with no hint of irony, no hint of resignation that a married man must utter certain words to get along regardless of his feeling or believing them to not be conduits of deep truths or intimate expressions. Albert is not and never will be a sweet-nothings husband, Mary knows, but she wouldn't mind the occasional persuasive lie.

For now, she'll settle for a partially reconstructed picture of his life these past three weeks, for knowing where he's been beyond the camp and what he probably purchased. Mary sips her Captain's Daughter, logs in to their bank account, and scrolls down the list of debit-card transactions. Except for a fifty-two-dollar debit charge at the last gas station Albert passed on 95 three weeks ago and a hundred-dollar ATM withdrawal less than two hours after that at Bear One Stop, about twenty miles from camp, there are no expenditure bread crumbs on his trail. A hundred dollars in three weeks? She knows he must have purchased ice once or twice at the Garland Store. And since she knows his predilection (his obsession, really) for consolidating errands so that their accomplishment occurs in a single automotive trip, he likely also bought the *Bangor Daily News*, the *Morning Sentinel*, and beer reinforcements on those one or two ice trips. Was that the extent of his human interaction? How long could it take him to tear down a cabin that was falling down already? Two days? Three? What does he do with the rest of his time, those other unappointed, non-laborious days?

She sips her Captain's Daughter, logs off their bank account, and goes to a psychology site she likes to visit when she feels like criticizing Albert's personality. She peruses the familiar list of basic personality traits (openness, conscientiousness, extroversion, agreeableness, and neuroticism) and remembers needling Albert when he deserved it about his lack of openness, his lack of conscientiousness, his lack of extroversion, his lack of agreeableness, and/or his abundance of neuroticism. Under such assaults, he typically shrugs and says, "I am what I am. Too old to change now." She scrolls down the page and clicks on a link that she does not believe she's clicked before. The topic is the personality's plasticity after age thirty. Not surprisingly, the personality isn't very plastic at that stage of the game, which, according to the article, is not to say that, with a little will exertion, one can't act contrary to one's character. So Albert is wrong on that account. He could change if he applied himself. Acting thus, however, tends to be a stress inducer, and, according to the article, "To counteract that stress, you'll need to revert back to your true self for a bit: To use the classic example, when introverts are forced to act extroverted at a party for a few hours, they'll often need to 'recharge' with some alone time afterwards." Maybe the essential Albert, she thinks, is simply up there shucking the illusion of the teacher and recalibrating, via quietness and isolation and expenditure reduction, the delicate psychic scale. *Maybe*, she thinks, *he does belong up there*. Avoid illusion. Avoid recalibration. Maybe they would all, the boys, herself, Albert, be healthier up there, the people they are meant to be.

Maybe.

Mary logs in to her email account and composes a message to her husband re: July's Mortgage Payment: "Albert, do you want me to pay the mortgage for July or to begin the strategic default that we discussed before you left? I went to the DCF Open House tonight, and I think we should adopt. I also think that if we default now it will seriously hurt our chances for adoption. If we could wait six months, it would be a big help. I realize that you will not read this message until you've gotten home, but I know that you'll complain whether I pay the mortgage or default. So at least you can't say I didn't try to communicate with you. I'll wait a day to see if, somehow, you reply. If I don't hear from you, I'll pay the mortgage. Come home soon. I'd like to talk to you in person about adoption. Miss you. Mary." She presses *Send* and feels unburdened.

Mary finishes her Captain's Daughter, drives over the Portland Bridge, through town and past the fairgrounds, past where Albert administered the head-butt, past the gas station, up the hill, and up their gravel drive. She sees three deer beside the shed. "Oh, shit," she says, remembering she hadn't left out corn for them before she left for Sweet Harmony. She promised Albert she would feed them in his absence, although she sees no need in the spring and summer. She unlocks the basement door and tries to lift the fifty-pound cracked-corn bag from the metal garbage can without compressing something in her back. As Mary lugs it toward the shed, the deer snort and retreat a few steps deeper into the woods. She pulls the bag's rip cord and pours the corn into a slightly dusty pile. She puts the bag in the recycling bin and leaves the deer to inch back down for the dusk's repast.

Inside, a light in the room above the basement door goes on. She walks to and from a bureau. The light goes out. Mary lies down on the bed, her panties off, her legs spread. The sound of a contented beehive fills the room for several minutes. Then the light comes on again, and Mary knits until she feels the weight of sleep accumulating on her eyelids.

Chapter Ten

Albert's pen taps the graying whiskers on his chin. He's puzzled. Stumped. He's read and reread this cipher of a crossword clue ("O") and cannot tell where it is meant to lead him. It is early and his coffee is still sinking in, the slow matutinal infusion. He rests the folded paper on his scratched lap and leans his head back in a basking posture to entirely appreciate the lilting of the nearby hermit thrush and the agape-quality response its partner in the distance lilts back. Unseen. Small wonder of the world. The cows low, faintly. Watts rustles in the tent and repositions. For a moment, there are no entanglements, no desires. Then, like a stone the Agitator high arcs and plunks in Albert's dead-calm brain pond, it hits him that he's obligated to a lawn three states away, a lawn that's been extending toward the sun in silent worship for the past three weeks, a lawn a lot of nominal Christians pass each day and judge. *It's hard,* thinks Albert, *to practice pure detachment, to stay focused and remain in that elusive zone in which the little hacky-sack of human being is just going with the cosmic flow, afloat, serene and airborne, kneed or sandaled up or somehow kept aloft, above the summoning earth.* And, in thinking that, he's back to earth. Basking, in short bursts, has its place, its purpose, lets him know that something intellectually improbable is out there and provides a peek, a gander at the way. He nods. Earthbound isn't bad when you are this far from the road, the trafficked road, the paved road, the real road. Albert gets up and stretches like a grass blade, walks out to the Morton Road, the discontinued road that isn't, in his from-away opinion, properly a road. Watts emerges from the unzipped tent and follows. Albert looks up the Morton Road and down. Trees encroaching. Rocks and ledge. The narrow way. Last night's rain still trickles like a timepiece toward the stream.

"Well?" he says to Watts. The tail wags. "Lead the way."

Coyotes were close by last night before the rain. Watts looks down the road, turns right, trots ahead at independent distance, stops at intervals, and deploys his nose like a detector over the ground. Albert wonders what it's like to have that sense of smell, to have *a* sense of smell. He can remember smells pre-accident: dank weed, corn muffins, cut grass, bad farts, Brut. But they are like things he saw years ago and summons via memory. Figments of the mind's eye. The mind's nose. So he remembers pine smell, but he doesn't smell the pines; remembers cedar smell but doesn't smell the cedars. He sniffs like Watts, and there is simply air. Smell. Smell. Sometimes he believes it is a matter of the will. He watches Watts for odor cues, for danger signs, and thinks *Reduced to.* He depends on Watts, but he supposes, if a sense must go, it's best that it's olfactory.

Watts looks back, confirms his master's presence, and continues. The road is half rut, high grass, tree fall, erosion. About two-hundred feet down, orange tape dangles from a branch. Boundary. Legal claim. The history of the country's post-Columbus settlement writ small. Washington was a surveyor, if Albert remembers correctly. A man of metes and bounds. Watts pauses over a pile of coyote shit, the fur of some devoured creature threaded and protruding, undigested. The pile sits upon a rock of dinner-plate proportions. Watts lingers over it as if in deep appreciation of the careful presentation, lifts a scrawny hind leg, and spritzes. Onward.

The Morton Road is interrupted by the stream, which curves left past modest boulders and disappears past ferns and hemlocks leaning streamward, proprietary in their humble way. The discontinued road picks up across the stream curve, comes out to the Campbell Road, a maintained, graded dirt road, about a mile on. Before the curve and across, a trail winds slightly to the right, muddy, puddle-mined. Watts runs through the stream. Albert rock hops. Everything is evergreen and fern green and shades of brown. There's no one. Not a soul. Albert wonders briefly if it makes good sense to join that vocal portion of America that feels secure in bearing arms. *In bearing is implicit an abiding fear. And what is there to fear? If it's disquieting to be unarmed and in the woods,* thinks Albert, *don't be venturesome. It's not disquieting. It's quiet. Tread lightly. Move on.*

Without a watch, he isn't sure how far they walk, but he and Watts emerge from the shadow of the woods and squint like moles in the cornfield light. Albert does not want to trespass or to see a person, but he wants to linger for a minute in the light, to think about and mentally applaud the unsung, dirty role that small-scale agriculture should play in his life, to stare agape-style with his blue eyes at the dragonfly that has alighted on a cornstalk and smiles unreservedly as if to say we're not so different, you and me, as if to say rejoice with me for pausing in the sunlight here, however long. Albert smiles, bares his crooked, jaundiced teeth, does so broadly and without self-consciousness in the sunlight. He decides that he will stay as long as this companion dragonfly abides. This unmined jewel of a dragonfly, all iridescent greens and blues, transparent wings, observant eyeballs, all fragility and staying power, all effusive smile, is fixed on Albert, a curious form if ever one there was, and Albert feels deeply welcomed, not at all the violent, boundary-drawing alien, and thinks about the touching *ET* scene in which the two extended fingers, one ET's, one Eliot's, converge and, that easily, remove the distance and the fear and the suspicion one so often harbors for the Other. For two minutes, three, the world hangs thus. And then a green and yellow hummingbird, its neck and chest tinged red, materializes, hovers, and, for two illuminating seconds, there exists in life a scene that Albert wishes he could capture via paint and frame and turn to when he wants to feel this sense of pure alignment once again. And then the air is cleared, the cornstalk vacant. The idyll is dispersed, and it's just Watts and him returning on their six feet to the apparently enduring woods, which do not seem to care if Albert and Watts come in or if they go.

"All right, Watts," he whispers. "Let's head back. Today's a burn day."

On the way into the woods and past the same sights that he saw before but now reversed and up the discontinued Morton Road, Albert wonders how much of the world beyond the cornfield he should venture into, how much he should keep imaginary, keep as someplace dealt with purely in the mind. But he suspects the latter options won't be possible for long. You can only walk so far before something venturesome inside you says walk farther and you yield. He could Google Earth the unknowns when he goes home, but Google is a great remover of enigma, terra incognita, ambiguity, mystery—those fields on which the hero must contend—a great remover, therefore, of legitimate discovery, the individual's first-person, sensory engagement with the world whose story is only partially told, whose reality is only partially experienced through the medium of the computer screen. Screen dependence, zooming in and zooming out, seems counter to the purpose of his plan. *No Google*, he resolves, *for hinterland exploration.* He submits his resolution to the Proenneke test, and he is satisfied that Dick would not have Google Earthed a territory he had yet to walk on foot. The resolution passes. He'll continue to rely for landscape information on the *Gazetteer* and on his feet to gradually get him to what map points sing to him. On foot, or undiscovered. That would make a nice motto, something to translate into Latin and stitch beneath the family crest and shield. *Yes,* he thinks, *it would be sweet to have a family motto.* Sweet to have a crest and shield. Sweet to have two sons. What's the point of motto, crest, and shield if no one after him becomes the standard bearer striding proudly through the world? He'll try the motto out on someone when the conversational drift might make the utterance seem appropriate, and he will gauge by words and body language the reaction. *On foot, or undiscovered.* In Latin.

Call it a coincidence. Call it the unseen, too long in hiding, coming out to see about the slight commotion, what the sextet footsteps mean. Albert and Watts, like hunters, pause at a hint of movement to their right. From the rock wall peeking through the undergrowth, an ermine, light brown, eel-lithe, ditches camouflage and fortification and up-periscopes itself in the direction of the six stalled feet. Watts growls but will not venture farther, maybe sensing that a compact killer, even if it looks adorable, should be respected, differentiated from the vegan squirrel, with respectful distance.

"Knock it off," Albert whispers. Watts obeys. Albert exchanges with the ermine the exuberance of curiosity. "What's up, buddy?" he inquires of the ermine, who looks from Watts to Albert and registers particulars. "Just passing through," says Albert as he and Watts move on.

The ermine down-periscopes and parallels their progress,

weaving in and out, over and around all obstacles. All ease and silence. Fifty feet. A hundred. Albert, traditionally, involuntarily a scatterer of wildlife, feels as if he's been conferred an honor, feels, if not accepted exactly by this woodland native so attuned to life out here its coat is seasonal, at least not feared. He thinks how long ago was Port Jeff Station, Albert's dense hometown, all woods, hospitable to otherness. How long ago was Portland, where his house is now, not primarily a place of yards and houses, overtaking, always threatening to overtake what naturally grows? How insulated and exclusive are the places Albert has called home. How territorial. Proprietary and incurious. How locked and paved and well-lit and delineated and computerized. How inhospitable to any but the least offensive species. How the least offensive suffer oftentimes regardless. How unwild. No wonder he has wandered so far from the graves of his ancestors. Not without regret, but he has wandered. No wonder he has walked through middle life the bearer of a personal apology he cannot find descendants of the slaughtered and displaced to grudgingly accept. Sure, at home the squirrels and the chipmunks and the birds accept his seeds. At home the deer accept his corn. But here, without enticement, in the middle of the woods, the ermine says hello and lets him be. Albert likes the sound of ermine on a field vert. He makes a mental note to look into heraldic symbolism when he goes home and has access to the internet again. The ermine disappears, the unseen world, but Albert feels privileged for the friendly glimpse, the seasonal introduction. As he reaches his property line, he wonders when the ermine's coat began to change from white to brown, how long the transformation took. Such metamorphosis can't be the province of the ermine only. How does one resolve to be more open to impressive change?

He thinks about the transformation mechanisms and the agency of resolutions as he brushes his right foot to and fro over the boggy driveway grass and watches as the startled frogs again broad jump to the wheel-rut ponds and situate their bulbous eyes at water level to determine what this huge enigma will do next.

He passes into the clearing, stands beside his tailgate, and looks to where the sagging cabin is no more. Most of the pine-board siding he piled carefully, the bark facing up, the nails extracted or bent back, about fifty feet to his right beyond the sapling cedars and the sapling hemlocks vying for a long-term situation on the fringes of the clearing where the sun, unfiltered, shines for several hours each cloud-free day. He piled the boards so that there is a small slit for an entry, piled them so that in the center is a hollow, snug and dry, that he envisions as a fox den next winter. What he will do when Watts and the envisioned foxes get too close and snarl for territory next June he has not thought through. The remaining boards he lay in a similar-looking pile, sans entry point, sans hollow, over the decommissioned outhouse pit whose depth he never had been clear about and which he feared, uncovered, might ensnare a deer in flight or any range of passing beings not expecting to descend into a pit of years of excrement. If he ever does become a father to those boys, he told himself as he positioned the boards above the muck, he will impress upon them the life-and-death importance of the careful step. By way of illustration, he will point out that such lack of care caused many California dinosaurs to perish viscously. The boys might not remember anything that he says lesson-wise about the careful step or the advantages of caution, but they won't forget the image of a T-Rex or a stegosaurus as it slowly sinks and wallows, crying out for succor to the prehistoric world. And from that, without his saying so, he hopes that they infer how precious a commodity is sympathy.

All the other untreated wood, the thick, mossy slabs of hemlock that had been the deck boards, the old-time two-by-four cedar that had been the ceiling joists, the one-by-six pine boards that had been the inner walls, Albert lay in several tidy piles deeper in the woods, all nails extracted or faced down or bent back to minimize the threat of incidental puncture, refuge for the toad, the newt, or for whomever the inviting crevices and hollows of the slowly decomposing world can be, without shame, without the feeling of a diminution of their station in the world, called home, called nothing, just a place to come across and enter with their little hearts and be relieved of their exposure for however long relief is necessary.

What remains is just the floor. Twenty feet by twenty-four. The plywood and the painted wood are piled there beneath a tarp. He sawed the wood to pieces that would fit, without his geometrical finagling, in the fifty-five-gallon drum that squats at the floor's edge, facing streamward.

Albert carries two buckets to the stream and fills them. He inspects each one for captured fingerlings, and the water in the bucket that has caught one he pours back in the stream. He dips the bucket and refills, rechecks. Free of fingerlings. He walks uphill and lifts the buckets not quite chest high and sets them, sloshing, by the drum. He clambers onto the floor, stands up, and wipes one hand against the other three times. He looks around—at drum, camp chair number two, tarped wood—and, not seeing what he's looking for, walks up to the clearing, to the truck.

From the passenger side, he takes a Sealtest milk crate, which contains a small fire extinguisher, a read and reread *Bangor Daily News*, and lighter fluid. He pats his pocket to confirm the lighter. From the camp chair by the tailgate, he picks up the paper he held earlier and puts it in the crate. With both hands, he holds the crate and pauses like a window shopper by the cooler. Certainly too early for a beer, although compatibility standards, those unwritten guidelines that suggest that this particular thing achieves its full expression and exists most beautifully when it aligns with this particular sidekick, sort of dictate that, if he is going to ignite and tend a fire, it is only natural that he have a beer to complement and to intensify the gazing tendency inspired by the mesmerizing dance that fire does. Albert tells himself to focus on not burning down the woods. With last night's moisture still abundant, he does not believe he'll burn the forest down, but drum fire is still fire and he knows how alcohol can sand the edges off the wariness and reasoned fear whose purpose is to see that simple things don't mushroom and become complex because the momentary lapses alcohol is famous for take over. Then he wonders why he often has these little conversations with himself regarding beer. The answer is historical, too tentacled to enter into right now, the stuff of dusk reflection.

"I used to sing in finished basements with abandon, Watts." He looks out at the woods. "The days of the communal roof-incineration song have passed me by." He wonders why the bonds of friendship lose adhesion over time. Watts wags his tail as if linguistic comprehension isn't necessary to appreciate assertion and the palliation it can offer to a person who reviews the decades and is not encouraged by his record of extraordinary transformation.

"All right, Watts. Let's burn this motherfucker."

Albert carries the crate to camp chair number two and sets it on the seat. He checks the date on one of the papers and begins to separate the pages, crumpling each one to the desired density (not too loose, not too tight) and dropping it in the drum. When he deems the bottom of the drum sufficiently combustible, he folds the tarp back on the plywood pile and selects five rectangles that he sets lengthwise in the drum, each piece extending to a point about a finger length beneath the drum rim. He squirts the lighter fluid on the paper and the plywood and returns the can to the crate, which he relocates a logical distance from the drum. Although the stream is running high from last night's rain and trees drip and the floor is still slick, Albert tilts a water bucket at a slow-pour angle and directs it in a circle around the drum and works his way out about five feet. He sets the bucket down and takes the matchbox from the crate. He strikes a wooden match, shields his face from what he judges is the worst denomination of disfigurement, extends his hand beyond the rim, and parts his thumb and index finger so the match drops in.

Ignition.

Albert watches as the fire gains momentum—the paper burst, the flame crawl, the inner plywood yielding. This is a responsibility, a reason to be mindful, sober. He watches as the flames leap, and he thinks, as he is prone to do when he is close to fire, about those photographs of Quang Duc, the monk who sat erect and burned beside the gas can in the Saigon intersection, sat serenely, meditatively, and burned, becoming black inside the flame, in protest of the South's oppression of the Buddhists. Few Americans regard the South as the oppressor. *Extraordinary transformation*, Albert thinks. *Makes most others seem mundane.* But Albert can't remember Quang Duc's name. He isn't sure he ever knew it. There is solace in believing that. He holds his splayed hand over the fire. He draws it back. So many roads to martyrdom. Why would the guy choose this one?

A steady heat develops. Albert monitors, and, when the energy declines and space opens up, he brings another batch of plywood pieces over and leans them against the left legs of camp chair number two. He lays one on the drum rim, slides it in, and judges. Lays another on the drum rim, slides it in, and judges. Sparks go airborne, waft for seconds, lose their forged glow, and descend. A few land glowing on the old floor, fizzle in their own sort of martyrdom, and go out. Albert gazes, sharp in his sobriety. "The Tyger" enters his mind a few times. Even that he has not memorized. The dead sparks, the high stream, the calm interior that fire under reasonable control produces in a human grant him sufficient leave to get a sandwich and some drinking water and some cookies for the sweet conclusion to the feeding interlude.

He carries back to camp chair number two a paper lunch plate and a plastic water cup and looks around like a preemptive-minded park ranger sans pressed uniform, sans mesa of a hat. He sets his plate and cup upon the floor, retrieves the recent paper from the crate, and sits down slowly in the camp chair, which bends inward with his weight.

"Git," he says to Watts, whose nose draws toward the sandwich.

Albert unfolds the paper, lifts his plate. He takes a bite of his sandwich, reads the newswire summaries of national news, and suspects he caught a contact high from breathing the incinerated plywood glue; but it is not enough to render written words nonsensical or fuzz their edges much. He chews. He sniffs to isolate the fume. He reads about the uphill battle regulators face in trying to prevent more oil trains from exploding in the boom in Bakken crude. No mention of the grassroots outrage. No glory for the regulatory. Albert looks up at the smoking, flaming fifty-five-gallon drum, which probably held oil once or kerosene or something no one wants extracted, shipped, or spilled in their vicinity.

Albert chews. His attention shifts to a longer article beside the newswire summaries of international news:

"Russian performance artist Pyotr Pavlensky broke new ground on Sunday when he walked onto Red Square at lunchtime, stripped, and nailed his scrotum to the cobblestones of Russia's most famous public square.

"'The performance can be seen as a metaphor for the apathy, political indifference, and fatalism of contemporary Russian society,' Pavlensky said in a statement.

"Pavlensky has a history of self-harming, including sewing his lips together to protest against the jail sentence given to members of Pussy Riot and wrapping himself in barbed wire outside a Russian government building, which act, he said, symbolized 'the existence of a person inside a repressive legal system.'"

Albert chews and wonders if these solitary protests ever work, if they are even pebbles that create the vanguard ripples in the water body that is human history, or if they simply make the sort of person who is prone to read the paper feel unusually adjusted by comparison, a person who may have issues with society but who, regarded in the light of certain martyrs, gadflies, hermits, malcontents, and freaks, feels pleased his constitution hasn't pushed him to exhibit such antagonism, such extremity.

Albert almost finishes his sandwich, flips the last sixteenth to Watts, plucks a cookie from the paper plate, and masticates as if to help chug cogitation. What does he owe to such people as Pyotr Pavlensky, Quang Duc, Dick Proenneke? What does anyone owe to the mortifiers of the flesh, to the ascetics, to the people who proclaim by deed against the usual way? A hearing at least, a listening, an entry in the inventory of our consciousness, a meaningful incorporation of their sacrifices in our lives, our thoughts. Albert makes a mental note. He plans to read more thoroughly about Pavlensky's views when he goes home. He plans, when he goes home, to burn the name Quang Duc in his brain and maybe, if he ever has another dog, to name that dog Quang Duc. He plans, when he goes home, to be divested, piece by piece, of what is keeping him from living as Dick Proenneke lived because he thinks if he can live as Dick Proenneke lived there is no need for immolation at an intersection, for impaling to the public cobblestones a private part of his anatomy.

Albert finishes his cookies and throws the plate into the fire. He sips his water and stands.

"Whew," he says to Watts. "These fumes are sneaky."

He backhands his brow sweat, swats the air above his head to keep the deer flies unaccustomed to the unmolested landing, Mr. Blondes it to the plywood pile, and supposes that the burning will continue some way into night. He looks up at the sun about to clear the trees. He looks back at the fire, picks up, one by one, five plywood pieces, carries them at his right side like a book stack of unusual dimensions. He leans the stack against the camp chair legs and walks up to the clearing where he stands a moment. Without society, without its schedule and commitments, his is the unfiltered voice, the sole determinant. He lifts the cooler lid, stares in diagnostically, and dips his right hand in the watery ice, withdraws an IPL and says to Watts, "We're running low." He pops the top off with a teaspoon. At a rate he predetermines will produce an aromatic-looking head, he pours the beer into a tilted tulip glass, decants the bottle as though there is nothing in the world worthier of his focus and his ardor than this lager. When he gently shakes the last drop from the bottle's lip, he says to Watts, "There's a time for water, and there's a time for beer." He sips and says, "My goodness." It is as if the angels sing.

Albert returns to camp chair number two with caution, careful not to agitate his nectar, and he pulls the chair a few feet farther from the drum. "Shite," he says to Watts, "it's hot." He sits and stretches out his bitten legs like lamb shanks toward the drum. The condensation slides down the glass's belly to the stem. He squints up at the sun, which cleared the trees and will not be attenuated by arboreal impediment for several hours. Watts lies next to him and lightly pants. "It's gotta be eighty-five," Albert says. He takes a long drink. "Hu-mid," he says as he pulls the center of his t-shirt from his skin. "Time to feed the fire," he decides.

He finishes his warming beer and feels inspired to be living in this manner, at this time. He slides three plywood pieces in and pulls back from the dense heat. "Whew," he says to Watts. "I think I singed a few on that one." He inspects his forearm like a solitary primate, and, convinced his core identity is more or less intact, gets three more plywood pieces, which he leans against the two already leaning on the camp chair legs. "All right," he says, looking with a single eye into the depths of his curvaceous glass. "To the cooler."

He shepherds afternoon to night this way—from camp chair number two to drum to plywood-pile resupply to cooler back to camp chair or to floor's edge for a leak as he looks toward the stream and sways a little like a cedar seeking equilibrium in intermittent breeze. He's fished the last beer from the cooler, and he's pulled the camp chair closer to the drum because he's slid the last piece of the plywood in and there is no light but the drum glow and the hermit thrush is tucked in and the temperature has dipped since sundown and his contemplation nightcap's transformative power is proportional to drum proximity. So Albert holds his glass in both hands, and he leans in toward the drum, his face warm and his moth mind drawn to the light. With mind and body thus configured, almost anything seems possible. With such alterations (intellectual, emotional, postural) comes the pleasant misconception that perhaps he's overestimated standard hardships. Build a modest camp. Resettle. Raise two kids. Make do. Pass on. The two kids take the passed baton. They bear the standard Albert has passed down, the family motto proudly kept in circulation by those two adjustable boys: *On foot, or undiscovered.* Albert stares into the glowing drum and wonders at paternity, the father's mortal spark kept glowing when the father himself has gone out.

Must the link be biological? He thinks about his father's crawling cancer and the radiation at the Lab, his father telling him the day before he died he couldn't have asked for a better son.

Albert sips his beer and thinks about the deathbed pep talk, an incentive to walk proudly in the world and prove his father right post-mortem. *More about the spirit,* he considers, *than the flesh or the genetic.*

He slumps back in the chair and takes a long drink. He rubs his skull where the fracture was, the place that sometimes tingles when he drinks, and wonders if there always is a reason for what happens.

Albert takes a drink and leans in, gazing on the bright reaction in the drum.

"The evidence for metamorphosis is everywhere."

Watts thumps his tail against the floor as if in indolent applause.

Chapter Eleven

For sixteen years now, Albert's harbored slightly traitorous misgivings when it comes to pledging his allegiance to the flag, but he has risen every school-day morning, placed his right hand over his heart, and said the words without the fervor as he stared up at the angled classroom flag and felt his acquiescence was a practical betrayal of the principles of someone his age who believed he really knew what the Republic was about. And no one occupying a position of authority could answer why the population of an all-boys Catholic school was told to rise each morning and recite those lockstep words that bound it to the secular, that bound it to a sprawling entity whose God supposedly was nondenominational and not a deity for whom Albert felt the flock's affection or to whom he felt he could turn unless the matter under prayerful speculation had to do with national interest, with how he might make his humble offering to the ever alms-seeking State. So in September, on the Tuesday after Labor Day, the first day of the new school year, Albert stood up with his class when told to by the intercom, but he did not recite the Pledge words. When the students sat down afterward and the announcements of the day were broadcast, Albert stood at his lectern before the white board and looked out at the hairless faces of his honors-freshmen English class and asked, "Do you know who Quang Duc was?" Some students shook their heads. Some looked down at their ruled paper as if shamed.

"Quang Duc," continued Albert, "was a Mahayana Buddhist monk who sat down in a Saigon intersection in 1962. A fellow monk poured gas on him and lit him up. Quang Duc sat there in the lotus position, perfectly still, or as still as you can be, I guess, while being consumed by flames, until the fire overcame him and he fell. Does anyone know why he did this?"

Silence.

"He was protesting his government's brutal persecution of the Buddhists," Albert answered. "Can anyone tell me who his government was?" Silence. "What his country was?"

A student wearing a pressed shirt and short tie raised his hand. Albert pointed at him.

"What's your name?" asked Albert.

"Tim Elliot."

"What was Quang Duc's country, Tim?"

"Vietnam?"

"South Vietnam. Does anyone know what government supported South Vietnam in 1962?"

Tim raised his hand again. "The United States."

"The United States. Exactly." Albert looked around as if allowing time for this cruise ship of a point to sink in. "All right. Let's review these course guidelines," he said as he licked his index finger and began to pass fresh copies to the first row.

The next day, after rising for the Pledge, reciting nothing, and then listening to the announcements, he inquired of his students, "Ever heard of Pyotr Pavlensky?"

One student near the front raised a tentative hand. Albert pointed at him.

"What's your name again?"

"Ryan Murray."

"All right, Ryan Murray. What say you?"

"Is he a hockey player?"

"No," said Albert. He then explained Pavlensky's mode of protest against the Russian government and its record of oppression and abuse. The students winced and smiled and looked at one another. He concluded, "If he were an American, he could as easily have nailed his scrotum to the cobblestones in a U.S. city in protest of *our* government's record of oppression and abuse. He'd be as justified."

The next day, after rising for the Pledge, reciting nothing, and then listening to the announcements, Albert inquired of his students, "Anyone ever heard of the Tuskegee Syphilis Experiment?" Silence. "From 1932 to 1972, the U.S. government ran a program that set up a clinic in Tuskegee, Alabama. Rates of syphilis were high among the rural poor, mostly sharecroppers, mostly African-American men. So the government advertised that anyone with syphilis could receive free medical care for their condition at the clinic. Guess what happened?"

A student in the middle of the classroom raised his hand.

Albert looked at him and said, "What's your name again?"

"Mark."

"All right, Mark. What happened?"

"They cured syphilis."

"That's a humane and reasonable conclusion, but no. The government doctors administered placebo medications. They weren't offering any treatment at all. They simply studied the effects of the untreated disease as it progressed in these poor, uneducated, rural, African-American citizens. Untreated syphilis can lead to terrible lesions and deformities, blindness, deafness, brain damage, dementia, death. The doctors could have treated them with penicillin by the 1940s, but they didn't. They just watched. Watched, studied, and took notes." Albert paused. "In 1997, I think, President Clinton, the Lewinsky president, publicly apologized to the few surviving participants of the study. Let that be a lesson to you."

The next day, Friday, after rising for the Pledge, reciting nothing, and then listening to the announcements, Albert inquired of his students, "What is a subprime mortgage?"

A few students tried to explain but missed the mark.

"One example I remember," said Albert, "involved a couple from California. Their gross income, *gross*, was about ninety-thousand dollars, which means their take-home was probably around sixty. With no money down, they bought a house for $590,000. What's wrong with this picture?"

One student said, "They could never afford that much on that income."

"Exactly," said Albert. "So why would the bank give them a loan? Why would the government allow the bank to give them a loan?"

Another student said, "Because the bank knows it will

eventually get the house."

"That's part of it," Albert said. "The bigger part is that the bank packages the mortgage into a security, obscures the obvious risk, and sells it to an investor, a pension fund or whatever. Greed. Materialism and greed."

Another student raised his hand. "Are you a Democrat?" he asked.

"I don't vote," said Albert. "It's not a Democrat-Republican issue. Clinton's administration was the one that got the Glass-Steagall Act repealed. That Act kept a firewall between the investment and depositary arms of a bank. It prevented a bank from dipping into a depositor's money and gambling with it. I agree with Ralph Nader, who said that, except for certain ideological issues like abortion or gun control, there's really no difference between the parties. What he means is that the Republicans and Democrats are so deep in the pockets of the corporations and are so beholden to them that the business of the government is the business of the corporations. Corporations are the politicians' real constituency. Not the people."

By November 10th, Albert delivered forty-nine such disquisitions on such topics as the Wangunks' dispossession, Chief Seattle's desolation, Brookhaven National Laboratory's peaceful nuclear intentions, Ben Bernanke's rounds of quantitative easing, Wendell Berry's sane and reasoned advocacy of the agrarian ideal, legitimate jihadi grievances—whatever seemed to justify refusing to articulate the Pledge. He made a point of delivering each five- or ten-minute disquisition to his other four classes so a symmetry was formed and he could easily remember what specific topics he had covered with what classes since he covered each one with them all. Pedagogically, he knew repeated failure to remember what he said the day, the week, the month before would be the kiss of death, would undermine what thin authority he wielded as a lower-order intellectual repository. Even students who obey a dress code and have hair that's neatly trimmed above the ears and volunteer on Saturdays to feed the indigent and homeless will enumerate among themselves the mounting failures of their teacher's memory and make a parlor game of taking their advantage when the person who drones on before them grows forgetful. Thus he entered in his composition notebook each day's disquisition topic and the date that he delivered it.

By November 10th, he was fairly certain who was philosophically aligned with him. The students who agreed with his perspective had decided their allegiances lay elsewhere and had ceased their recitation of the Pledge. They didn't all stop at once. The earliest decided by the middle of September. One stopped pledging after disquisition forty-eight. Although Albert felt a teacher's pride in this recruitment by example, by osmosis, he predicted, when he saw the first boy saying nothing while the others pledged, that he would be called down to someone's office in a time to be determined by administrative variables. Because the periods rotate each day (first period on Monday becoming seventh on Tuesday, second becoming first, and so on), each first-period teacher who had Albert's conscientious objectors started handing out detentions and reporting to the dean of discipline the seemingly spontaneous withholdings of allegiance. So the summons to the office on October 23rd was hardly unexpected. Albert even thought it was a little overdue.

Albert sat in a narrow, cushioned chair before a large desk and suffered the interrogation with aplomb because the check for fifty-thousand dollars (his share of the settlement the DOE decided was sufficient reparation for the slow death of a patriarch) had arrived by registered mail two days before, a windfall he could not help feeling opened up some wiggle room for him.

"So what's the problem with the Pledge?" asked Nick Gironda, who closed the door and settled in behind the desk. He had a round head, black hair shaved close to the scalp, and a chinstrap beard that took the long way ear to ear. He was about fifteen years Albert's junior.

"Well," said Albert, "I don't really like what the Republic has become, I guess."

Gironda stared at him for several seconds.

"You can't tell the kids not to say the Pledge," Gironda said.

"I didn't tell them not to say the Pledge. I just stopped saying it myself."

"You have to say the Pledge. You're the leader in your classroom. Students follow the example you set."

Albert said nothing.

Gironda said, "What about these monologues I hear you're giving at the start of class?"

"They're just ideas. Discussion points. I usually manage to make them fit the lesson."

"They're disruptive. Albert, you know these kids are impressionable. You can't go telling ninth- and tenth-grade boys it's okay to nail their scrotums to the cobblestones because they have a problem with the government."

"I didn't tell them it's okay. I told them about a Russian guy who did it and why. His name's Pyotr Pavlensky."

"You're not hearing me. You're splitting hairs. You're supposed to be a role model, but it sounds like all you're doing is promoting discontent."

"How is mentioning what goes on in the world promoting discontent? What's disruptive about standing up respectfully and saying nothing?"

"You've been saying the Pledge for years. What changed? Why start this now?"

"I had some time to think over the summer. I don't take this lightly. It's no caprice."

Gironda shook his spherical head.

"Look," he said. "I've gotten calls. Some parents are not happy. One parent thinks you're a socialist."

"A socialist? How am I a socialist? Socialism is—"

"I'm not getting into a socialism conversation with you. Take a minute out of your day and set aside your principles and say the Pledge and knock off the monologues."

"I don't know if I can turn this ship around," said Albert.

"Start tomorrow. This isn't *Dead Poets' Society*. You are not

Robin Williams."

What a dick, thought Albert.

"All right," Albert said as he rose. "Have a good one."

The next morning at 8:15, the bell rang. Albert rose with everyone and faced the flag, but he did not recite the Pledge. He noticed several students who'd abstained from pledging in the past few days returned to recitation. When the class sat down, Albert wondered how he should proceed. He wondered if these backsliders would report him to Gironda after class. He slightly shook his head because a grown man should not fret about a schoolboy tattling on him. A grown man should not shrink back from his conscientious inclinations.

Albert stood like a third-party candidate behind the lectern and asked, "Is anyone familiar with a character named Bartleby the Scrivener?" A wall of silence. "Bartleby gets a job with a law firm as, essentially, a human copy machine. A scribe. A scrivener. He competently does his job for a few days. When his boss tells him to examine the accuracy of a particular document one day, Bartleby says, 'I would prefer not to.' Every time the boss tells him to do something, Bartleby says, 'I would prefer not to.' This puts the boss in a bind. The boss finally fires him and tells him to leave, but Bartleby replies, 'I would prefer not to.' The boss moves the whole firm to another building. Bartleby still won't leave. He gets arrested. Then he dies. The boss is left to wonder what the hell went wrong with Bartleby." Albert paused. "Who wins here?"

A student raised his hand.

"Noah," said Albert.

"No one."

"No one," said Albert. "It was a Pyrrhic victory for Bartleby. Still a victory, I guess." He paused. "Like Emerson said. I think it was Emerson. 'Whoso would be a man must be a nonconformist.'"

In the ensuing days, the anecdotes rolled in. Albert sat in the faculty lounge and gazed at his computer or corrected, and he overheard the teachers, rippling with indignation, when they put their bags down and began to vent about their wiseass students, who, when asked to conjugate a Spanish verb or to approach the board and solve an algebra equation or to read aloud a paragraph about the slaves-sugar-rum configuration of the triangular trade or to explain some ways the media distort the Church's teaching of such doctrines as infallibility, replied with maddening equanimity, "I would prefer not to." Day after day, Albert overheard the teachers when they talked about attempting to recover from the childish rebuffs, explaining to their charges the importance of obedience in moderation and of academic inquiry and of understanding that at their age students often are unable to make out the forest for the trees and thus get deeply lost; and Albert overheard the teachers when they said in wounded tones that those brats calmly brushed the admonitions off and said, as if descended from the Transcendental troublemaker, "Whoso would be a man must be a nonconformist."

"I mean, I'm impressed that they memorized the line, but what am I supposed to say to that?" Jim Latham asked the teachers sitting at the various tables one morning. "I'm a science teacher. It's not my job to teach the virtues of conformity."

The teachers shook their heads in solidarity.

"Just give the fuckers their detention slips," said Brendan Tell.

"I have been," Latham said, removing his glasses and rubbing the nose-pad indentations on either side of his upper nose. "But some of them refuse to go."

"Then it gets doubled," Tell said.

"A couple still refuse to go."

"Fuck them then," said Tell. "Gironda should suspend them. If they want to be nonconformists, let their parents deal with them."

The teachers bobbed their heads in solidarity.

Latham looked at Albert and said, "Nothing from the English department?"

Albert looked up from his computer and said, "All I did was mention Emerson one day last week. And Bartleby the Scrivener. It's not like I issued a directive."

"No," said Latham, "but Gironda might not see it that way."

"Probably not," said Albert. "No, the odds are not in my favor."

"I still say suspend them," Tell concluded. "Problem solved."

The teachers bobbed their heads in solidarity.

The imaginary force field that is tenure magically emboldened Albert to keep listening to the subversive voice inside his head, the voice that was a mellow baritone urging him to hew to principle. The alternative appeared to be to thoroughly capitulate and to suppose that in capitulation he'd be leaving everyone with an erroneous impression of the character he knew he actually was, the one that in his occupation he had stifled for so many years but that should be at liberty now, considering that, come June, the only thing that he would leave behind would be the unadulterated, all-in-type impression of his character, unbuttoned, on the minds of all his docile colleagues who would keep on aging here and envy him, upon the minds of mere boys who would think on his example during crucial moments in their future, compromising lives as emulation worthy, an unshackling ideal. But what exactly did it say about him that continuing as an emboldening ideal depended on his trusting in the tenure shield? Can you ever be all in with tenure? This conundrum would anon be solved for him.

On Friday, November 7th, at 2:56 pm, as Albert performed his final departure rituals for the day, he checked his email one last time and saw a bright red exclamation point beside an inbox message (Subject: MEETING, Sender: Principal John Hughes) that had arrived at 2:55. Like Cardinal Spada opening the letter that invited him to dine with Caesar Borgia and the Pope, Albert clicked. The message, cc'ed to Headmaster Brother Aloysius, read, "Albert, I've scheduled for you to meet with Brother Aloysius and myself on Monday, November 10th, at 3:00. See you then. Have a good weekend. John."

"What the fuck," Albert mumbled.

The tradition of delivering unpleasant news on Friday afternoon or evening is, in modern hierarchies, where the management prefers to veil aggression, well established. Veiling institutional aggression is a dark art, but the signifiers must be generally intelligible to those on whom the darkness and the artistry are practiced. Omission, for example, must be understood as the beginning of the mind-fuck, leaving the bewildered underling to guess at management's intention while said underling believes he's fairly certain that he knows what's going on. Apparent cordiality expressed in first-name usage and such platitudes as "Have a good weekend" must be read as written with a smirk because why leave a valued person hanging during days of rest and tell him to enjoy the hanging—unless, that is, the management, in saying so, manipulates its hands in wizard-like formations to effect said mind-fuck. The mention of the extra person in the meeting must be taken as the management's conveyance of numerical superiority, designed to get the underling to think all weekend on just where he will be sitting in relation to the two superiors—essential to the mind-fuck since the seating possibilities are endless if the underling thinks hard enough.

But what really bothered Albert and made him wonder how two men whose Catholic faith was openly professed each day could be so calculating and vindictive was that they conspired to appoint a meeting time intended to create the greatest inconvenience for Albert and to open up a second front on which to pummel him with his own mental agitation. At 5:30 on the tenth, the parents whose last names begin with letters ranging A to L would be arriving for their parent-teacher conferences, some parents simply wanting formal introductions, some asking pointed questions, some conveying with an eye twitch or a tone that they pay twelve grand for tuition and believe their boy is better than a B, but all behaving so politely (some sincerely, some for show) as to hand over no legitimate incentive for a weary teacher to resort, as he is wont to do with students, to the vivifying refuge that is snark. John Hughes and Brother Aloysius knew, like good behind-the-curtain men, that shortening the interim in which Albert could relax and could prepare, in which he could rehearse a little patter in his mind, establishing a parent-teacher-conference rhythm that would ease him through the night's inherent awkwardness—they knew that shortening the interim would be a visceral reminder of whose time he was on.

On Monday, then, at the appointed hour, Albert sits stiffly on a wooden chair before the window that Linda, practiced in the pleasantries of school reception, slides not quite halfway to her right and says with half a smile, "They're ready for you."

As casually as circumstance allows, Albert enters the administration labyrinth via the remotely unlocked door, and he proceeds, not jauntily but not as if he's on the first leg of a death march either, past administrative instruments great and small, past art that's meant to soothe the stressed delinquent or the parent who has sat a long time in a hard chair, turns left, and pauses like a footman on the threshold of his master's door.

John Hughes sits burgomasterly behind his high-end casket of a desk, his forearms at rest on either cushioned arm of his high-backed leather chair, his hands a-dangle. His hair is brown and gray, cut high and tight, suggesting a historical Marine, although the principal has never served. Before his desk are two chairs. Brother Aloysius, sitting in the left one, turns to look at Albert, who in his weekend thinking didn't spend much time on this particular configuration. He assumes that its intent is to convey administrative distance and proximity at once, to let him know without the words that they're beyond his reach but they can touch him when they like.

"Please close the door," says Brother Aloysius, white-haired and bespectacled, his clerical collar torqued a little in the turning. Albert has always admired the precision of his part. "Come in." Brother Aloysius holds his upturned palm out to the chair beside him. "Have a seat."

It all begins with pleasantry, forced humor, but the clock runs quickly out on that.

"Look," says Hughes. "I think you know why you're here, right?" He rests his hands on the enormous calendar that's centered on his desk. "We know you're a good teacher. You know your subject. Your students like and respect you. You're never absent. You've always been a steady presence."

Brother Aloysius looks at the carpeted floor and nods.

"But," says Hughes. "These past two months. What's going on?"

"You mean about the Pledge?" asks Albert.

"The Pledge, the monologues, the 'I would prefer not to,' the insubordination. Nick was clear in your last meeting, right, that this stuff had to stop. Why didn't it?"

"I don't have an explanation," Albert says.

Brother Aloysius leans in toward the desk and picks up a black binder, which Albert recognizes as the Faculty / Staff Handbook. He opens it and turns to a page that has been flagged with a fluorescent orange sticker, and with two hands holds it out to Albert.

Brother Aloysius says, "Please read what's written in bold at the top of page thirty-nine."

Albert clears his throat and reads, "All classes at Saint Francis are to begin with a prayer."

Silence.

Albert sits as if he's letting something of the highest order of profundity sink in.

"Do you begin all your classes with a prayer?" asks Hughes.

The question is rhetorical, Albert tells himself. *Say nothing.*

Brother Aloysius reaches over and takes back the binder, which he closes like a sacred text and lays upon the desk. He picks up a stapled set of papers and relays the set to Albert, who looks down and reads the top line to himself, "SAINT FRANCIS HIGH SCHOOL CONTRACT OF EMPLOYMENT."

Brother Aloysius says, "Please turn to the appendix."

Albert turns.

Brother Aloysius points to a passage on the page. "Read this, please."

Albert reads aloud a sentence that declares unlimited causation and then prefaces the termination stipulations.

Brother Aloysius moves his finger. "And this."

Albert reads aloud a sentence that commits the signatory to compliance with the rules that will be stated forthwith.

Brother Aloysius moves his finger. "And this."

Albert reads aloud a sentence clarifying that participation in a public scandal or in turpitude or in behavior counter to the general good is hereby categorized as termination worthy.

Brother Aloysius moves his finger. "And this."

Albert reads aloud a sentence in which insubordination is the path to termination.

Brother Aloysius points to the bottom of the appendix. "Is that your signature?"

"It is," says Albert.

"Do you see what we're saying here?" asks Hughes. "We're not having another meeting on this."

Albert nods.

"If anyone tonight brings up the Pledge issue or the monologue issue or whatever, just tell them you were trying something out educationally and it didn't work the way you thought it would. Assure them that things will return to normal tomorrow."

"Tomorrow is Veterans' Day," says Albert.

"Assure them, then, that things will return to normal on Wednesday. Then steer the conversation back to the student's performance, how you can help him to improve, and so on. Understood?"

"Yep."

Albert unwinds himself from the administrative wing and walks back to his classroom. He sits down at his cluttered desk and pulls his school calendar from his slumped bag. Starting with November 12th, he counts each school day, month by month, and stops on June 1st. Excluding exam days and potential snow days, he counts 118 class days remaining in the school year.

It's doable, he thinks. 118 Pledges, fewer if he factors in the days he doesn't have first period. He clicks the calculator feature on his laptop. 590 prayers. *It's doable.*

By 5:15, he sees the first arrivals slowly passing by his classroom, glancing at the number on his door, then looking at the schedules in their hands to check for any matches. When the parents suddenly materialize before his door, he is supposed to smile and be bright eyed and adopt the easy graciousness of the secure in case the passersby turn out to be the parents of a student under his tuition, is supposed to put on the Samaritan demeanor in case the passersby turn out to be disoriented and befuddled by the logic of sequential numbers. Yea, the two great smilers have deprived him of his nap, and Albert has already become a wretched watcher of the clock. How many minutes is 118 class days?

"Mr. Lesiak?" a woman asks, air-knocking on the open door. "Am I too early?"

"Not at all," says Albert, rising, trying not to characterize American ennui. "Come on in."

They extend their right hands.

"I'm Nora Salter. Frank's mom?"

"Sure," says Albert.

"He's in your freshman honors class."

"Sure," says Albert, expending mental energy to visualize the boy and summarize with accuracy the boy's accomplishments and/or deficiencies without resorting to the gradebook right away because such sudden consultation often makes the parent feel the teacher does not truly know the son. Albert slides a student desk so that it roughly parallels his own and slightly lessens the inherent awkwardness in the posterior presentation necessary for this sort of sit-down.

So early in the evening, so early in the academic year, Albert's loath to dash parental dreams, and so he speaks in code.

"Well, Frank's done well at times this quarter. The first quarter, I mean. I don't believe, though, that he's working to capacity."

Mrs. Salter nods and waits for data to support this disappointing, if foregone, assertion. Albert takes a moment, trying to incite his memory to pull specific figures up, but he can say no more of substance without the gradebook, which he opens to a page that is a green-and-white grid crowded with neatly black-inked checks and numbers, documentary evidence from which a boy's trajectory in life is, in part, to be divined and on which strategies for nurturing the child's inner genius or remediating the encroachments of his inner dunce will be, with faith in the potential of a boy at that age to be open still to molding, based. No one mentions drugs.

"For example," Albert resumes, "Frank had a ninety-five on one vocabulary quiz but sixty-five on another. So he's shown that he can do the work. Consistency, however, is an issue. That's not difficult to address, especially if Frank comes before or after school to extra help so we can talk one on one about how to optimize his study time."

Mrs. Salter's lips show signs of melancholy pleasure.

Albert continues, "What concerns me is his performance on the reading assessments. Again, he's got some halfway decent grades, a seventy-five, for example, but he's also got a forty and a fifty-two. He's also got a zero on an in-class assignment that was five questions based on the previous night's reading."

"That was the mythology?"

"Right," says Albert. "Now, I don't believe that it's a comprehension issue."

"No," says Mrs. Salter, shaking her head. "I agree. It's lack of effort."

"That's what I'm inclined to think. Typically, when a kid gets a zero on that sort of assignment, he just didn't read. The question is why. It's hard to answer that, it's hard to say it is or isn't a comprehension issue, until Frank comes to extra help and he and I can talk one on one about what's going on. I can check his notes. I can ask him some diagnostic questions to get a better sense of where he's at with reading comprehension."

"I like that idea. I think that will help."

"I did read a study recently that showed a different part of the brain is activated when a person reads something on a device compared to when he reads that same something on a page. It has to do with the glow of the screen, the pop-up ads, the ability to scroll."

"Distractions."

"Basically. When a person gets conditioned to reading on a screen, the other kind of reading can apparently be harder."

She nods. "He's always reading on a screen. His phone, his Kindle, his computer."

"They all do. That's the challenge these days." Thus absolving himself, without a mediating presence, of responsibility for Frank's deficiencies, Albert says, "Look. Why don't we do this? Have him see me in extra help before the next reading quiz, and I will email you after I grade the quiz and then we'll see where we stand."

By six o'clock the line outside his door extends because he does not usher any parent out when his or her allotted time is up despite the periodic and polite reminders on the intercom to limit conferences to five minutes and to schedule an appointment with the teacher if the parent would like additional communication. So far no one has explicitly complained about the Pledge omission or the monologues, but several parents have expressed how interesting their historically disinterested sons have found his class, especially the little talks that Albert gives before he starts the lesson proper.

"Thank you," says Albert each time. "I appreciate that."

The closest someone comes to violating the implicit code of geniality that rules the night is when a father leans back in his student desk and says, "It just doesn't ring true to me. In real life a boss would fire a guy like Bartleby immediately and not look back." He rises, shaking his head. "That's literature, I guess."

"That is literature," says Albert.

As the realist departs, Albert prepares to greet the next parent. Before he registers the entering face and matches it to one that hangs in superannuation somewhere in the shadowed gallery of his mind, he says by reflex, "How's my line out there?"

"It's substantial," says the man. "I suspect you'll be here for a while."

They shake, and Albert's visited by what he feels must be a vision.

"Bill Huckabone," the man says.

"Huckabone," says Albert.

"Kyle's my son. Honors freshman."

"Sure," says Albert, studying the countenance with an intensity that goes beyond what is acceptable in normal salutation. Albert then sees the narrow, birdlike features, and he sees the man who woke him when he slept beside the river last June, the man he pitied for his fathering four children, the man he watched the dancing sandhill cranes with. He recognizes Updike. Huckabone is Updike. "Please have a seat," says Albert with a cordial gesture. "I suppose we didn't have a formal introduction when we met the first time."

"No," says Huckabone, whose lankiness settles in, "I don't suppose we did."

"How go the sandhill cranes?"

"I'd guess they're leaving Indiana, if they haven't flown already, heading down to Georgia or to Florida with stops along the way."

"You don't seem too surprised to see me here."

"I saw your picture on the website in September. That surprised me. I've seen you sometimes when I've come to pick my son up. I admit you seemed out of context at first."

"Did you, by any chance," Albert ventures, "mention last June's indiscretion to the principal or anyone?"

Updike/Huckabone shakes his head. "Your free time is your own."

"I appreciate your discretion," Albert says. It then occurs to him that Updike/Huckabone might know what happened to the driver to whom Albert had applied the head-butt, but, on second thought, he reckons that, if Updike/Huckabone knows nothing and now learns about a turtle-motivated cranial assault, he might decide such violence crossed a non-negotiable societal line and might decide that Albert isn't worthy of discretion after all.

"My wife and I decided to adopt," says Albert.

"No kidding," Updike/Huckabone replies, uplifted by the mention of a changed heart toward paternity. "That's wonderful."

"We're about halfway through the process. Two boys. Brothers."

"Good for you. That's great."

Mr. Morehead, academic dean in charge of underclassmen,

comes on the intercom and says, "Please pardon the interruption, but I'd like to respectfully remind parents and teachers to limit conferences to five minutes so that all parents who would like to visit a particular teacher have time. If any parents feel they need more time, please make an appointment with the teacher. Thank you."

"Okay," says Albert. "I'd better move along." He flips some pages in his gradebook. "Kyle is an easy one. His homework average for the first quarter was ninety-five. His vocabulary and grammar average was a hundred. His reading average was ninety-seven, and he got an A, a ninety-five, on his essay. His writing is articulate, mature, and well organized. He participates consistently in class. He's just a great all-around student so far."

"That's good to hear. He loves the class. He likes that you're a bit . . . unusual."

Could be a compliment, could be a dig, thinks Albert. *Let's wait for qualification.*

"That one day you talked about the dispossession of the Wangunks, he was fired up. He's been researching indigenous Connecticut place names and tribes since then."

"Wow. The boy's got some follow-through."

"That day you talked about Wendell Berry's view of 'The Great Economy,' he came home and kept saying to anyone who came in, 'Did you know it takes five-hundred years to make an inch of topsoil? Do you know how much life is in an inch of topsoil?'"

Albert smiles. "I'm not really supposed to say those sorts of things anymore."

"Why not?"

"Ideological differences, I guess. So those little talks don't bother you?"

"Bothered by a little independent thought? No."

"Do you mind if I ask what you do for a living?"

"I'm a lawyer."

"Oh," says Albert with a tone dip. "Nice," he says, more

upbeat.

"An environmental lawyer, actually. I work for a nonprofit called Earthjustice. We've sued the government for species protection, habitat restoration, that sort of thing. We've sued corporations over air and water pollution, land preservation. We just got one company to stop making methyl iodide, which is a pesticide that's linked to various cancers and to late-term miscarriages."

"Well," says Albert, "you must not lack for cases."

"No, unfortunately."

"Do you have any questions about the class or how things have gone so far?"

"No," says Updike/Huckabone as he stands up. "I think that covers it. It was good to meet you under different circumstances. Thank you for your time."

"My pleasure," says Albert. "Thanks for coming."

They shake with firmness.

"Good luck with the adoption. Nothing's better than fatherhood."

Albert wonders if that's true before another parent enters on behalf of a beloved boy.

Chapter Twelve

"Did you pledge allegiance to the flag today?"

"Yes," says Albert.

"Did you open each class with a prayer?"

"Yes."

"Did you keep your views about the government and so on to yourself?"

"Mind your business."

"We can't afford to lose your job until we get these boys adopted," Mary says.

"I am aware," says Albert. "That point has been established."

Mary puts her bag down on a kitchen chair. She scratches Charlie Watts behind the ear and says, "I'm nervous."

"What now?"

"It's the first time we'll be meeting them. What happens if it's not a match?"

"Gina said it doesn't work that way. We meet them, they meet us, and everyone works through their reservations at their own pace. She said you can't become a family in a day."

Mary walks down the narrow hall and into the bedroom where she changes out of work clothes.

Albert calls up an imperial pilsner from the beer fridge, pops the cap with his birch-handle opener, and pours, in three stages, the respiring elixir in a Duvel glass. After an appraising sip, he says, "Besides, we get to have the first meeting here instead of at her office. We have home-field advantage."

"I don't want an advantage," Mary says from the bedroom. "I want them to be comfortable."

Albert shrugs and sits down in his chair, about a body length from the firebox in which the fire has developed an intensity. He unfolds the *Rivereast Bulletin*, which is delivered in the mail each

Friday, and he reads in their entirety the more incendiary letters to the editor. He reads the previous week's arrest reports for his town and the one adjacent, where he used to live, in search of names he knows. He scans the town news and the ads. He looks at the addresses on the public notices to see if anyone applying for a variance might also, in the process, be applying for the town's permission to diminish Albert's quality of life, although he doesn't do this last bit with the vigor that he used to since he figures that his time here doesn't stretch the way it used to. But one never knows, and sometimes vigilance, leisurely pursued, is just good practice, something that, internalized, might keep a man from being steamrolled down the road.

"What time are they supposed to be here in the morning?" Albert asks.

"Ten," she says, entering the kitchen. "So please don't overdo it with the beer."

***

In the morning, Albert's clear and orderly and free of Saturday's occasionally unshakable vibration that suggests for no good reason, other than induced depression, looming gloominess.

The desire to present oneself as one would like to be presented, free of the afflictions and dilemmas that lap like tidewater at one's emotional well-being and make standing with self-confidence and empathy and love in front of others such an exposition risk that the traditional predictive strategies are shorn of mystery—that desire is ascendant not just in Albert's chest this morning, but in all his seats of feeling: stomach, head, nape hair, groin, esophagus, and the extremities whose tingling cries, "Reach out, you stunted fool, reach out for once in your emotionally impoverished life."

Albert listens to the radio and sips his coffee, and he tries to put his finger on approximately when he started having trouble with expressing the affection that he no doubt felt inside, that did not wane in his reality because a wallflower reticence was fond of whispering, "Let's not get too effusive or too joyful lest some danger in effusion or in joy, some danger we're not privy to, has somehow by sincere expression started on its course."

He dates this aspect of his character *before* the fracture of his just-post-adolescent skull, but he cannot be sure the fracture and exacerbation of the tendency now under his consideration didn't coincide and then cooperate to lead him to this juncture. Then, he thinks, there's Uncle Joe, his father's eldest brother, fond of alcohol, like Albert, childless, like Albert, not a great articulator of interior emotion, certain that possessing the capacity for speech did not mean he was obligated to the utterance, dead now like his father, cancer-sent to the Reunion Albert hopes that kinship and the afterlife are all about.

Albert stares into the fire and holds his coffee to his chest. He is about to go deep with Uncle Joe reflection when the radio transitions to another song and Glen Frey of The Eagles sings about the Tao of stress reduction.

Albert is about to softly sing along when Mary turns the volume down, diminishing his sense of song-based liberation, and he understands this means that they will talk.

Mary stands in the kitchen, at the counter, doing something, Albert guesses, with a sponge. Above her is an arch that spans the counter length and gives the ceiling beam support that wall studs once provided. The space thus opened, roughly ten by three, lets the living room and kitchen share the light, inviting occupants in each room to communicate across what used to be a sheetrock boundary. Mary cannot see her husband's head beneath the pine sill, but of course she knows it's there atop the rest of him, trying independently to ascertain, without resorting to their language right away, why she has fiddled with the tunes.

Albert looks out the bay window at the leafless weeping cherry tree and at the upper reaches of the pair of sycamores across the road and at the three perched crows in the broader one and at the other trees across the road and at the blue sky. He likes that when he sits here and looks out from this position, sunken in his armchair, legs propped on his ottoman, he cannot see the road, his hilly yard a buffer zone. He looks at the reflection in the television's black screen, and he sees the ceiling fan, the Bierstadt print, the couch, the coffee table, the fern, the ottoman, the chair, himself. Behind him he can see his wife's head and her shoulders and a fraction of her torso. She appears to sway a little, side to side, like someone skating.

"What are you doing?" Albert asks.

"Cleaning the counter."

"What's up with the tunes?"

"Remember, when they get here, before you ask them anything, to use their names when you address them. That helps them focus."

"I know."

"And remember to mention their special interests. That also helps them to focus."

"I had the same training you had."

"You're not good at small talk. You don't like to talk about what interests other people."

"Who does?"

"That's one reason why you don't have any friends."

"I have two," says Albert. "Two's enough."

Mary tears a sheet of paper from a notepad on the counter, and she dangles it beyond the pine sill, just above her husband's head.

"Here's the list with their interests," she says. She shakes it. "Take it."

Albert holds his left hand up and moves it to and fro until he grasps the paper. Though he's read it many times before, he reads it once more in the interest of review. Both Jake and Ryan columns list dinosaurs, computers, drawing, animals, and cards as interests. Ryan's column also includes stones, cars (especially headlights, tires, and rims), foam letters, and Mickey Mouse. Jake's column also includes doors, certain trees, and Dr. Seuss. Albert thinks about the specificity of human interests, and he understands the dinosaurs' appeal, the lure of the computer and the cards, the attraction of the drawn line, of a color manually applied, the gravitation toward an animal that runs or hops or crawls or slides or flies away or stays put, saying nothing, the inaudible suggestion of the ageless stone whose language is tactility. But what could be so interesting to a ten-year-old about a door? The lock? The knob? The being hinged? The division of the world between the inside and the out? Why would a ten-year-old prefer to spend time with a headlight or a tire or a rim rather than to sit behind the steering wheel, imagining control of the entire vehicle? Albert thinks about the times he tripped and how the unsung surfaces of the material world (his epidermis, raindrops, grass blades, car grilles, walls) became so wonderfully endowed with sentience and with life on those occasions, and he makes a mental note to not abandon this investigative avenue, to keep in mind what he has learned about perception from his recklessness.

"Speak clearly," Mary says, still at the counter, looking over a tips-for-dealing-with-autistic-children checklist. "Don't mumble like you normally do. If they can't understand you, it induces more anxiety."

"Really? Good to know."

"No sarcasm," Mary says. "No irony. No figures of speech. No stupid jokes. It just confuses them."

"I need my ambiguity."

"Don't be an asshole. Please."

"Why don't you just forget about this special-interests list and leave out the toys and drawing stuff we bought?"

"Because it has to be a low-arousal environment," says Mary, entering the living room and sitting on the couch.

"I don't know about you, but I'm in high arousal," Albert says, looking at his wife and jiggling his package.

"Please don't be an asshole today." She looks around the living room. "No music, no TV, no ceiling fan, no clutter, no offensive smells as far as I can tell. And come to think of it, we shouldn't have a fire going in the stove either."

"Too late now. What's the big deal? I installed the child guard."

"They might not like the smell. The sight of the flames might bother them."

"She said their triggers are auditory," Albert says.

"Mostly auditory." She looks around the room and into the

kitchen. "Otherwise, I think we're childproof. No sharp edges. Outlet protectors. No glass. No chemicals. Cabinet locks."

"With three adults, I don't think supervision is an issue."

"Don't forget to put Watts in the back room before they get here."

Albert nods. "We have an hour."

"Do you have your flashcards?"

"Right here," Albert says, picking up his deck from the table to his right.

"Don't forget to take a shower."

"Before I do, could I get a hummer in the interest of achieving low arousal?"

"Please don't be an asshole today."

"Language," Albert says.

About an hour later, Watts, who has been lying lengthwise on the couch in Albert's study, springs up at the sound of tires passing over driveway gravel and looks out the elevated window, vocalizing his displeasure with the sudden territorial encroachment.

Albert walks in the room and says, "No bark."

Watts listens, and the sublimation of his bark occurs inside his throat and out comes a sputtering, elongated growl which Watts then further muffles when his master kneels beside him on the couch and smooths his risen hackles and looks out the window with his boon companion and says, "Relax, Watts. No growl." And then it's just a silent man in a collared shirt and decent slacks beside his silent dog, observing from an elevated window over the garage a physically attractive social worker getting out of a sedan and opening the back door from which, after she apparently delivers some instructions or encouragement, two boys who shared a womb emerge. The empty-handed boy, Albert guesses, must be Jake, and Ryan must be he who holds the Dynavox before him like a lunch tray. It then occurs to Albert that if he is ever to present himself as fatherly he'll need a finer differentiation standard to identify his sons.

"What are you doing?" asks Mary from the kitchen. "Leave the dog alone. They're here."

"Be good," Albert says to Watts while closing the door. "I'll introduce you later."

Albert is not a fluid greeter or a person who erases introduction boundaries with a cheek kiss or a hug. He's stiff, reserved as was his father, as was his Uncle Joe, and is relieved that, in this situation, physical expression isn't requisite. In fact, according to his copy of his tips-for-dealing-with-autistic-children checklist, the conventional approach is to allow a wide berth, to remember unsolicited tactility can be an overload inducer and a meltdown trigger. He's relieved as well because another checklist point suggests that the adult should not bombard the child with the many questions the adult who is adopting hopes will narrow the intimidating gap in which so many unknowns hover it is hard to figure out which one to first demystify—which point, when broken down to its essentials, he interprets as "So take it easy." If the child tenses or withdraws, reduce communication. Limit words, limit body language. Just be.

I can do that, Albert thinks. He pauses in the hall and pats the pocket on the heart side of his shirt to reassure himself the checklist is in there and easily accessible in case the basic interaction tenets he has studied suddenly elude him in a pressure situation.

Mary slides the kitchen door open, steps out to the patio, and does not close the door behind her. The squirrels, goldfinches, titmice, sparrows, cardinals, chickadees, and house wrens scatter to the trees. The boys, whom Gina Dunn escorted to the concrete stair top, pause at the dispersion flutter. Gina crouches to the level of the boys and points to a suet pack on which a downy woodpecker slightly swings.

"Ryan," she says, "what kind of animal is that by the tree?"

Ryan looks in the direction she is pointing and then looks down at his Dynavox. He presses one box on the screen and then another.

A digitized voice replies, "Woodpecker."

"Right," she says. "Woodpecker. Great job, Ryan."

Ryan moves his shoulders slightly, but he does not otherwise reply.

"Jake," says Gina, turning her attention, "what letter does *woodpecker* begin with?"

Scrunching up his face so all his features gather round his nose, Jake looks up at the leafless sugar maple and says, "Mmmmmm. W."

"That's right, Jake. W. Great job."

Jake unscrunches.

Albert thinks but does not say to Mary, *You're letting all the heat out.* This may arise as a discussion topic when they're once again alone and high arousal's not the atmospheric problem that it could be now. He makes a mental note and joins her on the patio. In a gesture he considers selfless and symbolic of a welcoming that's unconditional, he also does not close the door behind him. He crouches next to Mary, and he wonders if the others sense his selflessness and grasp his symbolism. But, except for Mary, he supposes, how can they appreciate how much it bothers him to be extravagant with energy? *They can't,* he thinks and therefore reassures himself their inability is proof the gesture's altruistic.

When the boys come closer, Mary smiles more intensely, tries to look directly into Ryan's eyes, and says, "Hello, Ryan." She tries to look directly into Jake's without becoming a contortionist and says, "Hello, Jake." She puts her hand above her breast and says, "I'm Mary."

Then she puts her hand on Albert's nearest shoulder and says, "And this is Albert."

Jake looks at a goldfinch bobbing on the clothesline and, as if he wishes to be free of obligation to the awkwardness of introduction, says, "Hello."

"Hello," says Ryan's cheerily robotic proxy voice. "It's nice to meet you."

"It's nice to meet you, too," says Mary. "Ryan, Jake, would you guys like to come inside?"

Neither looks directly in her eyes.

Mary waits a couple of minutes to allow for processing. She remembers that the checklist says, in structuring one's questions, it is helpful to present some options to allow the child to experience some measure of control. So when she's confident that a response is not forthcoming and she doesn't notice any undue indications of anxiety, she says, "Or we could stay outside."

Jake, his gaze directed at the paving stones, says quietly, "Inside."

Then Ryan's proxy voice chimes in, "Inside."

"Good idea," says Mary, standing up in stiffened unison with Albert. "Let's go inside."

"Ryan, Jake," says Albert, "please follow me."

They do.

Then Gina Dunn, her eyebrows raised, seems pleasantly surprised and says to Mary in a register above a whisper, "So far, so good."

***

The living room is small, rectangular, cozy if the occupants and circumstance align, compressed if not. The couch is flush against the short wall opposite the wood stove and situated so that it prevents the front door, which is rarely used, from being opened more than a quarter of the way. During her initial home visit, Gina emphasized that prior to the children being placed here this arrangement must be altered so the door can open all the way. The exit must be clear in case of fire.

"Of course," said Mary. "We can move it back here," she said, indicating the wall the living room and kitchen share, "where it used to be."

Albert nodded as if he and Mary were the sort of couple that was used to speaking with a single voice.

Albert now stands beside the coffee table on the wool rug, and the two boys stand about three feet away as though he is invisible. A potted fern is on a stand before the door side of the picture window, and its fronds describe green arcs in all directions. Jake inspects the fern for several moments. Then he reaches out his hand and runs it along the fronds, beginning toward the center of the fern and, in no rush, proceeding out, and in the repetition Albert believes there is communication taking place that he is not quite privy to.

In terms of feng shui, Albert's happy with the fern's position and the positive reception it inspires, but he looks left toward the couch arm blocking conflagration egress, and he sees an obviation failure, an indictment of his parenting chops, a sign that his circumscribed imagination hasn't sufficiently envisioned the infinite potential tragedies, the four young smoke-filled lungs, for instance, overcome because his pre-parental feng-shui sensibility insisted with the mystical authority of the unvisited East that couch and wall and door were cosmically endorsed and confluent. Albert does not feel paternal. That prerogative has not been earned. He stands about three feet away from silent pre-adoptive boys and wonders if he must pass through some secret father-forging stages that will gradually impart to him the wisdom to instruct the boys on whether, in a situation like the present one, they should sit or stand, the wisdom to intuit whether a particular moment is a teachable one or should be left, like a harmonious shrub, alone. He looks at Jake's hand gliding like a breeze along the fern and looks at Ryan looking at the wool rug, and he thinks he understands a little what it must be like to know there is a thing expected of you and to not know what exactly that thing is or what it is you have to do to get across to the expectant the response that satisfies the various perspectives in the room, your own included. It suddenly occurs to Albert, in violation of the ancient code of hospitality, that there are other things he'd rather do, that there are habits he's spent years conforming to and is not comfortable abandoning summarily. For instance, on a normal anti-social Saturday he would be in his study working on his breakthrough poem at this hour and then reading, by eleven, several pages of a novel, which for months has been Vollmann's *Fathers and Crows*, and then, by one, venturing with Watts into the woods and then, by three, unwinding with a nap, which he believes slows down the effects of the clock biology keeps tightly wound. *It isn't fatherly,* he thinks as he attempts to jury-rig remorse, *to fret about your personal routine's disruption when you're meeting your prospective children for the first time. Feign interest if you have to. Focus.*

Mary had gone down the hall with Gina Dunn and now returns with items she had bought as inexpensive offerings, as evidence that these two people Jake and Ryan do not know have somehow tuned in to a few of their abiding interests and, on that account, might merit an abridgment of the distance that the boys perceive between themselves and many people, young and old, whom they have met before. Because the plan at first is to engage them sans enticement, Mary puts the items on the kitchen counter for the present, and she walks into the living room with Gina. As she does so, Mary narrows all that's ocular and aims at Albert the stink eye, but she's careful not to emanate too confrontational an air because the boys, although they do not look at her, may sense the possibility of high arousal and intuit in their bones that this environment is not for them. She unconstricts her gaze as soon as Albert registers her discontent.

"Did you offer the boys a seat?" asks Mary in a dulcet tone that's faux.

"Not yet," says Albert. "I wasn't sure if that might be a group decision."

Mary blinks a less than one-one-thousand blink and shakes her head once, quickly to the right and back to center, just enough for conveyance of exasperation or disgust. To the untrained eye it could have been a tic.

"Ryan, Jake," she says, trying to attract their gazes via timbre modulation, "would you like to have a seat on the couch?"

Ryan channels his attention from the wool rug to the Dynavox. His index finger presses once upon the screen and then again. His proxy voice says, "Yes, please."

"Excuse me," she says to Albert, whose presence is obstructive. He takes two steps back and sits down in his chair, but judges that his lower legs upon the ottoman would seem too casual a pose. He must keep both feet on the floor. He must lean forward.

"Ryan," Mary says, "please come this way." She makes a movement as if she intends to take him by the hand or guide him by the shoulder, but she checks herself because he holds the Dynavox with both hands and because she is reminded that a sudden touch might be too much.

Ryan walks around the coffee table and sits down on the door side of the couch. He looks down at the Dynavox upon his lap. His index finger presses once upon the screen. His proxy voice says, "Thank you."

"You are welcome, Ryan. You are so polite." She pauses. "Jake," says Mary, "would you like to sit beside your brother on the couch?"

Albert admires Jake's relentless interest in the fern and is reminded of the tininess and vastness of the world.

Mary looks at Gina, who says, "I'll sit over there," and points to the Queen Anne sort of chair beside the TV. She sits, a clipboard on her lap, and seems inclined to be as unobtrusive as a corporal being could, in such a living room, expect to be.

Because the basic plan, discussed over coffee during Gina's prior visit, is to start the bonding process via unforced interaction, insofar as possible, a period of rustling quietness ensues. Mary sits on the couch end opposite Ryan. Like a primatologist observing from a distance not deemed threatening, she eyes the boys and hopes to see some subtle signs suggesting that abridgment is acceptable. There may or may not be noblesse oblige apparent in her placid gaze. Albert continues with the earnest-seeming lean, but he is careful not to overdo the earnestness and not to hope that steady gazing will attract the longed-for contact. He has read some Temple Grandin and some studies in respected journals, and he's troubled by the lack of a consensus, by the experts' lack of resolution as to what to do about facilitating neuro-typical/autistic communication, by the multiplicity of quirks he has to be on guard for, by what remains in many quarters to which people go for answers still a mystery.

For instance, recently he read an online *Scientific American* article entitled "Eye Contact Triggers Threat Response in Autistic Children," which at first he thought enlightened him: "The results of a new study provide additional insight into why autistic children avoid eye contact: they perceive faces as an uncomfortable threat, even if they are familiar." Although the article gave no advice on how a neuro-typical person, which he was not sure he was because of doubts that lingered long after the re-knitting of his fractured skull, might mitigate the threat appearance, he at least considered what it offered good to know. And so he scrolled down to the bottom of the page to Comments, and he read the following:

"For me, as a person with Asperger's Syndrome, I find the study holds true in what they see on the MRI, but the motivations you have described here are wrong, at least for me.

"I don't like round things—convex, concave, or flat, and I DO NOT like images or models of eyes and feel physically sick when I look at them. Because people try to 'chase your face' to make eye contact, something completely unnecessary in a conversation, you usually have to pick a place on their foreheads to look at so they will stop trying to do whatever it is neuro-typical people do when they insist on making that kind of violating personal contact. It makes as much sense to me as if people needed to hold each other's privates to communicate."

When Albert first read this, he was struck by the commenter's specificity of revulsion. Who would ever have considered that convexity, concavity, or basic one-dimensional roundness could be so provocative? Who would have thought the image of an eye could make a person sick, could make a person so inflamed he felt it necessary to employ the caps lock in his comment to a *Scientific American* article?

Albert reread it and was struck by how articulate and comma conscious this autistic person was. Except for the shift to the second-person pronoun in the second sentence of the second paragraph, this person wielded language beautifully. The biting sense of humor at the end with that comparison made Albert aware of how requiring an ocular component to verbal communication could seem odd, invasive, overbearing, offensive, even sickening to a person of a slightly different neurological tribe. He was not sure how he'd feel if someone kept trying to cup his balls in casual conversation. Flustered? Roused? Appraised? On guard?

And so his reading on the subject took an anecdotal turn because he figured that, though science was a necessary mediator in negotiating the approach to certain kinds of understanding, it would be more practical to listen to those people who had written on what it was really like to be autistic. He discovered quickly that his anecdotal reading would reveal no unified theory of autism, no one-size-fits-all approach; but, in reading through the blog posts and the commentary posted on a galaxy of sites, he inched his way, word by word, along the great divide and found that simple statements free of jargon yielded insights, points of clarity he might apply to real life.

One blog Albert read repeatedly was subtitled "This is the story of a boy who could not talk, but learned to make his thoughts known by spelling on a letterboard and typing. This is his path from silence to communication." In one post the boy responded to a woman who inquired why her autistic nephew found it so hard to make eye contact. The boy wrote, "I am letting you know about eye contact. My eyes see very well. Most people seem to have a need to have to look long and hard to make sense of a picture. I can take in a whole picture at a glance. Each day I see too many petty details. I look away to not get overwhelmed by a lot of little bits of information. A seat on the side keeps me focused on your voice and not on visual distractions. I am assessing many sounds too. I have to erase some stimuli to access my answers to people's questions and meet their demands. That is why I don't make eye contact. I am always listening. I listen to a lot of voices. I so love when people talk to me and are not talking like I am not there. I am active because I am unable to feel my body well. People think I am being rude but I can't help it. I need to move to feel my body, but sitting down at least helps me not walk away from you. Please talk peacefully to your nephew. Let him know you understand. I am sad when people think I don't like them. I love people. Love, Philip."

The rustling quietness continues—Mary and Ryan seated opposite each other on the couch, Jake in contact with the fern still, Gina in the chair a slight diagonal across from Albert. Albert gets his wife's attention as he moves two fingers toward his eyes as if he means to poke them, indicating to her that she's trying, in his estimation, too hard with her eyes. She squints at him.

He leans forward still, his forearms resting just above his knees, his gaze now redirected on the ottoman.

"Jake, Ryan," Albert says in his flat voice, "I don't like to talk much either." He pauses for processing time. "But I communicate what I am able." He pauses for processing time. "I'm good with silence."

For a few minutes, Albert still looks downward at the floral-patterned ottoman, plays back what he just said. The parsing yields no irony, no snark, no double anything, no word to indicate the refuge of the wiseass. *Interesting,* Albert thinks. *Maybe this is fatherhood beginning.* But a person his age cannot extricate himself so easily from a tradition in which the sincere expression is detained and told to go forth in the world with gruffness or a strut, a sort of stiff-arm to inform the people who would like to hug him and exchange affection for affection that he may or may not be impervious and therefore has the upper hand because he has created in the other the retainer of uncertainty. How many times has Mary been offended when he's stiffened like a possum at her touch? How many times has she remarked to someone hugging him in greeting, "See how stiff he gets? It's like hugging a mannequin"? How many times has Albert said, "I can't help getting stiff. My dick has a mind of its own"? And how many times has Mary, or whomever, separated from him, saying with a head shake, "You're disgusting"? *His* involuntary stiffening or *his* reluctance to commune is one thing. Someone else's in response to *his* obtrusive presence, which in general he believes deserves at least a welcome, is another.

Though he mentioned earlier to Mary the advantage of the home field, he is not attempting to attain the upper hand here. The traditional defense is pointless. He is trying to communicate, but how do you communicate with someone else when basic wavelengths do not coincide? You can tell yourself a housefly sees the world through compound eyes, but that in no way makes you privy to its worldview. Albert experiences internal castigation, asks himself what's wrong with him, how could he be a father, truly, if he has it in him to compare these boys so cavalierly to a housefly.

Jake has shifted closer to his brother and has moved his right hand to the couch arm, where it vibrates like a sander set to low. Ryan seems to take no notice. Albert looks to Gina for a quick interpretation or some guidance, but she's writing something and is either not aware that Jake has moved or sees no reason for alarm.

Albert looks to Mary, who has arched her eyebrows and lifts her index finger like a searching inchworm from the couch arm and seems to point it at the flashcards on the coffee table. Albert is unclear as to what he is meant to do with this direction.

"Well," says Albert, "I am thirsty. I need an ice pop. Is anyone else here thirsty for an ice pop?"

He walks into the kitchen, slides the freezer drawer open, takes an ice pop from the box, and slides the drawer shut. The boys tense a little as the plastic wrapper crinkles, and they shyly look toward Albert standing in the kitchen. Albert looks across the living room and out the bay window at a cardinal, brighter than the ice pop, in the sprawling rhododendron. Meditative. Metronomic.

Jake says in a tone of pure instruction, "You're not supposed to eat an ice pop if you're thirsty."

"That's right, Jake," says Mary. "He's just being silly."

Jake looks down at the couch arm, and he almost smiles. Gina jots another observation in her notes.

Mary asks Jake, "What is he supposed to do if he's thirsty?"

Jake, still looking downward, leaning on the couch arm, says, "Get a drink."

"That's exactly right, Jake. Good answer."

Albert holds up his ice pop like an incandescent bulb whose filament has fizzled and conducts a serious inspection. "I believe you have a solid point there, Jake. If I'm eating an ice pop, I must not be thirsty. What must I be?"

No response. The guidelines say give options, but they also say allow the child sufficient time to formulate his own response. But temporal sufficiency is highly variable. The momentum of the breakthrough is at risk. Albert restructures.

"Jake, Ryan, want an ice pop?"

Jake nods, chin to chest, and Ryan's proxy voice says, "Yes."

Albert gets two more from the freezer, leaves the empty box upon the counter, and hands them to Mary, who unwraps each one and passes it along.

Albert resumes his kitchen post, continues his erosion of the ice pop, and again looks out the bay window at the sprawling rhododendron, where the cardinal is no more. He isn't sure exactly what, if anything, is being shared communication-wise at this time, but he guesses there's at least a gustatory, tactile commons they're partaking in, a sensory communing it would make no sense to try to verbalize. It's not exactly sitting side by side on the front stoop with his father, drinking silently their beers and interjecting random thoughts and watching cars pass by and birds pick bush berries in what seemed like summer's inexhaustible light. It's not exactly lying on his back beside his buddies in the year or so before their bond began to weaken, dilated pupils peering at the night sky, whose immensity and grandeur mushrooms made apparent to them were not meant to be demoted to the homely province of their word stores.

But this is something. This is an experience. It may just be water, strawberries, sugar, carob bean gum, natural flavors, guar gum, citric acid, color (beet juice extract, turmeric color), and ascorbic acid (vitamin C) connecting them right now, but this is the beginning. This is like the newborn reaching out and grasping the paternal finger for the first time. Maybe. It is hard for him to tell since even he is not accustomed to such gaze aversion. But he's pretty sure he feels some gustatory, tactile link that is embedded hereby in the three of them and will be felt in years to come as the formative contact. He imagines sitting in the woods with them eleven years from now, each sunk in his respective camp chair, each in charge of his respective beer, the silence and the spare words and the sense that it is too hard to articulate what binds them—so they sit and drink and sometimes utter platitudes when silence is too much and understand what it is like to love and be loved and not need words to pass that understanding down the line. But then he wonders as he's left with just a pop stick if autistic people are allowed a beer. He makes a mental note and then reminds himself to not get carried away.

"Does anybody want anything while I'm up?" asks Albert.

"Nothing for me, thanks," says Gina.

Mary says, "I'm good."

Jake and Ryan work their ways stickward.

Albert returns to the chair and ottoman, the heady unity vibration emanating from the ice-pop synchronicity becoming less and less apparent. He wonders if his father used to feel this way when Albert departed after two or three beers from the stoop in order to imbibe more with people he felt chemically attracted to or philosophically aligned with, if his father sat there trying to imagine how to offset drift and separation, how to get across what he would like to get across, and how to get whatever *that* was accurately interpreted, linguistically or otherwise.

Albert picks the favorite-animals flashcard deck up from the table to his right. He studies the polar bear and shifts it to the bottom of the deck, the chimpanzee and shifts it to the bottom of the deck, the Holstein Friesian cow and pauses, thinking that this color photograph of the black-and-white Holstein Friesian cow might offer common ground on which the three of them might somehow come to a consensus on a shared interest in milk or ice cream or the sacredness of cows in certain regions of Nepal and India, but then he shifts it to the bottom of the deck, deciding that you can't be too suggestive or insistent when it comes to special interests and the bonds that might be forged therefrom. Albert wouldn't, after all, if Jake and Ryan's wiring were more mainstream and a free and easy conversation could just flow, bring up a random animal depicted on a card and say with great cheer, "Let's talk about the ring-tailed lemur for a while." So why believe that these two would be up for that? His wife was right. Albert is not and never has been great at small talk. Why the hell would he be good at this?

He flips the cards to pass the silent time and pauses when he comes to the dog card on which a field of goldenrod extends and blurs to the cornflower-blue horizon. Anchoring the foreground is a golden retriever in the prime of life, its pink tongue lolling to the left of its lower canine like a sign of recent vigorous activity, affirmative of life, the corners of its mouth turned up, the corners of its soft eyes angled in expressions of good humor, jollity, the features of a tranquil and expressive soul, a true companion in whom there is no hint of the ancient marginal angst or wildness, no sense that when it looks at you there is misunderstanding or a wish that you were someone else.

If this is someone's only image of a dog, then Charlie Watts, an Italian greyhound and Chihuahua mix, will be an existential letdown. Watts is over twelve in human years. His head will sometimes start to bobble nod like Katherine Hepburn's toward the end, and he will nod off while he's sitting upright and forget, when he comes to, that he was begging. His eyes have gotten overcast, and he prefers, for reasons no one has divined, to sometimes not be spoken to or touched. At such times, when he is addressed, he will, if seated on the Queen Anne sort of chair, look out the window or at the chairback, making you invisible until you cease your violations. And at such times, when he will not consent to physical communion, he will dodge affection and depart the room, abandoning your loving hand to the air without an explanation. But he's not by nature committed to the shun. Watts will smile, if not as photogenically as the retriever. Watts will be convivial and loving; but he's no retriever, no inspiring distillation of the canine essence, and no kennel club will recognize his kind and dignify how far it's journeyed from the legendary darkness of the lupine. Still, Watts is a dog. That fact, despite the card, will not escape these boys.

Albert holds the card up so that Mary sees the beautiful retriever, and he cranes his neck and tilts his head once toward the back room where, in his opinion, Watts has been behaving admirably—no scratching at the door, no whining—and has therefore earned the right to be admitted to the wider world. Mary shakes her head and holds her hand out, beckoning him to pass the card along. He typically would not so easily accede to a request like this because between them, prior to exchanges, a dynamic marked by pointless confrontation must play out; but there are strangers present, people to whom he is not bound by legality or blood, and so appearances must be kept up. What must it be like to accord your usual behavior to the standard of appearances even when you know you are not being watched? What if your first reaction to the spousal request, ridiculous or otherwise, were "Yes, dear," cutting out the process whereby the allotment of disharmony was arbitrated, offering no pushback, no power play, no stiff resistance? Would capitulation eat you up inside, or would it soothe the organs that heretofore have clenched during those negotiations, freeing you to just be—like a golden retriever in the prime of its short life, no gripes, no grudges, no regrets or sad fixations on the future or the past, no undertow of angst or wildness, just a flow of gratitude at what life it's been granted? *Maybe,* Albert thinks, getting up, *this is what having children is about, sublimation and a built-in audience to keep your best self on its unballetic toes, to glean from you the secrets of the happy life.* Like Mr. Blonde from *Reservoir Dogs*, Albert takes three stutter steps toward Mary, hands her the retriever card, and takes three stutter steps in reverse to show that her request, in fact, accords with his desire.

Mary holds the card up so that Jake and Ryan, if they look in her direction, could see the sociable retriever. She says, "Can anyone tell me what animal is pictured on this card?"

Jake, who has been gently raking his denuded popsicle stick along the couch arm, looks askance and then returns to raking like a farmer who has witnessed what he needs to of the world. "That's not a hard question," he says. "It's a dog."

Mary smiles and says, "That's right, Jake. It is a dog. I thought that might be too easy for you. I was just testing. What about you, Ryan? Can you tell me what letter *dog* begins with?"

"That's not a hard question either," Jake says, raking still.

Ryan's proxy voice says, "D."

"That's right," Mary says. "Good job, Ryan."

Without looking up, Jake says, "The paint is uneven where the walls and ceiling come together."

Albert says, "That is an excellent observation, Jake."

"Well," says Mary, "sometimes I have trouble staying within the lines. I get distracted. Plus, I'm not very tall. I tried."

"I thought the man is supposed to paint," says Jake.

"That is an excellent observation, Jake," says Mary.

"I get distracted, too," says Jake.

Mary says, "We all do. Life would be pretty boring without distractions, wouldn't it? Speaking of distractions, would you like to meet our dog?"

Jake and Ryan look directly at her, their four eyes widening, preparing to accommodate the scope of wonder and the wavelength alteration that attend an unexpected animal introduction into human company.

Ryan's proxy voice says, "That's an excellent idea."

Jake asks, "What's his name, and is he friendly?"

Albert walks down the hall to get the dog.

Mary says, "His name is Charlie Watts, but usually we just call him Watts. And, yes, he's very friendly. I know he'd like to meet you two. If he gets too friendly, too close, just say, 'No, Watts,' and gently push him away."

Jake carefully lays his spent popsicle stick on Ryan's on the coffee table and makes sure the edges are aligned and flush.

"Why does Watts get close?" asks Jake.

"Dogs depend on their sense of smell a lot more than we do. They like to smell your sneakers and your pants, whatever they can, to figure out who you are and where you've been. Their noses are very sensitive. So, if Watts's nose gets too close and you're not comfortable, just say, 'No, Watts,' in a nice tone and gently push him away. That will tell him where your personal space is. He'll understand. Sometimes he'll sit on that chair over there," she says, pointing to the Queen Anne sort of chair where Gina sits. "When Watts does that, he's telling you where *his* personal space is."

The rhythmic tap of Watts's nails upon the hardwood floor grows louder. In he trots, exuberant and spry, revived by liberation, like a being in whom malice or resentment could not possibly reside. He bristles with the joy of meeting, with the revelation of encounter. His entire body says hello, and loose hairs fly from him as if containment and appearance are the provenance of dour souls, the sorts who do not want themselves to be so plainly known. He takes the path of least resistance, past the coffee table, over the wool rug, past the ottoman, to Gina Dunn, whom he has met before but whom he greets as though the interval of absence has necessitated all the fuss of a reunion. So he sniffs and wags and sheds, and Gina says, "Good boy," and pats him, as a prelude to departure, on his head.

Jake has squeezed in next to Ryan on the couch, their feet up off the floor, their arms and torsos lightly tensed as though a ball will soon be sailing their way. The boys, conjoined in curiosity, observe this interaction closely, studying Watts, who moves so naturally, unlike the rest of them, who wiggles unreservedly and is not stinted or discouraged when effusion, when unmitigated feeling, when kinesis as expression of the blissful inner canine state is not returned proportionally.

Jake says, "If he's too close, say, 'No, Watts,' in a nice tone and gently push him away."

But what he seems to mean is send that sensational dog this way because your stiffness and tepidity are insufficient greeting modes in this particular circumstance, are illustrative of a failure to appreciate without reserve what happiness has come before you.

Albert clinks the cookie jar when he puts back the top. He hands two dog biscuits in the shape of little bones to Mary, who then hands one each to Ryan and to Jake.

"That's Watts's favorite snack," says Albert.

Watts, having heard the jar clink, has developed interest in these boys now and approaches, black nose angled high. Jake and Ryan hold their biscuits high, above their heads, the natural human inclination to protect the foodstuffs.

"Don't hold them so high," says Albert. "Watts will think you want him to jump." He steps back in the kitchen and takes another biscuit from the jar. "Hold them this way," he says, concealing the biscuit in his palm and holding it mid-thigh. "Come here, Watts. Sit. Shake. Good boy," he says, revealing the biscuit to Watts, who gently takes it from his hand and then returns to the far side of the coffee table to investigate the latest example of biscuit concealment.

Albert's a devout believer in the palliative potential of extending, literally or figuratively, the human hand to feed an animal, to draw what's wild or marginally wild or not, at least, conventionally articulate toward one who is involuntarily descended from a lot of elbows and a lot of boots, a lot of wood and clearing, as a form of saying, "Look here, I won't kill or run you off or be the sort of dick you have a lot of reasons to believe I am." With dogs, the trust flows easily, the product of habituation and unspoken symbiosis recognition. When Albert rises in the morning, he and Watts say nothing, but they are as understanding of the other and aligned as any two cohabitants who share a language and make small talk over coffee prior to the sunrise. Stripped of pretense, stripped of ambiguity regarding what's to be exchanged or what's to be perceived, stripped of the necessity that they acknowledge there must be a future, some point that has not materialized but toward which they should aim, the current matutinal peace be damned, communication is a simple matter of just being present and available to basic pleasantry in which their gestures of affection aren't lesser currencies because they're spare. So the extension of a biscuit is enough, the tactile wee-hour reacquaintance is enough, the letting be some mystery between them is enough.

Standing in a posture of expectancy beside his seated wife and watching Jake communicate with Watts, who sits when Jake says sit and offers up his mottled paw when Jake says shake and stares at Jake so that they both feel something they would not feel otherwise if they confined exchange to their respective species, Albert's nudged to reassess the recently concluded popsicle epiphany as more or less a minor pleasantry that flowered from mundanity. Jake does not smile when the biscuit passes from his hand to Watts, but Jake glows with the pride of the provider, and he sits back, eyes glued to the wordless, masticating wonder that is Watts, whose consumption vigor is itself a gratitude expression that is universal and requires no translation. Albert imagines all the other instillation opportunities, the vast expanse of Master chances to pass on the values he espouses to the Grasshoppers, who will carry them some distance in the world, alongside Albert at first and then in front of him, and they will someday bear those values in memoriam and pass them on to people smaller than themselves as though, in taking care of the tradition of the delicate succession, they exert what force is granted them upon the always looming end.

Albert grooves to what he tells himself must be the inner, soothing rhythm of tai chi, the contentment of the body moving with apparent smoothness through the world as though the frictional were just a myth erected long ago because a child struggled to appreciate the flow.

"You have a friend for life now, Jake," says Mary.

Albert continues his recruitment. "*You* try, Ryan. Watts seems interested in you. He wants another friend for life."

Ryan, hiding still the coveted biscuit in his left hand pressed against his chest, has been waiting for this moment with a coiled focus. His finger taps the screen. The proxy voice says, "Sit." Watts betrays no recognition of the digitized command. His finger taps the screen again. The voice again says, "Sit." No recognition, no exchange. Ryan studies critically the Dynavox as if to troubleshoot the flaw. His finger taps the screen once more. The voice once more says, "Sit." Communication breakdown.

Albert kneels beside the coffee table, and a part of him feels vindicated by this limitation of technology. He says, "Ryan, Watts can't understand that you can speak through a computer. So he doesn't understand that you're the one who's telling him to sit. He doesn't have experience communicating that way. But you can still be friends with Watts. You don't need words. Hold on." Albert gets up, steps into the kitchen, and retrieves another biscuit. "Watts can respond to signals. Watch." He hides the biscuit in his left hand and holds the hand out chest high. Watts comes over to investigate the hand extension. With his right hand's imperial finger, Albert points to the floor. Watts sits. Albert kneels and holds his right hand out. Watts shakes. Albert confers the biscuit, pats him on the head, and says to Ryan, "See? You don't need words with Watts."

There is a moment when the elders present think independently that Ryan is interpreting this Plan B as a denigration of his Dynavox and all that it has done for him, but then he slides it on the couch between himself and Mary, and the sudden separation doesn't seem to be a prelude to anxiety. He stands and juts his left arm out with closed fist, drawing Watts toward him.

Ryan sidesteps to his left, arm still extended, so that he eludes the coffee table and removes it as a barrier between himself and Watts. He points the imperial finger of his free hand toward the floor, and Watts sits. He bends the elbow of his biscuit-holding arm and kneels as if to say that his apparent bossiness should not be held against him and is not what he's about. He holds his free hand out. Watts shakes. He opens up his left hand and extends the biscuit. Watts accepts his generosity and plucks the biscuit from his palm, and Ryan's lips relax. The flatline bends a little, ripples from an undercurrent that is joy. Ryan puts his arm around Watts when Watts is finished with the biscuit. Watts accepts this burst of close affection, this acceleration of familiarity, to a point, and then he wiggles out and puts a little space between them. Maybe it's too early. Maybe it's too much. But Ryan isn't crushed or otherwise deterred and seems to understand that Watts is not averse to hugs on principle and is negotiating boundaries whose redrawing will require the elapsing of some acclimation time.

Ryan kneels still, a forearm resting on the coffee table. Watts sits on the wool rug at a distance. There are adjustments to be made. That much is certain. What is going on between them is transpiring with the eyes. And then the adaptation spirit suddenly asserts itself in Ryan, who picks up the topmost popsicle stick that heretofore had lain upon the bottommost that heretofore had lain along the coffee table's edge and tosses it toward Watts in one of those time-is-slowing-down anomalies that we have all experienced but find so difficult to actually believe. Following the high arc, Watts emerges from his element like a dolphin or a brook trout and reclaims that piece of woodwork from the air, and when he comes back down to earth he runs around and around the cramped room, slipping, sliding, showing everybody, as though some elusive pinnacle of being has been reached. And everyone, according to their various capacities, is smiling as though what has been proposed, in common and inside their private heads, these past few months might work.

As Mary, Albert, and Gina, in their separate attitudes of observation, watch the boys, who practically levitate with joy, the application of arousal modulation, in this living room right now and with this dog as the arouser, seems to them shortsighted, an example of the forest-for-the-trees mentality. The grown-ups share a round of raised eyebrows. In the back of their minds, of course, the spotty scientific literature's determination on arousal levels looms, and in the back of their minds, of course, there is the anecdotal evidence, related to their inner ears in earnest and unclinical tones. These resident adults are willing, though, to let Watts run wild and are willing to let Jake and Ryan process Watts's concentrated energy because, if eyebrow elevation is any indication, they have come to a consensus, tenuous perhaps and not submitted to the scrutiny of peer review, that high arousal can be therapeutic in the proper setting and the right conditions and because they know the old dog cannot keep this Cassady impression up much longer.

Watts winds down eventually. The moratorium that his kinetic burst imposed on certain forms of recognition and the social business of acknowledging with words the presence of the others in the room is lifted. Watts hangs his tongue and sits down on the wool rug until his front paws shimmy him the whole length to the floor, where he lies parallel to the coffee table, dignified, an unimposing, heavy-breathing little sphinx whose gaze is fixed on something no one else discerns outside the bay window.

"Well, that was fun, huh guys?" says Mary to the boys. "Watts is so excited to see you guys."

"He likes us," Jake says with the evenness of someone who's explaining to an ignoramus in the simplest terms a basic element of natural law.

"He does," says Mary. "He warmed right up to you guys."

Albert goes back to his chair, decides against ottoman employment, and wonders how things would have gone if, years ago, they paid a thousand dollars for a golden retriever and the pedigree instead of paying several hundred to the Sato-Project people, who found Watts in Puerto Rico on Dead Dog Beach and shipped him with the others via airplane to Connecticut. Is there something in the hearts of the abandoned that can recognize in fellow travelers the hi-sign of abandonment, regardless of how long ago the tether snapped, regardless of the subsequent admission to a circle of relations? Is there instant camaraderie, affinity, commiseration as exists between two veterans, for instance, who have never met before, the usual niceties of introduction vaporized by mutual recognition of their similar experiences—even if the one has somehow had his life put back together more completely (his emotional needs addressed to a stability-encouraging degree, his ontological interrogations, the confounded *Why me?* of it all, addressed in part by some authority he cannot put his finger on) than the life the other guy must day by day contend with? Albert remembers scrolling through the rescue websites, searching through the earnest profiles of pit bulls, old dogs with cloudy eyes, bait dogs, mongrels—all of them in need of saving—but he never saw a golden retriever featured, waiting to be driven home by someone who experienced a visceral connection on the basis of a photo, waiting to be rescued on the basis of a few words (euphemism, understatement), words intended to express in the most positive light, without resorting to the lie, that this dog is more than the depressing sum of past abuses and abandonment. How can a kid like Jake or Ryan, who's been featured on a website in a last-resort appeal to someone out there who might have a glimmer of parental interest that's not blood-dependent—how can that kid formulate a wavelength synchronicity with someone, even someone of the same age, same sex, same approximate geographical coordinates, with someone who has no anxiety about whose care he will come under, no uncertainty about where home is, no unanswered questions as to why he was relinquished by the people who were obligated to respect the blood connection, why two strangers would desire him when his experience is pretty clear that he is not desirable?

As Albert observes the unwound dog, the unwound boys, the slow progression toward familiarity and hominess and wanting to be here, it suddenly occurs to him the unnamed couple who paid fifty-thousand dollars to the blond, blue-eyed, statuesque, and Jewish Yalie for her ova would not want these boys, whose lineage continuation down the road, in the opinion of some people, might create more problems for the commons than the promise of the new lives would be worth. It isn't lost on Albert that he himself would not have thought about adopting them if Mary hadn't sold him first on the utility of stipend money. He considers the progressive and persuasive nature of desire, how, when one day you discover you desire to protect a being no one else desires to provide protection for, you feel all savior-like and pretty good about yourself and choose to not recall the years you didn't give two shits about whom Fate had flicked around, those souls whose flicking landed them in foster care, on Puerto Rican beaches, in or on the countless elsewheres. Albert tells himself he'd take these two without the stipulated money, but he keeps the purity of his intention to himself and briefly wishes for a catastrophic budget shortfall so that he can tell the heartbroke folks at DCF he will adopt these two boys with the stipend or without.

Albert does what many saviors do. He sits back like the Memorex fellow from the old commercials and is practically blown away by manifestations of his savior capabilities. He stares at Watts at sphinx peace on the wool rug, free to go outside or lick or doze and squirrel-dream because of the security provided via human love, and he imagines that, without his loving intervention years ago, Watts probably would not have made it past the first years of the century, would probably be bleached bones without integrity or infinitesimal parts per billion of the Caribbean Sea. Though Watts at present looks away from Albert, when he's gazing into Albert's eyes, where he is wont to gaze, Albert senses the awareness of what might have been and feels from Watts a gratitude vibration, which may be, he sometimes thinks, a biochemical reaction, a serotonin jolt perhaps that floods their systems with the blissful, symbiotic vibes. He wonders what he has to do to replicate that gaze in Jake and Ryan.

"What should we do," asks Mary, "while Watts takes a rest?"

The boys don't answer. Watts's ears stiffen upward when he hears his name. Jake notices the ear reaction. As if experimenting with a thing whose power has been rumored, Jake says softly, in a tone without affection or emotion, "Watts." Watts pricks his ears up once again and turns his head, and Jake betrays no facial satisfaction with his confirmation of the rumored force.

"Jake, honey," Mary says, "let's give Watts a chance to rest. In the meantime, we can play a game." She takes a new set of flashcards from the right-side coffee-table drawer. "I've heard," she says, flipping through the deck, "about some of your interests and was wondering if what I heard was true." She pulls out two flashcards. "Since I heard that you like dinosaurs and drawing, I thought we'd play a dinosaurs and drawing game. Jake, this card is for you," she says and slides the stegosaurus flashcard to the left side of the table. "Ryan, this card is for you," she says and slides the brontosaurus flashcard to the center.

Jake picks up both cards and hands the brontosaurus one to Ryan.

"Okay, good," says Mary. "Bear with me." She takes two sketch pads and two markers from the drawer and opens each pad to a blank page. "Okay, in this game we need a dot drawer and a line drawer. To begin, if no one minds, I'll be the dot drawer and you guys can be the line drawers."

No objections are in evidence.

So on the first pad she imprints a lot of green dots, enumerating them as she goes. "One. Two. Three . . ." She does the same thing on the second pad except that there the dot configuration is a figurative departure from the one she imprinted on the first. She slides each pad before the boys and hands them each an uncapped marker. "Okay, as line drawers you guys connect the dots and make the picture. You're the artists. Remember what you saw on your flashcards."

They hold their markers for a while, rolling them between their thumbs and fingers, possibly reluctant to commit to an artistic vision that has been too easily prescribed—no suffering, no self-examination, no perception wrestling. Ryan ventures first and slides his buttocks tableward. He works from right to left and pauses several times as if considering directional fulfillment. Jake takes an interest in his work but does not interfere. When Ryan finishes, he contemplates the now-delineated brontosaurus, does not cross-reference it with the flashcard brontosaurus, and accepts the praise from Mary as he would a minor perturbation of the air.

"You can color him if you want," says Mary. "Maybe give him

an eye. Some texture."

While Ryan thinks about his coloration options, Jake begins his dot connection. He takes a shortcut past a couple of the backbone spikes and doubles back to hit the unconnected dots, but it is evident when he is done that he has limned a stegosaurus.

Mary says, "Wow, you guys have done a beautiful job." After a tranquil coloring interlude, she says, "I didn't know you guys were such great artists. These are better than the flashcard pictures. If you don't mind, I'd like to put these on display." In the absence of objection, she removes each drawing from its pad and tapes it to the narrow wall between the arch and doorway leading to the kitchen. She takes a step back for curatorial perspective and admires each one in its affirmation-rich location.

The general feeling is the game should be continued, with perhaps a variation here and there to freshen things.

"We can play the game the way we played it," Mary says. "Or one of you can draw the dots, and I and the other can draw the lines. We can take turns."

"I can draw the dots," says Jake, who turns out to be squarely camped among the representationalists.

Things flow pleasantly for a while thus, and Albert, observing from his short remove the slow development of interpersonal familiarity and embryonic trust, the gradual evaporation of the foreignness of place and personality, believes the satisfaction of the ova buyers, even if the zygote was, according to the plan, transformed into a blond and statuesque and sexy Zionist egghead, must be limited because their sacrifices weren't much beyond the usual ones attending the transactional, were not the ones that Albert and Mary made and will continue making: the paperwork, the training, the scrutinizing visits to the home, the bureaucratic slow roll of adoption, which outlasts gestation, the perception rearrangement, trying to perceive and think and feel the way autistic and untethered ten-year-old boys might, the internal fretting over the duration of dependence (What do we do with two autistic boys when they turn eighteen?), the imagining and visualizing bonding opportunities that might, if they are lucky or watched over by a rectifying force or chemically aligned, believably approximate the bloodline-quality adhesion. Albert thinks about the ova buyers and their expectations for their child, and he wonders, *What if their child aforethought turns out to be a redhead or a little person or a little slow or Buddhist-minded? To whom could they complain? Yahweh for his failure to direct a little bit of his omnipotence their way? The Yalie for her failure to recall the whispered family lore about the havoc, shame, or mild discomfiture once visited upon a distant generation in a close-knit Eastern-European village by a sleeper cell of a recessive gene? The doctor whose extraction or insertion of the ova might have been substandard due to his preoccupation with a hitch he recently developed in his golf swing or due to her dissatisfaction with the Affordable Care Act's financial impact on her practice?*

Albert decides he will not impose acceptable-child preferences upon these boys. He won't insist that they emote or focus more conventionally or try the clarinet or soccer. Maybe the difference between Albert and the ova buyers is that he does not envision Jake and Ryan bearing his genetic material onward in the world the way the ova buyers' child will bear half of theirs. Perhaps, as such, the ego doesn't enter into it as much for Albert, who made his peace with his truncation of his branch of the family tree after artificial procreation didn't work for him and Mary. Still, he thinks, he would prefer it if they took a liking to the woods, would like it if they leaned back with him, looking up through the canopy toward treetops, searching out a porcupine or hermit thrush or just admiring the intricacies of bark or needles or the hydrological complexity of uptake, feeling more integral and human there than they can manage feeling elsewhere. If not, what then?

Temple Grandin said she recognizes, based on reading their accounts, that neuro-typical people often feel a sense of peace and reverence when they're in the presence of the woods or waterways or mountains but that she does not feel what they feel, does not experience their endorphin rush, their flood of well-being. What if Jake and Ryan couldn't care less about the woods? Worse, what if they perceive his eighteen acres as antagonistic, inhospitable, emitting bad vibes with its shadows, dampness, and mosquitoes, an environment of high arousal? Most of the literature, though, suggests that when autistic children spend significant time outdoors they experience anxiety and stress reductions and cognitive-functioning improvements.

Albert glances at the popsicle sticks, and he recalls the story of the four-year-old nonverbal boy who threw things or hit in order to communicate. After spending an hour a day for several months in his program's outdoor classroom, one day he walked over to a woodpile and removed three sticks, which he placed in a wheelbarrow and wheeled to the pavement. He removed the three sticks one by one and laid them on the ground, forming the letter A. He made three more trips to the woodpile, taking first two sticks, then four, then two, making an L, then an E, and then an X on the ground. A verbal declaration. His teachers were stunned. That is the anecdote that Albert returns to when he wonders if a move to Maine is fair to these two. There is even a movement afoot called Free-Range Kids. Livestock and poultry associations aside, Albert likes to think that his will be the freest.

"Anyone want to take Watts outside?" asks Albert.

Watts, whose existential preference always lies outside, springs up. Mary glares at Albert as if to say that now is not the time to alter the arousal level.

"We're in the middle of our game," she says, returning to her sketchbook page on which the dots she has thus far connected seem to be directing her toward the delineation of an alligator. Ryan, likewise, is engaged in his koala-bear delineation. Albert looks at Jake, who looks with managerial detachment at the figure that's materializing dot by dot on Ryan's page.

"Okay," says Albert, opening the door for Watts, who bounds out as if entering a realm from which he's been restricted for too long. The squirrels free-fall from the feeders, and their nails grate on the tree bark as they scramble up and out of reach and twitch with indignation.

There is no leaf left on the trees. Low-intensity smoke wafts from the chimney, evidence of the choked-back stove. Because the boys had no reaction to the suffocating fire in the box, he figures there would be no harm in stoking it and letting it breathe when he goes in.

If Albert smoked, he would smoke now. He looks toward the dwindled pile beside the shed and makes a mental note to put a bag of corn out for the deer this afternoon. It then occurs to him that a nice high-alcohol stout would hit the spot after that. And maybe a little music to accompany his sipping.

Albert sings the first few lines of a Drive-By Truckers' song about a father and a son who fish and sort of genuflect beside a dam that they seem grateful was constructed by the TVA. "All right, Watts, let's head in." He slides the door open and waits. "Watts, let's go." He looks around and doesn't see him. He claps his hands. Watts comes from the side of the house. They enter. Albert slides the door shut.

As Albert heads toward the living room, he hears the thermostat click. The boiler in the basement rumbles. Water gurgles through the baseboard pipes.

Shit, he thinks, *I should have stoked the stove before I went out.*

The water gurgles, pressurized, a closed system. The pipe comes up through the floor on the far side of the living room and runs underneath the bay window toward the left arm of the couch before going down through the floor again. Perhaps because the gurgling's source is hidden or insistent or in concert with the unseen basement rumbling, Ryan drops his tranquil marker on his sketchpad, claps his hands over his ears, and makes a steady noise that is half hum, half growl. Jake does likewise, and the stereophonic half hum, half growl achieves possession-like intensity.

"What happened?" Mary asks. "What's wrong?"

Gina takes a pink sheet from her clipboard and holds it so that Mary and Albert can see. They recognize it as the Sensory Overload troubleshooting sheet, and they separately try to recall the basics: "Try to determine the trigger and remove if possible. Do not treat the reaction as a behavior. Allow the child to come out of it on his own. Do not try to talk the child through it."

Albert lowers the thermostat. The boiler shuts off. The gurgling subsides. Watts approaches the boys, who still have their hands covering their ears, who still half hum, half growl. The six of them ride out the aftershock of high arousal, waiting for their nervous systems to confirm that all is fine.

Chapter Thirteen

The process of divestiture begins in earnest on the first of January. For the first time in their stellar credit history, they do not slip a light-blue check into a windowed envelope and lick the oddly pleasant strip of glue and raise the red flag on their mailbox as a signal to the passersby of their devotional remission of their mortgage payment, yet another small step toward the promised day when they would look back with accomplishment at how they incrementally got out from under principal, interest, PMI, and whittled down the amortization schedule to the beautiful Arabic numeral zero. As with the termination of any long-term relationship, they have their second thoughts about the separation, they experience the possibly coincidental bowel upset of remorse, and they, because the sanctity of honoring one's debts, one's signature, was dutifully instilled in them when they were children, are conflicted by the specter of betrayal, by their sudden occupation of the existential no man's land of being in arrears. They are, however, in possession of $1,835.54 they otherwise would have remitted to a person they have never met in Sioux Falls, South Dakota, a sum that would have trickled up to the obscenely wealthy CEO, and Albert reminds his wife that, whereas in 1965 the average CEO made just over twenty times the salary of the average worker, the average CEO now makes 354 times as much. That fact, coupled with the windfall default money, soothes their consciences and regulates their bowels so that they're not wracked by physical and psychological reminders that they have crossed a line past which their word is immaterial, past which they will be known as credit risks.

Defaulting is a huge risk, one that Albert and Mary have submitted to exhaustive kitchen-table scrutiny. Early in the submission process, Mary floated the idea that maybe they should look into the possibility of selling the house to see what they could get for it and just in case their severance from society did not pan out and they might need to use their credit scores to help secure a proper shelter. Albert objected on the premise that the build-up to a house sale would add another complication to a plan that was unwieldy as it was, and he objected on the premise that he wanted to chalk up one small victory against a mortgage company; but he agreed to have a realtor conduct a market analysis anyway because it wouldn't cost them anything but time.

"You have a nice big yard," the realtor said. "A little hilly, but nice. A lot of mature trees. The house is set back from the road. It seems to be in good shape. The problem is you bought it near the height of the market. You'd be lucky to get what you owe on it, but I can run the numbers and see what comes up. We could put it on the market and see what kind of interest it generates."

The other risk, more intimate and vital, is, if the Connecticut Department of Children and Families does another financial background check and sees default on their report, the last few steps toward finalizing the adoption will be scrubbed and Jake and Ryan will be softly told they must remain in limbo for a while longer, for a time to be determined. But there have been articles in the paper on the fiscal woes the state is suffering, and one piece in particular said, because of budgetary shortfalls, agencies, including DCF, are short-staffed and the situation is a slow-motion tragedy for those who depend most dearly on state government. Albert and Mary have adopted optimism and agree it is unlikely DCF will double back and check their credit once again, although they asked themselves one night across the kitchen table in dim light why would they take the risk. Could something in the composition of their ids have driven them to take unnecessary risks and sabotage the process seemingly without volition, thereby freeing them of serious parental obligations while allowing them some plausible measure of deniability to help them get to sleep at night?

"You do want to continue with the adoption, don't you?" Mary asked.

"Yeah," said Albert. "By the time the default even shows up on our record, the adoption will probably be finalized. I don't believe we're jeopardizing anything. I think we're good."

That night they played a long, untimed, silent game of Scrabble.

When Albert gets home from work on the Friday after Christmas break, he opens a California barley wine he has been aging for a year. He takes his credit card from his wallet and dials the 24-Hour Customer Service number listed on the back. A feminine computer voice welcomes him to the company. There is a flurry of Spanish before the voice resumes in English.

"Please say or enter your account number." Albert enters. "Thank you. Please say or enter the last four digits of your Social-Security number." Albert enters. "Thank you. In a few words, please tell me what you're calling about. You may say something like 'I want to pay my bill' or . . ."

"I want to cancel my credit card," says Albert.

"I'm sorry. I didn't understand your response. You may say..."

"I. Want. To. Cancel. My. Credit. Card."

"I'm sorry. I didn't understand your response. Please hold for the next available representative."

Albert puts the phone on speaker and lays it on the table to his right. He listens to promotional tie-ins followed by soft rock followed by the feminine computer voice assuring him, "The next available representative will be with you shortly."

More out of an innate belief in self-expression than out of any sense that someone is listening or that the call is actually being recorded, Albert says, "Fuck Bank of America."

Albert holds his tulip glass up to the light streaming in from the bay window.

"Tawny," he says and then realizes he is not exactly certain of the definition. He sips the beer and lets it lie upon his tongue a moment. He's no swisher. "Oh, yeah," he says as if receiving a massage. He puts the glass down beside the phone on the table and picks up the *Webster's New World College Dictionary*, autographed by Mario Van Peebles, which he keeps on the floor to the left of his chair.

He reads to himself, "[[ME *tauny* < OFr *tanné*, pp. of *tanner*, to TAN[1]]] brownish-yellow; tan **–n.** tawny color **–SYN.** DUSKY – **taw′·ni·ness n.**" He leaves the dictionary on his lap, holds up his beer to the light once more, and decides that *tawny* is not the word he was looking for. Why did it come to him?

"The next available representative will be with you shortly."

The mystery of etymology engulfs him as he sips. He pays the Toto song about the rains down in Africa no mind. He doesn't understand why in his free time he does not investigate word origins deliberately instead of waiting for these moments in abeyance when investigation simply helps to pass the time. He feels he should allot to etymological investigation a capacious time slot of its own, invest it with the dignity of a pursuit or avocation in which he is free to delve and thereby deepen his existence as a human. He flips backward to the region of the C. **Coriolis force/cornfed**, **cornfield/corporal**, **coulter/counterespionage**, **crab/-craft**, **crazily/credit**. Credit's etymology is "[[Fr *crédit* < It *credito* < L *creditus*, pp. of *credere*: see CREED]]." He sees *creed*. The etymology for *creed* is "[[ME *crede* < OE *creda* < L *credo*, lit., I believe (< *credere*, to trust, believe < IE *kred-dhē-, to attribute magic power to, believe < base *kred-, magic power of a thing + *dhē-, to place, DO[1]]]."

So, thinks Albert, *Bank of America trusts me, believes me, attributes magic power to me. I am to them an unseen moneymaker. That's my magic power. But the power goes both ways. Without the one, the other is diminished.*

Albert sips and stares at the magical card, the shiny logo in the top right corner, three pairs of thick lines configured so that one pair parallels another and is perpendicular to the third. An evergreen forest in the foreground from which blue-gray mountains rise, WORLDPOINTS blazoned underneath the rightmost ridge. Cardholder since 1990. This card is capable of conferring on him goods and/or services worth fifteen-thousand dollars, capable of conferring on him the fifteen-thousand dollars itself. That is a magic power, a conflation of the bound and unbound. He is not sure he should give the power back.

"The next available representative will be with you shortly."

As long as he is burning bridges and strategically defaulting, why not seize what power he can seize, be fifteen-thousand dollars richer, let the debt-collection drama play out on computers while he tries to alter long-held habits and adjusts to daily life without electric power in his paid-for woods? Because the strain of relativism to which he has long ascribed is here applied, he flips forward to the W's and on the first try lands on **weepie/welcome**: "**welch** (welch, welsh) **vi.** [Slang] *var. of* WELSH."

The word reminds him of his father for a reason he can't pinpoint forthwith, though it stems most likely from a card game that was formative memory-wise for Albert the child because his father dipped into the bill-money on that afternoon to cover his losses over the objections of his mother, who was not moved by her husband's honor-based defense that he was no welsher. "**welsh** (welsh) **vi.** [[19th-c. slang, prob. < fol., with reference to alleged character traits of the Welsh]] [Slang] **1** to cheat or swindle by failing to pay a bet or other debt **2** to evade (an obligation) Often with *on* – **welsh´er n.**" Albert has been unsettled by his temporary entertainment of his stepping over to the welsher's side and singlehandedly undoing an intrinsic generational prohibition, which would be, if disregarded, a dishonor to his father's memory and very probably the memories of his grandfather and forebears he has never met. But isn't mortgage-skipping a species of welshing? Relativism lets him argue that the mortgage papers he initialed here, here, here, here, and here and signed here, here, here, and here were, despite the legalese, quite clear the loan was of the non-recourse variety, meaning, in the event of a default, the bank would take the house but was not granted in these papers the authority to pursue beyond that any assets. Besides, Albert put a new roof, including sheathing, on the house, re-sided it with cedar shingles at five-inch exposure, redid the bathroom, put in four-inch red-oak flooring in the kitchen, had the driveway graded once and re-graveled, planted over fifty trees and shrubs around the property, and lived here gingerly for less than ten years—so the bank would get back a better house than he was loaned and so the ignominy of the welsher will not stick to him because of the default.

"The next available representative will be with you shortly."

Since that is settled, he peruses. **Welsh corgi**, **wel·ter**, ***Welt·schmerz***, **Wemb·ley**. He goes back. "***Welt·schmerz*** (velt′schmerts′) **n.** [[Ger, world pain]] sentimental pessimism or melancholy over the state of the world."

"Hmmm," says Albert. "That about sums things up."

He sips, and he peruses. **Wend**, **wentle·trap**, **wer·geld**. "**wer·geld** (wʉr′geld′, wer′-) **n.** [[ME *weregylt* < OE *wergild* < *wer*, man (see WEREWOLF) + *geld*, payment: see GELD[2]]] in early Germanic and Anglo-Saxon law, a price paid by a person who has killed another to the family of the person killed, to atone for the killing and avoid reprisals: also **were′·gild′** or **wer′·gild′** (-gild′)."

The circulating alcohol makes him a little misty-eyed. He turns the wergeld concept over in his mind. There is a tribal logic to it, an acknowledgment that deep harm has been done. He isn't clear on how the early Germans or the Anglo Saxons settled on a price, how much of it was predicated on atonement, how much on avoidance, how the widowed or the fatherless or motherless or otherwise bereaved reacted, how the windfall might have changed their lives and given them new options, how it may have soothed them and induced in them the guilt of the accepter, the collaborator, now complicit in reducing the existence of a kinsman, of a *kinsman*, to a figure everyone involved could live with more or less. Where went the bloodlust? Who first championed the vengeance sublimation? Why did expiation via wergeld finally give way? Albert realizes that it yielded to a penal system but that it was not abandoned absolutely by the world that came to be. He now sees that the Department of Energy, the overseer of Brookhaven National Laboratory, paid the wergeld, the man-price, to his mother to facilitate the appearance of atonement for his father's death and to avoid reprisal and the negative publicity. His share of the wergeld, fifty-thousand dollars, earns an interest pittance in the bank. His share of his father's life. He wonders how many of the early Germans and the Anglo Saxons took the wergeld because they knew the world was stingy and would be legendarily reluctant to offer them anything else. Here comes the Weltschmerz. Albert blinks to contend with the ocular mist.

"The next available representative will be with you shortly."

The opening piano chords of Journey's "Don't Stop Believin'" pick up Albert's spirits, tempt him to resist the tempting pull of Weltschmerz when a human voice, a female voice, cuts short the stirring song and says, "I apologize for the wait. How may I help you?"

"I'd like to give back my magic power."

"I don't understand, sir."

"I'd like to cancel my credit card."

"Okay, I can do that for you. But first can I get the last four digits of your Social?"

"Three, eight, zero, six."

"Thank you. And could you tell me who I'm speaking with?"

"Albert Lesiak."

"Thank you."

He expects to hear keyboard clicking in the background, but he only hears a hollow, channeled sound, which may not actually be a sound but does exist to Albert's ear and registers as something poltergeist-y going on between two land lines.

"Just to confirm. You said you'd like to cancel your credit card."

"Right."

"I'm showing that you have a zero balance on your card."

"Right."

"Have you experienced any problems with your card?"

"No. It's been a good relationship."

"Is there a reason that you want to cancel?"

"Weltschmerz."

"I'm sorry?"

"I've had it."

"You've been a valued cardholder since 1990, and we'd like to do what we can to keep your business."

"I'd like to sever ties."

"Since you've been a valued cardholder since 1990, we'd like to offer you an interest-rate reduction to 3%."

"What's my interest rate now?"

"23.9%."

"Hmm. One might interpret such a generous reduction as an indication that I've been severely overcharged since 1990."

"We've actually never charged you interest since you pay your balance in full each month. Interest only accrues on that part of your balance carried over to the next billing cycle."

"So why would 3% be an incentive?"

"May I ask if you are looking at other cards in order to extend your credit limit?"

"You may."

"We can extend your credit limit to twenty-thousand dollars, if you'd like."

"I don't put a dent in the fifteen-thousand I have now."

"So why not hold onto the card in case of an emergency? It doesn't cost you anything."

"I'm trying to simplify."

"May I put you on hold a moment?"

"Is this like calling a timeout so the opposing field-goal kicker has more time to doubt himself?"

"I apologize, sir. It will only be a moment."

The line goes silent. Slight static. No music. No promotion. Albert imagines her in ecru pantyhose, maneuvering her swivel chair to face her well-groomed supervisor whose philosophy is that he doesn't like to lose, which causes Albert to consider if not liking losing can be categorized as a philosophy. It strikes him more so as a mindset, an illogical ability to think that if you think on a retention problem long enough and use the right incentives and just focus there will be no letting go, no loss. What will such a person do when it is time to die? Inside his head Albert hears the ever twenty-seven Janis Joplin sing her version of the song about a truck and nothingness and liberation intertwining.

"I apologize again for the wait, sir."

"Do you know what Weltschmerz means? I learned, while I

was on hold earlier, that it's a German word meaning *world pain, a pessimism or melancholy over the state of the world.* Do you ever feel that way?"

"I try to be optimistic."

"Like if you keep smiling, things will go your way?"

"I'm only twenty-five."

"If you care about me as a customer, then set me free."

"I will, sir. Please hold."

Chapter Fourteen

Albert's pretty sure the rock that just engraved its mark into his undercarriage wasn't there the last time he was on the Morton Road. The sedimentary, upraised by some external force, can be that way.

His brother-in-law, who flew from Texas for the summer to participate in the construction, says, "I wouldn't worry about it. It probably just hit the skid plate."

Albert, still driving under five miles per hour, the laden trailer still in tow, says, "I should have paid the extra money and gotten the off-road package with extended skid plate."

Contemplations of this sort transcend mere disappointment and extend the chain of associated blame to points unknown, as if decisions he made years ago had led inexorably to this particular upsetting incident with friction and all that it suggests about the paths that he has taken in this life. He should be surging with a pioneer resilience, brushing off such minor setbacks, grateful for the chance to show what he is made of.

Albert stops before the cable strung across the entrance and gets out. He fiddles with his keys like a custodian, inserts one in the lock, and moves the cable to the side.

"I'm not good at backing up the trailer," Albert says. "You want to drive it in?"

"We can unhitch and move it by hand when we get in."

Albert pulls into the clearing. They unhitch the trailer, push and swivel it, attain mobility, decide on a location that's accessible but unobtrusive, and commence the broke-down-car push to that spot. Albert gets in his truck, performs a many-pointed turn, and parks so that it's facing toward the road. When he gets out, he walks to the front of the truck, kneels down, lies on his back, and wiggles himself beneath it.

"It definitely got the skid plate. Gouged it pretty good. It might have hit the transmission. I can't tell. And the strut or whatever you call this part," he says, tapping something Steve can't see. "That's got some deep scratches, too. I'm going to put some newspaper under there, just in case," he says, wiggling back out.

"In case of what?"

"In case it leaks."

"But it's not leaking."

"Not that I can see."

Later, when Albert grows tired of waiting for the leak to manifest itself, he will remember certain lessons from two courses that he took on Buddhist thought in college. He will be reminded of desire and attachment and will understand or not-understand that wanting something like his truck or himself to be what it was yesterday or last week is an example of desire and attachment chaining him to suffering. He will also be reminded of Professor Sung-Bae Park discussing skeleton meditation, whereby the devoted monk sits in the presence of a corpse and understands or not-understands reality to be in the detachment, in the decomposing and the transformation. Albert will, at some point, while sitting in a camp chair, meditate with a distracted mind upon his altered truck and will understand or not-understand that it will someday rust to nothing but the tires and the plastic, glass shards, oil stains; but that day will come long after he is gone, and that will make him wonder what he worries for at all. That will not be sufficient for him to attain enlightenment, but it will remind him that there have been masters.

For now he takes the classified section of the paper from the truck, unfolds it, and slides it underneath the hypothetical leak zone.

"And what's your plan if it leaks?"

"I don't know," says Albert. "Who plans for leakage?"

Steve takes a dip tin from his pants pocket, where the tin's impression abides despite the absence of the tin. He twists the tin top, takes whatever is a step up from a pinch between his thumb and first two fingers, nestles it between his lower lip and gum, and looks around. "You've got a real nice spot here," he says. "Now this is something of value. This is something you hold onto." He spits toward the woods and surveys. "You said eighteen acres?"

"Yep."

"Paid for? You own it free and clear?"

"Yep."

"Good. Very good."

His bulging lip, his squint, his punctuational expectoration, and his cogitative pauses lend his observations and interrogations an authority and heft they would not have if he were sucking on a lollipop or chewing gum or even taking slow drags on a hand-rolled cigarette. He could pass for a run-down Josh Brolin but without the Thespian intensity and the entitlement. He wears a khaki baseball cap whose bill perimeter is frayed. An inch or two above the bill, a U.S.-flag patch sewn or heat-pressed on may represent a certain point of view. He wears a salt-and-pepper mustache and a chin beard that's more uniformly gray, a thick-gauge stubble to the left and right. He wears a khaki button-down shirt whose sleeves are folded to the elbows. From the left-breast pocket peek the spiral binding of a pocket-sized, flip-up notebook and the push-button mechanism of a decent pen. He doesn't give the impression of a man who relishes his butter and his ice cream and his meat until a breeze or posture change removes the fabric billow from his shirt, revealing paunchiness in disproportion to his body as a whole, which stands in work boots at a height of five-feet-ten. Clipped to the waist band of his jeans, a leather carrying case contains a folded multipurpose tool whose parts are properly lubricated. He seems like a man who understands unpleasantness can flow from unpreparedness.

"Okay," Steve says, looking at the four stakes where the cabin will be built. "The trailer can stay where it is. That's out of the way for now." He looks to the other side of the clearing. "When Dexter Lumber comes tomorrow, do we want to stack the materials over there?"

"We do."

Steve walks to that side of the clearing and stares for a minute at the ground. He takes out his notebook and flips past a few pages. "So concrete pads, six-by-six pressure-treated posts, two-by-eights, two-by-sixes, two-by-fours, three-quarter-inch Advantec flooring, three-quarter-inch plywood, half-inch OSB for the walls. That's all that's being delivered tomorrow, right?"

Albert looks at his invoice without really reading it. "That's it. We've got the fasteners. We've got the gravel for the pads."

Steve nods, spits toward a sapling mob, and puts his notebook back in his pocket.

Albert says, "We just need to unload what we need for the night."

They spread a tarp out on the ground and silently unfold the tent and orient it so that the zipper faces toward the road. They clarify the purpose of each color-coded grommet and insert the proper graphite poles whose flexibility allows the dome shape to materialize. They stake the perimeter grommets, overlay the fly, stake the fly grommets, and achieve desired tautness.

In setting up to camp, there is presumption and humility coincident.

It is, in one sense, an invasion, a displacement or disturbance of the seen and unseen beings who were born here and exist on what is here, no clutter and no importation, and whose roots are so deep that to contemplate them undermines your presence here, and you are forced to think in terms of the priority of size and therefore do not check your moral compass overmuch when you say to a colony of ants, whose harmony you ruined when you picked a mossy piece of hemlock lumber up, "I need this piece of ground for my own purposes. I mean you no harm, but you'll have to move." You basically announce on your arrival that you cannot make it on your own here and do not possess the wherewithal to integrate. Hence the vehicle, the tent, the water jugs, the camp stove, the propane canisters, the pots, the pans, the silverware, the plates, the cups, the sponges, the garbage bags, the Weber grill, the charcoal, the spatula, the flashlights, the batteries, my God, the batteries, the matches, the lighters, the coolers and their processed bounty, the coffee pot, the tooth-decay preventatives, the antiperspirant, the soap, the shampoo, the toilet paper, the radio, the footwear, and the clothing—all of it announces you are not at home here.

Despite the civilized belief that life is better and more dignified with intermediary-vended goods of manufacture and of produce and despite the average camper's practical adherence to this passed-down line of thought, the camper tries at least to put aside his prissiness and temper his conditioned superciliousness and keep his eyebrows relatively level when he lies down for the auditorily quite happening night in a Chinese tent that offers no substantial safeguard from a suddenly toppled tree or from a sniffing presence on the dwindling list of predators who still possess the heart to take a human out. None, except the oddly comforting assurance that he's covered. The camper tries at least to honor the indelicate biota, to unknow what knowledge he has of bacteria, let's say, when he uncovers his posterior and squats to defecate remotely in the woods and wonders why this seemingly intestinal contortion, which in fact is more conducive to a smooth and healthy movement than a sit-down, was abandoned for the privy seat, the toilet seat, the ersatz pine scent, the desire for enclosure. Waking unharmed in the morning on the ground or walking back from an evacuation that reminds him where he's really from and where he's going, the average camper senses something so impressive in the woods that it is only proper to resist less the interior upwelling of humility and to be quieter, to not be profligate with water or with light, to wonder more and more, as minor deprivations press upon him, about the lives of unforthcoming woodland creatures, and to ask himself some questions. Do they require REM sleep? How do they survive the lean times? Could I build a shelter using only what I find around me in the woods and make a life here? If not, how long could I survive without my store-bought clothes in the woods in winter? How insanely tough and unsung are the unforthcoming woodland creatures? How do they know just what to do when it is time to raise the young? How do they cope with loss? Where are the dead? Why are there not more dead?

So Albert and Steve presume and have their share of intermediary-vended manufactured goods and produce, but they also practice a reduction of the standards of their nation and their time and do without what standards many of their countrymen and their contemporaries are Panglossian in pointing out were nonetheless developed, nonetheless preserved for the betterment of life, which seems therefore to argue the directive force thought better of their being done without. And who is anyone to second-guess the will or flow of the directive force? And who is anyone to hint by action at recalibration?

Steve removes the camp stove from the trailer and centers it upon an old shed door that lies across the tops of two long-decommissioned fifty-five-gallon drums the previous owner kept in the decrepit shed for reasons he did not disclose at closing. Steve goes back to the trailer and removes a propane tank. He sets it on the ground beside the second drum and threads the camp stove's nipple counterclockwise into the tank threads. He turns the gas on, holds his lighter to a burner, flicks his thumb, and turns the burner knob to verify that they have carried in their way the gift of fire to another outpost.

"We have ignition," Steve says.

Albert positions the provisions cooler near the tailgate, and he slides a jug of water likewise. He positions the libations cooler so it parallels the wheel well on the driver's side and is within range of moderate arm extension. It allows as well the two of them, when it is time, to take two proximate beers and rest their arm parts on the gunnel of the bed as they imbibe and talk construction or become familiar in a guarded way with one another or say nothing and let their drinking and their barroom postures and their staring into woods suffice for sociability and bonding when the recognition somehow comes across as mutual that language would be almost sacrilegious and would buzz-kill the arboreal, near-solstice, thrush-set mood.

Steve says, "We'll need to figure out a spot to set the sawhorses."

"True."

"Are you sure you don't want to cut down some trees? Make things easier. Let in some extra light."

"I'd like to tread lightly," Albert says, setting camp chairs near the vestibule of the tent. "I'm all about the treading lightly."

Steve throws his pillow, sleeping pad, sleeping bag, and duffel bag into the sleeping quarters of the tent. "You have a preference for a side?"

Albert shakes his head. "I'm ambidextrous."

Steve ducks and enters. He unfurls, fluffs up, unzips, gets situated. He lies down on his smoothed-out sleeping bag and puts his hands behind his head. "Do you carry a pocketknife?" he asks.

"No."

"You know, not long ago, certainly within my lifetime, it was common for a man to carry a pocketknife. What changed?"

Albert wonders if this is Texas talking. Steve grew up in Marlborough, Connecticut, but left home when he was eighteen to take a plumbing job in Houston. Albert is not familiar with Marlborough's personal-armament views of thirty years or so ago when Steve left home, but he suspects that they were not as ideological and yahoo as those views a teenage transplant, wanting to fit in, might have absorbed and taken for his own in Texas, even in an urban setting such as Houston, since then.

"I don't know," says Albert. "A shift from farm work to office work. A decline in whittling. Come to think of it, I can't recall the last time I observed a whittler in action."

A curious phenomenon accompanies communication through a tent. Your interlocutor is unseen, so, in one sense, it is like you're talking to yourself and therefore you're inclined to be more liberal with expression than you might if you were talking face to face. You can talk and touch yourself or talk and mine the dark canal for ear wax, as Albert does now, or talk and give your interlocutor the finger, and the only thing that makes it through the tent is what you say. You do not have to be concerned about your interlocutor examining your face for flaws or subtext. It is a liberating way for people to communicate and keeps the interaction intimate and local, human in a way the cell phone or the internet cannot.

"Maybe," Steve says, "but I believe it's more subtle than that. It's more, uh . . . What's the word I'm looking for? It has to do with messages and advertising."

"Subliminal?" Albert offers, taking the grill from the trailer and setting it on the ground.

"Yes, thank you. Subliminal. Subliminal," Steve says as if to conjure up the essence of an old acquaintance. "I believe it's more subliminal. It has to do with criminalizing, gradually criminalizing, behavior that isn't criminal. If you get pulled over in a traffic stop and don't give your consent to have your car searched, which is your right—illegal search and seizure, it's in the Constitution—and the cop asks you to get out of the car and pats you down and finds a pocketknife, what happens? You get arrested for possession of a pocketknife, a concealed weapon—if he wants to arrest you. You don't need a license for it, you didn't do anything criminal with it, but it could get you arrested."

"Are you a Sovereign Citizen?"

"No, and I'm not saying this happens all the time. But it happens, and I'm asking why. What's the point?"

"You carry a pocketknife *and* a multipurpose tool?"

"Do you know how many people ask me, 'Steve, can I borrow your knife for a second?' or 'Steve, do you have something I can use to fix this problem with the chicken wire?'"

"A lot."

"Here's a hypothetical. A boy gets a brand-new fishing pole for his birthday, which occurs before the start of fishing season. He just wants to get a feel for the pole, imagine what great things that pole and he will do come fishing season. So he walks to the lake, unlocks his rowboat, rows to the middle of the lake, and sits there imagining his glory. After a while, a DEP officer notices him out there and gets in his official boat and makes a beeline for the boy. The officer says, 'You can't fish outside the season. I have to confiscate your pole and issue a citation.' 'But I'm not fishing,' says the boy. 'I'm just sitting here with my new fishing pole I got for my birthday.' The officer says, 'How do I know you weren't fishing before I came out here?' The boy says, 'I have no lures. I have no bait. How can I fish without lures or bait?' The officer says, 'You could have dumped the bait.' The boy says, 'But I didn't.' The officer says, 'How do I know you won't row to shore, dig up some worms, row back out here, and start fishing when I leave?' The boy says nothing because he knows the officer can't know that, human nature being what it is. The boy surrenders his beloved pole, accepts with due humility his citation, rows to shore, locks his boat, walks home. It's the same with the driver carrying the pocketknife. No crime has been committed, but the person yields to the police because what other option is there?"

"And you think that accounts for the dearth of whittlers?" Albert asks, opening a beer.

"I'm saying that it happens, and it gets in people's minds."

"Well," says Albert, "I think your knife is safe from the police out here."

"It should be safe from them all over," Steve says as he emerges from the tent and scoops out the dip wad with his index finger, disposing of it with a sidearm, jai-alai sort of motion into the woods.

"What did you do with the dip spit you produced while you were in the tent?"

Steve pats his stomach. Opening the cooler and taking out a beer, he says, "I need something to wash it down with."

"When my dad was in the hospital for his cancer operation," Albert says, tilting back his head and letting his consumption lend his anecdote a little gravity by utilizing the convention of dramatic pause, "for two days he had a roommate who was thirty and recovering from having had the left side of his jaw removed. He said through pursed lips that he started on the dip when he was nineteen. Eleven years of marination later, he was the proud owner of a prosthetic jaw."

"I know. It isn't good." He swigs. "Mmmm," Steve says, looking at the label, "this is not your ordinary beer."

Albert looks over. "That's a ten-percent Scotch ale aged in bourbon barrels. From Grand Rapids, Michigan. Nice, right? I love that stuff, but it's dangerous. Goes down too easily."

"Boy, that is good."

Albert notices the flare-up of a Texas accent.

They look around at the woods, experience the pleasant mellowing of brain activity as extraordinary beer dilutes their bloodstreams.

"How many people," Steve asks, "would do what you're doing?"

"In terms of what?"

"In terms of moving out here. You know, starting over, building something, giving up suburban life."

"Dick Proenneke."

"Who's that?"

"You never saw *Alone in the Wilderness* on PBS? About the guy who cut down trees, towed them back with his canoe, built his cabin in interior Alaska? It's on at least once a year."

"Yes," says Steve, lifting his index finger from its supernumerary support position on the bottle neck and pointing it in Albert's direction, "I have seen that. I didn't know that was his name. Yes, *he* would. He *did*. Is he still alive?"

"He died in a convalescent home. Or at his brother's house. I forget."

"Okay, so he's out. Who else would do what you're doing?"

"I don't know. I'm sure some people do."

"Some do. But why do most just pay their mortgages, do their jobs, put money into their retirement accounts, and think, if they just keep doing what they've been told to do and have faith in the system, things will work out in the end?"

Albert shrugs and shakes his head. "Because things have worked out in the end before?"

Steve lifts the same finger from its supernumerary support position and declares, "Because things have worked out in the end before. It's natural for people to ignore what's different. That's why the internet is so great. For a guy like me, who never went to college, there is so much information out there that I wouldn't have known existed otherwise, and I can get at least a sense of what's going on in the economy, in government, around the world. Without the internet, I wouldn't even know what to read. Have you ever read Jared Diamond's *Guns, Germs, and Steel*?"

"No."

"Oh, great book. Have you ever been to *Zero Hedge*?"

"No."

"Such a great site. All sorts of smart people who really know what's going on contribute there. Economists, professors, former government officials, writers, intellectuals. Breitbart's on there. Chris Hedges, former *New York Times* writer, he's on there. Paul Krugman's on there. And you can engage in discussions with these guys. You can ask them questions. I had an exchange with Krugman about quantitative easing a few weeks ago. Very interesting."

"Why would Krugman be on *Zero Hedge*?"

"Because people like him can only say so much in the mainstream media. You don't get truth in the mainstream media. For example, the *Times* will talk about the financial crisis and what the government tells them about unemployment or what the Fed says, when the Fed says anything, but they won't really try to connect the dots. Like they won't say, like someone said on *Zero Hedge*, that these things historically run in eighty-year cycles. Roughly eighty-year cycles."

"What things?"

"Crashes. In 1929, you have the stock-market crash and the start of the Great Depression, which lasted through the thirties. What happens almost eighty years later, 2008? Another financial crisis."

Albert performs delayed subtraction in his head. "Was there a crash in 1849?"

"Good question," Steve says. He puts his beer on the tailgate, takes his pen and notebook from his pocket, writes, "Was there a crash in 1849?" and returns the pen and notebook to his pocket. "I don't know the answer to that. I'll have to look that up when I get home. I think there was a depression in the 1800s, though."

"Seems like a pretty small statistical sample."

"Maybe. You might be right about that."

"And we pulled out of the Great Depression."

"Thanks to World War II and a period of income equality that lasted more or less into the seventies. Then what happens? Nixon takes us off the gold standard, inflation, the rise of two-income families, the widening gap in income inequality. You see, the mainstream media will report on these things, but they won't report on the *reasons* for them. These things don't happen by accident. There are reasons things aren't as good as they used to be. Do you think our generation is better off than our parents'? Do you think the generation after us will be better off than us?"

"I don't know about the eighty-year-cycle stuff, but, yeah, I see your point about the rest. Beer?"

"Thank you."

"My grandfather retired from AT&T with a full pension when he was fifty-five. That was 1978, '79. He didn't work a day in his life after that, and he lived pretty comfortably."

"Those days are over for most workers. In the private sector, anyway."

"My brother works for the Long Island Railroad. He'll still get that sort of pension. Twenty years and out."

"Even for those guys, I think their days are numbered," Steve says. "Look at what's happened to the unions. Look at that asshole Scott Walker."

Albert nods. They sip. They mentally digest.

"You smell that?" Steve asks.

"What?"

"Cow manure."

"There's a dairy farm up that way," Albert says, pointing west-northwest. "We passed it coming in."

They decide without a dialogue to sit a manly distance from each other in the camp chairs that they take from near the vestibule and set an arm's length from the grill.

"Do you keep your money in the bank?" Steve asks.

"Right now, yeah."

"You think it's safe?"

"More or less."

"Why?"

Albert shrugs. "It's insured."

"By the FDIC. Your deposit is insured up to $250,000, right? Most people have confidence in that. There's no fine print on the sticker on the window at the bank. So why, in 2008, when McCain was in the middle of his presidential campaign and seeking the advice of financial *experts* on what he should say about the breaking crisis, why were those advisors leaving the room and calling their wives and telling them to take out thirty-thousand, fifty-thousand dollars from their bank accounts?"

"*It's a Wonderful Life*. The fear of a run," Albert says.

"They knew the FDIC can pay out less than 1% of the money it insures. If a crash wiped out the depositors' money, the FDIC has less than 1% on hand to pay them back. Why isn't that on the sticker at the front of the bank? And what does it mean that those financial *experts* were panicky?"

"I thought these things don't happen by accident."

"They don't."

"If those guys didn't know, then where's the orchestration?"

"Someone higher up than them is running the show."

A barred owl hoots four times from the woods.

"Barred owl," Albert says.

"Do you know anything about the shadow-banking system? It's this unregulated corner of the financial system, where the biggest lenders can have the power to crush some of their competition, even at the risk of harming the overall economy."

"What does that have to do with 2008?"

"Subprime mortgages. All I know for sure is we'll never get the full story on what happened to Bear Stearns and Lehman Brothers, and that the biggest banks made out like bandits. Fucking Paulson was a Goldman Sachs guy. Geithner. I think Geithner was a Goldman Sachs guy. Rahm Emanuel. Robert Rubin under Clinton. That should give us some idea of who's running the show."

"I should start a fire," Albert says.

"But none of that is out here. None of what happens in New York or Washington really matters here."

Albert crumples newspaper and arranges it in the belly of the bisected orb.

"We're not exactly in the wilderness," Albert says. "There's a Wal-Mart twenty miles away."

"But the kind of life here, you're not tied into things the way the others are. A financial collapse, a power-grid disruption, a terrorist attack—you might feel the outer ripples, but, when you get settled here, you can weather shit most other people can't."

Albert chutes the charcoal into the belly of the bisected orb and sets fire to the paper.

"You ever heard of Quang Duc?" he asks. He stares at the fire and explains. "You ever heard of Pyotr Pavlensky?" Albert asks. He leans from his camp chair toward the fire and explains. "Sometimes I feel like Quang Duc right before the conflagration, but without the guidance of religion. Sometimes I feel like Pavlensky right before the hammer drives the nail in, but minus the resigned conviction of a Russian."

"Perfectly normal to have doubts. You don't think those guys had doubts? It's normal to be nervous on the eve of an adventure."

"Did you just say, 'It's normal to be nervous on the eve of an adventure'?"

"That's good," Steve says. "I should write that down."

When Steve is finished writing, Albert says, "It's not just *my* body that I'm lighting up or *my* sack that I'm nailing to the cobblestones. Once we're here, we're here."

"You know how many people *say* they'd like to do what you're about to do?"

"But they don't leave their decent jobs without notice and ignore their mortgage lender's dunning agents and assume the two autistic kids they just adopted will experience a metamorphosis and butterfly it through the sun-dappled woods. They go camping for a week or two in the summer and return to their societal commitments and the comforts of the infrastructure."

"Remember the Old Milwaukee commercial with the guys around the campfire, and the one guy says, 'It doesn't get any better than this'?"

"That beer sucked," says Albert, imposing the lid on the intensifying fire. "Good commercial, though. Evocative."

Chapter Fifteen

In the peopled world, so much depends on what is level, what is plumb.

Where the four stakes were are now four circular concrete pads, each eighteen inches in diameter and each a hundred pounds. Albert rolled each one to its location and was careful not to catch his fingers when he let it fall flat on the gravel he had smoothed out with his hand. Unsystematically, without the basic understanding of the methods of construction that applied, he thought about the pyramids at Giza, the cathedrals that drew medieval eyeballs skyward, how they started with a block, he guessed, a weight positioned in a surveyed place and leveled, how the builder put his faith in that block as a champion of immobility, a representative of density that would resist the pressure to adjust or sink or shift, to undermine the edifice of which it had the honor and the burden of serving as the everlasting cornerstone. They say that you can get a sense of what's important to a people when, on entering that people's town, you see the tallest buildings and discern the structural devotions. Albert guesses that in Garland, which is not a concentrated town, the tallest building is a barn or silo or the church that's not affiliated with the formal piety of Rome. He wonders what a small camp at the bottom of the Morton Road will say to someone slowly passing by on horseback ages hence, will say to someone less reflective passing much more quickly by on something touted as a conqueror of all terrain. Here lived a person who was humble? Here lived a person who was hoping he would not be seen? Here lived a person who had issues, otherwise why would he have forsaken what the world could else have offered—sunlight, lake views, distance from what trickles down, from moisture dwellers, from mud?

"Hold this on center," Steve says, handing him the dumb end of the tape measure. Steve walks backward to the concrete pad diagonally across from Albert. "If the distance between these two points is the same as the distance between those two points," he says, pointing to the other two pads, "we're square. Right now, we just need to be close." He puts his end of the tape on the center of his pad. "Thirty-three feet, ten inches. All right, move over there and put the tape on the center of that pad." Steve rotates to the next pad and puts his end of the tape on center. "Thirty-three feet, eight inches. Close enough for now."

"The old Pythagorean theorem more or less," says Albert, releasing his end of the tape.

"What is that, the square of the hypotenuse is equal to something?"

"The square of the other two or something like that. I don't think about Euclidean geometry as often as I should. For some reason, though, I do know that Pythagoras believed in the transmigration of the soul. He stepped in to stop the beating of a dog once because he heard the cry of his dead friend in the dog's bark." The truth is, Albert once wrote a poem on the topic after he discovered that about Pythagoras, but he is conscious that a revelation of that sort, in his experience, does no one any favors.

"All right," Steve says, "let's make sure these pads are level."

They each take out a six-inch spirit level from their tool belts, crouch by their respective pads, and place the level on center, waiting for the Tic Tac of a bubble in the level's little window to stop moving.

"I'm off this way," Albert says, turning the level clockwise ninety degrees and setting it crosswise to the first position. "Not bad this way, though." He puts the level in his tool belt, pries the low side of the pad up with his left hand, has his right sweep gravel inward, and is optimistic that redistribution will effect desired levelness. Laying down the level in the first position, Albert says, "Now that's what I'm talking about. Perfect this way." He turns the level counterclockwise, sets it crosswise to the first position. "Shit. Now I'm off this way." For several minutes, levelness appears elusive, a theoretical condition that resists its imposition on the real world. Albert looks around. It seems that nothing natural's level, nothing natural's plumb—unless by accident, without premeditation. A bird's nest or an ant hill doesn't need a level to establish equilibrium or functionality. He looks from pad to pad and understands with sinking heart that settlement will come, and all they've done in kilter's name will be undone by increments of fractions of an inch.

"I don't know," says Albert, "maybe we should just dig holes and set the posts in some cement."

"You'll still have settlement," Steve says, spitting to his left. "This way, when it settles, you can jack it up and make it level."

Albert nods. The two of them go back to lifting heavy pads with one hand, redistributing the gravel with the other, and experiencing the hope of humans at the outset of construction that, when they set down the pads again and form the basis of the edifice, their bubbles will be centered and the order of the universe will be affirmed in microcosm and the two of them will rise and look at the imaginary square and picture habitation like a hologram within.

After lunch, Steve walks down to the duffy rise that overlooks the stream and hangs his nylon hammock between two trees and lies in it as though his body has become a mark of metrical unstress.

Albert pulls a two-by-eight and measures to confirm the eight is nominal. "Seven and a quarter," he says and keeps saying as he pulls a three-quarter-inch sheet of plywood, tilts it up, and carries it like a plate-glass window to the sawhorses on which he lays it flat. He hooks his tape measure on the plywood's edge and pulls the tape a little way across the sheet. "Seven and a quarter, seven and a quarter," he repeats and makes a pencil mark. He pulls the tape a little farther. "Fourteen and a half." Another pencil mark. A little farther. "Twenty-one and three quarters." Another pencil mark. A little farther. "Twenty-eight." Another mark. A little farther. "Thirty-five and a quarter." Another mark. A little farther. "Forty-two and a half." Another mark. He makes the same set of marks on the opposite end of the plywood sheet and snaps a chalk line from mark to corresponding mark, beginning with the seven and a quarters. When he's done with the sixth line, he blows the blue dust from the plane and measures his marks on both sides one more time. He puts the circular saw on the plywood, checks the extension-cord connection by performing what appears to be an isometric exercise for quitters, and walks over to the generator. He chokes it back and flips the start switch. All sound is drowned out by the seismic rumble that is portable electrical production. He waits, unchokes, flips the breaker switch, and goes back to the plywood, checking on the snugness of his glasses as he goes. He lines the blade up with the first blue line and sets the blade a blade's width from the plywood's edge. He pulls the trigger, and the blade bites into wood. The generator noise dips and then redoubles with the power surge. What does the saw's metallic whine inspire in the mice? Albert squints despite prescription eye protection and tries hard to honor lineation, hewing to the line as if in lineation is the wisdom and the way. He lays his left hand on the plywood as he starts to lean in with the progress of the saw. Although he knows there should be nothing but the saw blade and the line, he sees his hand there and recalls the boy afflicted suddenly with severance in the famous poem. Albert thinks how much easier it is to lose a hand to this saw, which is not fixed like the buzz saw in the poem and is opener to inattention. He slides his hand a little farther to the left, and he continues down the line, his inner speaker interjecting "Amputation!" now and then as a jinx, whose inspiration would be psychological and murky, difficult to parse, or as a caution to be mindful.

When he is done, he pulls another sheet of plywood, snaps three lines, and guides the blade as truly as he can. When he is done, he lays the saw down like a beached ship on the uncut plywood and shuts off the generator. It is as if the auditory world is summoned to resume. Silence, birdsong, flutter, rustle, breeze. But they have been there all along, and Albert feels good that his sounds are the temporary ones and that, when the generator does generate and the circular saw does circulate, the other sounds, the ones not owing to the engineer or the machinist, go intently on.

Limbs safe, body in no danger of disfigurement, he cleans his glasses on his shirt and lifts his shirt up, exposing abdomen, to sop the sweat up from his face and brow. He puts his glasses back on and looks toward Steve still in the hammock. He looks down at his fingers, which feel thick from recent gripping, and he tries remembering the name of the disorder that he read about in the *The New Yorker* years ago. *Body dysmorphia,* he thinks, *or body something or other disorder*—something Latin, something Greek.

But he remembers reading in the article about a man whose ideal image of himself was as a man with one leg and who went recumbent in his bathtub to effect the severance with a chainsaw but passed out before it went clean through and was discovered. His reattachment surgery was a success, but he became depressed and vowed to learn from his mistakes and did eventually effect a total severance with a chainsaw and was even somewhat cheeky to the people who had tried again to save the leg. Albert does not remember if the amputee reality and the amputee ideal turned out to be equivalent for that rare example of the can-do attitude, although, Albert guesses, as with many dreams, fulfillment likely wasn't all the pre-disfigured man had cracked it up to be. *Or maybe it was,* he reconsiders, flexing his fingers. *Maybe that's what bothers people.* Albert makes a mental note to reread the article to fortify his memory when he has access to the internet again.

Albert pulls a two-by-eight until he's roughly in the center of it, and he carries it to the imaginary square and lays it flat across three concrete pads. He pulls another two-by-eight and bears it to the same place, but he sets this one on the ground and leans it against the same three pads. He folds the oilcloth tarp back on the trailer, finds a caulk gun, loads it with a tube of Liquid Nails, and sets it on the two-by-eight that spans the pads. He goes back to the trailer and grunts as he lifts the air compressor, which he sets about the cord's length from the dormant power source. He unplugs the saw and plugs in the compressor. He goes back to the trailer, loads a coil of framing nails into the chamber of the gun, and sets the gun upside down against the two-by-eight that leans against the pads. He goes back to the trailer and removes the red compressor hose, the blue extension hose, and makes the requisite connections. He begins to wonder how much motion conservation matters to the master builders, and he wonders how in wood construction fastening was done before the advent of the nail. He wonders then about the nail's invention. It was prior to the Crucifixion, certainly, but how prior? Back to the Ark, he guesses. Earlier than that? Did it predate the wheel? He is troubled by how much he doesn't know without computer recourse.

Confronted with such stubborn ignorance, he redirects his

energy toward the accomplishment of something practical. He clips the spout tip off the tube of Liquid Nails and finds an 8d common nail to puncture serially the tube's protective seal. He walks to the far end of the two-by-eight that spans the pads and pulls the caulk gun's trigger and applies the Liquid Nails across the board's length in an undulating line whose peaks and valleys are approximately equidistant, like an outline of a well-proportioned mountain range. He sticks the 8d nail into the spout and sets the gun down on the ground. He picks a piece of power-sawn plywood from beside the sawhorses, blows each side and swipes his hand across each side to dislodge unblown particles and blows each side again, and lays it down upon the two-by-eight, aware of the encroaching fixity and how the three sides must be flush or free at least of level-ruining protrusion. Careful not to dislodge what he just took pains to lay, he sets a second strip of plywood on the two-by-eight and then a third.

"Steve," he says. "I need a hand."

Steve lifts his USA cap from his face and says, "I'll be right there."

He groans the existential groan of later middle age and stretches out as he walks up the hill. His back is shot from plumbing.

Albert completes this side's Liquid Nails application by the time Steve arrives.

"Take that end, please," says Albert, indicating the two-by-eight aslant against the pads, "and gently set it on the board."

They handle the two-by-eight with the care of marble wielders and inspect all sides with hands and eyes for flushness or at least the absence of protrusion.

"Good?" Albert asks.

"Good."

Albert starts the generator and adjusts the psi on the compressor. Steve holds firmly his end of the almost finished floor beam. Albert clamps his end with his left hand and shoots the nail gun with his right. He shoots low, slides the nail gun to his right six inches, shoots high, slides it, shoots low, and on occasion shoots one in the middle for the permanency illusion. When he nails to Steve's side, he returns to his own, they rotate the beam, and then he nails a complementary pattern on the flipside.

They manufacture two more floor beams in that way—gluing, sandwiching, nailing.

When they finish, Albert asks, "Do you know why a two-by-eight is one and a half by seven and a quarter?"

"I'd guess that someone found a way to make some extra money on his boards one day, and it probably caught on." He writes in his notebook, "Why are modern lumber measurements not true?"

They eyeball the topography and determine which pad will support the highest post.

Steve saws a six-by-six in half for handling ease and sets one four-foot section upright on that pad. Albert takes the other post and sets it likewise on the pad diagonally across.

"About this high?" Steve asks, his finger pointing to a spot not quite three quarters of the way up the post. "Remember, we want to keep enough space underneath the camp in case you ever need to jack it up."

"That looks good."

Steve keeps his finger on that spot and lays the post down on the pad. He taps a nail in where his finger was and stands the post back up. Albert walks over and hands him a spool of neon-yellow nylon string whose end Steve knots into a loop and hangs upon the nail. Albert takes the spool, walks backward toward the pad, unraveling, maintaining modest tension, stops to hook a line level on the string when he gets halfway, and continues backward to the post to which he holds the string at several points.

"Does that look level?" he asks.

"Don't pull too tight," Steve says, letting go of his post and pausing for a moment to decide if present tension will allow it to stand independently. He checks the line level. "A little lower. Lower. Good. Mark it. We'll cut the post a little high to be on the safe side."

About three hours before the sun sets, confident that finally the floor beams will be level and the pressure-treated posts will be plumb, they fasten tie plates to the beams and posts with hot-dipped galvanized nails and stand each beam upon its post and pad and set the three-foot level on the beams nine times, nine verifications of the stilled and centered bubble, level all, and you would think, to look at Steve and Albert as they stand back in attitudes of satisfied appraisal, that they dragged twelve slabs of dolerite from distant hills and raised up nine as posts and raised up three as lintels to construct three trilithons arranged so they could worship the arrival of the summer-solstice sun and stun the future pilgrims to this nondenominational locale with the uncanniness and the precision of celestial alignment.

Chapter Sixteen

Without the gradual transformative experience of gestation, nine months to get used to, on the inside, the idea of motherhood, to the idea that you and an incipient other are inseparable, a union in the blood sense, the genetic sense, the sense that you are passing the ontological baton to someone who will still be running when you fade, without a husband who is nearby or at least is in possession of a cell phone and in calling daily technically adheres to parenting's participatory ideal, without a village or extended family in state to contextualize the raising and to offer its collective rearing wisdom, it is sometimes hard to put your heart into creating something monumental out of Legos with the twin boys you went into training to provisionally adopt and who behave at times, for reasons that have glimmered like addressable conundrums in the literature, as though they do not see you and do not appreciate the interpersonal dynamics and the sacrificial nature of the mother-son relationship in these, the final years before they move on to their teens.

"What should we do here? Should we build up?" Mary asks, flourishing her hands above the embryonic structure like an amiable magician trying earnestly to conjure interest in her act.

"Or should we build out?" Her hands expand toward the coffee table's ends.

***

On the first of June, about a month ago, she tied two yellow ribbons to the mailbox flag and watched them tauten as the pair of blue balloons they were attached to went as high as they could go, and she was happy with the image (blue balloons, yellow ribbons, red flag, green mailbox) and its buoyancy and how it seemed to complement the life-affirmative impression that suffuses later spring. As she and Albert drove down the driveway, she began to worry that the helium would dissipate and the balloons would seem to signal that a celebration had occurred at this location but was over by the time that she and Albert arrived home as probationary parents for the first time with the boys. When they got home, she smiled when she saw that they were still afloat and turned to Jake and Ryan in the back seat for reactions. They looked at the balloons with the mild interest of two chauffeured passersby whose only outlet was to look, and, when Albert turned in the driveway and drove past the green mailbox and the red flag and the yellow ribbons and the blue balloons, they seemed to think no more about them and did not inquire what the colorful arrangement meant or who could have arranged it.

"Welcome home," said Mary when the truck stopped.

In the kitchen, hanging banner-wise above the entry to the living room, eleven linked and glittering letters spelled out WELCOME HOME and fluttered slightly with the atmospheric change of human presence. From the chairbacks of the four chairs pushed into the kitchen table, four yellow ribbons tethered four aloft and blue balloons. Jake approached the nearest chair and touched the chairback and the yellow knot. He looked around the kitchen, walked around the table, and peeked inside the living room.

"Where's Watts?" he asked.

Albert said, "He doesn't hear as well as he used to. He's probably still sleeping. Hang on." He went to the back room, and the floor creaked when he entered. Watts opened his eyes and blinked and wagged his tail against the chair and yawned. He rose from the chair and arched his stiff back like a cat. He stepped onto the ottoman and stared down at the floor, reluctant to perform the leap without consideration. Then he leaped and led Albert to the kitchen. When he saw the boys, he wagged his whole body and jumped on each of them in greeting, and the boys could not have patted him on the head with more conviction or have stroked his loosened back with greater tenderness or have been happier when they scratched his rump and Watts inclined his snout toward the ceiling as if basking in the sun.

"He's smiling," Jake said, and the corners of Watts's mouth were turned upward and were difficult to read as other than the oral upturn universally interpreted as signaling one's happiness.

"He's happy to see you guys," said Mary. "He's happy you're home."

Albert put their luggage and their other boxed and bundled personal belongings in their bedroom. In consultation with Gina Dunn, Albert and Mary had agreed the boys should share a room until the newness of the situation wore off and the settlement of the familiar made them edge for separateness. Until then, Albert's study, the back room, which they'd told Gina would become the extra bedroom when the boys were ready, housed a smattering of age-and/or ability-appropriate diversions, and the boys were free to enter and disturb his sullen privacy without knocking or reserving an appointment or considering the premium that certain types of people place on personal space.

After dinner, Mary set an ice-cream cake impaled by four lit candles on the center of the table. Its icing spelled out WELCOME HOME in cursive.

"Okay," said Mary, "there's one candle for each of us. One candle for each member of this family. Before I count to three . . ."

"Where's Watts's candle?" Jake asked.

"You are absolutely right, Jake. I completely forgot about Watts," said Mary, who stuck another candle in and lit it. "Watts is lucky to have you and Ryan watching out for him. Okay, before I count to three, let's make a wish." They paused as if in prayer. "When I count to three, let's blow the candles out."

On three, all four exhaled with various degrees of vigor.

"I blew for Watts," said Jake, "because he loves me."

Ryan looked down toward his lap and tapped the Dynavox, which said, "Me too."

In honor of the value of parental dedication and to give attention to the finer household details that before the new arrivals hadn't seemed to need an everyday attending to, Mary took that first week off from work and made conventional breakfasts each day, which Albert did not partake in because the sudden introduction of a breakfast into his matutinal routine of only coffee would induce in his already unpredictable digestive system elevated stages of the socially inhibiting condition of vociferous irregularity, and drove them both to school and walked them in and hugged them to affirm the temporary nature of their separation and drove home wondering if during lunchtime they'd communicate to one another their opinions on her sandwich-making capabilities and her decisions vis-à-vis the snacks.

Albert administered his finals that week and so was home each day by twelve-thirty at the latest. He had lunch each day when he got home, spent an hour or two in the back room mostly grading the day's exams, and took a nap when he got tired. On Thursday he did not go in at all because he had no classes scheduled for exams. Because he knew that he would not be running into anyone in a restrictive setting until that afternoon, he breakfasted with everyone that morning and felt, as he had felt at recent dinnertimes, a little of the chest puff of the patriarch.

Aside from Mary, he had not told anyone that he would not return to Saint Francis High School in September. He had opened his manila envelope like any other faculty member, spent a few obligatory moments reading over the familiar terms and calmly threatening conditions stipulated in his contract, signed his name, with middle initial, on the line above Employee's Signature, and wasn't bothered that he signed with no intention of upholding his end of the bargain this time, had no qualms about the honor-sullying he was thereby perpetrating on his family name because, for quite a while, he'd considered nominal honor as a legal fiction, an invention of incorporated issuers of contracts as a shaming mechanism, one designed to gather in the blood relations under ignominy's wide net just in case the threat of personal disgrace was insufficient to induce compliance. He wasn't even overly concerned that, when the paychecks for the upcoming academic year would start to be deposited directly into his account in mid-July and he would not be seen or heard from in September, they would sue him to recover the amount of those four checks and probably to get some stick-it-to-him money for the contract breach.

At that time of the year, the finals wind-down, summer near, the coming of the heat, the light, Albert usually felt enlivened, optimistic, westerly Buddhist in his being on board again with non-attachment and the letting go of suffering or putting it in its proper place at least. All the teachers, except perhaps for those who needed extra money and signed on for three weeks of summer school, felt likewise. It was like completing a prolonged experience with dentistry—your other problems didn't also disappear when it was over, but you faced them with a new insouciance now that the centermost affliction of your being was displaced.

But, that finals week, Albert exuded an existential lightness that transcended his colleagues' annual June relief. He felt superior to them, above them, because they all, at one time or another, fantasized about departures from Saint Francis but allowed their summers to eviscerate their fantasies and suck the Huck Finn right out of them. They would, like caribou, continue on the ancient migratory path and walk the same way with the safe herd come September, year in, year out, unless a natural gas or oil company decided it would like to drill on school grounds and diverted them in some direction that tradition or genetics hadn't mapped as a diversion route before.

Albert imagined them at continental-breakfast time before the first meeting of the school year, huddled in their fluid subsets, asking one another where he was, had he been seen or heard from, was he all right, did something happen over the summer that had not been properly disseminated to the school community just yet, was he not coming back. And when, in coming days, the knowledge torch would touch each hand and it was clear that he was sprung, for reasons that would multiply like murky legend, Albert's status would be elevated with each fabrication, and its unofficial recognition would, ironically, receive the imprimatur of authority when the administration sent the email memo out that no faculty or staff member should discuss, among themselves, with students, or with parents, the departure of Albert Lesiak. When teachers would begin referring to him as He Whose Name Must Not Be Uttered, Albert's institutional apotheosis would be final.

So he was all about the new adventure when he picked the boys up after school. Each day, his exams graded and his grades recorded and his inner being nap-refreshed and clarified, he summoned Watts at 2:45, told Mary he was going to pick up the boys, and walked down the concrete steps, whose widening crack was properly a chasm now and separated step three from step four in a sort of continental drift, which didn't bother him because he was no longer paying for the house and June was good, with all the nesting and the birdsong and the budding, June was good about reminding him that curb appeal, repair, and resale value were the worries that succeeded the worries that attended a house presumably at the mercy of a merciless geology, the worries that preoccupied a person when he wasn't rested and was under the illusion that he was his ranch house and his ranch house, built in 1955 and needing maintenance, was he.

Albert drove, arm resting on the door sill, and he took deep breaths and looked pleased, like a person at the tail end of a television ad for respiratory medication. Watts stood on the passenger seat, his window rolled down halfway so he could project his head and neck and partial torso out and meet the jet stream like a canine version of those nautical figureheads that graced the bows of ancient boats for purposes, Albert guessed, of good luck or intimidation. That was yet another thing that boosted Albert's serotonin. Whether it was Watts's figure or another dog's, the pure projection of a dog's head and neck and partial torso from the open window of a moving vehicle was as significant a liberation image to him as *Washington Crossing the Delaware* or Neil Armstrong hopping on the moon. In the deepest reaches of his childhood, before the advent of his conscious memory but verified in photographs in which a baby said to have been him was playing with a German shepherd in the presence of relatives he could identify as people in the last years of the sixties, Albert had lived in the presence of a dog.

He glanced at Watts existing in the deathless moment, Canis Minor reveling in the speed at which the sensed world hurtled by, unburdened, Canis-wise, by nitpicks and adulterations and anxieties and possibilities that there were freer states of being elsewhere, and Albert was doomed to wonder when the life of Watts would end. He estimated, given Watts's veterinarian-approved condition and their long hikes in the woods, that Watts had three good years remaining, which would get him to sixteen, ripe but not unreasonable for a dog of his dimensions. Besides, according to the Guinness Book, the oldest dog on record was a border collie who defied the actuarial tables, assuming the actuaries actually had such tables tabulated for the dogs, and lived past twenty-nine. *Past twenty-nine*, which, if you went with the dog year being equivalent to seven human years convention, was two-hundred-three years old. *Two-hundred-three*. So why couldn't Watts hit eighteen, nineteen, even twenty, which would still fall far short of the record?

Albert suddenly tapped his brakes and swerved, anticipating that a chipmunk on the roadside would play chicken, but the chipmunk reconsidered and retreated to the borderland of brush and grass. Albert checked his rearview to confirm.

"Sorry, buddy," he said to Watts, who, thanks to his experience with prior unannounced momentum shifts, had managed to retract his head and neck and partial torso and, in doing so, to lean his seventeen or eighteen pounds so that they fell against the cushioned seat-back and avoided a collision with the fairly unforgiving dashboard. "I thought he'd cross."

That week, each day after Albert picked up the boys from school, he put their backpacks on the floor in front of Watts, unless he sensed that dispossession could be an arousal trigger, which he sensed on Wednesday and was proud of sensing, and made sure their cores would be essentially immobilized in the event of accident and wondered if the visionary who would one day render canine seatbelts standard, or at least a basic option, in American vehicles was born yet. The four of them did not say much.

On Monday afternoon, the four of them rode silently along the river where it splits around Gildersleeve Island, crucial habitat for the endangered Puritan tiger beetle, which is only found along the Connecticut River and, six-hundred miles away, along the Chesapeake Bay. Fewer than a thousand still survive at three sites in New England, 99% of whom are in Connecticut, and most of that percentage was, at that time of the year, emerging from the sand around the island and preparing for the existential numbers game that was the propagation ritual. Because it troubled Albert that few who drove by the island knew how grim the prospects of the Puritan tiger beetle were and those who did know didn't care because the beetle didn't have the grandeur of the eagle or the wisdom symbolism of the owl, Albert planned to tell Jake and Ryan all about the insects who inhabited that island and the daunting odds they faced. He planned to weave the theme in of respect for life across the species lines. But he thought that pointing at the island and explaining these things would be more effective if he had pictorial assistance and the boys could visualize the pressured creature (six legs, long antennae, black and white, with jaws like ice-block tongs) that he seemed oddly passionate about. He made a mental note to search for images when he got home.

He scanned for turtles on the road and slowed as he approached the fairgrounds entrance, near where he'd administered the head-butt right around this time last year. The gate was open, but he parked to the side instead of entering. The four of them got out. He put a leash on Watts and held the looped end out toward Jake and Ryan. Ryan took it, and the four of them walked on the grass and followed the direction of the paved road. When they got to where the road curved, Albert pointed at Watts, who sat, and held his hands up to the boys in a "Wait here" gesture. He waited on the margin of the road for two cars to pass and ran across with torso bent like someone doing what he could to get low just in case of sniper fire and came back with a retracted painted turtle who had been about to do the slow crawl across the road to their side. He set her on the grass in the direction that she had been heading, and he held his hand out to relieve Ryan of the leash. The boys kneeled and ran their fingers gently over the turtle's back until its shelly texture lost the power to amaze and waited patiently for the emergence. After a duration of collective observation and no sign the turtle would let down its vulnerable defense, Albert moved her back a greater distance from the road and set her on the grass again in the direction that she had been heading. They resumed their silent vigil, trying telepathically to will the turtle out with peaceful vibes. Albert took the leash off Watts, who trotted toward the meadow, where the sandhill cranes had done their dance around this time last year, and paused from time to time for scent investigation. The boys followed Watts, and Albert followed them, imagining their futures.

If, in modern times, there's still room for the idyll, that week, from approximately 3:15 to 5:30, could be fairly termed idyllic. Two expanding brothers and their reinvigorated dog and their paternal figure strode by breeding meadows and stood by the tidal river and observed the heron grace and did not fling stones to disturb the grace. They stepped with care the following day past plinking frogs and sunning black snakes as they crossed the narrow isthmus leading to the two-tier observation deck and looked at the beaver's domed lodge and the cranberry infrastructure and the lily-padded bog. They saw the next day where had been the fire tower and traversed the fire-tower ridge and passed a lot of massive rocks deposited millennia ago by a retreating ice mass and examined fingerlings suspended in the stream that fed the reservoir and walked the path around the reservoir and took inside of them the surface calm of ducks and did not fling stones to disturb the surface calm. The following day they disregarded faded Posted signs and found the hidden pond and sat in Adirondack chairs or on the grass and watched the reigning snapping turtle bask and took the secret passage out. The next day, with binoculars, they went back to the tidal river, and they took turns looking toward the island where the Puritan tiger beetle somehow held on.

The problem was that such a week established an idyllic rhythm they could not sustain since one day it would rain or there would be no animals in evidence or they would have to drive up to the airport as a family to get Steve, who would exist among them for a couple days and then depart with Albert to Maine to do the manual work of actualizing what a good part of our literature suggests would be a more authentic way of life.

"You're not taking Watts," Mary whispered in the bedroom the night before the Maine departure.

"A camp dog's a necessity," said Albert as if reminding her of an inalienable right.

"You're so fucking selfish."

"Selfish?"

"You would really take the dog from them."

"What's the big deal? They'll be in school for two more weeks. They wouldn't see him that much anyway."

"That's fucking selfish. Start acting like a father."

"What the hell is so unfatherly about a camp-dog requisition?"

"You're not taking Watts."

"Let's leave it up to Watts."

"You're *not* taking Watts."

They reached a point where they experienced a word depletion and were forced to wait a moment for their language stores to be replenished.

Mary resumed, "In the last week, how many times has Jake said Watts loves him?"

Albert had to admit that taking Watts in light of that reminder would have been supremely dickish and a lasting blot upon his reputation as a father, one that probably would irk him like a Fury unto death.

"Fine. Watts can stay. Deprive him," Albert said and went to drink another beer with Steve.

***

Moments when unfocused manual manipulation yields a major insight are so rare that, when the insight suddenly appears and its substantial nature clarifies, its stricken and involuntary conjurer may have to sit among the unstruck for an equilibrium-reclaiming while, worrying something like a Lego piece before contributing again to the construction and deciding that she will incorporate the insight into the amorphous structure that was heretofore her life. Of course, decisions of such heft can't bear excessive scrutiny and can't be thought about so much that they begin to ramify and must, as far as possible, be implemented forthwith if the conjurer is serious. If there are children present, she must facially dissemble and excuse herself by saying something common in a steady, moderately cheerful tone. If rising causes a betraying wobble to run through the legs, she must intuit that it is permissible to look a moment out the window and to write the wobble off as circulatory reassertion after a compressive period of sitting. If the rising causes dizziness, she must walk through the dizziness and know it's not a matter for the limbs. And then, in order to confirm the ho-hum nature of her movements, she must ask of anyone who might be onto her if they need anything. It may be helpful to suggest two basic items to enhance the overall impression that there's nothing ripple-worthy in her going forth.

So struck, Mary rotates a yellow rectangle of a Lego piece like an ear of corn between her index fingers and her thumbs and contemplates the burden of the lie and its amassing quality and how, if she does not act now, the lie will never have a half-life and will never be inert. She gets how people can be twisted by complicity, by a windfall, by a husband who believes complicity and sudden money to be signs that he should do what he has talked about for years and live a somehow truer life, a life apparently more Emersonian or whatever than the one he's lived thus far.

She wishes that she never mentioned that enticing stipend as inducement to adopt and wishes that she never mentioned that the surplus could go toward the renovation of the old camp. What meager powers of prediction had she needed to foresee what would come next? She wishes that she just said *Fuck no* to strategically defaulting on the mortgage, to his cabin tear-down last year, to his giving up his job without a word to his employers, to his cabin rebuild, to his wanting to become a version of Thoreau or Dick Proenneke or Eustace Conway or whomever else he idolizes as Authentic Man. But if, on second thought, those wishes could come true, she probably would not be a probationary mother right now. Things tended, she assumes, as they were meant to tend. Without her husband here, however, she is free to undo what she's able to undo.

"It looks like we've decided to build upward," Mary says to Jake and Ryan. She inspects the structure and connects her yellow piece, the general theme of verticality progressing thereby. She waits her turns and adds a few more pieces, following Jake's and Ryan's leads. "I can't believe how high we're getting." She purses her lips and nods.

"Believe it," Jake says.

"Very impressive. But I need," she says, untangling her legs and rising, "to take a little break because I just remembered that I have to pay a bill." She stretches one leg, then the other, to facilitate the blood flow. She looks out the window and reports, "It's so nice out. We should take Watts out for a walk later." Her notice of the pleasant weather and her setting up a tentative, short-term plan subdues a little of the buzz of conjugal rebellion. "While I'm up, can I get you guys anything? A juice box? Carrot sticks?" A pause. "Okay. You guys keep working. Keep an eye on Watts. I'll be right back."

Mary walks to Albert's study and feels apprehensive, as if merely entering instills in him, 350 miles away, an intuition that a shift he cannot put his finger on has just occurred at home. He keeps the checkbook and the bills atop the Seamus Heaney, Geoffrey Hill, Tony Hoagland section of his bookshelf underneath his Hondius World Map c. 1641. She removes the checkbook and the latest notice from the mortgage company. It's been six months, and Citibank has not begun foreclosure proceedings on them yet. She flips the checkbook open. The current balance is $77,410. It is to her a mountain of a sum, an almost liberating sum.

In the kitchen, Mary takes her bank card from her purse and takes a pen and calculator from a counter drawer and scribbles on an envelope to judge the pen's utility and finds the phone and goes back to the living room. She pauses in encouraging appraisal of the incremental, elevating structure and then sits in Albert's chair. She scans the latest notice from the mortgage company. With late charges, they owe $11,403.24. She taps that number into the calculator, adds July's payment to that number, writes $13,238.78 on the bill, and dials. She gets past the automation and informs the human representative that she would like to make a payment so that they're no longer in default.

"I can do that for you," says the female representative with customary optimism.

Mary reads aloud the number on her debit card, the expiration date, the three-digit number on the back.

When she concludes the call, she enters into the calculator 77410 – 13239 and writes in the checkbook, "6/29 Mortgage (January-July) 13,239." In the Balance column, she writes, "64,171." She stares at the number for a while and, although she sort of feels like she's committed infidelity, decides that number does not carry adequate dissuasion weight. That is, when Albert discovers it, although he'll feel enraged and baffled and financially and philosophically betrayed, it will not be a diminution of severe-enough proportions. It will not inspire him to scrap his independence plan betimes.

Mary thinks about the sort of people who have knowledge of investment vehicles, of risks and yields and fees, and how they are unlikely to be frightened when it comes to allocation of the right sum to achieve a clear investment goal.

She picks up the computer on the floor beside the chair and types in "low risk investments." She reads about CDs and modest interest rates and calculates that, if she deposits fifty-thousand dollars in a five-year CD at 1.81% interest, compounded annually, she will have $54,692 in five years. Then she reads about the early-withdrawal penalties and thinks a penalty of some severity would be enough of an incentive for Albert to contemplate maturity, to let the money be, and to admit defeat. She clicks to learn more about the penalties and is disheartened to discover they are relatively mild. For maturities of less than one year, the typical penalty is merely ninety days of interest. Not enough dissuasion weight.

It then occurs to her, as she observes the ant-like focus of the boys as they continue to erect, that, if she summons fortitude and steeliness and singleness of purpose centered on the welfare of the boys, she could just put the money in a CD and refuse to tell Albert where it went until the summer really wanes and school starts and he starts to come around to her perspective and, by various means, agrees an off-the-grid existence is impractical with two autistic boys and no job and an outhouse and no inclination to destroy an animal and no experience in gutting and preparing and preserving one and general pressures that a guy like Proenneke, who had no wife and children with him in Alaska, never had to face.

Mary lingers on the benefits of Albert's absence and the boldness it engenders in her. Then she pictures him returning, storming through the sliding screen door, brandishing an ATM receipt as evidence of a disastrously diminished balance, and demanding, never minding that his voice might be a high-arousal trigger for the boys, demanding, "Where the fuck did all the money go?" She pictures telling him, to spare the children in the short-term, that she put the missing fifty thousand in a five-year CD as a sort of protest, an exertion of her recognition of the wrongness of expecting these two boys to readjust again, expecting them to be his sidekicks in his fantasy of self-reliance and remoteness and return to nature. The resolution of the picture isn't great beyond that, but she sees the fifty thousand, minus the withdrawal penalty, reallocated, and she sees the staking out of their positions in the arguments that must ensue.

She thinks that she could bear the arguments, that they could move beyond them, if he really lost the means to carry out the radical remove.

Mary scrolls down the page and moves on to another. She reads brief, perplexing explanations of Treasury Inflation Protected Securities, Money Market Funds, Municipal Bonds, and so on. She comes across a site that mentions debt reduction as a strategy that could be better than investment, and she clicks around and learns that there is no consensus as to whether it is better to pay down a mortgage and reduce the bondage years and interest or to put the earmarked money in a risky place from which it may not ever find its way back to the wizening investor.

Mary clicks a Mortgage Payoff Calculator and enters the Existing Loan Balance, which she rounds to $163,000, the Interest Rate, which is fixed at 3.25% because of their refinance three years ago, the Period Remaining on Existing Loan, in Months, which is more or less 144. Next to Number of Months From Now You Want the Loan to Be Paid Off, she enters 120 just to get things going. A one-time-only payment of $24,457.77 would knock off two years on the mortgage and save them $9,385.89 in interest. She clicks the back arrow and replaces 120 with 96 to knock off two more years. A one-time-only payment of $48,489.02 would save them $17,198.65 in interest and the mortgage would be done in eight years. She and Albert would be fifty-three by then. The boys would be nineteen.

Mary pictures how the day they make the final payment will be shot through with such lightness. Albert will have no reason to bemoan indentured servitude. They will look back on this day as the expediter of release.

"Are you playing a computer game?" Jake asks.

"Sort of," Mary says as she picks up the phone to call the mortgage company again. "It's like a numbers game for grown-ups."

"I hope you win."

Chapter Seventeen

Albert and Steve discuss their fastening needs as they stand at the Dexter Lumber register and say good morning to the capped and mustached counterperson when he walks out of the office in a manner that suggests his legs are not of equal length or that his occupation has its perils. Albert says he'd like to place an order and removes a well-worn piece of paper from his back pocket. The counterperson watches with an expression that betrays no bias of the mind as Albert unfolds it three times.

Steve turns, looks left and right, goes right, and disappears down the aisle at whose entrance squats an efficient-looking pellet stove. A period of clanking then ensues.

Albert reads the list of the materials they need for the roof. He reads deliberately, pausing after ordering each item to allow the counterperson's index fingers ample time to hunt and peck. And when the man looks up at the enormous, antiquated monitor to check what he has entered and his fingers hover like a pianist's above the keys, Albert waits one beat and resumes as though there were no limits or contemporary pressures on his time.

"Delivered?"

"Yeah," says Albert. "We're on the Morton Road in Garland."

"The Morton Road," he says as if in contemplation of a crossword clue. "I thought I knew all the roads in Garland."

"What road don't you know?" asks a voice from the stockroom. A bald, bespectacled man, a mustache-sporting man, emerges and looks inclusively at Albert, who recognizes this man as the deliverer of their initial order. "Put down on the invoice Hi-Cut boys. We've been there before." Without a formal sign of greeting or departure, he returns to the stockroom.

The counterperson redirects his attention back to Albert and asks, "That'll do it?"

Steve returns and sets on the counter a cardboard box in which are piled grayish silver galvanized hurricane straps. Albert picks one up, admiring its complementary geometry and how what should have been a corner of the one rectangular plane becomes an isthmus leading to another plane that lies at a constructive ninety-degree angle in relation to the first. He holds it vertically and pictures how the top plane would be fastened to a rafter, how the bottom would be fastened to the two-by-fours that form the cabin's top plates. Albert sometimes finds himself involuntarily amazed by metallurgy and the alchemy of manufacture and the multiplicity and specificity of ties and fasteners that it produces.

Steve hands Albert a pocket-sized *Simpson Strong-Tie Wood Construction Connectors Catalog.*

The counterperson, unfazed, asks, "How many?"

"Twenty," Steve says.

"That'll do it?"

"That'll do it," Albert says.

"Did you get two rolls of Typar?" Steve asks.

"No."

"And two rolls of Typar," Steve adds.

"Nine foot?" asks the counterperson.

"Nine foot."

"You want some Typar tape?"

Steve considers. "Yes. Three rolls should do it."

"That'll do it," Albert says, holding out his debit card.

"Everything delivered?"

"We'll take the hurricane ties, the Typar, and the tape," Albert says.

"Typar's in the first bay to your left when you go out," the counterperson says, handing Albert the invoice and his debit card. "Tape's right there," he says, pointing to a rack behind them.

Flush with widened human interaction and participation in the honest commerce of the nation, Albert and Steve survey the flanking products with an eye toward future need as they approach the door and joke as men not beholden to a pressing obligation are inclined to joke.

The sky is lightly overcast. The sun seems on the verge of breaking through, but it does not break through, and so the atmospheric tenor feels mercurial or noncommittal and the sense of rain perhaps a-coming makes the two of them appreciate the progress of a dry spell.

Steve sets the box down in the truck bed, and they head toward the first bay, looking here and there, impressing harder on their memories the details of a landscape memorized thus far in the initial broad strokes characteristic of the early visit.

They are suitably impressed with the dimensions of the bay and gaze up at the ceiling, maybe thirty, forty feet high, gaze up at the ceiling with the bared throats, humbled eyes, and not quite slack jaws of cathedral tourists.

"Can I help you guys find something?" someone who enters behind them asks.

"We need two rolls of Typar," Steve says, leveling his gaze.

"It ain't up there," the man says. He is about fifty, suntanned, with close-cropped hair and a tended mustache somewhere on the reddish-blond side of the spectrum. He wears a clean blue t-shirt tucked into his jeans. "That all you need?" As he passes Albert, Albert hands him the invoice almost as a reflex. "Hi-Cut boys? What you guys got going on on Hi-Cut?"

"Building a camp," says Albert. "On the Morton Road actually, across from Hi-Cut. About half a mile down."

"I used to fish the brook back there when I was a kid. I don't live too far from there. I'm on the Millet Road." He waits for a sign of recognition, and, when it is clear they do not know where the Millet Road is, he says, "Where you guys from?"

"I'm from Connecticut," says Albert. "He's from Texas."

"Texas? Long way from home."

"Steve Batchelder," Steve says, extending his hand. "Originally from Connecticut."

"Robert Pingree." They shake.

"Robert, nice to meet you. Beautiful country up here."

"Albert Lesiak," says Albert, extending his hand. They shake.

"Just building a hunting camp down there?" asks Robert.

"About that size," says Albert, "but I plan to live there year-round."

Robert has a look of mild puzzlement. "You got power down there?"

"No. Well, a generator," Albert says.

"You got a well?"

"No."

"Hmm. Hard living. My parents both grew up without the indoor plumbing."

They are silent for a moment to envision such a youth.

"What's your plan for water?"

"We have five-gallon jugs we fill up in the stream. We add a little bleach to treat the microbes."

"Yeah, I don't know if I would drink that water. There's a spring right off the Exeter Road. It's frozen in the winter, but it's flowing now. You know where the Exeter Road is?"

"No."

"You know where the Corinth Road is?"

"No."

"You got a *Gazetteer*?"

"In the truck."

Robert leads them to the rack on which the boxed rolls of Typar lie and slides one out, which Albert takes, and another. Robert says to Steve, "I got it."

The boxes, situated in the bed, stick out three feet beyond the tailgate. There is brief discussion on the prospect of their shifting when the truck is underway, and Steve, a staunch proponent of securing even relatively stable loads with rope or bungee cords or crank straps, takes from a compartment near the tailgate a fluorescent-orange crank strap, hooks one end, raises the crank and strap above the boxes, hooks the other end, smooths out the strap so it lies flat upon the boxes, and cranks until the boxes start to compress. Steve puts his hands upon the boxes, tries to wiggle them, cranks twice more, tries to wiggle them again, cranks once more, wraps the excess strap around the boxes, and secures the loose end to the taut strap with a knot.

Albert admires Steve's facility with knots and how that knowledge has been passed down serially, ingrained, without a formal course, and how Steve summons it without a conscious effort and without considering it remarkable, the way a monarch butterfly whose forebears wintered down in Mexico does not regard its fluttering in Massachusetts as a miracle of navigation or kinesis. Albert recalls a distant morning he accompanied Steve's father to the transfer station. Steve Senior, in the process of securing what they'd loaded in the trailer, showed Albert how to tie a half hitch and a loop knot and a slip knot and a timber hitch, including in his demonstrations explanations for the purposes of each. And after that day, Steve Senior showed him how to tie those knots again and others, Albert retaining almost nothing but the interesting names. Albert wonders now why he is not blessed with that particular strain of the utilitarian, which would allow him to size up a nautical or lading situation and determine that it calls for, say, a half hitch and be expert in the execution of that half hitch so whatever is secured by that knot does not qualify his manhood and become unmoored. *Of all the things to envy someone for,* he thinks. He follows that by thinking that Dick Proenneke must have been a master knotsman.

Albert gets the *Gazetteer* and hands it to Robert, who on the first try opens it to Map 32. Robert sets the map on the right angle that the quarter panel and the tailgate form and places his index finger just below the black dot where the Garland Road bears right and then becomes the Corinth Road. The three of them become a human arc around the map.

"The Garland Store's here. You know where that is. Go past the pond," he says, his finger moving east along the Corinth Road. "Then turn right here. That's the Exeter Road. Before you hit the first house, turn left down the dirt drive. It's not on the map, but it's there. The spring house is tucked back there."

"Easy enough," says Albert. Then his attention wanders eastward to a sprawling, disproportioned feature outlined in a tannish-brownish-pinkish band, PENOBSCOT INDIAN TERRITORY, which extends past the Interstate and ends just shy of the PENOBSCOT RIVER whose name is in the blue that is the river and appears to flow serenely by the little archipelago whose tannish-brownish-pinkish hue means it belongs to the Penobscot. "What does *Penobscot* mean anyway?"

"It's an Indian name," says Robert.

"But what does it mean?"

Robert shrugs. "It's Indian."

Albert says, "Like *Connecticut* means *the place of the long river* or *beside the long tidal river*."

"It's Indian is all I know."

"Well, thank you, Robert," Steve says. "It's good to know that there's a spring."

Steve questions Robert on the quality of the well water in these parts. Robert relates what he has heard of arsenic, uranium, and radon concentrations from the people who conducted tests.

"I use the spring myself," Robert says.

Albert makes a mental note to learn the etymology and meaning of *Penobscot*, and he wishes that he had the discipline to keep a notebook and a pen on standby in his pocket so his mental notes could benefit from documentary respect and he could be relieved of trying to retrieve another fleeting victim from the endless mental shuffle.

Robert's revelation of the hidden water source is filed in the category of rendered service and indebts Albert and calls for him to make an offer that conveys his gratitude and sociability and recognition of reciprocation. Civilization used to really champion hospitable exchange between its crossing strangers to remind its members that society was its foundation and had proven to be more conducive to the good life and the long life and the celebrated life, the life continued in memoriam, than solitude. Perhaps because he grew up in a suburb of increasing density, Albert casts the stink eye on such championship, but water is a life force, an elemental resource over which, according to predictions, governments will someday wage war, and the man who voluntarily performs the office of the dowser without the promise of remuneration or a favor should, Albert knows, be offered something like a seat around the fire.

"Robert," Albert says, "you should stop by some night. Any night. We have plenty of beer, plenty of food. We're always there."

"I might just take you up on that," he says.

As Albert drives onto the Garland Road, he asks, "You think he'll stop by?"

"He might," Steve says. "He seemed interested."

As they look out the windshield and the open windows at the farms and homes and stretches of apparently unpopulated woods, it is as if a sign they separately registered before but did not talk about because it was sporadic suddenly acquires topical significance despite its meaning having not been clarified and its appearance having not attained to regularity since their initial, tacit registrations on their passage into Dexter.

"I wonder what that yard sign means," says Steve. "That's the third or fourth one I've seen."

"I was wondering the same thing."

The signs they pass are all the same, so there is evidence of centralized coordination. In a red-bordered rectangle, oriented so the longer lines are vertical, is a red-bordered circle bisected by a red line slanting at an angle of about forty-five degrees, which line is meant to symbolize without equivocation that whatever else is in the circle is not wanted. In the hemisphere above the line is a W in red, and in the hemisphere below is likewise an E. Below the prohibitive circle, in a smaller font but seeming somewhat stouter than the aforementioned letters and blunter because of the reduction, is an unmistakable linguistic prohibition: NO CORRIDOR. But what the corridor is or is to be and just where in the west and where in the east its terminuses are or are to be and why the corridor is so unwanted that some citizens decided to engage in grass-roots activism, fixing to a wicket a laconic sign and sticking in the earth the wicket legs to a sufficient depth for sturdiness and hoping passersby would be by signage moved to join the cause, could not be known without some context.

"We should have asked Robert," Albert says.

"We should have asked Robert," Steve agrees. "It never crossed my mind."

"It takes a while sometimes for a thing to be called in from the periphery."

Steve writes something in his notebook.

By the time they reach the Morton Road, they've seen a few more signs and, though the modest signage numbers do not have the power to invest the centralized coordination with the gravitas of an unstoppable organic movement generated by an almost geological resistance to the schemes of corporate entities, they sense that something has at least gone airborne from the Weltschmerz-wracked sporangium.

***

It is the sort of day undesignated for accomplishment. Humidity and heat are on the rise. It feels like it could rain. Because the roof materials would not arrive until late afternoon the next day, they could wrap the walls with Typar in the morning and install the windows after that and still have time to wait with a libation for delivery. The enterprise is in abeyance, but they feel no guilt or shame for their industrial lull because, like idlers in no rush to ditch the granted respite, they attribute their inaction to the sometimes not unpleasant forces outside their control.

Steve swings slightly in his hammock for some moments as he settles and goes still.

Albert zips the vestibule screen and crawls into the tent to take an early nap and sees the tag of origin again and wonders what the lowest worker in an Asian factory would think if his or her superior approached with an intimidating clipboard and announced, "You're free to take an early nap. Production has been up. You've earned a little rest." Would he or she regard the napping offer as a test or trap, the only rational response a deferential head shake and perhaps, with eyes averted, a bizarro-Bartleby expression of the preference not to?

Albert lies upon his sleeping bag and closes his eyes and breathes the way Professor Sung-Bae Park taught him and his fellow primarily Judeo-Christian undergraduates that Buddhists who are practice masters breathe in meditation. He takes a steady breath deep down, beyond the trachea, beyond the lungs, below the level of the navel even, and lets go a small percentage of the self in exhalation and inhales the air again and lets the inhalation go and really focuses, in his Occidental style, on the letting go.

When Albert was twenty-one and off Dilantin and more sanguine as to prospects since his skull and brain had seemed to weather fracture and contusion admirably, without a seizure, and devoted to his consciousness the way a person who believes he nearly died must for a while show devotion, he approached the teaching seriously and practiced breathing each night in his bedroom in his parents' house for months and tried to meditate himself beyond the pesky consciousness of the five senses and the consciousness of the mind and the consciousness of the ego to the eighth consciousness, the storehouse consciousness, the primal consciousness that would eliminate duality, erase the false divisions, disabuse the mind of the delusion of the subject and the object and the whole attachment apparatus. Albert, however, always tried to meditate while lying down or sitting like a person being hand-fed grapes in his recliner, so, when meditation was progressing well and he was on the verge, let's say, of moving past the consciousness of touch, he'd fall asleep and yield to REM and dream and finally come to and, in that nanosecond of coming to, made no distinctions and was therefore only as enlightened as the general population and was more than ever mystified by how the Quang Ducs of the world let go. His practice, therefore, was reduced to the utility of sleep aid, but he took some solace in his somnolent breathing as a practical application of a fraction of a credit of his liberal education.

Albert, alone in the tent, supine in the tent, breathes meditation-quality breaths until the labor laws of other nations trouble him no more, until the tag of origin is not a separate thing from him, until there is no him supine upon the sleeping bag, no him who has to wrap the camp, no him who has to put the windows in, no him who has to calculate the roof pitch, no him awaiting a delivery, no him on whom three people in Connecticut depend.

They sleep about a hundred feet from one another for about an hour and a half and wake at the insistence of a raven whose intelligence is underrated by a lot of folks because, among other reasons, it is hard for people to get past the scavenger lifestyle and the grating caw.

They listen to the raven as they clarify.

Steve caws thrice from his hammock.

Albert caws thrice.

The raven caws no more.

Then they are just two guys who cawed without success, who have no secret knowledge of the languages of wildlife. So they arise at more or less the same time and approach the cooler as if walking toward a vehicle that will not start. Albert traverses the shorter distance. He is first and holds the cooler lid up with his left hand while he peers in like a mechanic at an engine that betrays no obvious malfunction. He wonders if it makes sense on this day of idleness to be judicious on the alcohol-by-volume issue in selecting for the two of them a beer to pair with post-nap conversation. Though it might make sense, considering the empty stomach, wise decision wouldn't help to foster the desired air of moderate abandon that a day like this seems made for. A well-hidden 8.2% seems middling on the scale of recklessness. He fishes out two beers, lets the cooler lid down gently, and extends one by the bottleneck to Steve. Albert pops his own top with a metal spoon and sips.

"To a day of rest," he says as Steve pops his top with his multipurpose tool and sips.

"A day of rest," Steve says, raising his bottle slightly and sipping again, dispensing with the clinking of a proper toast.

They sit in camp chairs near the grill and sip and stare appraisingly at the unwrapped, roofless camp.

After they are silent for a while, Steve says, "Building Seven."

"Building Seven," Albert says.

"Why would Rumsfeld say he never heard of Building Seven? What is gained from that lie?"

Albert tries to arch an eyebrow in the style of John Belushi.

Steve continues, "Salomon Smith Barney occupied thirty-seven of the forty-seven floors of Building Seven."

"That's a lot of sevens."

"My point is, Rumsfeld was *chairman* of the Salomon Smith Barney advisory board until he became Secretary of Defense. Fucking *Cheney* was on the board."

"But what would be the motive for blowing up the building?"

"Who knows? The CIA admitted that it ran a front out of Building Seven. It didn't admit what the front was, but the Secret Service, the IRS, DOD, SEC were all listed as tenants in Building Seven. The SEC lost a lot of documents. Who knows what the motive could have been?"

"I hate the fucking DOD," Albert says. "No, wait. I hate the DOE. Can you imagine the shady shit they actually did that no one knew about if they gave my mother and all those other people $250,000 out of the blue?"

Steve nods. "It's all about the cover-up. And I'm not saying the government necessarily blew up Building Seven. What do I know? But it had all the earmarks of a controlled demolition. It wasn't mentioned in the 9/11 Commission Report. And why would Rumsfeld deny knowledge of its existence?"

"What's the point?"

"I don't know."

"I mean," says Albert, "what's the point of worrying about this stuff. If you didn't have the internet, you probably wouldn't know about it anyway. You can't do anything about it."

"No," Steve says. "No, but you can't just let it go."

"I guess. Yeah, I guess sometimes someone has to give a shit."

Steve nods.

"Reminds me of Flight 800," Albert says.

"TWA. Flight 800. Fuel-tank explosion."

"My friend's brother took his boat out that night from Center Moriches. He swears he was looking out at the horizon, a flash or something comes up from the ocean, streaks up and arcs toward the plane, explodes on impact. No question in his mind it was a missile. Hundreds of people gave essentially the same account. The FBI or NTSB, whoever it was, said the flash and the streak were optical illusions. Fucked up," Albert says, finishing his 8.2% and getting two more beers whose ABV is similar.

"Plausible deniability," says Steve. "Deny, deny, deny."

"When the plane exploded, Tom sped out toward what turned out to be the debris field. It was already secured by the Coast Guard by the time he even got near it, which was minutes after the explosion. A police boat turned him away."

"If the government wants it to be a fuel-tank explosion, a fuel-tank explosion it will be. And if someone raises questions, goes against the official explanation, the government will make that person out to be mistaken or misguided, maybe not quite right in the head. At first. But, if that person keeps on, then the government will attack his character, threaten something dear to him, put child porn on his computer—whatever it has to do."

They sit in contemplation of the obvious conspiracy. What redress avenues were open to the common man, the honest man, the man who has no friends in lofty places?

"I think I caught a buzz on that last one," Albert says.

Steve sips and nods simultaneously.

Albert says, "I wonder why so few Americans are willing to mortify the flesh in protest of the government. Why does no one nail his nutsack to the cobblestones to register dissent? Why is self-immolation such a rare mode of civil disobedience? Does anyone even go on hunger strikes in this country anymore?"

"Let's assume you have a cause," Steve says. "In that cause's name, how long do you think you could go without food?"

"What's the cause?"

"I don't know. Human-rights abuses."

"Make it Arctic drilling. No. I don't really want to die for that." Albert sips. "If someone said go on a hunger strike and silverback gorillas will no longer be endangered or even a species of concern, I'd get on board with that."

"All right. In defense of the gorillas. How long could you go without food?"

"You mean how long could I possibly last? Because I think Gandhi went three weeks without food. I'm fairly confident that I could outlast Gandhi."

Steve chuckles.

"You don't think I could outlast Gandhi? That guy was a toothpick *before* the hunger strike. I can't compete with him in terms of moral fiber, but I'm the better physical specimen. I weigh like two-ten."

"So you think you could go three weeks without food?"

"With or without water?"

"With."

"Then, yeah, if Gandhi went three weeks without food, I feel that, personally, anything less than three weeks would be a personal defeat."

"Care to make it interesting?"

"No, I'm pretty hungry actually. And I don't think that starving myself would help the silverback gorillas' situation anyway. No one has the wherewithal to make that guarantee."

"I think that's the difference right there," Steve says, tipping his bottle top toward Albert. "We're not the freelance mortifying-flesh type anymore. Most of us aren't anyway. Unless our suffering is guaranteed to show some positive results, we take a pass. We aspire to the product, not the process. When's the last time you heard about a martyr in Connecticut?"

As two drinkers in a conversation such as this will do, they sit in silence for a while, shorten up their sipping intervals, and think about how best to follow up what Steve just said.

"I don't know," says Albert. "All I got is Nathan Hale. I know he was born in Connecticut. We have a million Nathan Hale elementary schools, but I'm not sure where he died."

"What did he do again? Did he inflict injury or death on himself for a cause?"

"He was hanged by the British as a spy."

Steve shakes his head. "That's a military issue. That's different. We're talking about a person from civilian life who recognizes that a moral wrong is being perpetrated and believes a letter to the editor or to his congressman won't rectify it. He's past the point of posting words on social media. He's basically saying that he can't continue as he has been while the moral wrong continues, and the only thing he has control of to convey his depth of grievance is his body and the only thing that he can think to do to show how deep the grievance is is to mutilate his body or to stress it deathward. When's the last time you heard about a person in Connecticut who did that?"

"You're fucked up."

"I'm fucked up? You're the one who keeps bringing up Quang Duc and the Russian scrotum nailer."

"Where does Dick Proenneke fit on the protest scale?"

Steve shakes his head. "That's not martyrdom. He made some tough choices, no doubt. He made a statement. But he just did what humans have been doing since the beginning. He had some issue with where he was living, so he moved."

"That's the American way," says Albert.

"Why mutilate yourself when you can move?"

They nod grimly as if they have suddenly arrived at a depressing truth and are constrained by it and stare, with both pairs of their legs extended, lounging-like, with beers resting on the slopes above their waistlines, at the covered grill as though it steams or glows or plays coy like an oracle.

"You ever wonder where we'd be," Albert asks, "if we just stayed in Africa?"

"Humanity?"

"That's right.

"Makes you wonder."

They adopt befuddled looks and hold them for a period that honors the conjecture.

"What do you think Gandhi first ate when the hunger strike was over?" Albert asks.

"I can't picture Gandhi eating," Steve decides.

"He had to eat."

"I know he had to eat, but I can't picture him eating."

"The alcohol's diminishing your powers of imagination."

"What do *you* think he ate?"

"Okra maybe," Albert says. "Something vegetal and fibrous, I would guess."

"How many chicken burgers do we have left?"

"Four or six. Why? You want to eat now?"

"No. In a beer or two."

Albert gets up and checks the cooler. "Six," he says, closing the provisions cooler, opening the libations cooler, and selecting two beers. Albert takes a sampling sip of his and says, "I should have been a sommelier of beer."

"A what?"

"A sommelier of beer."

Steve enunciates the syllables of *sommelier* a couple times and then pronounces the word in full.

"People would say, 'What do you do for a living?' I'd say, 'I'm a sommelier.' They would say, 'It must be nice to work with wine.' And I would say, 'I am a sommelier of beer.' They would say, 'Is there such an occupation?' And I would say, 'There is. A sommelier of beer is known as a cicerone.'"

"Reinheitsgebot!" Steve interjects gutturally.

"Gunter glieben glauten globen," Albert says.

"Why does that sound so familiar?"

"It's printed on the back of all U.S. currency."

Steve looks askance.

"I wonder what Jimmy Page is doing right now," says Albert.

A period of wonderment, in which the image of an English manor figures prominently, ensues.

Eventually, they sup and, after supping, sit and stare intently at the glowing charcoal through the smoke wisps and the shimmery heat and think about the distant past, prehistory past, and carnivores who kept their distance from the fire glow and how the whole lupine/canine domestication process came about. They shoo mosquitoes, but their shooing vigor wanes. They still have hours left of daylight.

When Steve hears bovine lowing in the distance, he says, "The cows are home."

"What?"

"You don't hear that?"

Albert nods, looks up at the sky, and says, "I haven't seen a bat since we've been here."

"It's early."

"I mean the whole time we've been here. I used to see a lot of bats here."

"Could be pesticide-related," Steve says.

"Could be the fungus syndrome," Albert says. "The bats leave their caves in winter and die of exposure."

"Could be both," Steve says. "Or neither. Beer?"

Albert tilts his bottle for a volume check. "You're a gentleman."

They drink and stare at coals.

"Did you know," asks Albert, "that a single bat can eat up to a thousand mosquitoes in an hour?"

Steve raises his eyebrows in admission of his ignorance.

"Imagine," Albert says, "what happens if they don't rebound."

They stare into the glowing coals, imagine what could happen if the delicately calibrated bat-mosquito balance tips, and do not share what they imagine. Many minutes pass, but they are less inclined to think in terms of minutes than they were when they arrived originally.

Albert eventually gets up and John Waynes it over to the sawhorse on which lies the silver speed square. He inspects one side, flips the speed square over, and inspects the other. He brings it to his camp chair, and he studies it from the seated-man position.

He reads, "COMMON RAFTER CONVERSION

INCH RISE / FOOT = DEGREES".

He studies the four rows of conversions. Then he holds the speed square up for Steve's inspection. "Do you know how to use this to figure out the roof pitch?"

Steve says, "I am ashamed to say I really only use it as a straight edge."

Albert looks back at the speed square and tries to make sense of the information etched there. "We should be able to figure out the angle of the rafters using this. What do you think the pitch should be?"

"Shallow enough so you can walk on the roof when you need to."

Albert looks at the speed square. "Eight?"

"Eight. Somewhere between seven and nine, I'd say. We'll experiment tomorrow."

Albert walks back to the sawhorse and moves it so it lines up with its companion sawhorse. He takes a leftover two-by-four and lays it across the sawhorses like a footbridge. He sets the lipped part of the speed square flush against the long end of the board so one end of the square's hypotenuse lines up with the top corner of the board.

"Okay, so this angle," Albert says, tracing his finger down the hypotenuse, "has to be forty-five degrees, right? Forty-five degrees is," he says, pausing to refer to the third conversion column, "a twelve pitch. So how are you supposed to get an eight pitch or a nine pitch?" He says this more to himself than to Steve. He scratches the top of his head and rubs his palm across his forehead. He sighs like someone who could use more oxygen. He focuses his attention on the right angle formed where the two legs of the speed square meet, where it says PIVOT, with a curved arrow indicating that the pivot motion should be upward and to Albert's left. He pivots it accordingly, but the resulting angles get progressively precipitous. He tries to pivot downward, but the lipped part of the speed square catches the board's edge. To pivot downward he would have to yield the fixed point. He shakes his head and flips the speed square so the right angle and the pivot point lay on the upper corner of the board, the pivot arrow curving upward and to Albert's right. He doesn't even have to pivot it to see that that was not the secret either. He sets the lipped part of the speed square on the bottom of the board so the hypotenuse runs one way and then reverses its situation so the hypotenuse now runs the other. He sets the lipped part of the speed square on the side of the board so the hypotenuse runs one way and then reverses its situation so the hypotenuse now runs the other. "This makes no sense," he says, but what he means is that he knows the sense is in there—he can see that it is sensible—but something, a deficiency of common sense or a reluctance to embrace the medium, obscures it. How can something he has sheltered in his toolbox for so many years befuddle him like this? How can something seemingly so logical, something meant to simplify the application of geometry, be such a cipher to him? "Where the hell is the internet when you need it?" He takes a moment to regroup. He sits down in his camp chair, drinks his beer, and looks around as one would look who seems unburdened by his placement in such scenery. He comes back to the speed square in his lap.

"This part here," he says to Steve, "HIP-VAL, TOP, CUTS, COMMON, that's got to be the measurement arena for the rafter cuts, right?"

Steve takes the speed square. "This row of numbers looks like it's for cutting rafters for a hip roof. You know, a gambrel roof like on a barn. This bottom row is for the regular roof. This open space in the middle of the rows has got to be where you mark what you want the pitch to be." He pivots the speed square up and down on his lap, flips it over, pivots. "But I don't see how you're supposed to position the square to get the angle you want."

Though there is a single person who can testify to his

befuddlement and though that person has professed himself to be befuddled as to function divination re the speed square, Albert feels publicly unversed when, all things considered, he was feeling pretty versed in general carpentry compared to other people that he knew who would have hired a professional to undertake the sort of job that he and Steve have undertaken.

"Know thy speed square, carpenter," says Albert as he gets up and goes back to the two-by-four to carry on with his experiments.

While Albert's thus engaged in the pursuit of artisanal self-improvement, Steve discerns a rumble in the distance. It is not a rumble traveling at high speed and it is not an atmospheric rumble, but it is heading steadily in their direction. By the time the rumble reaches the lower portion of the Morton Road, Albert looks up from the speed square. It is interesting how, when human beings isolate themselves, the onset of a passerby or possible arrival simultaneously arouses feelings of defensiveness and hospitality so that you don't know whether to start looking for the pitchfork or the candy dish.

The rumble turns left onto Albert's property, comes down the elevated section of the drive, and clears the cover of the trees. The rumble is revealed to be an emanation from a Kawasaki ATV on which sits Robert Pingree, extremities extended in the standard navigational configuration for this sort of vehicle. He slows and stops and turns the key. A certain kind of silence floods back.

"How's it going?" Robert asks, dismounting. He wears a t-shirt with a Dexter Lumber logo on the left breast and shorts that used to be long pants.

"You took the snowmobile trail?" Steve asks.

"Nope," says Robert, stepping to the rear of his vehicle and unsecuring the bungee cord that snugs his cooler to the rack. "I took the Camp Bell Road."

"The Campbell Road?" asks Albert, remembering the spelling on the map.

"The Camp Bell Road. Beer?" Robert asks, extending a Coors Light tallboy.

"I'm good," says Albert. "You live on the Millet Road you said?"

"Right."

"That connects to the Camp Bell Road?"

"The Millet Road comes out to the Corinth Road. Cross that and you're on the Cemetery Road. Take a right past the cemetery, that brings you to the Camp Bell Road."

"The Camp Bell Road's a paved road?"

"Dirt. Take a left off that and you're on the Morton Road." Robert sips his tallboy, looks at the unwrapped camp walls and the unused Typar rolls. "Didn't get much done today?"

"Today's a lazy day," Steve says. "Robert, while we have you here, do you know your way around a speed square?"

"I suppose."

The three of them walk to the two-by-four and speed square.

"If you wanted to make a rafter cut for an eight-pitch roof, how would you do that?"

"Well," says Robert, putting down his beer and picking up the speed square, "that ain't no big deal." He sets the lipped part of the speed square on the top of the board. "Assuming the end of the board here is a straight line, line this," he says, indicating the non-lipped leg of the speed square, "with the end of the board. See this here says PIVOT? Pivot up until this eight down here is even with the top of the board. Then scribe a line along here," he says, using his index finger to scribe an imaginary line along the non-lipped leg.

"Shit," says Albert. "How did I not figure that out?" He takes the speed square and replicates Robert's method with a seven pitch and then a nine pitch.

"He's an English teacher," Steve says. "What can you expect?"

"You're a plumber," Albert says. "I don't remember you imparting any pitch wisdom."

"Thank you, Robert," Steve says, "for clearing up that mystery. That information will be useful."

There are no hospitality extensions that surpass the ones that characterize such peoples as the Bedouins, the Bashkirs, the Ibo, no generational traditions whereby what is hostile in the world is held at bay. No invitation to remove his footwear and refresh himself by laving off the dust and stick of travel is extended. The hosts hold out no labneh, kumiss, kola nut. No pipe or snuff box makes the rounds. There is no mention of forestalling further travel on this waning day and sleeping off its rigors in their tent when they are done conversing. Granted, Robert isn't from afar.

Still, there are extensions.

Albert extends his open hand toward the camp chair he had occupied, an indication that the chair is high up in the seating hierarchy here, and says to Robert, "Have a seat." Albert takes a third chair from the trailer and unfolds it and situates it in conversational proximity to the originals and sits.

For a while, conversation focuses on the fundaments of Robert's life. How is working at the store? Does he have weekends off? Does he have kids? A wife? Commiseration on the situation with his former wife. Has he ever gone by Bob? Is he a hunter? Does he fish? Why is he a brook-trout man and not a bass man? How was childhood around here when he was young? How are the women now? What truck is he the owner of? They ask the sort of questions meant to draw their guest out into personhood, and, when he answers, they respond verbally and tonally and body-language-wise to make it clear that they are interested in his personhood and find his mode to be compatible with theirs, though there are differences and so they hold things back.

There comes a point when all three tilt back their heads to maximize their beverage love, then eye the bottom of their empty bottles or rattle the empty can to verify their emptiness.

Albert gets up and opens up the cooler and says to Robert, "Care to try one of these? They're a little stronger than the Coors Light."

"I had a couple before I came over," Robert says. Then he shrugs. "All right. Let's see what this is all about."

Albert extends an imperial pale lager from Connecticut to him. "That's at least two Coors Lights alcohol-wise right there."

Robert takes a sip and raises his eyebrows and rotates the bottle to inspect the label. "That's different," he says.

"Good, right?" Albert asks.

"Different."

"So, Robert," Steve says, "what do you think about those meltdowns at Fukushima?"

Robert shakes his head once. "I don't watch much news."

Steve summarizes the situation, explaining how much radiation is reportedly leaking into the Pacific Ocean and how the reports most likely downplay the magnitude of the actual discharge and how cesium would get into the fish and how the fish would infiltrate the people.

Robert says, "That's something. Kind of far away to worry about, though."

Steve asks, "Are there any nuclear power plants in Maine?"

"I think there's one down around Wiscasset. Never heard of no meltdown, though."

There is no tension in the air—everything is mellow, amiable, and free of confrontation—but Albert, as owner of this property, believes that it is not hospitable to focus on a topic in which Robert is not versed or interested.

"What is *Pingree*?" Albert asks. "Scottish?"

"Don't know."

"Where does your family come from?"

"Maine."

"What about four or five generations ago?"

"Always been from Maine as far as I know."

"I like your perspective, Robert," Steve says. "There's a wisdom in it that I wish I had."

"I don't know about wisdom," Robert says. He sips his IPL. "I'll tell you what, though. There's something in this beer, and it ain't wisdom."

They laugh the laughter of inebriated men, and, when the

laughter dies down, all three focus on the grill glow. The silence isn't forced or awkward. Beer, fire, woods. A kind of trinity of manhood. Robert Bly. They think their separate thoughts, but they are also all aware that each thinks something similar at some point about the beer, the fire, the woods. These are things that do not need discussion. Once sufficient time transpires, they begin to think about transition topics, what they might say when conversation starts again as they are sure it must because disbanding wordlessly is not an option.

Albert looks up at the slowly dimming sky and asks, "Have you noticed a decline in bats this year, Robert?"

"Now that you mention it," Robert says, looking up at the sky as if to contemplate the countless tragedies that go unnoticed. "It has been a while since I seen one."

"Robert, let me ask you," Steve says, "do you know anything about the E/W signs?"

"Oh, there was a meeting up in Dover three or four months back. You started seeing signs not long after that."

Albert's on the verge of interjecting for a clarification when the possibility occurs to him that this sort of answer in abeyance is a narrative decision Robert made, reflective maybe of his following an oral tradition in which full disclosure requires some unfolding, maybe of his own inherent recognition that a good guest should bring something with an entertaining structure to the table. Maybe it reflects both.

"Chinco wants to run a private two-hundred-twenty-mile toll road from the Stud Mill Road to Coburn Gore. Four lanes, fenced off, two-thousand-foot right of way. 95's right of way is only three hundred."

"What's Chinco?" Albert asks.

"Construction company down in Pittsfield."

"Why two thousand for a right of way?"

"Pigue didn't say. Just said you can't predict what future uses might come into play. People think it leaves room for a pipeline."

"An oil pipeline?"

"Yep."

"Where's there oil in Maine?"

"In Canada. The road would run from Canada on the Coburn Gore side to Canada on the Stud Mill side. People think the pipeline would carry oil to some Canadian refinery on the coast."

"Who's Pigue?"

"President of Chinco."

Albert tries to conjure Maine geography. "What do people in Dover care if there's a road or pipeline from Canada to Canada?"

"Pigue said in the meeting the road would run just north of Dover or just south of Dover, crossing 15 somewhere."

"We're just south of Dover," Albert says.

"He showed one map where the road ran straight through here."

"Here where? Garland?"

"You got that *Gazetteer*?"

Albert retrieves it from his truck and hands it to Robert, who places it on his lap so they, with minor repositioning, can see the back cover, which is a map of Maine partitioned into seventy rectangles. Robert places his index finger on Map 36 and slides it just below a black dot on Route 1, just west of the Canadian border.

"You see this road coming off Route 1? That's the Stud Mill Road, a logging road." His finger follows the road southwest out of Map 36, southwest across Map 35, west across Map 34, into Map 33. "The Stud Mill Road ends here. At Costigan. The East-West Corridor would run this way." He traces a west-northwest line to the Canadian border at Coburn Gore. "In the Dover meeting, Pigue called this stretch the Hollow Middle, meaning, basically, there's nothing here. That caused quite a stir apparently. Now," says Robert, opening the *Gazetteer* to Map 32, "Kelly at the store who was at the meeting said one of the maps Pigue showed had the highway running right through here." He traces a line between the Center and Campbell Roads.

"So the highway's coming right through here?" asks Albert,

gesturing toward the woods.

"Well," says Robert, closing the *Gazetteer* and handing it to Albert. "Technically, they're calling it a Transportation and Utility Corridor. And they been trying to get an East-West Highway or whatever you want to call it put in on and off since the forties."

"How would they get all that property?"

"Eminent domain," Steve says.

"That's a lot of dispossession," Albert says.

"Well, supposably, it's a private road," says Robert. "Pigue said they can't use eminent domain. I don't see how you get all the people along a two-hundred-twenty-mile stretch to sell without eminent domain."

"I've seen it in Texas," Steve says. "If they want the road, they'll figure out a way."

"I don't see it," Robert says. "Too much opposition."

Albert does not like what he is hearing, and he wonders if the disappearance of the bats is only the beginning.

Chapter Eighteen

Even for a person who has taken two undergraduate courses in Buddhist thought and still thumbs through the dog-eared course texts now and then and rereads passages he bracketed in black ink over twenty years ago and tries to go against the Western grain and seriously apply his former studies to his present life when he finds himself in situations or in states of mind he knows he should regard as mere delusions, fabrications of the ego, which he's also pretty sure is a delusion, Albert feels emptied, physically emptied, hollowed, as he stands before a Bangor Savings Bank ATM in Dexter on a mid-August morning, holding his receipt in front of his recorded face and saying in the stunned undertone of a person who has witnessed an atrocity in lovely weather, "What the fuck?"

As an exercise that he devised to try to pinpoint where he landed on the scale of Buddha worthiness, Albert sometimes closed his eyes and pictured in the darkness his reaction to a diagnosis of a cancer in the brain. The exercise idea occurred to him because he'd read an article on CAT-scan radiation's cumulative effects, which weren't properly feared in 1987–1988 when Albert slid into the cylinder for his scans to reveal the detailed images of his brain and its contusion damage and how its recovery progressed from scan to scan. Because he did not have, as far as he could tell, a cancer in the brain, the exercise was easy to perform and pointed to a Buddha worthiness not typically associated with a person who originated on Long Island. He only had to think of an imaginary tumor and his actual body as delusions of the ego, temporary things that by their nature had to pass. He only had to think of his true nature, his Buddha nature, as transcending all attachment, separate from a suffering that couldn't last and therefore was delusion. In theory, it was pretty easy to Quang Duc it.

When he had occasion to, he'd move the exercise outside the theoretical arena. One day, for example, he was stacking firewood in his woodshed when the temperature was in the twenties. He was in the process of stacking up a new row when, in the interest of improving manual dexterity, he removed his gloves. He placed his right hand flat upon the new row. As he reached his left hand toward the unstacked pile, there was a slight redistribution of his weight and then a piece of firewood from above dislodged and landed lengthwise on his right thumb. For a moment, he invoked the exercise: pain and thumb and body over here in one compartment, Buddha nature over here where it transcended all compartments. And then the pain intensified. He took his suffering and thumb and body and Buddha nature inside the house, and Mary said how pale he was. When the pain subsided to a pulse and the facial perspiration dried up and his stomach calmed and his head cleared and his color came back and Mary smiled and remarked on his fragility, he knew he was not worthy, and he understood there were no shortcuts around the path that Quang Duc took.

Standing at the ATM, Albert stares at his receipt and does not even try to implement the exercise because he's staring at an absence and he cannot set aside an absence as he can a thing that *could* be there, like an imaginary tumor of the brain, or as he can attempt to set aside a thing that's sensible, like thumb pain. Before the split log landed lengthwise on his frigid thumb, the thumb pain wasn't in his consciousness. Before he read the CAT-scan-radiation article, the tumor specter wasn't in his consciousness. Their nature was not-there. He conjured them, he didn't suffer or he suffered the delusion of attachment, depending on the rigor of his exercise, and they returned to being not-there, sort of proving the detachment point.

But the money, the absent money, is supposed to be there, its nature is supposed to be his ticket to detachment from the decent salary and the taxes and the neckties and the mortgage and the home phone and the power and the cable and the wireless connection and the mercy of the weekend and the three-day weekend and the bittersweet vacation stretches and the easy drift of being middling and the tantalizing sense that the authentic, unbeholden life he should be living will be his if he can just hold on until retirement.

Albert folds his receipt, inserts it in his wallet, turns away from the dispensary machine, and walks like Auden's Unknown Citizen across the street to Reny's. Even in the midst of troubles, Albert admires how the drivers in these parts defer immediately to those who use the crosswalk. On the sidewalk, he walks past the plastic Adirondack chairs in non-arboreal, pastel colors, past the yard tools, past the kiddie pools. He pulls the door, the little bell above which tinkles to announce him. He walks in a little way and comes out of his slouch, assumes his full extension, so his vantage is improved by several inches. He peers over the savannah of stocked and half-stocked shelves in search of Steve, who entered earlier to purchase batteries, and sees him in the footwear section studying a sandal engineered for the adventurous.

"The prices aren't bad here," Steve says. "These don't seem like they're irregulars."

"I need to borrow your phone."

This expression of necessity has Steve return the sandal to its place in the display. He reads the density in Albert's face and reaches in his pocket for his phone. He hands it to Albert and asks, "Everything all right?"

"We'll see."

"There shouldn't be a problem with reception here."

Albert goes out the tinkling door, flips open the phone, and dials. He paces while a wonder of the invisible world plays out. When Mary answers, he says, "What happened to the money?"

"Don't get mad."

"So it's not a bank mistake." Because his tone attracts attention, he walks down the sidewalk, past the storefront, and turns into an alley.

"I was going to tell you," she says.

"Yeah, after I checked the balance."

"You should get a cell phone."

"Where's the money?"

"I paid the late mortgage payments, including August. We're no longer in default."

"What the fuck for? The whole purpose . . ." Albert's quiet for a minute while he does the rough math in his head. "That's only about fifteen thousand. Where's the rest?"

"I looked into putting some money in a CD or a money market for the interest."

"And."

"And I saved us over seventeen thousand."

"Where is it?"

"I used fifty thousand to pay down the mortgage. It cuts off—"

"Wait a second. Let me get this straight. You're telling me you took the money *my* mother gave *me* as *my* share of the settlement that was basically the federal government's non-admission admission of complicity in my father's cancer death and *you* used all of it—fifty-thousand dollars—to pay down a mortgage we were getting rid of anyway?"

"She gave it to both of us."

"And you decided to get rid of it on your own."

"We can't move to Maine right now."

"No shit."

"I mean if we move now we could lose the monthly stipends because of the probationary period." Mary doesn't know this for a fact, but she believes she may have read it somewhere or been told about it once when she was sipping tea with Gina Dunn. Either way, potential stipend revocation has the air of plausibility. "We need the stipends, don't we? I already lied to Gina once about why you weren't here when she visited."

"Long-term, yeah, we need them," Albert says as if talking to himself. "Could sell the house and salvage this." He pictures dealing with a real-estate agent and the showings and the things that need to be repaired. The View-Master in his mind ker-clicks and now he's picturing himself arriving at the continental-breakfast portion of the opening of school retreat for faculty and staff in two weeks or so. He'll have to leave the woods and urinate indoors and be unnaturally punctilious about his hygiene and be mildly self-conscious about his beige teeth when he smiles because you have to smile at the continental-breakfast portion of the opening of school retreat or else your elsewhere wish will be revealed. He'll have to clear his throat more often to muffle the accordion truth that his digestion is impeded by society and its appointments and its many ears. "Fuck," he says, "I gotta go." He shuts the phone and leans against a brick wall in the alley, and, instead of trying to employ a precept from the East to separate himself from suffering that wouldn't qualify as suffering in countries that require more than angst, he thinks of Walter Mitty smiling in the face of an imaginary firing squad. This is what you do when you do not possess the Buddha nature of Quang Duc. You lean against a brick wall, which reminds you vaguely of the premium once placed on craftsmanship, and rue. Albert rues his emulation strategy and sees how flawed it was from the beginning. Though Dick Proenneke and Eustace Conway weren't members of the he-man-woman-haters' club, as far as Albert could tell from what he's seen and read about them, they did not take a wife and did not procreate or adopt and did not sacrifice to the idea of lineage or loneliness their visions of how they were meant to pass through this existence. They held fast.

Albert does a half shimmy, and his shoulders push him off the brick wall. He walks out of the alley to the sidewalk, into sunlight. He stops in front of the storefront window, looks down with contemporary skepticism at a flimsy Adirondack chair, is momentarily in contemplation of the mystery that shrouds the process by which it was rendered pastel blue, and sits down like a rheumatism sufferer, the chairback flexing as he settles in, reminding him of the preponderance of planned obsolescence in contemporary industrial design. He watches someone who is probably a pensioner look left and right before he limps his way through the crosswalk. It occurs to Albert that everything is built for obsolescence, but contemporary manufacturers have taken it too far. He watches as a car stops in honor of the crosswalk social compact. Albert notices its tires, and he wonders if it's true that tire companies possess the knowledge to produce a tire that will never wear out but will not produce it because, well, where's the obsolescence. He wonders if there is a cancer cure that someone who is not a team player safeguards in an antiseptic room. Then the car moves on, and Albert's thoughts turn once again to spousal perfidy and what percentage of the perfidy that spouses perpetrate is known to the betrayed.

The doorbell tinkles. Steve and Robert exit Reny's, each holding in his left hand a plastic bag of purchases.

"What are you doing out here?" Steve asks.

"You guys have been divorced," says Albert. "What's the downside?"

"It's expensive," Steve says. "It's emotionally draining."

"Everything's an argument," Robert says.

"You wouldn't get the dog," Steve says, "without concessions. Even then it's doubtful."

"I didn't think about that. Or the kids." Albert leans back further in the chair, testing its tensility.

Steve and Robert look out toward the road as if in contemplation of concessions or the children of divorce.

The doorbell tinkles. A lady acting in a managerial capacity approaches Albert and says, "We don't mind you sitting there, hon, but please don't lean back so far." She scrunches up her face and shifts her voice down to a whistleblower whisper. "They tend to break."

"Okay," Albert says as he moderates his lounging. When she goes back in the store, he tilts his head in her direction and says to Steve and Robert, "Julian Assange over here."

"What happened?" Steve asks. "She cheat on you?"

"Who?"

"Mary."

"Sort of. Here's your phone."

Albert hands it over and recounts to them what he has learned. They process.

"I feel, I don't know," says Albert, "hungover sort of. No nausea really. No headache. But that cranial fog. That fog that's like clarity."

"Could be a sign," Steve suggests.

"What could?" Albert asks.

"This development."

"A sign. It's not a sign. It's fiscal infidelity."

"It could be good," says Robert. "Look. You ain't set for winter anyway. No stove set up, no firewood, no well. Sort things out. Move up next year."

"It's just a year," Steve says.

"Easy for you to say. I can't live off in-law money like you and work here and there when I want to." Silence. "I don't mean to be a dick."

"And what about the highway?" Steve asks. "You don't want to move your whole life up here and find out they're putting a highway next door to your property."

"No, that's true."

"The money's not gone exactly. It's equity. Next year, you sell the house and get it back."

Albert stares at the crosswalk, and he wonders if the penalty for killing someone in a crosswalk is more severe than the penalty for vehicular extermination outside the protective zone. It has to be.

"It's not right what she did," Steve says, "but it's done."

Albert thinks of Lady Macbeth.

"You're not getting a divorce," Steve says. "You just adopted two kids."

"I did do that. Hasn't felt like it up here, but I did do that." As men with facial hair will sometimes do to amplify a contemplation, Albert deploys a thumb to one side of his mouth, an index finger to the other, and runs them in a fu-manchu direction down the facial hair and brings them up to linger in the soul-patch region of the chin. The facial hair is like Zen-garden sand, the fingers like a pair of soothing rakes. "All right," he says, arising, "fuck it. Let's go."

They use the crosswalk and continue to the parking lot behind the Bangor Savings Bank.

"I'll stop in Milo for some worms," Robert says. "You guys can get a three-day license there."

Robert's GMC Sierra heads north out of Dexter, and the pop-up trailer that it tows rattles on the patches where the frost-heave damage hasn't been remediated. The spaces between the houses widen in proportion to their distance from the town until the houses cannot be considered as existing in relation to each other anymore because, when one appears to interrupt the woods, it has the aura of a homestead circa 1862 and you envision pickled vegetables in Mason jars and a root cellar and a bean hole and stoic people who are comfortable in solitude when it is ten below. A good percentage of the places they pass, as evidenced by signage, are inhabited by people who oppose the East-West Corridor.

Albert doesn't know what it is about being a passenger and looking out a window at some country that inspires longing, but he longs now, even though he understands that longing is just suffering for what he doesn't have and even though he figures Quang and Dick and Eustace didn't long much. Suddenly he wants to be with Watts and Mary and the boys, which is unusual because, except for some nights, his omission heartache really only centered on regretting that the camp-dog residency that he reserved for Watts was every day not filled by Watts. He understands why the Elizabethans were suspicious of emotion as a force that could befog one's reason. He knows, when he goes home and satisfies this current longing outburst, he will want to be back here, the longing process like a boomerang and living in the moment as elusive as a wolverine.

They pass through Dover, stop in Milo for the worms and licenses, and drive north through Brownville, past the log trains. They pass through Millinocket, vacant storefront after vacant storefront. Robert turns onto Penobscot Avenue and points to a two-story building, its lower half sided with half-round cedar logs, its upper half cedar-shingled. The bottom story extends along the road a little longer than the top, and, where the second story stops, the blue cab of a logging truck is mounted on the roof of the first story. To the left of the truck, red letters fastened just below the windows of the second story spell out:

PELLETIER LOGGERS

FAMILY RESTAURANT

BAR & GRILL.

Two Pepsi symbols, waves of red and white and blue, flank BAR & GRILL.

"You ever seen that show *American Loggers*?" Robert asks.

"I think I've seen it," Albert says.

"Not *Ax Men*?" Steve asks.

"Not *Ax Men*. *American Loggers*. The people on that show, the Pelletiers, that's them," says Robert, pointing to the restaurant as they pass.

"Looks closed," says Steve.

"I wonder how they got that truck up there," says Albert.

"It is closed. They've been trying to sell it for over a year."

"Town seems pretty deserted," Steve says.

"You should have seen this place in the seventies and eighties. Graduate from high school, get a job in the mill the next day. Money everywhere."

Robert takes the Millinocket Lake Road out of town. "On your right," he says, "is Millinocket Lake. On your left is Ambajejus."

"Ambajesus?"

"Ambajejus."

"What does it mean?"

"Got me."

"Ambajejus," Albert says. "Interesting name. Good dog name."

Robert looks left and says, "I done a good bit of ice fishing out on Ambajejus."

"How did you tolerate the cold?" Steve asks.

"Schnapps."

They all look out the open windows at the water and imagine winter and the warming properties of German liquor.

"This is the Golden Road we're on now," says Robert.

"This is the end of the rainbow?" Steve asks. "This is where the money is?"

"Used to be. Not so much no more."

"It's pretty hollow up here," says Albert.

"Actually," says Robert, "at one time or another, there was talk of making this the East-West Highway."

"Why didn't they?"

"The talk fizzled out."

Here and there the softwoods part and mountains in the middle distance are revealed. Their proximity and clarity stun something ancient in the torso. Robert begins to descend a hill and slows and pulls the truck off the road. "I brought my camera," he says.

He and Steve and Albert get out. Robert looks behind them and walks into the middle of the road to get a clear shot.

"What mountain is that?" Steve asks.

"Katahdin," Albert says. "It's got that sort of humpback thing going on." Albert extends his hand as if to touch the mountain, and he makes a sort of humpback motion, following the ridgeline.

"You hiked up that?"

"A couple of times."

They stand and stare at the granite monolith rising from the evergreen.

"This is a view," Steve says, stepping into the road to take some pictures of his own.

"It is majestic," Albert says.

"The next part of the Golden Road ain't so majestic," Robert says, returning to the truck to put away his camera.

"You can't see the mountains?" Steve asks.

"Oh, you can see the mountains," says Robert. "But the road ain't tarred like here. It's a workout for the leaf springs."

They resume their observational positions in the truck and feel like relatively stationary figures looking out their open windows at what seems a mostly stationary world, except when they catch glimpses of the river or look up and see some scavengers or raptors spread out in the air, and lose a fluctuating portion of their stationary sense some miles down the tarred road when the asphalt artery that links them to the tire hum of smoothly run America is severed and the tires crunch the road's geology and care for the components of suspension must be taken and the way becomes as dusty as an urgent scene employing horses in a Western.

Where the Golden Road goes chasmic, Robert slows and swerves, but otherwise he drives at highway speed through shallow potholes, over frost-heave extrusions, over washboard stretches of the road with brand loyalty and confidence that engineers at GMC designed a vehicle equipped to handle shallow potholes and extrusions and washboard stretches even with a pop-up camper jangling in tow.

Albert considers the velocity at which they would be traveling if he were driving his truck on the Golden Road and knows that it would be so low that it would be ridiculous to use the word velocity to gauge their progress. He knows that he would wince each time a tire hit a pothole or extrusion or washboard rib and would inwardly lament the damage he'd imagine their desire to go fishing cumulatively inflicted on his undercarriage and suspension. It occurs to him as he inspects the back and side of Robert's head that Robert is at home with this machine and understands its parts and their capacities and purposes.

When he and Steve arrived at Robert's in the morning for departure, Robert showed them the 1934 GMC pickup he was in the early stages of restoring, how he rigged a system up to lift the motor out, and where he thought the trouble he was having with the differential probably originated. While Steve and Robert talked about the project and commiserated, troubleshooting in the midst of automotive sorrow, Albert was trying to recall that line from *Zen and the Art of Motorcycle Maintenance* about the Buddha's whereabouts.

Albert looks out the open window, confident in Robert's navigation of the Golden Road and comfortable his own truck is at rest, and then looks down at the Styrofoam container and imagines what it must be like to be a worm deracinated and confronted with the stymieing conundrum that there is no way beyond this cup of soil, its penetration skills, applied with vigor and persistence, yielding nothing but dead ends. He thinks about what little he can think about the Jains and wonders how their reverence for all life, including gnats, mosquitoes, pill bugs, worms, does not induce in them the paralytic fear that they, in simply being, may by breath or footfall be the killer of a being they believe has as legitimate a claim to this existence as themselves. Albert writhes a little as he thinks he does not want to sheathe the hook inside the worm. He guesses that the Jains do not have many branches in America.

Robert points to the right of the windshield at a clearing and says, "My father used to work up here in the seventies when I was a kid. All along here would be logs stacked thirty, forty feet high. He'd stay at one of the worker camps for a month or two at a time, and me and my mother would come up on weekends and stay with him. It was hairy up here in the winter."

"They don't log this anymore?" Steve asks.

"No, they do. It just ain't like it was. It used to be you'd see log trucks in and out of here all day, constantly."

Albert looks out his open window at the tannish clearing, at the desiccated-looking interruption of the woods, and does not say that, though he understands the economic toll the market shift has taken, he is glad the lumber industry has eased up on extraction and that market forces, in this instance, are for once apparently protecting woodland somewhat from the depredations that the depredators like to euphemize as forest management.

They approach the Abol Bridge Campground and Store, a poster of a massive sugar cone topped with a symmetrical scoop of strawberry ice cream prominently displayed on the side of the building. At the top of the poster are the words PROUDLY SERVING, and at the bottom left is the remaining one third of the declaration, Gifford's. Advertising, even on this scale, dilutes the sense that they are entering the fringes of a wilderness, and Albert regrets that the appeal is working on whatever is the brain receptor responsible for salivation due to two-dimensional ice-cream imagery.

"Anybody want anything?" Robert asks. "There's no other stores ahead."

"We're not staying at this campground?" Steve asks.

"No," says Robert. "Ours is up ahead a ways. It ain't as nice, but it ain't as crowded. And it's quieter. Closer to Hussrace."

They cross the Abol Bridge and see Katahdin from a new perspective, the West Branch of the Penobscot River flowing in the foreground.

"What it said on the bridge back there," Steve asks, "about yielding to logging trucks, is that a law up here?"

"They have the right of way," says Robert.

On the roadside, bolted to a four-by-four post implanted in the ground like an eternal, optimistic hitchhiker holding up his destination, a brown triangular slab of wood with rounded points announces HORSERACE BROOK, HORSERACE over BROOK as though the modest water body functions as denominator. Above the etched and yellow-painted words, the sign's creator carved a double-layered upside-down V at rest upon a horizontal line, conveying the quintessence of a tent, the symbol that you see on maps to indicate with spatial thrift a campground, saving the cartographer the effort and expense of spelling out the word across the landscape's features when a pictograph will do.

"Here we are," says Robert. "Hussrace Brook."

Albert is used to Robert dropping r's that are not followed by a vowel. Non-rhotic strains of English flourish in the upper mid-Atlantic states and in the Northeast, so Robert's leaving out the r in *Garland* or in *hardwood* does not arch Albert's inner eyebrows or offend his English-teacher sensibilities. In fact, when Steve, whose Texas-acclimated ears are more attuned to violations of rhoticity, poked fun at Robert's r-lessness one night around the fire, Robert went full rhotic and replied, exaggerating all the undropped r's, "In Garland, where Robert harvests hardwoods for the winter, Robert hardly cares about his r's is what you're saying, Mister Batchelder," and sounded like a caricature of someone whose rhoticity was just another air that he put on. Point taken.

But other interesting variations of pronunciation seem to have their roots in a tradition with which Albert is not familiar and finds harder therefore to assimilate as variants of Standard-English words he keeps on file in the dictionary in his mind. He tries to make allowances when he is able. So when Robert uses *tuba-four* in lieu of *two-by-four*, Albert tries to write the alteration off as an example of elision, which he likes to think is characteristic of a healthy local language. And when Robert says *Camp Bell Road* when the signs that Albert has seen read *Campbell Road*, conveying the implicit silence of the p, Albert figures that there must have been a Camp Bell on that road in the daguerreotype days or that there must have been an unnamed hunting camp once owned by someone of the surname Bell, the camp imploding in slow motion from the days of the daguerreotype to the day when someone holding an official rank decreed the road must bear a sign that bears its name and thereby suffered the conflation of the signman.

But *Hussrace* is a different case. *Huss* isn't *hoss*, which has a history that Albert's privy to. *Hoss* he can accept as an established variant of *horse*. He's old enough to have *Bonanza* images still resonating on occasion in his brain, and he remembers the endearing Cartwright they called Hoss, a draft horse sort of man. And he remembers from the Puritan-Age unit of his textbook long-dead Edward Taylor's "Huswifery," and from the title of that poem Albert knows that *hus* means *house*.

But why *huss*? He fears it's impolite to ask because, if Robert doesn't know, the inquiry will hang there, and who wants to go around saying something that he knows has origins he can't explain? The question Albert mulls over now is should he keep on saying *Horserace*, as the sign and map say, practically in inhospitable defiance of his guide, or should he quietly defer to Robert's usage, which must be legitimate by virtue of his nativity, and now say *Hussrace* as though *Horserace* never had a place in his vocabulary.

"This campground used to be a gravel pit," says Robert.

No poster of a mushroom-cloud-like ice-cream cone is posted near the roadside as enticement. There's no building to affix it to, no air of the commercial, no attempt to make the passerby believe that he or she is duly wanted here. And so when Robert turns right at the entrance, inconspicuous as a trailhead, the three of them experience a version of the ego boost you get when you walk down an uninviting alley and apply your knuckles to an uninviting door and someone opens it and studies you a moment to discern your worthiness and then admits you on the basis that you know a little something that the general population isn't privy to. But there will be so little spending here they also feel that they have entered a peculiar sphere, a realm left largely unadministered, no ranger present to project authority, a province where their money almost is no good.

Absent is the festive air they sensed at Abol from the road. They saw some people strolling there, enjoying the amenable commons. The Abol campers have electrical connections, coin-operated showers, relatively fragrant water-flushing toilets, laundry infrastructure, and the store. Their money's good there. Amenities abound. The campers are to one another relatively proximate, and such proximity, combined with alcohol in moderation and abundant leisure, yields conviviality and openness that more or less define the atmosphere, regardless of the weather. When the density becomes too much, the camper can seek solace in or on the West Branch or in the woods and then reenter, fortified by temporary isolation, the community of humans.

"We almost have the whole place to ourselves," Steve says.

"There's another section of the campground past those trees," Robert says as though beyond those trees teem people waiting to disturb the peace.

Robert tows the camper past the only site that's occupied as far as they can tell. A green Jeep Cherokee is parked beside a four-man tent with roof extension. The picnic table features an array of sundries that conveys a sense of tenure. A gray-haired man rummaging in the Jeep's rear removes his head and watches with a landlord's manner of detachment as they pass. He seems to be considering the levying of an intrusion charge, but then he sees that Robert will be driving farther on and elevates his left hand to a height of basic greeting and goes back to rummaging, his hand left raised and visible a second longer than his head.

Robert parks at a remove that indicates he values what the solitary rummager appears to value. Boundary reverence is established with the generous remove. Each camp can see the basic outline of the other from this distance, but is powerless to hear particulars or intimacies, and so the ruffling that accompanies new settlement is smoothed. Each camp now understands the other, understands the sympathies they share do not need validation via intercourse or condiment exchange. It all is rather lupine, how the imaginary lines are drawn, how the exclusion zones are settled on without a word.

Steve and Albert stand back with due respect for a procedure they have never had occasion to partake in and observe as Robert unhooks the camper from the hitch. They watch as Robert turns the crank to raise the camper's walls and roof. They seem impressed with human ingenuity.

"When's the last time you used the camper?" Steve asks.

"Last year. I raised it yesterday, though, to air it out. It's probably still a little musty in there."

They transfer their sleeping gear and packs from truck to camper and decide on the arrangements, who will sleep where.

"I call ledge," Albert says. He climbs up and lies down and stares at the ceiling for a while as if contemplating root causes of insomnia and whether sleeplessness afflicted native cultures prior to the nightmare that was white men. He then looks below, evaluating Steve's accommodations. "This could be dangerous," says Albert.

"What could?"

"Nocturnal emissions. They can be insidious. Some guy died a few years ago from breathing his own emissions while he slept."

"Who are you worried about here?" asks Steve. "Us or you? Gas rises."

"I'm concerned about the general welfare," Albert says, sitting up. "We're all at risk."

"Unzip that screen cover there," Robert says to Albert. "Emissions or not, we need to air this out."

The three of them unzip the screen covers nearest them. Robert props the door open.

"It's probably a painless death," says Albert. "But if there's three of us and only one of us is taken by emissions in the night, I wonder if the medical examiner could figure out whose methane was responsible for the fatality. And if he could, would there be charges?"

"I don't know," says Robert, exiting the camper. "But I can think of better ways to go."

"Like what?" says Albert, following.

"I don't know," says Robert, opening the tailgate, sliding a cooler toward himself, and carrying it to the picnic table.

"No, I'm interested," Albert says, picking up the camp stove. "I'm always thinking of how I *don't* want to die. Brain cancer. Colon cancer. Pretty much any instrumental cancer. Evisceration, like in *Braveheart*. But at least William Wallace had a cause. Ebola. AIDS. That flesh-eating bacteria. The hantavirus. Plague. I'm such a negative thinker. I should be focusing on how I'd *like* to die. So what do you think are some better ways to go?"

"Well, I suppose I'd rather go with a woman," Robert says, returning to the truck.

"You mean while having sex?" asks Albert. "I don't know. That's pretty awkward for the other party."

"Better than expiring because a person wouldn't take a Beano."

"I don't know. I just don't think I'd choose that passage for myself. What about you, Steve?"

"Something quick. On the crest of a wave, I guess. One second I'm surfing off Belize, and then it's over. Aneurysm. Stroke. Whatever." He pauses with his hands on the back of the camp chair he set down. "Don't get me wrong. If I could make it to eighty without dementia or a bowel cancer and just die one day from something quick, I'd opt for that. I'd like to see my kids grow up."

Albert sits in a camp chair and extends his feet so that they rest on the picnic table's bench seat. "No one wants to suffer anymore."

"When did anybody want to suffer?" Steve asks.

"I mean no one really wants to venture into the redemption possibilities of suffering." Albert leverages a lighter underneath a bottle cap and flicks it with a vigor that produces in the humid air a solid base-hit sort of sound. "There's something to be said, I think, for crawling to the finish line and humbling yourself to the conditions of the breakdown."

"I'd rather die mid-stride," Steve says.

"But *rather* enters into it so rarely I would estimate."

The three of them say nothing for a period of several minutes apparently allotted to allow for the morbidity to dissipate respectfully. They drink at intervals that once or twice appear Olympian and synchronized, perform perfunctory inspections of their fingernails and boot soles, shoo the airborne menaces that circle them in search of weaknesses, and stare like anthropologists at Jeep-man's camp and stare at the surrounding evergreens like former animists whose eye depth hints that they would dearly like to still believe.

Then they reanimate, shrug off the specter of impending doom, and finish setting up to camp, positioning conveniences and sheltering what would not suffer getting soaked in the event of sudden rain.

Robert lifts the beverage-cooler lid and asks, "We ready for another?" He passes out the fancy beers to Albert and Steve and keeps a Coors Light for himself. "Feel like taking a ride to see some sights?"

"Sure," says Albert, elevating his beer to toast the idea, "but what's the policy on drinking in the vehicle up here?"

"Oh, I ain't ever had a problem," Robert says.

They pass the Jeep-man's camp but do not see the man. They individually appraise his set-up and appreciate the man's apparent isolationist commitment.

Robert turns right out of the campground and heads west on the Golden Road. In two- or three-hundred yards, he slows and points left and says, "The Hussrace Trail's in there."

"How far in?" asks Steve.

"Not far." Then Robert seems to reconsider. "The trailhead's not far. The pond's about two miles from the trailhead."

After issuing the distance clarification, Robert demonstrates his fondness for acceleration, passing by the landscape features that he judges do not warrant commentary.

About three miles down the road, he slows again and points right and says, "Big Eddy's in that way."

"Who's he?"

"E, d, d, y. Like a whirlpool. People put in upriver and come whitewater rafting through this way. Supposably, when there's a penstock release from the dam, a discharge, things get pretty hairy on the river. Not tomorrow, but before we leave, I was thinking we might sit up there and watch a few of them come through."

This area of guidance thus addressed, the guide accelerates and silences.

About two miles farther on, he slows and turns right on a narrower road. His passengers' awareness of the water roar is gradual, but even Albert, hard of hearing, registers the din of hydrological constriction. In about a half mile, the road becomes a bridge that spans the Ripogenus Dam. At the entrance to the bridge, a sign posted to a guardrail reads,

WARNING!

WHEN SIREN SOUNDS

RIVER LEVEL AND

FLOW WILL INCREASE

RAPIDLY.

Adjacent to that sign, another reads,

NOTICE:

LIGHT VEHICLE

TRAFFIC ONLY

ON THIS DAM.

"Is this considered a light vehicle?" Albert asks.

"Light enough. They just don't want log trucks driving on

here."

Robert stops in the middle of the dam bridge to permit his passengers to gain an unobstructed visual appreciation of the lake on their left, voluminous, constricted, and the glacial pace of gorge erasure on their right, the swift vertiginous plunge that draws their gazes and requires them to wonder if the majesty of free-fall would be worth the suicidal impact. There is no full-blown discharge underway, but the cascading sound is everywhere, the tumult of high water seeking lower ground. They sip their beers and occupy an intermediate position on the question of human consequence. On the one hand is the evidence of human alteration power. On the other is the sense that there is no way to outlast the unexploded gorge walls. Once the atmospheric gravity has been assimilated, Robert lifts his right foot from the brake and lets it hover over the accelerator as they idle on, beyond a heavy-duty gear assembly, beyond a squat, rectangular, brick building whose three equidistant windows have been filled in, bricked perhaps, cement skimmed, beyond another heavy-duty gear assembly. Where the bridge transitions into dirt road, Robert pulls off to the right and parks parallel to the guardrail.

"Have a look around?" he asks, opening his door without delaying for an answer. Robert leaves his beer, and so the others leave their beers because so much depends on following the lead of one who knows the customs of the land.

They walk back to the bridge and stop in silent admiration of the second gear assembly, a sort of distillation of a certain kind of industry.

"What's this building?" Albert asks. "The powerhouse?"

"Nope," says Robert. "The powerhouse is down the river on the other side. This just controls the flow. The siren's up there."

"I'm surprised there's no cameras here," says Albert. "It'd be pretty easy for a terrorist to blow this place up."

They walk to the middle of the bridge and face the broad sweep of the lake.

"What's this called?" Steve asks.

"Chesuncook. Well, technically, this here is Ripogenus Lake. Over that way," Robert says, motioning toward the west, "is Caribou Lake. Over that way is Chesuncook, and way the hell past that is Moose Pond. But really it's all Chesuncook Lake."

"How deep?" Steve asks.

"I believe," says Robert in a tone that signifies the singularity of the approaching fact, "it goes down about a hundred-fifty feet."

"Good fishing?"

"I ain't fished it much. Too warm for brook trout, and too many other fish in here in competition with the brook trout."

"And you only fish brook trout?"

"I only fish brook trout. Except for ice fishing, but I'm getting too old for that."

Albert detaches from them as they enter into a discussion of the brook trout, whose piscine nobility is unimpeachable in Robert's estimation and is amplified considerably, claims Robert, whenever a lesser angler argues in favor of the bass—small- or largemouth, makes no difference.

Albert walks to the gorge side of the bridge and leans into the pipe fence, trusting its sturdiness and fixity, and stares down at the sheet of water sliding down the spillway. He is moved to spit, but he does not know how he'd judge depth on the basis of his spit's descent rate, even if he could determine its descent rate, and there is something disrespectful, he considers, in expectoration from on high. Most animals he can think of do not spit. Camels do and maybe certain types of asps, but, as a whole, animals are pretty good about not broadcasting their saliva. Albert thus refrains.

From this vantage, Albert decides that suicide is out. Forget about the temporarily uplifting flight between the spruce-capped gorge walls. He'd never clear the spillway. It would be like dying in an inundated skateboard park. He rubs that region of his skull in which a fracture line was knit. He's grateful, but he feels that he should be more joyful for the decades of survival. Where is the unmitigated joy? He pushes off the pipe fence and walks down its length a ways.

Where the spillway ends, a concrete chute extends from the dam for several hundred feet before it ends and gives way to the West Branch of the Penobscot. On the far side of the chute a set of steps leads downward toward a platform meant for maintenance or observation. Albert walks down the steps. The pipe fence here has chain-link fencing fastened to it by thick-gauge wire. Albert wonders why the pipe fence on the bridge, where accidental falls or pipe-fence penetration would presumably be in at least the same class of catastrophe, isn't likewise reinforced. He pauses on a step and looks up at the pipe fence on the bridge. He stares a moment to revise his memory because the pipe fence on the bridge is likewise reinforced. The unreliability of the eyewitness troubles him while he is stationary, but, when he continues down the steps, he tells himself that memory, like any product of the body, cannot be infallible and he was probably distracted on the bridge by the competing views, which understandably could make an item as pedestrian as chain-link fencing seem to disappear.

Albert walks down to the platform and comes closer to a chain-link fence whose installation was conventional. He wonders what went into the decision to install a standard chain-link fence instead of putting in another sturdy pipe fence, which aesthetically and safety-wise appears to make more sense. Even with its posts set in cement, he doesn't trust this fence with his existence as he did the pipe fence up above, and he merely rests his hands upon the top rail of the chain-link fence and doesn't pressure it and peers more closely at the chute and wonders what its purpose is. He looks back up at the spillway and the bridge and wonders, since the dam has been here for about a hundred years, what is the just thing. Dam or no dam? He sees Steve and Robert coming down the stairway.

"Don't jump," yells Steve. "You have a lot to live for."

"What is this?" Albert asks Robert. "Some sort of fish ladder?"

"Nope," says Robert, who possesses the ability to register restrained amusement at a person's ignorance of what, to Robert, should be common knowledge while also making sure that he does what he can to bring that ignoramus closer to the fold. "But they did consider building one at one time. Turned out to be too hard and too expensive. This is just a sluiceway. They used to run spruce logs, mostly spruce logs, through here and drive them as far as Bangor. That stopped in seventy or seventy-one, I believe, after the Golden Road was built. No sense driving down a river what you can move by truck."

Steve looks down the sluiceway. "What a loss of an interesting way of life."

"Yep," says Robert, looking down the sluiceway. "You know, up in Baxter off the Tote Road is the grave of The Unknown River Driver. There's a little marker on the side of the road along Nesowadnehunk."

Steve spits tobacco juice into the sluiceway and says, "Tough way of life."

All three look down the sluiceway and imagine what it must have been like to anonymously expire in a log drive.

"So what's the point of the sluiceway now?" asks Albert.

"Regulates the water flow. There has to be a certain rate of flow for fish downriver to survive."

"Impressive," Steve says. "I've learned a lot today. Much appreciated. Thank you for taking us down here."

"The day ain't over yet," says Robert.

Robert leads the way back up the stairs and back to the truck. Their breathing labors slightly from the moderate ascent, and so, resuming their positions in the truck, they do not straightway turn to words but hold their beers with votary solemnity and jut their whiskered chins out as they drink and rest their beers on the abdominal protrusions that provide utilitarian transition from their useless chests, and they look out the windshield and the open windows as if they will never be this way again.

"Well," says Robert, as if claiming conversational priority by means of interjection but delaying it a moment while he finishes his beer, "the Frost Camps are a few miles up this road here. Ain't too much to see there." He pivots in his seat and takes a Coors Light from the little cooler lodged behind it. "Ready for another?" Albert reckons it would be transgression on the guest's part to reject the host's extension, even if the guest's tastes do not favor offerings from Golden, Colorado. Robert hands out two beers. "So, I figure we can go a ways down this road on the right here and see the power station from across the river. Steve can learn a little something extra for the day, and then we'll head back for some supper."

The road he turns down is marginally wider than the truck's width and exudes a sluiceway attitude. Its sides curve up so that, counter to the common practice of the highway engineer, the road is actually a slightly serpentine concavity, a sort of trough, and there's a sense they are committed to descent until the forces—geological, hydrological, ontological—that shaped the road provide them with a widening in which to exercise the freedoms they are used to and to execute a turnaround, anticipating the victorious ascent. To the right, before the trees begin to thicken, they can see with minor craning of the neck the bridge and spillway from a vantage that progressively gets lower and diminishes until the bridge and spillway disappear because the trees achieve their natural density and they inside the truck have gone some distance down the road.

"How far is the power station down the river?" Steve asks.

"A little more than half a mile." Robert bucks from side to side with the suspension. "The road's a little rougher than I remember."

If the road possesses certain sluiceway qualities, the truck and they do not possess the qualities of water. Albert tries to anticipate the jounces and positions mouth and beer so that the jounces, mouth, and beer become a unity, but they do not. There's spillage. There's the clink of can on teeth. He holds his beer away from his body and imperfectly remembers an expression of the wisdom of Bruce Lee: "Empty your mind. Be formless, shapeless, like water. Now you put water into a cup, it becomes the cup. You put it into a teapot, it becomes the teapot. Water can flow and creep and drip and crash. Be water, my friend."

But how does one become the teapot? How does one become the cup? Be water, my friend. Was Quang Duc fire? When confronted with the violence of the state, did he become the violence of the state and thus incinerate?

What Albert's sure of is that you can't be water while you're seated in a GMC Sierra whose four-wheel-drive has just now been engaged to deal with the terrain. They could have walked. A half mile there. A half mile back. But he's aware vehicular conveyance through the woods, when possible, is Robert's way, which Albert believes, on average, is the American way. So why does Robert seem more watery to Albert than Albert, more willing to accept what lies ahead, more willing to descend on unnegotiated terms, more willing to just go and not say anything about the presence of a flow? *Be water, my friend.* Is this a koan that his efforts to reduce to sensibility reveal how humorously removed he is from understanding? He can't win with this approach. He looks out at the trees and is no longer certain that you can't be water while you're seated in a GMC Sierra whose four-wheel-drive was engaged not long ago to gain more traction on the fabulous terrain.

Practically no sky is visible at this depth. All is canopy, enveloping, protective, hiding them from satellites and drones, surveillance apparatuses that paper-cut to death the sanctity of privacy and of consent. Albert leans his head a safe way out the window, gazes upward at the layering and layering of leaves and branches, at the intricate reticulation, and is curious what evil genius was responsible for realizing Agent Orange, the defoliant par excellence, and how someone blessed with such an education, such a mind, could harbor in his heart such scorn or apathy for the arboreal. A red squirrel chitters at them from a tree, and Albert would like to know if it is true that, prior to the chop-chop European settlement, a squirrel, red or gray, endowed with an exploratory stamina and an expansive sense of range, could travel tree to tree from the Atlantic coastal forest to the Mississippi, never touching ground. He'd like to think so, and he thinks so, but he warns himself of the attraction of the mythic, and he lingers on the timeline of the country's progress, and he wonders if the rumor of a government-created drone reduced to the dimensions of a dragonfly is true and if it would be operational in woodland such as this, if density and layering would be enough to keep the peeking in at bay.

The trees begin to thin out somewhat on the right side as the road bends closer to the river. A sign posted on a white birch on the left side of the road announces DANGER! in bright red letters outlined in black. Below that, in less forbidding black letters in a less forbidding font size, the sign reads,

WHEN SIREN SOUNDS
STATION FLOW WILL
INCREASE.

On a white birch on the right side of the road, a sign whose WARNING! redness has been leached away absolves itself of culpability and hints at self-determination's perils:

THE UPPER GORGE
IS HAZARDOUS.
PROCEED AT YOUR
OWN RISK!

"What happens if the siren sounds?" Steve asks.

"I suppose," says Robert, "we would all be swept down river." He looks in the rearview mirror at Albert. "Now that'd be an interesting way to go, wouldn't it?"

"Be water, my friend," says Albert.

"What's that supposed to mean?"

"We'd die like The Unknown River Driver, but we wouldn't go unknown."

"I suppose that's true."

"The question is, I'd like to know, is would we struggle? Would we be water?"

"I suppose we would."

"Struggle or be water?"

"Struggle first. Be water second," Robert says as if that is the natural drowning order. "Anyway, I'm pulling your leg. The water don't come up this high." He pauses as he scans the road ahead and says, "Well, that ain't good." A tree of some girth leans across the road. "We ain't moving that." He stops the truck a few feet from the tree and says, "The power station ain't far. In the mood to ambulate?"

Be water, my friend.

Robert grabs his beer and gets out, so the others grab their beers and get out. Robert does not fret about their future egress, so the others do not fret about their future egress. They walk around the tree and down the road, imbibing adjunct lagers, breathing in the moisture droplets choired in the air, breathing in the dank entanglement of tree and soil smells, all the emissions and decompositions of the matter-steady world.

From a distance, at a quick glance, with pedestrian awareness that a quick glance can betray one's feet, the architectural persona of the McKay Station could be classified industrial-monastic. Like the more impressive monasteries, those that seem to emanate like geometrically impressive geological anomalies from the granitic landscape, this place overhangs the far bank of the river as if millennia or centuries ago an odd material coincidence produced the level concrete on which the rectangular and sober-seeming power station edifice was founded, not without the air of majesty that even modest elevation naturally confers.

As one nears, though, it is clear no men in brown robes are inside transcribing Western civilization's cultural inheritance or doodling in the margins of the manuscripts whose stunning brightness sometimes makes the modernist wonder, Viking depredations, plague, and whatnot notwithstanding, if the period in which those beauties were produced was as benighted as we're prone to think because we have experienced no scarcity of light.

The three of them emerge and stand with knees crooked at various degrees. They look across the river at the power plant, which, from this frontal vantage and this no great distance, seems more mill than monastery. They conduct their individual appraisals silently, attempting to delineate and maybe colorize a mental picture of the operation. They can limn the basics—water rushes in, a turbine spins, and water rushes out—but the transformative minutiae of the energetic enterprise, the engineering of it and the science of it and the patience and deliberation marshalled from inception to transmission, cannot be so easily or accurately envisioned, even as they sip their beers and focus all their mental powers on the visible facility.

"So this is the beginning of illumination," Albert says.

"Imagine boring out a penstock in the bedrock underneath the river all the way from here back to the dam," says Robert, who evidently has imagined this before.

"That is something," Steve says.

"Three penstocks, actually, I believe," says Robert.

Albert and Steve maintain their stable situations on their separate sets of rocks and nod and sip their beers and look across the river at the apertures beneath the concrete structure, where the water comes out, roiling that side of the river.

"That is something," Albert says.

Albert looks up at the concrete platform in front of the building. Behind a chain-link fence that runs along the platform's edge are three reinforced storage-container sorts of structures, roughly one-fourth the length of the building, roughly one-fourth its height. Each one is framed by rigging like the kind that frames an outdoor concert stage, and from the lintel of each rigging three lines rise, connecting to the grid, the larger rigging on the building's roof, and from that grid extend transmission lines that seem to vanish into woods.

"What's in those containers?" Albert asks.

"I believe," says Robert, "those are transformers."

"Not turbines?" Steve asks.

"I can't say for sure, but I believe the turbines are in the building itself. I remember someone saying that, but I can't say for sure."

Albert looks at the agitated water flowing from the apertures and tries to picture the beginning of the penstock near the dam and what the suction force must be.

"Do fish ever get sucked in the penstock at the dam and end up down here?" he asks.

"Smelt do."

"They don't have some kind of screen or filter where the penstock starts?"

"They do, but smelt get through. They only get this big," says Robert, holding his thumb and index finger apart to indicate a smelt length of about three inches. His tone suggests that human industry can only do so much in terms of its accommodations for the wee.

"So what happens to all the smelt?"

"They take a spin around the turbine. Some don't make it. Some get stunned, come to, and swim away." Robert squints hard at the water. "I don't see none now, but the dead and stunned ones make this an attractive spot for salmon. Salmon fishermen, those guys in here with waders on, now they're the ones that need to run come siren time."

Be water, my friend.

Albert lingers on the question of is it a proper application of the wispy moral law to say with equal parts indulgence and derision, "Look here, tree hugger, power generation is a greater good and renders smelt expendable," and not be troubled in the mind or soul by the demise of smelt by turbine and to even feel magnanimous because a number of the smelt just get their bells rung and to not spend one more second contemplating what a rung bell might mean for the survival chances and the quality of life for that spun, concussed, disoriented smelt that manages to pull through and adjust to river life after how long in the lake. If becoming water-like means letting smelt pass by without at least a sympathetic set of fingers in extension as a show of human-piscine solidarity and fellow-traveler status and commiseration, he does not believe that he can undergo the metamorphosis that Bruce exhorts.

"That's got to put a big dent in the smelt population," says Albert.

"No," says Robert as if dams and penstocks are just nature's way of saying it is not concerned with self-determination matters re the smelt, "it's a healthy population. They're abundant."

"Robert," Steve says, "thank you for showing us this place. It really is something that a lot of people never get to see."

"Sure."

"It is impressive," Steve says, looking at the plant. "This visit's really changed the way I look at power generation." He pauses, closes one eye, aims the other at his beer can, and shakes the beer can like the dice cup in a game of Yahtzee. "But I'm out of beer."

"I was just thinking the same thing," says Robert. "And my stomach tells me it's about time for some supper."

They depart the margin of the river and reenter the abiding stillness of the woods. One by one they pass the downed tree. Three doors slam in quick succession, and the truck moves in reverse. The power station and the river and the woods ahead recede, and Robert drives them backward at a speed that feels reserved for forward motion, navigating solely via side-view mirrors. They jounce and force their bodies not to give in too much to the dashboard declination, but of course they can't help being pulled that way.

Chapter Nineteen

If the architects of history's resistance movements could have met with their oppressors at the trailhead of the Horserace Brook Trail while the sun was still low in the east and stood together at the trailhead kiosk and explored the laminated map and read the laminated poster that provided information on the flora, fauna, geology, and history of the region they were entering and taken to heart the sign that read FIREWORKS ARE PROHIBITED and taken to heart the other poster that read "Please help stop the illegal stocking of fish" and understood by signs and posters that the upkeep and the preservation of the commons were the kiosk's theme, perhaps they could have laid the groundwork for a parley in which they discussed how best to sidestep bloodshed and how best to not let their munitions scar and litter, generation after generation, the land they both loved. If the principals of the resistance and establishment said nothing for a while except for commonplaces as they hiked the two miles to the Lower Horserace Pond and looked with new humility at spruce and fir and white pine and paper birch and aspen without knowing all the names until the head resister said them and, emerging, felt the privilege of discovering the pond and found the green canoe the head resister and his son had hidden in the woods and two of each group worked together so that they could safely enter the canoe and one of the oppressors paddled in the front and the preeminent resister paddled in the back, the two of them cooperating to describe a straight line to the pond's end, all four of them less egotistical as they looked north at talus and the granite cliff that has not tumbled, maybe posturing and war and even taxes could have been avoided. So Albert thinks as Steve and Robert paddle the canoe across the middle of the Lower Horserace Pond.

Robert pulls his paddle in and says, "Well, since we're out here, I might as well drop a line and see if I can get a nibble." He puts his fishing pole together, clips a lure to the leader, and casts, the whizzing of his freed line ending in a distant plunk. "Really it's too deep to be much good here, and I should be using worms. We'll see," he says, reeling in and casting out again.

"How deep?" Steve asks.

"Forty, fifty feet. It's cold down there, which is good for brook trout, but you have to reach them."

"Look at that cliff," says Albert. "Right up to the water. Imagine falling off that?"

"That is majestic," Steve says.

Robert reels in, casts out, and says, "You know, about a year ago, me and my boy came home from fishing up here, and, as we were unloading, two of those Mormons come by and ask if they could talk to us about God." He casts again. "I said I don't mean no disrespect, but we don't need to hear about God. We just got back from church." He's silent as he reels in. He casts and says, "This is my church. If you can't find God here, where else you going to find Him?" He reels in. "Okay, that's enough of that. Let's move on to the Upper Pond."

Steve and Robert dip their paddles to reorient the canoe and paddle toward the Lower Pond's northwest end. The three breathe like free and unaffiliated men and look down at the water on which they feel blessed to glide and look up at the tinged sky underneath which they feel blessed to glide and take the forest that surrounds them in, the cone trees ever casual in towering, and, though the three are certainly deficient in essential waterfowl perception hardware and interpretive capacities, they get at least a glimmer of what it is like to cross from the perspective of a duck or loon, those birds of placid wakes, those wakes as illustrative of our shared condition as Tibetan-Buddhist sand art but with water and without the intricacy and brightness and the robes and sashes of a beautiful religion.

"So what?" asks Steve as they approach the narrow stretch of shore. "We portage to the Upper Pond?"

"Portage?" Robert asks. He looks past Steve and at the shore, deciding where to land. "No, we ain't portaging."

"We're going to surfcast?" Albert asks.

"Surfcast?" Robert asks in disbelief.

"So what's the plan?" asks Steve.

"The plan," says Robert, "is for you to stick your paddle out and make us miss those rocks so we can get in there without tearing out the bottom of this canoe."

Steve sticks his paddle out and prods the rocks and pushes and provides resistance like a proper bargeman. Robert paddles once, twice, and then the keel grates on sand and pebbles.

"Be careful getting out," says Robert, sticking his paddle in the bottom of the pond. "It's tippy."

They each get out in turn and have a hand in dragging the canoe up, though it's not a three-man job. They take their packs and gear out, set them on the ground, and stand around the beached canoe. Robert spends some minutes looking into the woods and seems to find what he is looking for. He grabs the handhold at the front of the canoe and tilts his head back, indicating with his chin the direction he intends, and says, "Let's get this up in the woods." Albert grabs the handhold at the back of the canoe and follows Robert uphill. "Probably unnecessary," Robert says as he begins to bushwhack with his left hand, "but I'd rather not come back here later and discover that who knows has stolen our canoe."

They walk about a hundred feet uphill and reach a boulder that the Laurentide ice sheet in retreat deposited millennia ago, though Albert can't remember what the kiosk poster said about how many thousands and is briefly troubled by his poor numerical retention when it hits him that such facts don't mean too much out here except as points of interest and reminders of how carried away the average human gets with the traditional assumption of possession and succession. Robert sets his end down and looks downhill in appraisal of what someone passing by down there and glancing up this way might see or not see. Albert stands in admiration of the boulder and its crazy trip and staying power, and he transfers the handhold to his left hand so that he can lay his right upon the boulder's coolness and appreciate the boulder's composition and its sheltering proportions.

"This'll do," says Robert, picking up his end again. "Let's stash it back here."

They walk a few steps higher, rotate the canoe so that its keel is facing up, and lay it at the boulder's uphill-facing base. Robert collects some fallen spruce and pine branches and some deadwood and, with the suggestion of a system, layers and arranges them to camouflage the green canoe, and Albert does likewise since to bystand is to seem to harbor reservation. When all semblance of a Kevlar water vessel disappears and deep sight is required to discern that obfuscation has transpired here, the two of them are motionless and silent for a moment like two beavers processing the asymmetrical accomplishment that is their lodge.

Robert says, "That should do."

Albert nods uphill and asks, "Would anyone come down from that way?"

"Not likely. No trail runs through up there." He looks down at the stashed canoe. "No, this won't catch no eye."

When they come down the hill, Steve spits a jet of brown juice on lesser rocks and hooks his dip wad from between his lower lip and gum with his unsanitary index finger and propels it toward the woods. He wipes his finger on his haunch and spits out lingering tobacco flecks without the grace that characterized his economical expectoration and dislodges stragglers from his lower-lip and chin hair with his right thumb, which he pulls back and submits to an inspection as if this admittedly important digit is more precious to him than his tongue.

"I don't know how you can suck on that shit," says Albert.

"I plan to quit."

"I told you about the guy beside my father in the hospital," Albert says, hovering between a declaration and a question.

"I plan to quit."

"When my dad was in the hospital for cancer of the esophagus," Albert says, addressing Robert, as he places thumb and forefinger on either side of his Adam's apple and directs them downward, illustrating the approximate vicinity of one's esophagus, "for a day or two he had a roommate who revealed that he was nineteen when he started dipping. Here he was, eleven years later, at the age of thirty, with the left side of the jaw that he was born with"—here Albert puts his finger on the hinged part of his mandible and runs it to the middle of his chin—"sawboned and surgically removed and a prosthetic one screwed in, or however it's held in there, to substitute for the original. Dip took eleven years to do that."

"Maybe dip," says Robert. "Maybe something else." He takes his fishing rod apart and stows it on the left side of his pack. "My brother's down in Portland in the cancer hospital. Some kind of cancer in the brain, and no one really knows where that came from."

"How's he doing?" Steve asks.

"Well, a year ago, the doctors said he had six months. So if you go by that, he's doing better than expected. But he's drugged up and his memory's not good and he has seizures, and the cancer's in a place where they can't operate no more to get it out." He picks his backpack up and puts it on. "He is alive. That's something. But like he said to me the last time I was down there, it ain't everything."

At such conversational transition points, it's common to express one's recognition of the limitations circumscribing human agency and language and commiseration by just staring at the ground with a funereal intensity for a duration that the most afflicted will intuitively prescribe.

"Well," says Robert, "if we're all done being morbid, I suppose that we should get to doing what it is we come this way to do."

"Do you want me to put the paddles up with the canoe?" asks Albert.

"Nope," says Robert. "Bring them. Those we might be needing."

Robert turns and searches this extremity of woods the way a person fond of atmospheric figuration studies clouds, as if attention is what's requisite to scratch the surface of the underlying meanings of the world. He utters nothing as he shifts from stillness into motion. Albert and Steve move likewise toward the woods and follow Robert up to where the inclination levels briefly. The levelness becomes a palimpsest of a path that leads them left and from this elevation skirts the Upper Pond, whose glimmering they sometimes catch as though it were a naiad's hither-come sent through the sliver gaps despite the overwhelming density of trees. They clink and rustle down the path.

Robert's pace is workmanlike, not rushed but steady and possessed of that vitality that beams from just the right amount of bounce, his head and torso leaning forward as if braving wind, though all is calm.

"*In pede, vel irrepertus,*" says Albert.

"What's that?" Robert asks.

"A family motto I'm considering," says Albert. "Roughly translated, it means *On foot, or undiscovered.*"

"Ain't far," says Robert. "It's around here somewhere."

"What is?"

Robert stops and crouches slightly, trying to create a sight line through the underbrush and trees.

"This way."

They leave the trail and switch gears, heading downhill at a rightward slant. They inch around the densest deadfall tangles, pausing to release the snags, the forest saying *Do not go*, and moving on and climbing over trees more recently gone down and yet without the creepy growth and the botanical envelopment and the advanced decomposition.

"Bee's nest," Robert calls out, pointing with his left hand toward a hive that hangs like a piñata from a hung-up tree.

"Honeybees?" asks Albert, approaching the hive.

Steve passes him.

Albert stands still before the hive and lets the guard bees fly out unmolested to inspect him. "Honeybees. At least this colony hasn't collapsed."

He peers. The guards fly circles but are not alarmed by the intrusion, and they fly back to their guard posts, in position to observe the looming presence and react if it begins to harm their humming commonwealth. Their confidence in their defenses' viability, their blind faith in the apian traditions that have served their species for millennia, depress him because he sees in that dependent hive such fluid vulnerabilities that natural means are too slow to address.

"It's sad that this is what it takes to make it as a honeybee colony these days. Get as far away as possible from the Monsanto-, Bayer-, neonicotinoid-reliant farms." He looks around. No human hears him.

When he catches up to Steve and Robert, they are taking off the layered branches that were the camouflage for an aluminum canoe.

"Another one?" asks Albert.

Robert turns it over and says, "Well how else did you suppose we'd fish this pond?"

"You and your son carry this one too?"

"Carried it the first two miles. Then he got in the one canoe and I got in the other and we paddled across the Lower Pond. Then we carried this one the rest of the way. He wasn't too pleased about it. He didn't see the point of lugging this one in when we already had the other."

"What was the point?" Albert asks.

"Dry feet. Two canoes."

"It does add to the experience, Robert," Steve says.

"Is this the last of your canoe stash?"

"Oh, I have five or six at different ponds."

Steve and Albert pick up the canoe.

"Which way?" Steve asks.

They follow Robert down the hill and put in the canoe. They get in, Steve first, Albert, then Robert, who shoves off. Three men with three distant lives and this one.

Somewhere between five and ten Upper Ponds could fit in the Lower, and, although the Upper does feel fortified because of the surrounding evergreens and is rock-ringed, its geology lacks overt verticality and does not tower. There is not the need to set aside equivalent time for awe.

Steve and Robert paddle for a while and develop rhythm.

"The deepest part of the Upper Pond's about here," Robert finally says. He peers over the gunwale. "Only goes down about thirty feet, though." He holds his paddle in his right hand and dips his left into the pond. "The water's pretty cool still."

"Loon," says Albert, pointing ahead.

"Yep," says Robert, pointing with his paddle to the north. "Another over there." He strokes.

"How shallow does it get up ahead?" Steve asks.

"Oh, it gets to zero," Robert jokes. "One just jumped right there."

The loon that was in the direction they are heading keeps a red eye on them as it paddles north-northeast, maintaining relatively constant distance from the three men and the canoe.

"Are we using lead weights?" Albert asks.

"Swivel sinkers."

"Lead?"

"They're lead."

"Not good for the loons. They eat them when they scoop up pebbles for digestion and get poisoned by the lead. They die in two to four weeks. I read it in the paper the other day."

"As long as we don't cut no lines, the loons can't eat no sinkers," Robert says. He watches as the loon they pushed out disappears beneath the water and resurfaces a minute later farther north-northeast. "I have been meaning to switch over to them non-lead sinkers. I read the same thing."

Albert looks in the water and envisions hooks and lines and sinkers strewn, but he says nothing more about the article because there's only so much one man's sympathy and theoretical concern can do.

"This is good right here," says Robert, stowing his paddle so the blade end angles up from under Albert's seat and drips.

The blade end in the opposite direction also angles up from

under Albert's seat and drips when Steve stows his so that a shallow tide that's unpredictable and not connected to the moon moves bow to stern or stern to bow or side to side depending on the distribution of the three main weights and on the suddenness and vigor of the shifts.

Steve and Albert connect the male and female ferrules of their fishing poles and dangle two hooks out of harm's way. Robert hands an earthworm to Albert, who passes it to Steve.

"I can bait yours if you want, or you can do it yourself," says Robert.

"I can do it," Albert says, holding out his hand.

At times like these, Albert wishes he had never heard about the Jains, whose views on suffering suggest there is another way that he can be. At least, if Albert never heard about the Jains and their tradition of insisting that the fruit must fall before it's gathered, of allowing the mosquitoes to take up what they require for their lives, of donning cheesecloth masks to practically eliminate the risk of incidental inhalation of Shyama pokas, of serenely sweeping with a peacock-feather broom the path ahead to spare the life forms on the ground the hazards of the human foot—if Albert never heard about such practices and people, he could sheathe the hook inside the earthworm and be honest if confronted with the notion that this sheathing is a violent act and say he never heard about ahimsa. But he has heard.

And even if he never heard of Jains or of ahimsa, he has heard of Jeremy Bentham, who is probably more problematic than the Jains because he wasn't mystical like someone from the East or temple-bound or white-robed or sky-clad, but an economist, a jurist, a Utilitarian, an Englishman before the reign of Queen Victoria. If he, a Westerner like Albert, could say about two-hundred years ago, "The question is not, can they reason? Nor, can they talk? But, can they suffer?" with the understanding that it doesn't take a genius to discern the suffering of a bonobo or a veal calf or a worm, is it too much to ask of someone farther down the timeline to admit that writhing is a sign of suffering and that inserting a barbed hook into an earthworm or a brook trout or a human, into pretty much whatever is alive, is to inflict an injury and to cause pain, and is it too much to ask of someone farther down the timeline to not trivialize or will away nonhuman suffering by arguing that the inflicted does not feel pain as we do, as if we are the arbiters of all experience because our pain receptors and our spinal cords and our brain stems and our thalami and our cortices and our limbic systems are so finely calibrated that we'd suffer back pain and insomnia if twenty mattresses and twenty feather beds below us was a pea, a minor legume, when all other living beings would feel nothing and sleep soundly and, come morning, slither, fly, or otherwise continue on their unaffected ways?

Albert holds the hook in one hand and the earthworm in the other, and he knows that, if he says he can't go through with this on moral grounds and hands the earthworm back, then Steve and Robert will inquire with the certainty of pragmatists if he eats meat or walks about in leather boots or knows what animals his products have been tested on or ever ganders at his insect-spattered windshield. The themes they would develop would be manliness disdains the middleman and in what lives inheres demise. But even if they didn't make such inquiries and took the earthworm back with something like respect for his convictions and appeared to wish that they could manifest such fortitude when their defining moments crystallized and thereby granted him the moral victory, he knows the earthworm will be hooked by one of them regardless and the hooking will be merciless, with no reflection on the suffering, and will be more effective in enticing brook trout to forego peripheral nibbles and engulf the worm-socked hook.

Albert apologizes inwardly and hooks the worm through its intestines as it writhes and lets go castings, and he curls the worm and hooks it through its middle and involuntarily is careful not to pierce his fingers as he curls the worm again and hooks it through the stiff and wriggling end that holds its reproductive organs and its hearts—he hooks and curls and hooks and curls and hooks so that a good proportion of the worm is not impaled and theoretically does not, in that proportion, suffer as intensely as it would have had he run the whole worm through as would a more efficient angler, and he wonders if such measures constitute the bulk of human mercy.

He pins the line against the pole with one thumb, and he flips the bail arm with the other. For a moment, as if there is still a will and won't, the thrice-hooked earthworm dangles in the air behind him, then he whips the whole arrangement forward as would any scourging mortifier of the flesh and lifts the pinning thumb enough to free the line, and there's the whiz, the bola flight of swivel sinker, bobber, earthworm, and the distant plunk, the bobber observation, the attempt to picture what goes on down there, what bait thus introduced awakes.

"Reel it in a little," Robert says. "See if that does anything."

Albert reels it in a little, drags the bobber through the pond. To the bobber's right, a minor eddy swirls. The surface slightly breaks.

"They're in there," Steve says.

Albert's bobber dips below the surface and moves to and fro. He tries to picture what the fish has hold of, and he makes no sudden movements at this juncture when the proper angling thing to do is to perform the classic transfer backward of one's weight and jerk the rod tip up so that what's going on down there in terms of piscine nourishment is suddenly upended and the barbed invention of the wily human mind, tinkered toward perfection generation after generation, gets set in the gullet, gill, lip, or eye. The bobber comes back up, and Albert breathes.

"You had him," Robert says. "You let him go."

"My strategy is unconventional," says Albert. "I'm lulling him into a false sense of security."

"His sense of security seems pretty genuine to me," says Robert.

Albert suspects that Robert has identified him as a man of dual allegiance but is too polite to make him choose a side. The fact that Albert is not a hunter was established early on during the initial talk around the Weber grill, established by insinuation first since Albert, when it was his turn, had no stories in which he assumed the simultaneous perspective of the connoisseur of natural beauty and its killer, then by simple declaration, and the power balance and the sociability vibration did not seem to shift with its establishment. In fact, the conversation's scope appeared to widen, and, as if recounting the conversional experience that could have been depicted in a medieval woodcut, Robert spoke of sitting in a tree, his arrow nocked and aimed, a clear shot, at a doe serenely lapping water from the stream and lifting up her head when she had had her fill, rejoicing in hydration and her solitude.

"I don't know what it was," said Robert. "I was just about to shoot, and then I saw some water droplets sparkle on the side of her mouth and separate and drip down—the sun was shining on them—and I couldn't shoot."

"Did you stop hunting altogether after that?" asked Steve.

"No," said Robert. "I've killed plenty after that. I just couldn't do it then."

The anecdote's conclusion, its coda really, didn't have the moral lift that Albert was hoping for, but Albert, a fan of subtext, saw in Robert's story, whether Robert consciously embedded it in there or not, a sign that Robert understood why someone wouldn't have it in his heart to hunt.

But Albert senses that, in Robert's estimation, it is one thing to not want to hunt a fellow mammal and to drag it from the woodland like the quarry of a pre-agrarian man and to suspend it from a sturdy bough for drainage and to pose with predatory glee beside it and to butcher it or pay a butcher and to pay a taxidermist to preserve and mount the head and neck and to appraise your dwelling in the meantime for a proper elevated portion of a wall in some room that might feel less empty, cozier, if it were meditated over by a symbol of your capability as a provider and a killer, someone who will still be viable when finally the shit goes down, a symbol of your willingness to peer, without becoming sentimental, at an animal with warm blood like yourself or at the ruminant serenity and say goodbye—and quite another to extend your sympathies to creatures, legless and possessed of central nervous systems far less poignant than your own, existing in a class taxonomists are clear is not *Mammalia*, though the whale presents some interesting questions if you are inclined to rationalize from this perspective.

Yielding to the need to go unnoticed, Albert pretends to fish with interest and intensity. He reels his bobber in and sees the breaching worm. He swings the hook his way and grabs the line above it, studying the remnants of the worm, how those segments that had not been hooked were nibbled off by a double row of vomerine teeth. The worm is dead. Relief.

Robert casts and says to Albert from behind, "You need another worm?"

"I think I'm good," says Albert.

Concluding his investigation of his cleaned hook, Steve says, "I could use another one."

Robert passes up a worm, which Albert relays to Steve.

Albert casts, relaxes. Nothing at this moment suffers due to him. Nothing but the faintest ripples agitate the bobber for a while. The appearance of tranquility abounds.

Then Robert's bobber suddenly sounds. His rod tip flexes like a yogi, shifting suddenly from side to side as though become a divination instrument and the awaited sign requires only patience and a little dialing in.

"Big one?" Steve asks.

"Oh," says Robert matter-of-factly, reeling to an inner rhythm, "decent size it feels like."

A moratorium on the surrounding fishing is, in essence, in effect for the duration of the struggle, Steve and Albert observing Robert's method and the roiled water for a glimpse of what he's dealing with, their heads, at certain points in the intensifying drama, turning to and fro in silence with the spectatorial devotion of two noblemen at Wimbledon. Steve roots for Robert, Albert for the trout, which slaps the surface like a beaver tail and launches, arcing at low altitude for what, according to their inner time clocks, feels like longer than a fraction of a second, and the waterbound, the earthbound, and the airborne somehow coalesce for just a fraction of a second, time enough to feel they're right there on the existential cusp, the border of the out of body.

Robert reels with the assurance of a being whose entitlement and technological advantage are unquestioned, facts so natural and so long established they require no evaluation, reels against the fish resistance like a being for whom struggle of this sort is therapeutic and affirmative of full existence and without the worrisome accompaniment of risk. As Robert reels, prismatic beads of water cling like dew drops to the rising line and slide down or are shaken in the final stages of the struggle, and attributing to them respectful sentience is a leap that's difficult to make for even someone leaning toward the East because one moment you assume they are invested absolutely in the cling and are committed to experiencing evaporation from the floor of this canoe, and next you can't help seeing them as droplets harboring that species of regret that is reserved for the adventurous and wanting nothing more than integration with the pond again and anonymity. That is, it's difficult because you do not have a proper view of sentience.

Robert tips the rod up higher for the final burst of reeling. In the manner of a failing crane, the bent rod swings right. The line, bobber, swivel sinker, leader, hook, and brook trout follow with an orchestrated beauty, geometrical and fulcrum-based and torturous, the brook trout, like a medieval minder of his business suddenly accused by stoic men of heresy, at wit's end in defiance of a foreign worldview, struggling to spit out what a different order of intelligence has fashioned for it. The brook trout clears the gunwale and is gripped.

The sense of temporal compression is replaced by an impression of the marvel of corporeal variety.

With thumb and index finger, Robert dips the hook down to unlock the barb and slides this iteration of the dangle method of entrapment from the brook trout's bottom lip. The brook trout, sensing one form of release, attempts another and becomes tense with the effort, but the human grip predicts the effort in a nerve-communicated way and squeezes like an equatorial strongman to impress on it the fact of its captivity. Robert's manual security upgrade is such that he continues with the left-hand grip, his palm beneath the brook trout and his fingers wrapped below the visible gill, and adds a right-hand grip, his thumb and fingers wrapped around the brook trout's tapered rear end so that his palm obscures the squarish tail. He holds the brook trout just below the level of his chest and then performs an offertory-quality extension, but he keeps his elbows bent, toward Albert and Steve who have been watching with the interest and intensity of uninitiated countrymen.

"You guys said you ain't seen a brook trout before," says Robert, half declarative, half interrogative, as an observation invitation, as a sort of call to worship.

Albert and Steve lean in as though to let a man who has been through the ordination process lay a sacred baked good on their tongues, but they do not lean far enough in that direction at this moment to be elevated to the status of communicants. They simply stare like gallery visitors at the expiring brook trout's respiration efforts and its stunning variegations for a period of time whose passage is expression of their dual appreciation. They seem mesmerized by the accomplishment of the elusive stippler who was not content to leave this fish with yellow speckles, in a state of incompletion, but displayed the patience of a master intersperser, speckling the olive flesh with red dots circumscribed by blue coronas—so at first the yellow stipples overwhelm until the eye is drawn by contrast, by numerically inferior red dots rung blue, whose fewer numbers, indicating rarity, make Albert and Steve think they love them more. Then, as if another optic layer suddenly has been unveiled, they notice the transition zone above which all dots disappear, no red, no blue, and all the yellow has been rendered in abbreviated squiggles, like aquatic larvae motile in the dark pond out of which the dorsal fin arises.

Robert moves his finger from the tapered rear end, loosening his grip a bit, and points to a display of yellow squiggles.

"They call these worm tracks," he says.

Albert and Steve nod.

Albert takes in the colors and the patterns and the absences of patterns, and he wonders what advantages these squiggles and these speckles and these colors were selected for.

"What's a good size for a brook trout?" Steve asks.

"This ain't bad," says Robert. "Thirteen, fourteen inches, I'd say. They can get to sixteen, eighteen inches."

"Is that a male or female?"

Robert looks down at the suffocating brook trout to consider gender. "Male probably. Females usually have less color." He holds the brook trout up for an inspection of the belly. "When they spawn, the females usually have a reddish belly. But they ain't spawning now."

"Those are some beautiful colors, though," says Steve. "They really are a miracle of reproduction."

"Well, don't get used to them. They won't last long. Once the fish dies, the colors fade pretty fast."

"Really?" Albert asks.

"Yep. No different than a person dying. The color drains right out."

Robert loosens his grip to toss the brook trout in the bucket, but, as soon as it detects the slightest opening for release, it flaps and is unhanded and lands broadwise on the floor of the canoe and flops its way under Albert's seat and between his feet. It lies there for a minute, one eye staring up at Albert, its gill and mouth in search of usable oxygen after such exertion. Then it starts flopping once again, a little blood now mixing with the little water on the floor of the canoe.

Robert taps Albert on the shoulder with a wooden dowel.

"Knock him on the head with this," says Robert.

"He'll probably get tired," Albert says, not accepting the extended dowel. "I don't think he has much energy reserved."

Robert withdraws the offered dowel, and he drops it in the bucket. It hits the bucket bottom with a wood-on-plastic *thwhack* that makes it difficult to judge if Albert's roundabout refusal to subdue the brook trout with a dowel clout inspired Robert to propel it in there or if it was just a casual deposit. Albert reels his bobber in a couple feet and listens as the plastic lid is peeled back from the Styrofoam container and as Robert grates his rod against some part of the aluminum canoe in order to position it so he can bait the hook. Robert casts, and Albert does not discern judgmental vigor in the cast. But it is hard to tell.

The brook trout flops again between his feet as if to draw attention to a history of unaddressed injustice. Albert keeps his head up so that, from behind, it would appear he's focused on his bobber and is gamely trying to envision the activity of tempted fish and is untroubled by the struggle at his feet. His eyes, however, are cast down, and he would like to do the interspecies equivalent of directing one's index finger and middle finger at one's eyes and then directing them at someone else's eyes, indicating mutual observation and establishing an optical connection and a feeling that they're of the same mind or on the same wavelength and transcend the spatial or at least reduce the distance separating them by an appreciable degree. But there is no interspecies equivalent. And even if, in the expansive world of the hypothesis, there were, he probably could not perform it privately, beyond the notice of the man behind him and without inviting heightened scrutiny, which one should not invite when one is on a water body this deep in the woods and contemplating circumvention of a cherished folkway.

Albert thus pretends to actively angle, head turned portside just enough so Robert, if he looks, will catch the slanted profile and the eyeglass temple but will not be able to discern the downcast eyes or their Franciscan exudation, which, if witnessed, would be classified as unbecoming an outdoorsman. Albert stares concern down at the dying brook trout. Equivalency is but a pipe dream, a distraction softening the hard choice staring at him with a single lidless eye. He can do nothing and extend no mercy other than imagining how it must be to die in what is not your element beneath a massive figure of indifference. In this option, he is not the agent of destruction and, according to the letter of the law, is therefore sinless, but he tries imagining himself expiring via drowning similarly prolonged, a catfish of Devonian proportions hovering above him with its wavy whiskers as he works his bluing lips and flails and winds down toward acceptance and goes motionless and stares back at the catfish, whose suspension in the water and apparent unconcern are qualities of otherworldly wonder. This, the doing nothing, is the easy option and the one without which we would see a very different world go round.

Or he can proceed beyond the province of the ethical

conundrum and do the only thing that he can do to serve two masters, one who says to hurry up and end the poor thing's misery and one who says to do it in a manner that accentuates his masculinity. Albert reels a couple times and looks down at the brook trout's black eye, heart-stirred by the yellow ring surrounding it, a masterstroke of coloration, an exemplar of the detail in the service of the whole, and he does not believe he has it in him to pick up the brook trout in his left hand as if clement and in prelude to release and then to dowel clout it with his right and watch as if in vigil as the colors that bedazzled as if from the page of an illuminated manuscript bedim and lose what link they had to the sublime and leave him with a limp fish and an unchanged dowel and the digestive-system hollowness that's symptomatic of hypocrisy, the province of the ethical conundrum.

Or he can use that left hand, or the right, or both if he would like to lend a Eucharistic air to the proceeding, for a radical expression of a deep conviction and uplift the brook trout to the level of his eyes and straighten it so they are nose to nose and roughly eyes to eyes for something on the order of a second and then face the brook trout pondward, homeward, as he bears it past the gunwale threshold and then lowers it until the brook trout and his hand or hands are in the water simultaneously and he lets go and there is respiration reestablished, there the tail flick that propels the brook trout, there the stares and probably the expletives when he draws back his hand or hands within the bounds of the canoe, aware there is no explanation for the undeclared release. No Jain or Bentham reference would suffice. And these are men he has to spend at least another night with in close quarters. This is not his fish to give back. As the viability and promise of this final option fade, he thinks about Ed Mendel, who poached lobsters from Long Island Sound, and that imprinted day some twenty years ago when Albert picked up the lobster from the cooler and told Ed that he believed the lobster wanted to go free and Ed said, "Don't you throw that fucking lobster off this boat," and Albert kept harping in good humor on the liberation and the sentience themes and Ed kept saying, "Don't you throw that fucking lobster off this boat," and Albert held out the lobster past the gunwale and said, "Fly. Be free," and let the lobster go, the liberating plunk, and Albert was punched and stranded for a while in the middle of the Sound because he was committed back then to that sort of gonzo advocacy and didn't waver over how unorthodox it looked and didn't argue for consistency if it was mentioned that he was a hypocrite because he ate chicken and he ate cow and didn't fully register the scoffing when he said that if a chicken or a cow applied to him for refuge he would give it refuge and did not care if, when he was finished singing "Joy to the World," the person that he sung to stared at him, unmoved and unamused, and said he was an idiot.

Albert reels the bobber in and sees there's not much worm left, but he doesn't wait for Robert to suggest that he re-worm and casts it out again. He stares out at the bobber, and he wonders when the change occurred, when he initially experienced self-consciousness competing with conviction, when the theretofore unrecognized accountant in him came out, visored, pupils in the process of constriction after the diameter-expanding brightness of the banker's lamp, and showed him the cost-benefit analysis that itemized what Albert stood to gain in social capital by cultivating a persona predicated on a universal inoffensiveness and by denying the expression of his less expedient convictions. It had to be post-fracture, but how long post-fracture he has no idea. *Wait a minute, wait a minute*, he second-thinks himself. *What about the endless adolescent fronts and falsehoods?* He looks down at the brook trout, and, although he cannot say with certainty if it's alive or dead, he does believe its colors have begun to fade. What's the point of trying to affix a psychological development, which probably, when all is said and done, is quite a byzantine endeavor, to a single point upon a Julian-calendar-dependent timeline? And, as far as submarining deep convictions to enhance his public standing, didn't he last year apply a head-butt to a person on the basis of a deeply held belief that people should at least dramatically reduce their speed and take pronounced evasive action if they do not care enough to pull their vehicles over and get out to expedite a turtle-crossing with their own two hands? There was no denying his expression of his less expedient conviction then, so why deny expression of one now? For one thing, he supposes, masculinity is different in the finitude of a canoe, and it requires a withholding—of select emotions, of select affinities, of things in your interior you do not want to make accessible to men of certain leanings. For another, there is still the sacred bond between the guest and host. Implicit in the bond is the concession that they each must let some baggage go.

"The fish is dead I think," says Albert.

"Pass him back so I can put him in the bucket."

Albert picks the brook trout up and, in the process of the transfer, notices how far away and shadowy the colors have become. He wonders as he hands it over how long is the average lifespan of the brook trout, and he hopes that, when he gets home to Connecticut and asks the internet how long the average lifespan of the brook trout is, the answer isn't twenty years or more because, while twenty years is not a lifespan one would categorize as sturgeonesque or elephantine or tortucan, it is long enough to feel that something with some staying power, something intricate and noble and indigenous has been cut short, that something who's at least as worthy of its lease on life as him has had its unextravagant allotment requisitioned in the name of angling and has been deprived of the duration that biology and the divine force intended for it to shine forth.

"What's the limit, Robert?" Steve asks. "Five you said?"

"Five per person, yep," says Robert.

"That's enforced?"

"Supposed to be." Robert glances to his right and says, "Right side. Incoming."

One of the loons is making its final approach, and, in whatever region of the human brain the archivist-photographer resides, the loon is frozen in the attitude of avian extension, wings spread, feet tucked in a stick-the-ski-jump-landing angle, airy grace embodied prior to the minor turbulence of touchdown. Then it crashes in the water, tumbles like a spastic water-skier, quickly rights itself, shakes its head, and fluffs itself, resuming loon placidity.

"Well, that was awkward," Robert says. "He looks embarrassed."

"They always land like that?" asks Steve.

"First time in my experience. Could be a baby learning to fly. See how the other loon keeps an eye on him and keeps close by? That might be the mother."

"Maybe," Albert says, "he mistook a split-shot sinker for a pebble and ingested lead. Erraticism is a symptom of lead poisoning."

"He seems to swim all right," says Robert. "I think he's just young."

They watch the loon for signs of the irregular, and, when it seems irregularity has not undone the idyll, they return to fishing, Albert casting intermittent glances loonward.

"I need a worm," says Albert.

"So five per person keeps the population stable?" Steve asks.

"This pond ain't fished too hard," says Robert, passing up a worm.

"How strict is the enforcement?"

"Well, they only have so many game wardens for how many acres, so it ain't as strict as they would like. But you'd be surprised where you see those guys pop up. For all we know, one of them's in the woods and training his binoculars on us right now."

"Really?"

"Sure," says Robert.

"Have you ever taken more than the limit?"

"Never more than five in my possession."

"Never been caught?"

"Never been in violation that they know of, but I've seen them sneaking in the woods. I've been questioned. They're polite about it mostly. Sometimes, day's end, they'll be at the trailhead dressed like fishermen and ask about your catch to see what you'll give up."

Albert impales the worm with a diminished sense of culpability this time and hooks it as he did before, so that it isn't run completely through. He casts and tells himself that's something.

"There he goes again," says Robert, and they all observe the loon flap from the water and go airborne. He flies with waterfowl intensity in the direction of the Lower Pond and does not elevate above the level of the trees. At the eastern limit of the Upper Pond, he banks and flies with migratory urgency in their direction, coming down and down and down, and crashes in the pond again but with the awkwardness diminished somewhat from its first observed attempt.

"Well," says Robert, "that was an improvement, I suppose."

"I give him a four out of ten. He failed to stick the landing again," Steve says.

"I'm telling you," says Albert, "it could be that the lead leach of a split-shot sinker's throwing off his timing."

"I don't think so," Robert says. "His take-off wasn't bad."

"There it is," says Steve, whipping up his rod tip and reeling in a brook trout in the same length range as Robert's. He restrains it and removes the hook.

"Seems a little on the small side," Robert says.

"Dowel, please."

Robert passes it to Albert, who relays it to Steve. Steve stiffens for a moment, clubbing arm upraised, and clouts the brook trout where he estimates its brain to be and waits to see if he has clouted out all sensibility. He passes back the brook trout with his left hand, transfers the dowel from his right to left, and waits to pass it back until he hears the *thunk* of dead weight bucketed.

A practically religious transformation characterizes the expressions of the anglers in the next two hours, and that period is marked by plenitude and joviality and intuitions of pre-settlement existence. In the brief lulls, they are prone to utter to the others matters of interiority or random thoughts, which utterances do not necessitate responses, and the utterances and silences and three lines in the water are like bonding mechanisms, intimations of a grand connection to it all. Since the canoe is prone to rock when someone turns around and since they focus on their bobbers in this period of piscine frenzy, with a loon glance now and then, they talk to one another, and they listen to each other, facing mostly straight ahead, no eye to eye contact, which a lot of people claim you need to gauge a speaker's honesty or to assess a listener's reception. But, in this case, such claimants might agree there is in one's voice as reliable a gauge, in one's proximity and silence and perhaps one's aura as insightful an assessment. So Albert would say to the back of Steve's head but with the understanding that his audience included Robert, "I do not believe a biological connection is essential to the efficacious rearing of a child," and the other two would spin that declaration in their minds and someone's bobber would submerge and Albert's utterance would be internalized without the rigmarole of dialogue. Or Steve would wonder from the bow as if addressing, via deft employment of apostrophe, the pond or woods, "Are we not men?" and feel the lips upturn behind him as another bobber nosedives. Or Robert would say to the backs of both heads, "It makes you wonder if the effort is concerted down there or if every fish makes its decisions independently and runs like this are just coincidence," and he would see the subtle language of their bodies validating wonderment as someone's bobber sounds.

The spirit of accommodation often goes unspoken, and allowances are made without a word so that the interested parties minimize reminders of the frictional, those qualities embedded in a character that do not harmonize or jibe with qualities embedded in another character and therefore threaten to insert a pesky wedge between the characters who naturally would like to look back on an otherwise sublime experience in their decrepitude and be reminded only of the good vibrations, those coincident unearthly moments that released in them without intention or premeditation their endorphins, whose effect they would prefer in their decrepitude to think of as derived from more than biochemistry. So for about two hours, in that spirit, Albert fishes actively and does not slowly reel the bait away when there is evidence that nibbling has begun. And when the bobber sounds, he sets the hook and reels with sportsmanlike exuberance that masks the Benthamite and Jainist reservations and conveys to Robert willingness and gratitude for recent guidance.

As Albert reels the brook trout from the water and his rod tip flexes more than Steve or Robert's rod tips flexed, Robert says, "Swing him this way."

Robert handles the unpleasantness of landing. Robert takes the hook out. Robert clouts. He holds the brook trout lengthwise and declares, "We have a winner. Must be sixteen, seventeen inches. Biggest that I've seen from here."

Whatever ethical or philosophical objections Albert has to the notion of a trophy fish, he can't so easily dismiss the sense of an accomplishment, which you would think his recognition of coincidence and luck would temper, but a sense of diminution does not follow that awareness.

Rather, he is prone to side with those who think that evidence of blessedness is clear in good luck. Of the three men occupying this canoe, his brook trout is the longest. That's a fact that in the absence of a surer sign of blessedness-conferral must be twiddled seriously. His brook trout is the heaviest, the one that would confer the greatest calories upon his tribe if he were of a tribe, a fact that prior to the mercantile transformation of the Northeast would have had substantial existential value and begun conferring on him the attractive reputation of provider. Albert imagines that his native name would translate roughly into Long Fish, roughly since there's always something—nuance, intonation—that translation loses to the angel's share. It occurs to him as he impales another worm that, with the advent of the mongers and the markets, something naturally transactional was lost. A man could still fish for nutrition and provision, but a new world out there gradually insisted that he did not have to. And the having to, Albert reasons, must have been essential to a certain way of being in the world. Is not *the having to* the operating principle he's told himself he'd like to live by?

He casts as if he means it and supposes how his always being free from hunger is conducive to imagining there's something to be learned from hunger, something more than can be learned from Lenten fasting or the image-conscious dieting Americans are famous for. If he went independent of the merchants and depended like a person in these parts five centuries ago, or even four or three, upon the water and the land exclusively and did not come home one night with the anticipated brook trout in his creel, would he possess the stoicism and the wherewithal to not capitulate and travel via automobile to town and push a cart or dangle in his hand a plastic basket and traverse the aisles like a hollow forager, a superannuated hunter-gatherer, examining the products that were trucked there from afar and were displayed in ways suggesting the originator of such grocery design had known a thing or two about psychology? Could he, aware that he possessed sufficient legal tender to alleviate the growling, listen to his stomach for a night and listen to the stomachs of the people who relied on him as their provider and accept the spreading hunger as a temporary setback, an ennobling event in which the steadfast nature of their characters would be revealed and, as such, an event that just might be recorded in the annals, and arise before first light and walk back to the pond and sit in his canoe, his rod extended, unbowed by uncertainty or by petitioning?

Behind him, Robert reels in nothing and secures his wormed hook on an eyelet. He takes a single-burner camp stove from his pack and screws the propane canister in. He situates the stove assembly on the floor of the canoe and tears off a piece of foil, which he folds in half and sets upon the stove and crinkles so the edges angle up. He takes a brook trout from the bucket, and he lays it on the seat beside him for beheading. He drops the head into the pond and holds the brook trout so the belly faces up and so the tail points toward him. He inserts the knife into the anus, and he runs it at a shallow depth between the ribs and opens up the fish enough for the removal of the viscera, which he tosses in the pond. He dips the brook trout in the pond and agitates it slightly. When he takes it out, he agitates it slightly in the air and lays it on the foil on the stove. He makes a cut to one side of the backbone and removes the spine with thumb and index finger and discards it in the pond. He opens up the brook trout, butterflies it so the two sides lay flat on the foil, and he slides his knife beneath the ribcage structure and removes it, tossing it in the pond. His thumb and index finger grip an end point on the right fillet and lift the fine-boned skeleton out in one piece and discard it in the pond. They do likewise with the left. He turns the gas on and ignites it.

"What's going on back there?" asks Steve.

"Pipe down."

"Oh, I got another one," says Steve, who reels it in and clouts it. When he turns to hand it back, Robert tells him to just leave it on the floor of the canoe for now. So Steve deposits it behind him.

Robert dashes salt and pepper on the two fillets. A couple minutes pass. He picks up each one by the tail and flips it over, shaking salt and pepper on. When they are done, he puts the two fillets upon a paper plate beside him and removes the foil, draining the juices into the pond. He sets the foil back on the flame and lightly toasts the two halves of an oblong roll. He takes a lemon from a pocket of his pack, bisects it, and squeezes one half up and down the two fillets, which he then lays upon the bottom portion of the roll he holds. He sets that on the paper plate beside him and butters the top half of the roll, which he then lays on the two fillets.

"Pass this up," he says to Albert.

"Thank you, Albert. Thank you, Robert." Steve takes a bite and chews reflectively. He nods, indulging in the pleasures of ingredient identification. "Robert, you packed condiments? I'm tasting salt, pepper, maybe cumin." He takes another bite and chews, slow, steady, cuddish, granting the inquisitive tongue exploratory time. "You packed a lemon, Robert? You spritzed some lemon on there, Robert. Above and beyond." He takes a bite and chews as if to clarify his summary of findings. "Lemon, butter, salt, pepper, maybe cumin. Fresh brook trout cooked like this in a canoe," he says as though his powers to complete a simple sentence have been stripped by the ineffable. "Delicious. Thank you. Excellent. How'd you learn to cook like that?"

"Necessity, I guess. Trial and error. Common sense," says Robert, flipping Albert's trout. "Ain't no cumin in there, though."

"Robert, when the monetary system finally collapses, you will be left standing."

"You think so, huh? That's good to know."

"I'm serious. When the whole thing breaks down and the ATMs are empty and the trucks don't make deliveries, do you know, on average, how long the food supply in grocery stores will last?"

"Two days," says Albert.

"Two days. That's right. But, Robert, you could live out here indefinitely."

"I think in that scenario I doubt I'd be the only one out here."

"How long do you think the fish in here would last?" Steve asks.

"Oh, I don't know. How many people would be out here after a collapse? I ain't the only one who can cook a brook trout out here. And would the wardens still have jobs?"

"I suspect enforcement would be lax."

"We must be close to the limit," Albert says.

"Not after I finish with these sandwiches," says Robert.

"Do you eat the tail?" asks Steve.

"I do. Some don't."

"The fishing out here would be hard," says Albert, "if the collapse occurred in winter."

"Robert, do you ice fish much?" asks Steve.

Robert passes a brook-trout sandwich up to Albert. "Used to. Not so much no more." He takes a brook trout from the bucket and beheads it.

"Too cold?"

"The cold don't help." He cuts and guts the brook trout. "Last time I got too deep in the schnapps and coffee brandy. Had a hard time getting off the ice. After that, I told myself I'd quit while I was still ahead." He takes the spine and fine bones out.

"How long ago was that?"

"Oh, about three years ago or thereabouts. Well, no, maybe two."

"Have you ice fished since?"

"Nope."

"Gave the schnapps and brandy up too?"

"I didn't say that."

Steve sets down his paper plate and dips his paddle in the water for canoe reorientation, and he strokes thrice right, thrice left to glide the vessel back to deeper water. There is something comforting about resetting one's position after being carried for a while on a subtle drift. The loons shift likewise to maintain the distance buffer. Steve leans the paddle shaft against his seat and takes his pipe and pouch with minimal canoe disturbance from a cargo pocket. He packs the bowl and lights it, smoke rising, drifting as they had been drifting.

Albert establishes a mastication rhythm and observes on the aluminum floor of the canoe the brook trout Steve had clouted. Albert notices the colors haven't faded as they should have had the clout been of the giving-up-the-ghost variety. The skyward eye does not appear unduly cloudy, and he thinks that he detects an intermittent, super-subtle motion of the gill. He holds the brook-trout sandwich to his face and takes a bite and chews and tries envisioning the linkages of this biota's food chain. He recalls he never cared for that pyramidal depiction of the food relationships, the figure of a human, featureless, residing in that isolated little triangle at the top, the other beings fixed beneath him, sedimentary deposits in the strata of the epochs that had come before. He wonders if that sort of propaganda was intentional, if interested trade groups like the National Cattlemen's Association or the National Pork Producers Council or the National Chicken Association lobbied federal or state departments to ensure that any posters governmentally approved to hang in grade-school classrooms would convey with pictographic clarity and unity of theme the simple wisdom of omnivorism and its status as a natural law, the human as the uber omnivore, ordained by nature, which the children could appreciate, to eat without recrimination or a moral inventory anything beneath that line. It wouldn't do to trouble children with a picture of a stockyard or a beakless chicken or the basic operation of a slaughterhouse because efficiency demands a practical remove from nature, which remove, conceptually, is difficult for children who invest their very souls in singing "Old MacDonald Had a Farm" and understand that farm as a utopia—conceptually is difficult for children to corral because it takes them years to shake their innocence. He wonders in what year the pyramid fell out of favor and the food-relationships depictions started to include curvaceous arrows to suggest a natural cycle. So in one you'd have a yellow Sun, an arrow emanating from the bottom left of its corona, pointing to a water body in which Algae, undepicted, live, an arrow pointing from the Algae word to Small Marine Animals, which animals are represented by a crawdad or a shrimp, an arrow pointing from the shrimp or crawdad to a Fish, an arrow pointing from the Fish up to a rowboat and a representative of Humans, one guy in a long-billed cap, his rod tip flexing downward though no line is visible. The cycle ends with him. The guy gives nothing back.

Albert holds the brook-trout sandwich to his face and takes a bite and looks down at the brook trout on the floor. This is the first time in his life as a tertiary consumer that he's looked into the eye of an inferior consumer as he is consuming an inferior consumer of the same species as the one whose eye he's looking into. He wonders if the dimming piscine consciousness inhabiting the brook trout on the floor, the inner brainly business he believes he still sees flickering like mica in the brook trout's eye, is trying, with the one eye and the one gill, to impale his chomping consciousness, his apex-predatory heritage, with an equivalent of *How could you?* Albert asks himself how could he. Could he eat a burger as he sits a little ways above a dying cow, his feet so close that practically, with no extension, he could touch the bovine belly with either shoe toe to express a glimmer of compassion or with any of his real toes if he chose to go unshod and then beyond the glimmer to the intimacy of flesh-to-flesh expression? Could he chew like this and stare like this into the cow's eye until the eyelid came down, covered it to show the cow was sick of looking at his human face or dead, the shade that shut the mortal shop? Knowing that the cow has friendships and a social life and has a memory of length and has stood in a pasture, facing in the same direction as the other members of the herd, and felt contentment, irrespective of the weather, in the unity, how could he?

Albert dips his fingers in the pond and wipes them on his shorts. Steve smokes his pipe in front of him, and Robert eats his brook-trout sandwich with some lip smacks in the back. Albert rests his forearms on his lower femurs and observes the brook trout drained of color. An intelligence is lost.

Albert has, against his will, attended several presentations whose professors spoke with apostolic verve of Howard Gardner's *Frames of Mind: The Theory of Multiple Intelligences* and tried to make The Theory come alive. Though Albert never read the book, he had no choice except to listen to the speakers, take in Gardner's principles, and contemplate how they could be transformative if implemented in his teaching life and even in his life beyond.

He remembers the linguistic-verbal and the logical-mathematical intelligences, the ones you want for SAT success, but, even generously construed, he doesn't see those two as what this brook trout had to offer this biota.

Though he supposes there is something musical about the brook trout's path through water, something like those relaxation compositions that insomniacs may turn to to assist their passage into sleep, he doubts the brook trout's genius lay in the musical intelligence.

He doesn't know enough about the secret lives of brook trout to determine how the personal intelligences, the inter and the intra, might apply, although he does suspect it would be difficult for brook trout in a pond this size to coexist without some healthy trout-specific interpersonal intelligence.

He tries remembering another one and wonders if the memory alone is an intelligence.

The visual-spatial intelligence occurs to him, and, as he looks down at the brook trout's lidless eye, he figures that this brook trout must have had some navigational intelligence at least but wonders how much visualizing went on in the mind's eye.

He recalls the bodily-kinesthetic intelligence and looks down at the piscine sleekness and the squared tail and the fins, and he imagines how this brook trout moved through water with exquisite bodily control, with an intelligence of motion that surpassed what is embodied by the prima ballerina or the highlit wide receiver. The brook trout was water. That alone should be a reason to exist, a hedge against predation by the likes of Albert.

He is almost certain that another is the naturalist intelligence, the ability to render fine distinctions in the natural world. What being would know better than the brook trout who the flora and the fauna are in these parts? Still, this brook trout failed to make the obvious distinction that the floating sinker, hook, and worm did not belong down there. Maybe hunger always overrides intelligence no matter what.

Albert farts and says, "I'll take responsibility for that one. That one's on me."

"I'm eating back here," Robert says.

"My apologies," says Albert. "It's an affliction."

"Suffer in silence." Robert pauses. "My God, that's impolite," he says, fanning the air before him with his hand.

"All's I smell is pipe smoke," Steve says.

"Well, there you go," says Robert. "You spooked the loon."

They watch as the loon lifts from the pond.

Albert remembers one of the presenters saying that Professor Gardner was inclined in later life to think of existential intelligence as worthy of inclusion on the list, and he remembers thinking that he was himself a ponderer, a veritable savant in that department. He admires Gardner's open-mindedness.

The loon banks near the Lower Pond and flies back as before, a paradox of tuck and of extension, descends, descends, descends, and hits the water with an ease and grace that make your throat and chest and belly feel as though they have been touched by something you could call not physical. And, even if you never saw a waterfowl touch down before, you simply know that this is how it's done, and you are not concerned with what proportion of the landing is innate and what proportion has been learned. It's genius. It is genius.

Chapter Twenty

Lateral river marker 102 is fastened to a framework in protrusion from the top tier of a three-tiered scaffold structure whose four sides are each five feet wide. The marker is triangular and fluorescent orange, its perimeter fluorescent red, the color of the 102. The marker is about four fathoms higher than the surface of the river, and the framework in protrusion tilts it downward at the angle of a freshly airborne flying squirrel so that someone on the water looking upward for directional assistance near the riverbank will see that marker in relief, a clarity of outline, color, number, lo, an equilateral limpidity, a sign that humans who were here once and erected this direct him.

It is the middle of October, sixty-eight degrees, six higher than the average high, and it is not yet noon. The Wangunk Meadows, foreground sunlit, middle distance sunlit, background sunlit, open to the right. The books all tout the virtues of routine, stability, and movement, exercise. So Charlie Watts, Ryan, Jake, and Albert, almost always in that order, go for walks away from roads on Saturdays and Sundays if the weather's fair. And almost always, as today, they seem like separate particles coincidentally aligned, no outward sign of unity except the line, although they have been known to cluster in the presence of some mystery and to disperse linearly when they've come to terms with it. They walk single-file on an isthmus to the left and right of which are upper-shin-deep ruts the lift-kit trucks have left as evidence of ego, deep ruts filled with rainwater, little static wadis, and, as Watts approaches, late-season pickerel frogs spring from the sunny isthmus to the puddles, plunk on plunk, the turbulence of entering and sounding swirling puddle sediment so you can see the pickerel-frog trajectory, but that is where your pickerel-frog awareness ends in murkiness, or murk, or maybe nebulosity is here a better word to get across what now exists between the pickerel frogs and you.

Albert looks up at the red beacon light that is fastened to the top tier of the scaffold's north side and the solar panel just below the light and wonders, as he always does when he approaches or walks past it, what emergency would cause the beacon's activation, and he almost walks right into Jake, who is arrested by this business with the pickerel frogs.

Watts and Ryan amble on, evincing no concern for the amphibious evasions, none of the invaders' curiosity about the charming folkways of the natives, none of the jingo pride and inner boost that come with knowing your approach inspires the diminutive evasions, none of the attendant sadness, the invaders' puzzling mind-fuck, that suggests the natural order wasn't always this way, wasn't always such that to the existential table all you had the wherewithal to bring was fear, intimidation, the awareness, even absent malice, you were somehow dangerous and not to be engaged. They amble on, oblivious of Jake's arrest, and leave the isthmus, bearing right, two silent beings entering the meadow whose illuminated flaxen quality is almost most enticing at this hour. Albert stands like someone undergoing a conceptual advancement on the verge of a savannah and observes as Ryan holds his right hand out and runs his palm and fingers, slightly cupped, along the seed heads of the reed grass, each reed bending as he passes and then rising, emblem of resilience, like a limber person reinvigorated by his willingness to limbo. It's an odd thing to feel pride about, an odd thing to suppose could be an independence harbinger, but Albert remembers that he carries in his pocket two foam letters just in case the stimulation gets to be too much and Ryan needs to squeeze them, occupy his hands—the way that others fiddle with a paperclip or grip a beer—to feel he's in control of something.

Jake kneels down on both knees, lays his right palm flat upon the packed earth of the isthmus, and inspects the roiled water to his left. There was a time not long ago when Albert regarded such a stoppage as an opportunity to practice the paternal art of the rebuke. Although he didn't care about the tragedy of soiled knees and didn't think bacterial endangerment was markedly increased by getting lower to the ground and multiplying points of contact, Albert felt bound, by something not in writing, to enlighten Jake on laundry matters and the terrible historical toll exacted by bacteria and how a mother's burden is exacerbated by pre-soaking and the fact that antibiotic resistance in bacteria is on the rise.

Albert's reconsideration of parental intercession was initially occasioned when he read a newsletter article about the grief that parents undergo when they discover that their child is autistic. He was struck by what the author said about the root of such grief being the upending of parental expectations that their child would naturally be a person whose reception and interpretation and communication infrastructure would be like their own and would facilitate a free and easy interaction with a world there was no question he or she would be a part of. The author said that parents who wish their child was not autistic are, in essence, wishing their child had not been born. Because the autism and the child are interwoven, inextricable, one cannot be without the other, and to wish away the autism is to wish away the child. Albert repeated to himself that independent clause. *And to wish away the autism is to wish away the child.* And he wondered if that was what Jake and Ryan's parents had wished, wondered if they'd gotten mired in the wishing. The author said, instead of grief, some serious recalibration is in order, and he said the child may seem alien but isn't lost. He said imagine trying to communicate with someone whom you do not share a language with. It's like that, but the sense of the divide is greater, wider, more profound, beyond the alienation capabilities of the linguistic or the cultural. The author said, "You're going to have to give up your assumptions about shared meanings. You're going to have to learn to back up to levels more basic than you've probably thought about before." Albert had not considered the relationship as primitive in quite that way before. It goes to show how much is in the phrasing.

So, on these walks, Albert has progressively been less inclined to view himself as a director or a guide, a person whose experiences and sensibilities and even existential standards are to be imparted to his charges irrespective of the process they must go through individually to understand what portion of the limitless components of the world they can. This isn't such a simple process for a person so dependent on the combination of the letters of an alphabet to shed light on the world, for someone so dependent on analogy and metaphor and subtext to reveal to him a meaning. It's a process. It's a training of the consciousness to not be quite so jumpy. So, on walks, he started to instruct himself to check the tendency to issue a command or pointer, to instruct himself to not suggest the method of interpretation he observed was incorrect or inappropriate or inexpedient or insufficient or at odds with his or the majority's. So much of teaching, he believed, was imposition. How exactly does one turn the ship around, he asked himself, at his age? It's a process.

The injustice of the leash tug hit him as a violation of a fundamental canine right a few days after Albert read the article. It happened in September on a Saturday. The usual. They exited the truck in silence, Albert leashed Watts until they got some distance from the road, and, in the getting, Watts paused in the interest of olfactory perusal at a gatepost, at a fencepost, and at spots apparently unmarked or of invisible distinction on the way. Despite the absence of a schedule pressure, Albert experienced contemporary man's impatience with delay and tugged the leash, the collar a compression on the throat and neck, each time Watts put his nose down to detect a scent at least ten-thousand times below the threshold at which the proboscis of a human could detect it. Albert tugged him from the gatepost, tugged him from the fencepost, tugged him onward. But, as Watts pulled like a stunted draft horse toward the signpost, meaning in the form of article remembrance came to Albert, and he let go of the leash. And watching Watts inhaling stimuli around the signpost, on the signpost, stimuli that Albert did not possess the nerves to process, he understood how much he would not want himself to be pulled from a view or from a thrush song ramping up in June, how much the hand of the insensitive and the insensible was not aware of and denied. This was a breakthrough. Step two, in a sense. Article remembrance, then an application of the principle.

Meaning in the form of incidental personal remembrance came unbidden also, with no questions asked, as Albert slouched like a tobacco smoker outside the olfactory perimeter of Watts's signpost. What a memory from almost twenty years ago and from a geographical vicinity you haven't been in since then may lack in pictorial fidelity and flawless reproduction of the name of someone centrally involved and dialogue that is verbatim it makes up for by the fact that it has hung around this long and has retained enough of the experience for summoning and application at this relatively late date in its keeper's life.

Albert held his face up to the breeze and, certain H was the initial letter, certain that the surname was Germanic, maybe Frisian or Scottish, tried to conjure Ken's last name from his cerebral Rolodex. He tried out names with lots of consonants, some fricative, some guttural, but he came up with nothing. He was left with only Ken, Ken H., which was enough because the last name, after all, was immaterial because he knew Ken in the nineties was a hang-gliding, tango-dancing carpenter whose father was an admiral of a Navy fleet in some part of the world. Albert knew Ken's father wasn't fond of Ken's proclivities, but Ken believed in his proclivities, believed in listening to what his inner voice suggested, and was neutral on the subject of the admiralty. Ken had attended Yale with Thomas Lovejoy, who became the noted tropical biologist who hired Albert to perform the duties of a residential lackey, mostly watching after Skye and Eigg and Rum, the Shetland sheepdogs named for isles of the Inner Hebrides, and gardening and going to the store for items such as light bulbs and, in general, being present on the Georgetown Pike property, especially when Tom was in the Amazon. Ken materialized one morning with his aged German shepherd, and he knocked on Albert's slightly open screen door twice by saying, "Knock, knock," and requested access to the main house for a project he was undertaking, carpentry aesthetically consistent with the Jeffersonian, agrarian foundations of the house, which was constructed prior to the Revolution as an ordinary to accommodate the drovers who would pay for respite from the market drive. In those days, Ken and Albert were men of lenient obligation, so there was no rush to open up the main house and there was no principled objection to a coffee fortified with Benedictine, no insistence on matutinal sobriety, because they understood a shared nip in the morning was convivial, distinguished them from all the souls commuting at that moment toward the Capital. They sat at leisure's angle on the deck in Adirondack chairs and sipped their Benedictine coffees, watching as the four dogs, satisfied with their compulsory olfactory salutations, filed down the deck steps, turned right, and accelerated as if mimicking the urgency of wolves or hounds or war dogs, disappearing into the ascending woods that led to The Madeira School, where Jean Harris, who became notorious for murdering the Scarsdale Diet Doctor at his Purchase home in March of 1980, had been headmistress for a spell. The dogs returned in less than half an hour from their constitutional and took a more domestic spin around the yard. They sniffed at fruit and ornamental bushes, fenceposts, chicken wire, solar panels, weed tufts, tree trunks, peonies, and whatnot, lingered longer at some stops than others, pawed as if to agitate a scent toward its potential, sniffed, moved on, and circled finally before they lay down on the deck or on the dappled grass and slept or held their noses up at snooty, regal angles so that they could gather what was finest, unto scents at parts-per-trillion concentrations, in the air. Ken and Albert observed all this like casual behaviorists whom the operation of the second Benedictine quietly inclined to be less clinical.

"Every day they do this," Albert essentially declared, in his mid-twenties still, bemused. "Consider evolution. What advantage do they gain expending all this energy on smell identification?"

Ken was of no fixed religion and did not evince an interest in a life beyond the current one. Even when he spoke on weighty or on earnest matters, there was blithesomeness about him, which, rhetorically, was quite a gift. His Jackson-Brown-like hair was graying, and he was at least two decades Albert's senior, but he didn't try to compensate for the disparity in youth by issuing pronouncements in the privileged way that certain relative elders do, as if the issuance was predicated on the having reached an age at which one qualifies for access to the gnomic word store. Ken possessed the peaceful gravitas of someone who had hung a long time in the sky and thought up there about perception and the body and the world from a perspective land- or even plane-bound folks had not and landed, always, on his feet, which weekly danced the tango. Ken had liberal views that never hardened into partisanship, and he had given Albert such books as *The Poems of Catullus* and *The Selected Ezra Pound*, but Ken possessed the sensibility of someone who had moved a lot and understood that the ability to read and to articulate was evidence of an intelligence, but one that had its limits in the total world.

"It's like their morning paper," Ken, in essence, stated in a tone that someone mellow from a mountain region of the Far East might have used. "The same way that we read *The Post* and find out what's happened since we last read, they go up the hill and down the hill and round the yard to find out what went on last night." They sipped their Benedictine coffees and observed the herding dogs at rest. "It's just another form of understanding, of maintaining their identity." Ken sipped and did a qualifying head nod. "Granted, it is not the form you want if you intend to dominate the world or build a shelf or write a book, but why should that diminish its utility or its exquisiteness? Imagine what we'd know if we possessed their sense of smell. Imagine *how* we'd know."

Thus meaning in the form of distant incidental personal remembrance joins with meaning in the form of recent article remembrance to create in Albert a lurching willingness to not be so instructive or so masterly or so parental, neuro-typically parental, when he finds a dwarf wedgemussel on the riverbank and wishes that its rarity impressed the boys, or when Watts pulls the leash because he's caught in an olfactory magnetic field and Albert would like to act as counterforce, or when Jake kneels on both knees, lays his right palm flat upon the isthmus, and inspects the water roiled by the pickerel-frog propulsions to his left. Although Albert would prefer to say he thinks it's best to leave the pickerel frogs alone because would you enjoy a hand that dwarfs you hovering above you in your element while you are trying desperately to hide, he lets Jake put his left hand in the water and refrains from saying anything as Jake continues on to elbow depth and circularly trolls as though he were descended from a line of Southern noodlers.

Interpersonal expressions of affinity are problematic if the observational capacities of the excluded aren't given due consideration and then misdirected out of sensitivity and a respect for the illusion of neutrality and fair play. They are problematic, too, because they aren't necessarily verbal, often aren't verbal, and can be conveyed as clearly through the glint of eyes, or an unusual formation of the lips, or voice-tone modulation into Zappa whimsy, or an inclination of the head toward he or she the head incliner hopes feels likewise re affinity, or relaxation, slackness, posturally, an openness of form suggesting otherness is overrated, or the way an index finger rises to a tongue to moisten so the page can be more slickly turned, the way the index finger of the lesser or the younger person in the field of this affinity then rises to the lesser or the younger tongue for moisture and then flips the read page with a digital facility that studying the greater or the elder seems to have engendered. So it's hard to be politely conscious of expressions that are wordless, to refrain from doing what comes naturally because expressions do not come so naturally to whomever is outside the field of that affinity. Thus, when Albert reads to Jake the Seuss books in a Walken cadence in the evening or at bedtime and awareness of the aforementioned affinity expressions focuses and drifts, he feels both fatherly and favoritist because he knows that Ryan, who is in the room but unmoved even by the words of *Horton Hears a Who!*, is by the reading left forgotten and deprived of grooviness, that existential track, which, when you're in it, no one needs to tell you that you're in it or that you belong.

Parentally, the easy thing to do is parcel out the parenting, compartmentalize the family parts according to perception modes. While Albert and Jake, for instance, read or practice reading by dissecting morphemes and comparing phonemes and repeating the remarkable words and phrases, sometimes sentences in their entirety, until they separate at last from meaning as if spun in some linguistic centrifuge, Mary and Ryan squeeze the foam letters and arrange them or brush Watts luxuriously and hold the hair puffs in their palms or color or refine the signing system they've developed or retire to a separate room to watch the Disney mouse, a gloveless mouse until *The Opry House* came out in 1929.

So, this is what they mostly do, but sometimes, as a human, you just want to unify the whole experience. And often the apartheid method doesn't work logistically. It troubles Albert that he perceives neutrality and fair play as illusion, that, while he is reading or is listening to Jake read, he is trying to devise the misdirections that might sucker Ryan into thinking he is in the same zone. Albert therefore may suggest to Jake that they sit close to Ryan while they read, a gesture of corporeal inclusion, or he may adjust the book in Ryan's field of vision and point Horton or whomever out so Ryan has a chance to visualize what's happening linguistically or, if the character is admirable and has a name that is trochaic, Albert may say "Ryan" each time as a substitution, prodding his participation via such involuntary character insertion, but this latter strategy to Jake has proven irksome. And it troubles Albert that, regardless of the misdirections in the name of integration and inclusion, he is often not addressing head-on the essential matter, which occurs to him in flashes as he's setting up the feints, that Ryan isn't verbal in the way that Albert is, isn't verbal even in the way that Jake is, and to weasel him in a direction he is not equipped for seems unfatherly, unsportsmanlike, an abrogation of the duty to at least put forth an honest effort to perceive as this boy in particular perceives.

In the absence of experiential unity, a counterbalance of affinities is necessary. Albert has for some time been considering that Disney mouse that Ryan is so fond of. Unlike reading, even unlike reading Seuss books, viewing animation or cartoon art is a diversion Albert outgrew years ago when he put down the weed and even *South Park* and *The Simpsons* didn't tickle him as deeply as they used to.

"Does anybody remember laughter?" Robert Plant inquired one night in The Garden during the recording of *The Song Remains the Same*. Albert always took that line to mean that things had gotten rather serious by 1973, to be an invitation to renounce the recent tone of joylessness. What authentic joy could so commercialized a mouse inspire in the core of an adult like Albert? If it's not authentic, he is aiding and abetting once again illusion, practicing a prestidigitation of the limbic system, toying with what should be pure emotion.

As evidence of what can be accomplished with the internet and a desire to commune and to exert oneself a little in the interest of contributing to the conditions whereby like minds might be fostered, Albert had discovered several animated short films from the early Disney era that appeal, on different levels, but appeal regardless, to a range of family sensibilities and therefore technically do not provide a counterbalance of affinities but more or less an opportunity to practice the elusive unity and to approximate shared meaning.

The first, *The Barnyard Battle*, features Mickey and a lot of Mickey lookalikes in 1929 in boot camp and then marching musically to war against the cats in pickelhauben. Trenches and a Mickey-manned machine gun feature prominently in this one. The mice emerge victorious. Albert's joy in this short film is magnified considerably because of his uncovering an excerpt of a 1930s German editorial re Mickey: "Mickey Mouse is the most miserable ideal ever revealed. . . Healthy emotions tell every independent young man and every honorable youth that the dirty and filth-covered vermin, the greatest bacteria carrier in the animal kingdom, cannot be the ideal type of animal." He never mentions to the boys this droll component, this political dimension, this insinuation of a dark side, even though he values context and believes that an awareness of it is essential for the realization of the genre's and the era's comical potential. He prefers to let the boys enjoy what elements they have it in them to enjoy, prefers to not pose questions or declare his special knowledge so as not to complicate or vitiate the joy the mostly wordless world of early Disney sound cartoons evokes by other means. This preference starts out as a conscious thing and inches, root-like, toward a zone not governed wholly by volition, and, though he would not suggest the preference has, by inching into radical-behaviorism territory, been promoted to the class that emanates from second nature, he would say it has acquired the progressive quality of something hybridized, still in possession of the source material but branching out or inward, gaining power and resilience by reticulating as it goes. If Jake speaks up and asks a question or if Ryan via signs or Dynavox inquires, Albert will offer what he knows and try to be the sort of wise man he believes at times that he can be, but mostly he's become content to occupy the same vicinity as them and Watts and to observe without imposing and to learn what he can learn from them.

Because a figure over six-feet tall can be perceived by shorter people or by people in the process of amphibious inspection as a loomer and because the looming, though a great leap forward for our forebears in the grasslands, can obstruct the sort of observation he is interested in, Albert leaves the isthmus, laterally hopping over the little static wadi to his right, and walks two steps past Jake's position on the isthmus. He turns so that he faces Jake and hops back on the isthmus, kneeling so that he removes the aura of a shadow caster. He lays his left hand flat upon the isthmus, and he dips his right hand in the water to his right. Jake does not acknowledge Albert's repositioning except that he goes still a moment, water rippling slightly, sediment aswirl, awaiting its resettlement. Albert is unsure if the stillness is a bristling, body language for "Your presence has provoked in me discomfiture," or Jake attempting to instill in him the mindset one must enter prior to immersion. Albert is likewise still, his gaze averted, focused, as is Jake's, upon the water in which pickerel frogs continue practicing their inborn methods of elusion. They kneel there, each with one palm flat upon the isthmus, each with one hand and with some proportion of a forearm in the water, cool, embracing. It occurs to Albert, aside from the peculiarities of nervous systems and neurology and stimuli interpretation, aside from how sensation gets from point A to cerebral points beyond, there has to be shared meaning here.

Albert later asks himself what is the medium by which the meaning he is fairly certain of gets shared. It isn't language. Even with this boy with whom he shares a sort of semiotic, Wallace-Stevens-level understanding, or at least appreciation, of a good part of the Geisel canon, it's not language. The medium may be liquidity or water temperature, molecular transmissions to the sensory receptors, the beginning of the language of tactility. It may be otherwise organ-based, a visceral-abdominal transmission, wingbeats in each omphalos, anticipating grazing contact with some portion of the frog skin that could possibly torpedo past, the phantom language of tactility. It may turn out to be the chemistry of letdown when they do not feel what something maybe extrasensory prepared the both of them to feel. How can you tell if no one says a word? How many have been hoodwinked by reliance on the word?

At the tail end of their stillness interlude, three bubbles of approximately the same size from the depths materialize and float up in the dreamy-seeming way of jellyfish and bubbles, surfacing, as if allowing for the registration of their shimmer, bursting in succession as if atmospheric pressure or the observation they were under or just being bubbles got to be too much. Albert would like to take this opportunity to tell Jake what he knows about cutaneous gas exchange and how the pickerel frogs down there have ceased while underwater to be pulmonary breathers and are breathing only through their skin, but he decides against it. Jake lowers his shoulder so he can submerge his left arm deeper in the water, and he moves his arm toward where the bubbles were, its forward motion slowed as simultaneously he moves it with deliberation side to side, attempting to approximate the coverage of a dragnet. Since the tires that gouged out these ruts were monsters, Albert does not believe Jake has the reach to touch the bottom. Therefore, he does not fear overmuch the capture or the incidental harming of a pickerel frog, although the issuance of caution is a measure he finds difficult to mentally dispel.

Watts and Ryan come back to investigate these figures in positions that might indicate distress. Watts sniffs a representative proportion of the bodies and appears to certify that they are in good health, and then he bounds into the brush and down the riverbank and faces north, in opposition to the river coursing, nose inclined as if the vista and the coursing and the breeze of coursing and the scattered waterfowl legitimate him as essentially they would a biped who has come here from a cubicle and is at liberty until the morn.

Legitimation as an integration matter also carries on above without linguistic mediation. Ryan does not migrate to the isthmus, but he parallels it as he kneels and lays his right hand on the ground and dips his left hand in the water to a depth of middle forearm. He is not perplexed by absence of a rationale. The motion of his arm begins as lineal, a measured to and fro and yon and hither, covering an area uncovered by the others. A respect for sovereignty is evident in his averting the incursion and the overlap. He then transitions, midway through a line, to motion that is loosely orbital, hypnotic, like the motion of a slow-revolving, localized tornado from which the destructive force has been removed or of a dervish who resolved to take it easy with the whirling.

There is no need to dissemble. There is no need to say a word, no need to realign to manufacture the appearance of affinity.

Although you're not required to be in a watershed in order to experience the inner uplift of a moment to which the attachment of the modifier *watershed* would not be out of line, the poignancy of such a modification torques more when you're kneeling, arm submerged in frog water, with your rapt adopted sons on an October Sunday on the floodplain of a watershed that people long dead wrested from the Wangunks not that long ago in earth terms.

About the Author

Born in Port Jefferson Station, New York, one year after the beginning of the Summer of Love, John Popielaski attended SUNY-Stony Brook and American University. He has worked as a mover, lackey to a well-heeled tropical biologist, tent erector, lobsterman, and teacher.

His poems have appeared in such journals as *The Hollins Critic, New South, Post Road,* and *Redivider*. He is the author of several poetry collections, including *Isn't It Romantic?* which won the Robert Phillips Chapbook Award from Texas Review Press.

The Hollow Middle is his first novel.

About the Press

Unsolicited Press was founded in 2012 and is a nomadic small publisher based in Portland, Oregon. The team publishes unsung heroes and phenomenal writing. Learn more at www.unsolicitedpress.com.

www.ingramcontent.com/pod-product-compliance
Lightning Source LLC
Chambersburg PA
CBHW051003180726
48291CB00006B/1955

9781947021402